SEARCHING FOR LOVE

"You are free to turn back, Teran. I would not hold you to this."

He pulled her to him. All the emotion he felt for the flame-haired femina washed over Teran, threatening to drown him in a flood tide of sharp revelation. Though the admission was dredged from a place beyond reason, he could deny his fate no longer. They were bound, one to the other, until victory or death claimed them.

"Alia," Teran said, "don't you understand? I'm no longer free to leave. We are joined by more than words. My fate now lies with you."

The Knowing Crystal

KATHLEEN MORGAN

LEISURE BOOKS   NEW YORK CITY

A LEISURE BOOK ®

March 1991

Published by

Dorchester Publishing Co., Inc.
276 Fifth Avenue
New York, NY 10001

Printed in the United States of America.

PROLOGUE

Knowing Crystal, bright and fair
Secret of the richest gain,
Royal quest begins the cure
For barren empire, deepest pain.

ALIA STOOD BEFORE THE EMPTY STONE RECEPTACLE AND gazed down at the engraved words—words of an ancient, cryptic prophecy. Then, with an undulating swirl of lustrous white robes, she turned from the obsidian pedestal with its shimmering lines and walked out of the Sanctuary. She had already tarried too long. The High Priestess would be irritated.

Excitement churned within as her steps carried her down the smooth stone corridor, her sandaled feet echoing the rapid pounding of her heart. A scene flashed through Alia's mind, a remembrance of the whirling maelstrom at the pools of Cambrai. If feelings could be visualized, those waters would depict the emotions of this moment.

Yet another Test of Worthiness lay before her, only a few steps and secundae away, just beyond the dark, wooden portal that now separated her from the High Priestess' chambers. She hesitated, took a deep breath, then grasped the ornate handle, cleverly carved into the form of the famed mutant weaving spider of her planet. Pushing the huge door ajar, Alia entered a cool, sparsely decorated room.

Across the dimly lit expanse sat the femina who held her fate, in hands gnarled and grasping. The tall, dark form was backlit by the long slit of window behind her. "Come closer, child," the voice proclaimed from a face hidden deep in shadow. "Draw near and learn of your test."

Alia forced her legs to move, each step a stiff, painful effort. Her heart fluttered wildly in her chest. The reminder of her summons had been unnecessary. How could she forget the quest required of every novice of the most hallowed Sisterhood of the Crystal, a test both terrifying and irresistible?

Tales of it hinted at great pain and superhuman effort, of ignominious failure and, perhaps, even death. Yet all who aspired to final vows as a Sister of the Crystal faced the test with more willingness than dread, for it was a learning as much as an ordeal. Plumbing the depths of their courage, those who emerged unscathed of body would carry with them a heightened awareness of life and self. A test most worthy and a preparation most fitting, Alia reminded herself for the hundredth time, especially for one such as she, born into the ruling order of the planet Aranea.

She halted before the older femina's throne. "I come before you, most High Priestess, to beg of you my test." Ingrained from long horas of practice, the ritual words slipped from Alia's lips. "Pray that I am worthy of the most high honor and will incur no shame upon our revered order."

She knelt before the somberly clad femina and bowed her head. "With all my heart I await your words; with all my strength will I carry out the quest."

A twisted, cold-fingered hand briefly touched her head, an empty gesture that was nothing more than ceremonially correct. "Rise then, child, and hear your test."

Throwing back the flame-colored tresses cascading around her face, Alia climbed to her feet. Her gaze fell upon an empty throne.

"I am here," the icy voice of the High Priestess beckoned from behind her.

Alia turned to find the femina, who had virtually formed her from childhood, standing next to a map of the Imperium. Planets of various sizes and hues dotted the chart in a random order, as if thrown into the heavens by the hand of an uncaring god. The High Priestess' finger lay next to a large, tan orb.

Pale, expressionless eyes scanned Alia. The merest hint of a smile—if the upturning of the corners of the High Priestess' mouth could ever be called a smile— grazed the femina's lips.

"Here is your test—on the planet Carcer," she said, her head gesturing toward the chart. "You will journey there and not return, until your quest is complete."

A slight widening of the girl's honey-brown eyes was the only indication of her surprise. Thanks to the High Priestess, Alia's training had instilled a discipline and self-control far beyond her tender youth of 17 cycles.

"But, Domina Magna," she forced the words out of

a throat gone suddenly dry, "Carcer is the Imperium's prison. What is there on a planet of criminals that calls me to a test most holy?"

The hand of the stately femina slid from the map and fell to her side. "It is the Knowing Crystal that calls you. We have discovered it at last, on the planet of Carcer."

"The Knowing Crystal?" Alia could not hide the excitement that sprang, unbidden, into her voice. The long-awaited discovery of the ancient stone of power, stolen hundreds of cycles ago from its rightful place on Aranea, was more than even her iron-edged control could bear.

"My quest is the Knowing Crystal?" she repeated, her voice incredulous.

Dark eyebrows raised at the inappropriate display of emotion. Noting the femina's reaction, Alia quickly drew a veil of restraint around her. When she spoke again, her words were carefully modulated and toneless.

"Why have I been so honored to seek out the Knowing Crystal? I am least worthy of all the novices preparing for our profession. You, yourself, have admonished me time and again for my erratic control, my unruly emotions."

"Worthiness has nothing to do with it!" The words were uttered in a tone of sharp exasperation. "If it were mine to choose, the choice would never have been you. But the prophecy . . ."

As if to emphasize her next words, the High Priestess paused. "The prophecy clearly states only one of blood royal can ever hope to regain the Crystal. And you, most sadly, are the last of Aranea's ruling line. There is no one else."

Alia stood there, struck dumb by the import of the High Priestess' words. The engraved lines on the stone, the words that held such fascination, rose as a vision in her mind's eye. Those golden, glowing phrases, recounted by legend to have appeared after the theft of the Knowing Crystal—had they been meant, had they been waiting all this time for her?

She *was* the last of a royal line, the sole survivor of an ancient dynasty of Aranean rulers, but they had been a weak lot. Hadn't the High Priestess repeatedly told her that? Wasn't that why her own mother had failed to live longer than a few cycles after her birth? And hadn't that inherent weakness ultimately been the source of her mother's shameful death, the cause of which the High Priestess had yet to reveal?

But none of that mattered now. The test was before her. Though not one of her choosing, it was the one she must accept.

The ritual reply carried Alia through yet another difficult moment. "I accept my test and pray it finds me worthy. If I should fail, let me fail with honor and courage. If I should die, let my death bring glory to my people."

The pale claw of a hand once more settled upon Alia's head. "The trial is begun; the prophecy at last is set into motion. The Aranean people, as well as the peoples of the entire Imperium, await the outcome. The loss of the Crystal has tainted us all, in ways we have even yet to discover.

"But know this, Alia," the femina continued, raising her hand to quell the burgeoning eagerness she saw in the girl's eyes. "No one must suspect the purpose of your presence on Carcer. There are many who covet the Crystal's power. It must not be allowed to fall yet again into evil hands. Its rightful place, its only place, is here."

Glowing, determined eyes stared up at the black-gowned figure. "I will do what must be done. The

Crystal will be returned to Aranea."

A strange emotion flashed across the High Priestess' face, passing so quickly that Alia barely had the chance to wonder at the unusual display of feeling. As if seeming to remember herself, the older femina continued, her face once more a dark enigma.

"See that it does. You are our last hope."

Alia could hardly contain her eagerness. "When do I leave for Carcer?"

The High Priestess coldly eyed the girl, her displeasure frosting the already stone-chilled room. "You will be transported in three sols," she finally answered, her voice tight and clipped, "arriving at Carcer's claiming station. Merge into the crowd of Imperium claimants who are there to secure slaves of the planet's criminals. Seek out the man called Ferox. He has the Crystal."

She paused. "Unfortunately, there is no way to prepare you, no supplies nor weapons you may take, save the skills taught you these many cycles under the tutelage of the Sisterhood. To send you with anything else would call attention to your true purpose. All that you need must be found on Carcer.

"This Test of Worthiness is not only a trial of courage but also one of cunning. To succeed, you must be willing to use anyone or anything that presents itself, then toss it away when it ceases to serve you. Never make the mistake of encumbering yourself with something no longer of use. In the end it will only drag you down and divert you from the true quest, your holy mission—the salvation of our people."

"But how will I know where to go, where to seek the Knowing Crystal?" Alia asked, a frown marring her smooth brow. "Carcer is a large planet."

"If you are a true daughter of the blood the Crystal

will guide you, its voice growing stronger the nearer you draw. Open your heart, bare your soul to its pure call, and you will surely find the stone—as surely as it will find you."

Alia heard the note of finality. She bowed, then rose to her feet. "I will heed your words and obey them faithfully."

"See that you do. Now, I—"

A knock interrupted the High Priestess, who glanced at the door. "Enter!"

A Sister glided into the room. "Pardon, Domina Magna, you are wanted elsewhere."

Her nervous glance slid to Alia, then back to the High Priestess. "The matter of the mate of Jorna . . ."

"Ah, yes." The High Priestess turned to Alia standing so calmly before her, the only hint of her inner excitement the rosy flush that flamed her cheeks. "You are dismissed. In three sols time I will send for you. Prepare yourself."

Alia kissed the jeweled ring of sovereignty on the outstretched hand, then turned and strode across the room. Before she was halfway to the door, the Sister hurried to the High Priestess' side. Despite the whispered voice the words echoed off the stone walls, easily reaching Alia's retreating ears.

"So she knows? Does she suspect anything? How can you ever hope she will succeed?" the Sister babbled. "After all, she is hardly more than a child, and to go alone to a planet like Carcer!"

"Do I have a choice?" her superior bitterly snarled. "Well, no matter. The end will justify the means. And, small consolation that it is, aid is forthcoming. She will not be alone for long."

CHAPTER 1

ALIA CLOSED HER EYES AS THE TRANSPORT TECHNICIAN shoved the power lever forward on the control panel. A curious buzzing filled her ears, followed by a sensation of disembodiment. Heavy weariness, no doubt abetted by three noctes of restless anticipation, welled inside her. She felt exhausted, on the verge of collapse.

A scream forced its way up from some deep corner of her being. Alia concentrated on her strengthening inner focus, fixating on the mental image until the unacceptable impulse to cry out had passed.

The transport process had begun, and the terror of it paralysed her. Holding her flesh in a grip of iron, her mind swirled chaotically through the dark, sharp coldness of space. She felt torn apart, a literal splintering of body and soul. What if she died now and failed in her quest at its very start?

The thought froze her heart in a prison of ice.

Some travelers became lost in transport, their bodies fragmented into tiny atoms, to drift forever in the black loneliness of the universe. Was that fate now to be hers?

A low humming gradually rose in volume. It surrounded Alia with its harmonic vibrations, endlessly reverberating until the pulsations threatened to shatter her skull. She clutched at her head. The pain! No one had warned her of transport pain!

The rising din progressed in tone. The resonant clamor sharpened, until it acquired the semblance of voices—voices of nameless millions, crying out in agonized confusion, lost and adrift on the uncharted universe of ruined dreams and forfeited morality. They drew Alia, tugging at her heart until her mind swam in a chaotic dementia.

Yet, just when Alia thought she could bear no more, it ceased. Blessed peace flowed through her; a warm, soothing glow suffused her entire body. She tentatively inched one eye open.

She stood in a room of cool, gray-green hues. As she twisted her head around, Alia's finely strung nerves tightened to a dangerous tension. The room was empty. Where was she? What had gone wrong? The long suppressed scream rose again in her throat. This time only the Litany Against Fear could hold it back.

"I will not fear; I will be strong," Alia murmured softly, her words barely audible to even her own ears. "My courage true; my weakness wrong. I steel my heart; it will not last. The Crystal saves; my fear is past."

Her chanting filled the small room, rebounding off the smooth walls until it endlessly echoed, hammering at Alia's tortured mind. Slowly, she slipped into a near meditative state.

"Welcome to Carcer."

A flat metallic voice, speaking in the common language of the Imperium, forced its way into Alia's rapidly waning consciousness.

"Please exit through the departure portal."

As Alia glanced about her in helpless confusion, a partition to her right slid open. Inhaling a deep, steadying breath, she summoned forth her courage and stepped through the doorway.

The dreaded unknown on the other side was nothing more than a huge assembly room, constructed of the same minutely porous, gray-green stone as the transport chamber. Alia recognized the substance from her lessons on the videotutor. It was an air-diffusing rock called aerlapis, capable of efficiently cleansing the interior climate without allowing any of the suffocating heat or cold of the outside to permeate. Carcer was said to be uniquely cursed with an abundance of it, from solid mountains and underground caves to its gritty, pulverized form in the desert.

Her gaze continued to scan the large room. There were citizens of nearly every Imperium planet in the crowd. With some relief she was finally able to pick out several females, though all were alien to the humanoid species. Good, Alia thought. She had no desire to stand out in this particular gathering as the only one of the feminine gender.

Surreptitiously, Alia edged toward the mass of milling bodies. A male Simian lurched past. Hairy and hulking, he swung by, long, gangly arms swinging loosely in front of him. Alia tensed with barely concealed repulsion, his rank stench nauseating her long after he had disappeared into the agitated throng.

A high-pitched whine pierced the multitude's

muted roar, diverting the attention of all to the cubic video screen suspended in the center of the room.

"Welcome to Carcer, the prison of the Imperium," announced the same rasping voice from the transport chamber. "Attend to the following instructions for the claiming of a prisoner. You are free to acquire any being found on this planet wearing a govern collar."

The video panned in for a close-up of the collar. It appeared, to Alia, to be of a dark, leathery consistency, tubular in shape. From a small ring on the collar dangled something dull and metallic.

"The collar," the voice droned on, "is made of a virtually indestructible, beryllium-impregnated hide. Each collar is equipped with half of a key. You will receive the other half at the termination of this presentation. When the prisoner of your choice surrenders his key, you will be in complete control and claiming will commence. The two keys can be joined, when necessary, producing a painful deterrent that easily handles even the most unmanageable of felons. As long as the two keys are in your possession, total power will be maintained over your slave. Guard them well.

"Never forget your slave is dangerous," the voice continued. "All have been tried and exiled here by their home planets for a serious crime. Many will be more than willing to go with you, to subjugate themselves to a life of slavery. Their existence on Carcer is far from pleasant. A small kindness to be sure is this ability to choose the ultimate site of one's punishment. It is the only leniency ever shown these vile felons, but never forget there will be no gratitude or loyalty, save what the govern collar and its keys enforce."

Alia glanced around at the rapt, upturned faces. Though differing in a myriad of genetically incredible ways, all wore the same expressions of greedy anticipation. In that moment, they appeared little better than the criminals they so eagerly sought. She shifted restlessly, wondering how any of this could possibly help her. What she needed to discover was where the Knowing Crystal was to be found.

The video screen flickered briefly, then a map appeared. "This is a photo image of Carcer," the grating voice began again. "The provinces of Tarnor, Brodat and Nsate are the best areas for slave hunting. Avoid, at all costs, the province of Macer. It is the abode of the master criminal Ferox, the infamous traitor responsible for the massacre of Moraca. Macer is outside our sphere of influence. All dwelling there are foresworn never to be claimed. It would be foolhardy and, in most instances, fatal to attempt to enter this restricted area."

Ferox! The name shot through Alia with a jolting force. Ferox was in Macer! A wild elation exploded within her. At last the quest had some direction, pointing her toward the province of Macer.

"The video presentation is now terminated. Please exit through one of the three portals available on your right." The swoosh of partitions opening momentarily distracted the gathering. "Follow the corridors to the equipment rooms at the end of the halls. There you will receive your half of the govern key, supplies for seven sols and a transit equs. We wish you success."

The screen went black, and the room once again brightened. The low murmur of voices swelled to a discordant roar. As one, the crowd eagerly surged toward the exits, inadvertently drawing Alia with them.

*   *   *

Less than two horas later, Alia found herself mounted on a slightly sway-backed equs, a large bag of supplies tied to the rear of the saddle. Leaning over, she uncertainly peered down at the animal.

Over 20 hands high, the beast was a shaggy behemoth. Mottled gray in color, he possessed a bearded chin and long hair curling down the back of four, massive legs. The equs' hooves were cloven, a common practicality for all beasts of desert and rocky terrain. Only the large, wedge-shaped head, widely set eyes and tiny prick ears gave any hint of a basic intelligence and calm nature.

Well, Alia thought wryly, it wasn't as if she hadn't had experience with equs. They were common enough throughout the Imperium, but most of them just weren't quite so . . . so overwhelming.

As she patiently waited for the bulk of the throng to take their leave of the departure point, Alia busied herself rifling through the contents of the pouch. There was ample water, various food parcels, her half of the govern key and, joy of joys, a map, locator compass and stun gun. She smiled to herself, harking back to the lessons in the gun's use that Nonia, an old lay sister, had secretly given her. At least she now possessed some form of protection, however archaic.

Extracting the map and compass, Alia studied them. Then, glancing up at the brilliant red sun nearing its zenith, she quickly oriented herself to her location and projected route. Macer, apparently a mountainous province from the looks of the map, lay a full six-sol journey across a huge desert called Mors.

She noted an oasis located about halfway there. If she were lucky and didn't get lost, her supplies should last until she reached it. Food and water for the return journey would have to be replenished in

Macer—*if* she lived long enough to even get there, Alia thought, suddenly in a black humor.

Carefully refolding the precious map, she replaced it and the locator compass in the smaller pouch hanging next to her right thigh. Yes, there was indeed much to adapt to on this planet if she were to survive, much less successfully retrieve the Knowing Crystal.

Familiar only with Aranea's yellow star, Alia realized that, until her eyes adjusted, she would have to proceed with greater caution in the dimmer light of Carcer's red sun. And then there were the hostile flora and fauna of this unfortunate planet, heretofore the sterile, nonthreatening subjects of her studies. At the thought of them, she repressed a tiny shudder.

Glancing around, Alia noted that the majority of the crowd of potential claimants had departed. It was past time for her to be gone. Inhaling a deep breath to steady the pounding of her heart, she nudged the equs in the side. The animal obediently ambled off toward the carved aerlapis arches of the exit portal, leaving behind the relative safety of the transport station. The foreboding terrain of Carcer lay beyond. There was no turning back; the quest for the Knowing Crystal had at last begun.

It was high noon, three sols later, when Alia wearily reined in her equs at the top of yet another large sand dune. She wiped the eternally present aerlapis dust from her damp brow, her grit-reddened eyes scanning the horizon, desperately seeking sign of the oasis indicated on the map. It had to be somewhere in this vicinity, unless . . .

She refused to let the nagging, persistently doubtful little voice shake her confidence. Of course she had read the map correctly; the consequences of any other course were unthinkable.

Alia glanced down at the molded domare-hide flask hanging near her left thigh. There was just enough of the precious water left if she reversed her direction and immediately headed back to the transport station. But then what would she do except turn around and start out all over again? No, there wasn't any other choice. She would have to continue in the direction she was going. The oasis was bound to be over the next hill—or two.

Alia rode on. Her eyes swept the parched, barren land. Empty and pitiless, she mused, just like the look of the High Priestess that morning in Aranea's transport chamber. Had it been only three sols ago? It seemed more like three monates.

The High Priestess! Alia shuddered at even the memory of her name. For a few secundae, duty and revulsion warred tumultuously in her mind. Alone and far from her powerful influence, Alia's loathing for the femina briefly overcame her strict training. What unfriendly fate, she wondered, had ever led her into the hands of that femina?

As far back as she could remember there had always been the dark, unyielding form of the High Priestess, watching her every move, vigilant in her untiring attempts to discipline, to mold. But to mold into what and for what purpose? That was the mystery that plagued Alia, as much in sleep as in her waking moments, ever since she was old enough to marvel at the motivations of a femina who evidently bore her no affection.

Gradually, Alia became aware of an unbearably burning thirst, scorching its way into her contemplation. She reined in the equs and dismounted. Removing her water flask, she carefully poured a portion of the precious fluid into her hand. She offered it to the thirsty animal. He quickly consumed the meager amount and nudged her for more.

"Sorry, old boy." She smiled sadly at the giant beast. "That'll have to do until we rest this nocte, or reach that cursedly elusive oasis."

She raised the flask to her lips for a brief, blessed swallow and then, hanging it back on the saddle, remounted. With a despairing sigh Alia once more urged the equs onward, across the endless sands, toward a destination that promised to be even more harrowing than the blistering hell she now rode through.

The torrid red sun, even hotter than Aranea's despite its diminished brilliance, beat down, seeming to evaporate the very air around her. Drained of even the will to wipe the sweat dripping from her brow, Alia's thoughts began to wander in a confused manner.

The Sisterhood of the Crystal—why, oh why, had they given her such an impossible task for her Test of Worthiness? Perhaps they had planned it that way; perhaps they had never intended her to succeed and finally win her place in their hallowed order. But that couldn't be. With a violent gesture Alia shook her head, as if to mentally throw aside the treacherous thoughts. No, the High Priestess wanted her to find the Crystal, of that much she was certain. Yet it seemed more than mere devotion to duty that prompted the femina's engrossment in her and her education. Did it perhaps have something to do with the crown of Aranea? True, it was her birthright to eventually rule, but to attribute the High Priestess' motives to that was beyond belief.

In her heart Alia knew there had never been any hope of wearing the crystal crown. The people had long ago chosen the Sisterhood to rule rather than the frail, now nearly extinct Royal House of Certare. And if that fact were not enough, there was always the constant assurances of the High Priestess, endlessly disparaging Alia's abilities to reign.

Yet one inescapable reality remained—the almost unnatural interest of the High Priestess, an interest that bordered on obsession. The High Priestess seemed to need her with a desperate intensity that puzzled Alia. What else could explain the endless horas of personal tutoring, the frequent emphasis on self-control and logic in all things?

Everything, she realized with a sudden, insightful clarity, had been directed toward this ultimate quest, toward the prophecy that had insidiously entwined its words and purpose around her heart until ultimately it imprisoned her very life.

Even now, in a land forsaken by any living being, Alia could almost hear the words of the High Priestess. They echoed within her head, growing in force and volume until she thought the very sands were mocking her.

"Caring is a weakness, a luxury for the cowardly and dimwitted. Strength is to be valued over compassion. Control your emotions, or someone else will control you through them."

With an abrupt jerk on the reins, Alia halted the equs. She gripped her head in her hands, desperately holding together a skull that threatened to explode—yet the pounding persisted. The long cycles of training continued even now, as the programmed phrases built up to their final, overwhelming climax.

"There is no responsibility but to the Sisterhood, no morality except that of perfect, unquestioning obedience. Only in that way can we ever hope to regain the

Knowing Crystal and fulfill, once again, the sacred duty to our planet and the Imperium. As the Crystal's ancient keepers, our path is higher and more difficult. Only through our unquestioning faith shall we finally prevail, and the Crystal, with its power, shall be ours—this time for all eternity!"

The reverberating words slipped back into the hidden recesses of Alia's mind. She became aware, once again, of the desert's dead silence and the broiling heat. She cautiously opened one eye, then the other. Nothing moved, not a breeze to ruffle the endless ripples of sand nor a bird to dot the sun-bleached sky. She was alone, adrift on a lost sea of barren waste.

Despite the High Priestess' admonitions to the contrary, the Knowing Crystal had yet to speak to her. Her journey so far had been one based on sheer faith and the meager knowledge of where Ferox was rumored to be found. What if the Crystal never called her? How could she possibly go on without its aid? Was she a fool who was on a quest both hopeless and, perhaps, deadly? Yet what other choice was there but to forge ahead, however blind her faith might be? To do less would be unworthy, and then she'd never see her home again.

In a brave gesture of defiance Alia threw back her shoulders and straightened in the saddle. Her face shone with a resolute peace. She *would* succeed; all things pointed to it. She was the last of her royal line. The prophecy would not be denied.

With a joy she had not felt in many sols, she urged the equs up over a towering mound of sand and reined him to a halt. There, shimmering in the distance, was a large, heavily treed area. The oasis! Alia pushed her mount forward and rode as fast as the terrain would allow, her exultant cry carrying far across the desert.

The spring's cool, swirling waters called to Alia, beckoning her into its dark blue depths. She felt torn, wavering between an instinctive caution and the overwhelming desire to lower her naked body into the velvety fluid, undulating so invitingly before her. To wash away the sols of grit and sweat and finally be clean again—could anything be sweeter?

Surely it was safe. After testing the water for potability, Alia and the equs had drunk their fill without disturbance or hint of an intruder. At any rate, since she had left Carcer's transport station, there had been no sign of man nor beast. To be extra cautious, though, she could leave her clothes and stun gun within easy reach of the water's edge. With that reassuring thought in mind, Alia made her decision. Tying the equs a safe distance away in the trees, she quickly returned to the spring and disrobed.

The headgear she had devised to shade her head and face was shed first, followed by her tunic. Woven by the mutant spiders of her planet, the tan fabric, although airy, provided total protection against the sun's burning rays. High-necked, with long sleeves gathered in cuffs at her wrists, it fit her snugly along torso and waist, except where it opened below her throat. Her soft, ankle-high, leather boots and breeches, fashioned of the same cool fabric as her tunic, came next. At last, Alia eased herself into the inviting water.

The spring gathered her into its silky embrace, caressing her hot, feverish flesh and soothing her tortured nerves. She swam under the surface for precious invigorating secundae until the need for air

24

forced her upward. Pausing just long enough to gather another breath Alia dove again, to seek out once more the spring's dark, refreshing coolness.

She glided along the bottom, her shapely iridescent form weaving in and out among the dark green aquatic foliage. Her long strokes carried her halfway across the pond before her lungs again cried for sustenance. Surging upward, Alia's lithe, young body broke the surface. Gaily tossing her head, she flung her wet, flame-hued tresses from her face.

Alia froze, her finely tuned senses shrilling a warning of danger. She whirled about in the water, wildly searching for the threat, and, as her eyes came to rest upon the spot where she had recently disrobed, she saw him.

Long, muscular legs spread apart, his booted feet straddled her small pile of clothing. Alia's gaze traveled upward, past the dusty, brown breeches and wide leather belt embedded with hammered metal, to a broad, bronzed chest densely matted with black hair. A small jolt of apprehension shuddered through her at the sight of the pale, jagged scars that marred his upper torso and arms. Yet it was not until her glance reached his neck that the fear, stark and vivid, tore through her.

He wore a govern collar! Thrashing about in the water, she looked around for means of escape or for her stun gun. A sickening realization filled her. She had left the gun with her clothing. With a sinking sensation in the pit of her stomach, Alia warily turned to face her adversary.

"Looking for this, are you?" he asked in a deep voice, speaking what Alia recognized as the common language.

She raised defiant brown eyes to his, but not before her gaze had taken in her stun gun, clasped firmly in a large, masculine hand. "That's mine." She forced her statement out, her throat tight and dry. "Give it to me."

A dark brow quirked in amusement. "So, you want it back, do you? Then come and get it."

Alia made a motion toward him, then stopped. The only barrier between her and total nudity was the water. As if guessing her dilemma a wicked grin spread across the man's face, highlighting its ruggedly attractive planes.

She stood there, gaping up at him, mesmerized by the tall, powerful stranger. Gray eyes, glinting like silver lightning, smiled down at her. Her glance nervously moved over his face, noting the dark, closely cropped beard that did little to hide the square jaw and stubborn set of his chin. If anything, it only accentuated the raw virility of his already intimidating presence.

The man shifted his weight, but his casual stance did nothing to alleviate Alia's growing consternation. It was quite obvious he felt he had the upper hand. Watching him, she inwardly cursed his dominance over her, knowing all the while she had no other choice but to submit—at least for the time being. Alia forced herself to calmly await his next move.

"Well, what's it to be?" he prodded her. "Are you coming out or not?"

"Not until you leave!" she snapped back at him.

"And miss the best entertainment I've had in the past two cycles? Not likely!"

"Then I'm not coming out!"

The man shrugged and lowered his sinewy frame onto the grass. He ran a careless hand through his thick, wavy hair.

"As you wish. I'm a patient man. I can wait."

Alia's mind raced. Obviously there was no way to

outbluff this ruffian. Perhaps appealing to his sense of decency, if he had any, would work. At this point she was willing to try anything.

She gave him her sweetest smile. "Won't you at least turn around while I come out of the water and dress? A man of honor would do that much."

He threw back his head and gave a shout of laughter. "And give you the chance to knock me out or stab me in the back? I haven't survived on this miserable planet by being honorable, much less trusting someone enough to turn my back on them."

His eyes narrowed into hard bits of glacial ice. "You heard my terms, femina. Just be thankful I don't nail you where you stand."

"Well, then you may as well go ahead and do it!" Alia cried, her patience at an end. "I'm not going to come out while you're here, you . . . you uncouth mudpig!"

She spat the insult at him, her hands rising to a place of defiance on her hips. Oh, how she hated his arrogance and his position of control over her! She was certainly used to a more subservient manner from Aranean men.

"Mudpig, am I?" The stranger's mouth quirked roguishly. "That could be easily remedied by a bath. Is that an invitation to join you?"

Alia's eyes widened in horror, and she instinctively stepped further into the water. "Most definitely not!"

"Then as I said before, I can wait. That spring gets quite cold with prolonged exposure. You'll come out soon enough or freeze."

"Freezing would be a preferable fate," she sniffed indignantly.

At the same time, though, Alia began to notice the water's bone-chilling cold, and it wasn't long before her body began to shiver uncontrollably. As the secundae passed, she felt her feet and hands grow numb.

Her mind frantically searched for a plan, a way out of her harrowing dilemma, but found nothing. She was at his mercy, naked and defenseless. What a fool she had been to get herself into this position! The desert sun had obviously parched more than her body. Was it here her quest was fated to end, almost before it had even begun, ignominiously freezing to death in a spring?

Perhaps it would be better to swallow her pride. If she could survive whatever horrible things he surely had planned for her, there was always a chance of eventually regaining the upper hand. And there was more here at stake than just personal honor. An entire planet, an Imperium, was depending on her. Blue lips opened to acquiesce to his demands, when a new voice interrupted her.

"And what have we here, Teran?"

An aging graybeard sauntered out of the trees and over to where the younger man reclined. He, too, wore a govern collar.

Teran glanced up at the old man in ragged white robes and smiled warmly. "Nothing of any import, Teacher. Just a naked femina who'd rather freeze than come out of the water."

The man in white robes turned to curiously stare at Alia. Then he smiled at her, his expression gentle and strangely soothing. "Why won't you come out of the water, child? You're far too lovely to end your sols in there."

Alia's teeth chattered as she tried to answer. "H-he hasn't a sh-shred of honor and I-I won't come out until he leaves!"

"Then leave he shall." The old man turned to Teran. "You've amused yourself long enough at the femina's expense, don't you think, my son?" A stern frown spread across the wise, weathered planes of his face.

Teran shrugged. "I suppose so, Vates. Just don't turn your back on her. She could be dangerous." He rose and strode off into the trees, the stun gun still in his hand.

Alia waited until he disappeared, then directed her attention to the old man. If only she could win him over . . .

"Elderman," she began respectfully, "if now you, too, would leave . . ."

"We will await you beyond those trees. Do not tarry. My young friend Teran can be short of temper." He smiled one last time, then followed the path Teran had taken.

Barely had Vates left the water's edge when Alia jumped from the water. Donning her clothes in an awkward, fumbling manner, she considered her absolute stroke of luck at the old man's arrival. She would never have a better opportunity.

She must escape, with or without the stun gun. The equs was tied among the trees to the right of where the two criminals had disappeared. There was a chance, if the animal had not been discovered. If she could just get far enough away before they realized she was gone . . .

Forcing her numb limbs into motion, Alia stumbled toward the waiting equs. Heedless of the pain, she gave no thought to shield her face from the foliage that blocked her way. She fled the danger behind her, the branches clawing at her and attempting, in their mindless grasping, to further impede her path to freedom. The leaves slapped at her face until she was nearly blind from the blows, but still she staggered on. Her only thought was escape. She must not fail. The Crystal was waiting; her people were depending on her.

A hard, unyielding body suddenly appeared, barring her way. Strong arms encircled her. Alia screamed in surprise, then her finely honed battle skills instinctively took command. She fiercely stomped on a booted instep, feeling a grim satisfaction at Teran's surprised grunt. As his head came down in pain, she deftly raised a knee, aiming it toward his groin. At the same moment, her hand swung around to deliver a sharp chop to the side of his neck.

The next few secundae were a confused blur, as Teran reacted to her moves with razor-sharp reflexes. As quickly as it had begun, the fight was over. Alia found herself pinned in a hold beyond even her ability to escape.

Her struggles slowly subsided. She fell against him, defeated, trembling breathlessly in his arms. The rise and fall of his broad, naked chest gradually quieted her until they breathed in unison. A gentle hand on her head, stroking her hair, filled Alia with an odd sense of comfort. Her tense body relaxed against Teran's, her feminine curves intuitively molding into his hard, masculine angles.

For some reason beyond any reason, it felt right and natural to touch like that.

"Ah, femina," Teran suddenly groaned, breaking into the curious lethargy settling over her, "what are you doing to me?"

Alia raised wide, wondering eyes. And what are you doing to me? she thought. What are these strange new sensations? Are you casting a spell? I have heard of the ability of certain beings to steal the minds of the unsuspecting. Is this what is happening to me?

"Please, let me go. I won't try to escape. Just let me

go," she pleaded, her terror suddenly more fearsome than before. She struggled, but this time against the drugging sensations of Teran's body pressed into hers.

He flung her from him, his chest heaving from the effort and the long-repressed need. A hot desire flared within, and the blood surged through Teran's groin. How long had it been since he'd last lain with a femina—over two cycles now? Two long, gut-wrenching cycles! An eternity in the life of a man still as young and hot-blooded as he.

It was almost more than Teran could bear to see this beautiful, flame-haired femina standing before him and not take her, not finally satisfy his long-smoldering hunger. Yet, in that instant between desire and action, a stern discipline, tempered by an inborn sense of honor, rose to quench the fires wildly raging through his body. He could not, would not, have her against her will, no matter how agonizing his needs. With a deep sigh, Teran's tense body relaxed. He stepped even further away.

Alia stared back at him, fighting her own strangely whirling emotions. How quickly her feelings for the handsome criminal had changed!

A tiny voice droned a familiar warning. *"Control your emotions."*

From a place equally as deep, Alia retained her self-command. She cleared her throat. "Perhaps it's time we were getting back to your friend."

With a husky laugh, Teran grabbed her by the arm and shoved her ahead of him. "Get on with you then. Let's not keep Vates waiting."

Once again Alia fought her way through the dense foliage, this time with more care. She knew Teran was behind her, yet she could barely hear his footsteps. She wondered if his stealth were a survival trait acquired on Carcer or one learned in a life before his exile here. Well, no matter. Either way, he was a formidable foe.

The realization salved her wounded pride at being captured so easily. She vowed, however, never to let her guard down again. The importance of her quest provided little room for error, and Alia feared she had just exhausted any leeway granted her.

A firm grip on her shoulder startled her out of her thoughts.

"We are here." Teran's deep voice reverberated in her ear, sending a surprising chill down her spine.

"Here? Where is here?" Alia asked, as she glanced about in confusion. If anything, the trees and bushes were even more dense and overgrown in this particular spot. And there was no sign of Vates.

Teran strode over to a large bush. With the sweep of a powerful arm, he pushed the leafy mass aside. Alia's eyes widened. The dark mouth of a cave lay beneath the plant's camouflage, angling downward into the earth.

She walked over to Teran. "You've been hiding here, haven't you? No wonder I saw no sign of life when I arrived."

A wry smile touched his lips. "It's our hiding place whenever we visit this oasis, one of the few havens where we dare sleep without eternal vigilance."

He took her hand. "Follow me. It's dark and rocky."

She allowed him to lead her into the subterranean depths, though she inwardly shuddered at the thought of going down into such a gaping pit. The blackness quickly engulfed her. As they walked along, Alia had the eerie sensation of being swallowed, blind and helpless without her sight to guide her. Save for the rough grasp of Teran's hand and the sound of his breathing, she could have sworn she was alone, buried alive in the heavy darkness. And what additional horrors was he leading her to, once they reached the end of this particular journey?

A ponderous silence settled over them, until Alia felt she was entering a world with no hope of return. Reality merged with fantasy, until it was virtually impossible to differentiate one from the other. A growing need to reach out to Teran, to reconfirm that all this, however terrifying, was real, flooded through her.

"How . . . how can you tell where you're going?" Her voice echoed hollowly in the dank chamber of stone. "I can't see a thing, and you walk along as if it's sol bright in here."

A deep chuckle rumbled out of the darkness. How strangely comforting it sounded, even coming from a man who was a dangerous criminal and her despised captor.

"Well, I wouldn't say it was quite that bright," Teran laughed, "but after the cycles I've spent here, my eyes have adapted to Carcer's dimmer light. That, combined with a special plant native to this planet, has more than adequately aided my vision."

"A plant?" Perhaps if she, too, could acquire some of this vegetation . . . "What kind of plant could possibly help your vision?"

"A slender, deep orange vegetable with a green, leafy top. It's one of our staple foods here. If you like, I'll point it out to you sometime."

"Yes, please. That would be nice."

They lapsed into silence as the way angled sharply downward and the path became more rocky. Alia stumbled once, falling against Teran. The warmth of his body in the clammy tunnel was reassuring. She clung to him for an instant. When she forced herself to her own two feet, he pulled her back against him once again.

"Hold onto me," he commanded. "It'll keep you from falling. We're almost there."

Alia raised light-starved eyes and thought that, far ahead, she saw a slight, dusky tinge to the blackness. She gripped his belt and obediently moved on. This was certainly not the time to argue, no matter how much she loathed taking orders from him. The dark slowly lifted. Finally, as they rounded one last corner, the tunnel gave way to a brightly lit room.

Seemingly hewn from the aerlapis stone in which it lay, the chamber was circular in shape and spacious without being cavernous. Though Alia found the ceiling adequate in height, it was not meant for one of Teran's stature. He was forced to stoop slightly when they entered.

Vates looked up from a small fire he was stoking and smiled at Teran. "Ah, I see you convinced the femina to sample our hospitality after all."

His glance moved to Alia. "Come, come, child. Sit here beside me and have a cup of faba. It will warm you after the cold trip through the cave."

Hastily disengaging the fingers still clamped around Teran's belt, Alia stepped around him and walked over to Vates. Though she mistrusted the old man's attempts at friendliness, it was preferable to the disquieting closeness of Teran's body. There was a strange power in the tall foreboding man, a power that seemed to attract her.

She tossed her long, wavy hair defiantly at the thought. The solution was really quite simple, she blithely informed herself. Just stay away from him until she could escape, once and for all.

Alia sat down across from Vates and accepted the proffered mug of faba. The round, stone bowl felt warm and comforting in her hands, but, though the aroma wafting from it smelled tantalizing, she was loathe to drink it. There could be anything beneath the rich brown surface of the liquid—poison, truth drug, anything. Suppressing an urge to taste of the brew she raised her eyes to Vates, forcing her gaze to meet his with the same direct intensity.

"It is quite safe, child," the old man said, the smile on his face never wavering. "We mean you no harm."

"Then why do you hold me prisoner?" Alia's chin lifted belligerently.

Teran snorted in disgust as he lowered himself beside her. "Because someone had better protect you from whatever mad purpose has sent you here. Have you any idea what danger you're in, wandering about on a planet peopled with thieves and murderers?"

"As a matter of fact, meeting you has brought that point forcefully home!" Alia angrily retorted. "You're the most loathsome, stupid—"

"Stupid? And what do you call leaving your stun gun behind while you swim naked in the spring?" he growled. "The only stupid thing I did was save you from your own fatal idiocy!"

Alia set down her mug and scrambled to her feet, struggling to contain the rage that threatened to overwhelm her. "I never asked for your help and most certainly don't want it. So, if you're quite though 'saving' me, I'll be on my way."

She turned toward the cave opening when Teran sprang up, effectively blocking her way. Only millimeters from her, his eyes glittered dangerously.

"Sit down," he muttered through clenched teeth. "You're not going anywhere until we're quite through with you."

Their eyes locked, battling fiercely. Oh, how she loathed him and his overwhelming physical advantage! Even with her excellent combat skills, Alia realized she would never be a match for his power and lightning quick reflexes. *That* had been quite aptly demonstrated earlier.

A tiny voice teased the edges of her memory, inching its way into the seething anger of the present situation. What was it the High Priestess had said? Something about the mind being an even more lethal weapon than the body?

Alia relaxed, a slight smile on her delicately curved lips. The uncouth lout before her could be handled by less overt tactics.

"As you wish, my lord." She forced the honeyed words out, though the very thought of false capitulation nauseated her. "I know when I've met my match." *And when I haven't, too,* she mentally hissed at him.

Teran's gray eyes narrowed in amused suspicion. *This little cat has claws she prefers to keep well hidden for the present, but then, Vates and I have a few secret weapons of our own.*

He smiled down at her in apparent acceptance. "Then we understand each other. Now, sit. My teacher and I have a few questions."

Alia obediently lowered herself to the ground, her face an inscrutable blank. Vates, who had been quietly observing their interaction, broke the silence by clearing his throat. Two pairs of eyes turned toward him.

"Please forgive my young companion's lack of tact. Though we have survived on this planet by sometimes harsh means, we are neither cruel nor vicious men— perhaps just a little unpolished and blunt," he said, sternly glancing at Teran.

At his teacher's quelling look, Teran heaved an

exasperated sigh and rolled his eyes toward the ceiling.

Vates's gaze lingered on him for an instant longer, then returned to Alia. "Nonetheless, we are concerned for you, child. You wear no govern collar, so it is evident you are not a criminal. And, if you are on Carcer to claim a prisoner as slave, you are far off course."

He leaned slightly toward Alia. As he did, a light-headed sensation washed over her.

"Therefore, we can only surmise you have come here for some other reason," Vates continued.

His dark eyes burned brightly, searing Alia to the very depths of her being.

"What *is* that reason, child?"

CHAPTER 2

ALIA'S HEAD WHIRLED GIDDILY. SHE FELT WEAK AND drained, as if her thoughts and inner strength were being dragged from her, as if from a source outside herself.

Vates was using a mind seek!

Summoning all her abilities, Alia threw up a mental shield to the brain-sapping power of the old man. For long minutes she held out against the psychic hammering on her cognitive wall until she finally thrust Vates' probing aside.

She exhaled a triumphant breath. In her wildest dreams, never had she expected to need that particular lesson of the Sisterhood, yet at this moment Alia was more than thankful for the grueling horas of training. The High Priestess had prepared her well.

The expression on Vates' face slowly changed, first to confused frustration, then gradual realization and finally to one of respect. "I salute you, child. Whoever sent you has trained you well. I have not experienced a mind block as strong as yours in many a year."

"You have no right . . ."

The old man sighed. "That is true. I have no right. These are harsh times, however, since the Crystal was lost, and sometimes it necessitates harsh actions. I would not have used the knowledge I gained against you, if that is any comfort."

"Nothing you could say would be of comfort, save the gift of my freedom!"

"And that I cannot give, child. There is still much to learn from you."

Vates rose and walked over to where two crudely sewn domare-hide bags lay. He sorted through the contents, then glanced back at Teran.

"We shall require fresh fruit to stretch our meager supper. Why don't you take her along to help? She may need her supplies, and it would be wise to hide the equs, too."

He paused to smile at Alia's open-mouthed surprise. "Yes, child, Teran discovered your equs even before he found you."

The younger man unfolded his sinewy legs. In one fluid motion, he stood up. "With or without her equs, I think she will be more hindrance than help, considering her determination to run away, but if that is your wish . . ."

He turned to stare down at Alia. "Come on. You would be well advised to forget any ideas of escape, though."

Teran wheeled around and strode toward the tunnel opening. Realizing that she couldn't find her way through the underground shaft without him, Alia scrambled to her feet and raced after him. It might be just the opportunity to escape she'd been waiting for.

Behind her, she heard Vates chuckle to himself.

"Teran," she called just as he reached the cavern opening, "wait for me."

He halted, then slowly turned to face her. After studying Alia for a moment he offered his hand.

"Come."

She inhaled a deep breath before placing her hand in his. The show of trust, the false demonstration of cooperation, was necessary if she were to have any hope of winning her freedom, but how she hated touching him.

This time the journey through the black tunnel was less traumatic, if not less disconcerting. Hands entwined around Teran's belt once more, she followed him as they retraced their path through the darkness.

The subtle play of his hard back muscles against her hands wreaked havoc with Alia's emotional equilibrium. She marveled at how the slightest feel of him could set off such strange sensations within her. Perhaps it was merely because he was the first man she had ever been physically close to. True, Aranean men appeared just as imposing as this renegade whose nearness she was forced to tolerate in the darkness, but there had never been opportunity to know any, much less touch them.

Aranean custom dictated the two sexes be kept apart until the time of mating, and mating would be forever denied Alia, once she became a professed member of the Sisterhood of the Crystal.

For an irrational instant, she allowed herself to wonder what it would be like with Teran. The High Priestess had called it a degrading duty; the lust-crazed desires of a male were tolerated as a loathsome evil, an unfortunate necessity for species propagation. Yet despite the older femina's inculcations, Alia found it difficult to view Teran's commanding

41

masculinity in a disgusting light, even considering the short time she had known him. No, as innocent as she still was in matters of the flesh, he was far from disgusting.

With a mental grimace, she forced her meanderings back on a firmly disciplined path. It was a senseless waste of time, allowing her thoughts to wander off on such tangents. What she needed was an escape plan.

Lulling Teran into a false sense of security was the most obvious course of action, then, when he least expected it, she would execute a chop at the back of the neck and retrieve her stun gun. It should be easy enough, considering the overconfident lout he was. The High Priestess had said, time and time again, that males were little more than pompous fools.

The first glimmers of light caught Alia's eye. Once at the bush shielding the entrance, she paused while Teran stopped and listened intently.

"It's safe; there's no one about," he finally muttered.

Shoving aside the bush that hid the entrance, he climbed out. He offered Alia his hand. She ignored it and proudly, if awkwardly, crawled up out of the hole on her own.

Both blinked in the bright sunlight, slowly readjusting their eyes. Alia found Teran looking down at her, a bemused smile on his face, and she frowned, puzzled.

"Why are you staring at me like that?"

Why indeed? Teran asked himself. What was it about this femina that drove him to verbally lash out at her one moment and the next moment want to pull her into his arms? She was dangerous, this lovely creature obviously from a world beyond Carcer; her purpose here was both mysterious and foreboding.

42

Yet when she looked up at him like she was doing just now with those wide, melting brown eyes, he sensed a curious bonding between them.

Teran shook his head to clear his confused thoughts. In an effort to force himself back to reality, he turned his attention to gently disentangling a twig that had ensnared itself in her hair. How silky, he thought, just like the famous spun gold threads of the female weaving spiders of Aranea—and perhaps, he fiercely reminded himself, just as deadly.

When he touched her, Alia's breath caught in her throat. Her body tensed as he leaned close to carefully pull loose the twisted strands of her hair. She could feel the warmth emanating from his body and smell his musky scent.

Suddenly it was all she could do to keep from touching him, to feel the taut muscles of his arms wrap around her, to bury her face in the corded strength of his chest. The compulsion grew, until Alia was certain she'd go mad if she fought it a moment longer. What, in the heavens above, was the matter with her?

Uttering a soft cry, she wrenched herself free from Teran. She ran, fleeing the haunting emotions that threatened to tear apart her carefully constructed world. Alia fled for what seemed a long time and thought he failed to follow. Yet when she was finally compelled to stop, her lungs gasping for air, Teran was there.

"Why did you run?" he asked, his eyes dark with confusion. "I meant no harm."

She forced herself to meet his gaze, squeezing the reply past her constricted throat. "To escape from you, of course."

Though the words were a lie on one level, on yet another they were painful reality. All the cycles of training, the long horas of painful discipline, had melted in the heat of her unexpected response. When had she ever been prepared to deal with these most primitive of emotions?

Alia recognized them for what they were—the mating urge. The thought filled her with revulsion. How could she allow herself to sink to such primal desires? Yet perhaps this, too, was part of her test. It was said the trial could materialize when and where one least expected and be of the most degrading kind. This temptation, like all the others, would pass, if only she held to her training.

She squared her shoulders. "The sun is setting. We must hurry if we are to find fruit for our supper."

A slight hesitation glimmered in his gray eyes but only for an instant. Then, with a shrug, Teran strode away, calling to Alia as he went.

"Follow me. I think I remember seeing a cerasa tree over here. The fruit smelled sweet and ready for the plucking."

Alia moved her reluctant legs. Escape, at least for the moment, was beyond her emotional ability. All she could think of was fruit, sweet and ready for the plucking.

Vates was bent over the fire, stirring a pot of thick stew, when Alia and Teran returned. The aroma was tantalizing, considering she had eaten nothing but dehydrated food for the past three sols. Suspecting the chance of drugs in their food, Alia controlled her surge of hunger. Instead, she busied herself placing the armful of fruit she had picked onto a nearby flat rock. At least, she consoled herself, the fragrantly sweet cerasa would be safe to eat.

"Here, child, take some." Vates handed her a wooden platter of stew.

She shook her head. "No, I prefer my own rations, thank you."

Turning her back on the old man, Alia walked over to her bag of supplies. She rummaged through the various parcels until she found a dried meatstick and some bread.

Vates was still holding the platter when she returned. "Are you sure you wouldn't like some? Teran tells me I can make a feast out of most anything."

"Quite sure," Alia stiffly replied.

She was not about to let them feed her drug-laced food. They had made it more than evident they wanted information about her purpose on Carcer. Perhaps they were the very ones the High Priestess had warned her about, coveters of the Knowing Crystal's power.

Vates shrugged and handed the stew to Teran. "As you wish, child." He dished himself a serving before moving around the fire to sit between them.

They ate in silence. Alia doggedly chewed the tough meatstick, averting her eyes from the succulent slivers of meat and tender vegetables on the platters next to her. There were many kinds of torture to wear a person down, she thought, some more insidious than others, but somehow, someway, she would foil them.

"There is much I would ask of you, child," Vates said, interrupting her thoughts, "but I know you do not trust us. Perhaps in time . . ."

Alia flung down the rock-hard piece of bread she had been futilely gnawing upon. "Never, do you hear me?" Cold contempt dripped from her words. "Never will I trust nor confide in you. My business on Carcer is not your concern. I don't want your help nor need it. All I want is for you to let me go!"

With a low oath, Teran rose and strode over to Alia.

Grabbing both her arms, he roughly jerked her to her feet.

"Don't ever speak to Vates that way again, do you hear me?" he demanded, his face only millimeters away as he leaned over her. "Call me what you want, but treat my teacher with respect. He has suffered the torments of the damned these past two cycles on Carcer, and he has done nothing to deserve his exile here. Nothing!"

Caught in Teran's grasp, her feet barely touching the ground, Alia stared up into his angry eyes. Inwardly shamed by her discourtesy to the old man, she covered her discomfiture by glaring defiantly back at Teran. Vates had attempted kindness, no matter what his motives might be, and she had been taught to honor her elders.

She turned to Vates, pointedly ignoring Teran despite his disturbing presence hovering over her. "I am sorry that I was disrespectful," she said, in a proud, curt voice.

Teran released his hold. He stomped back to his place beside his friend and sat down, burying his face in his hands. "She's driving me mad, Vates," he muttered. "I've never treated a femina like that before. What's wrong with me?"

The older man laid a comforting hand on Teran's shoulder. "All will be revealed in time, my son. Have patience."

Vates smiled over at Alia. "Come, child, sit by me. Since you do not care to talk, I will tell you about us."

Alia hesitantly walked over and lowered herself beside Vates. When she was settled, he began.

"We are from the planet Bellator. Have you heard of it?"

"Bellator, the warrior planet? Yes, I know of it." Her brows arched in surprise. "But I don't understand. Of all the Imperium planets, Bellator has never exiled one of their own to Carcer. How is it you two are here?"

Vates and Teran exchanged a meaningful glance.

"Tell her, my son. It is important she know."

"Why, Teacher?" Teran scowled darkly. "She wouldn't understand, nor even care."

"Do it for me. I ask it of you."

Teran studied the old man, then gave a reluctant sigh. "For you, Vates, will I do this, and for no other. The planet of Bellator," he began, staring at the ground in front of him, "condemned me to Carcer for an act of cowardice."

He raised his eyes to Alia's. "Hardly the crime you'd expect of a brute like me, is it?"

There are many forms of cowardice, she thought, returning his gaze with an unwavering one of her own. His mercurial gray eyes narrowed, as if preparing for the verbal thrust he felt was sure to come. Yet beyond the steely barrier, Alia saw a curious vulnerability. Why does it matter to him what I think?

That glimpse of Teran's more private side unnerved her, and she quickly averted her eyes. "And what of you, Vates?" Alia asked, more than eager to speak of things other than Teran.

The white-robed man smiled a secret smile. "I? I was condemned for aiding and abetting in Teran's crime. As his teacher since he was a lad, I was held responsible for influencing him in his criminal tendencies, for encouraging his so-called cowardice. If anyone is the criminal, it is I, for I have ruined his life."

At his teacher's words the old loyalty, well-tempered by the cycles of suffering on Carcer, flooded Teran. He grasped Vates' arm.

"No, teacher, you did no wrong in sharing the

47

truths of your heart. It was my choice. I am a grown man and responsible for my own actions."

"A trait sadly lacking in the Imperium of late," Vates observed. "The loss of the Crystal has affected us all, and none for the better."

He paused to glance at Alia, his dark eyes intensely bright. "And you, child, what have you heard of the Knowing Crystal?"

Alia stiffened. Had his mind seek slipped through her barriers in some moment of weakness? Had he divined her secret? There was no way of telling. She swallowed hard and faced him, hungry to hear more of the Crystal, no matter how great the danger of discovery. Perhaps they would provide her with an answer to her continued inability to commune with the elusive stone.

"I know little of the Crystal," she began, "except it was stolen three hundred cycles ago, and that it was of great benefit to the Imperium. I would learn more, if you'd care to speak of it."

"With pleasure, child."

Vates picked up three cerasa fruits, one of which he handed to Alia. The other he tossed to Teran, and the third he began to slice for himself with a small paring knife drawn from his sleeve. "It is my well-loved craft, you see, to teach." He paused to thoughtfully chew a piece of fruit before continuing.

"No one knows from whence the Crystal came," Vates explained. "About seven hundred cycles ago, it suddenly appeared on the mother planet, Aranea. Hence Aranea's other name—Mother."

"One could hardly consider that cold, unfriendly orb a mother these sols. Better it remain known as the spider planet it is," Teran bitingly interjected.

Alia shot him a hostile glance. How she hated that name, when uttered in the derisive tones of those who did not know Aranea as she did. Turning back to the old man, she noted his raised brows. Alia cursed herself for the revealing action. Had Vates guessed? She vowed to exercise more restraint in the future.

"Do not judge any planet too harshly, my son," the old man cautioned. "All of us have deviated from the ancient ways in one twisted manner or another."

He returned his attention to Alia. "The Crystal's original purpose was to serve the Imperium as a resource unit to assist in the development of judicial codes. Unfortunately, it did its job all too well. Little by little, the Knowing Crystal was called upon to make more philosophical judgments. Unimpeded by the erratic emotions of living beings, its decisions were thought to be universally fair and logical.

"For a time, all was well. The Imperium enjoyed a prosperous reign, thanks to the sound advice of the Crystal. There were no wars. The people were fat and content. Only a few farsighted individuals realized the insidious damage being perpetrated under the conflict-free surface. As they abdicated their decision-making responsibilities, the people gradually lost that very ability themselves. All law, philosophy and religious beliefs degenerated, except for what the Crystal taught. The revered craft of teacher died out; books became nearly obsolete. Independent thought was unknown, save amongst those like myself, who secretly kept alive the skills."

A mass of questions swirled through Alia's mind. Why hadn't the High Priestess ever told her this? Why must she now hear the tale from men who were possibly her enemies? And could what they were saying be true?

"You make the Knowing Crystal sound almost evil," she said. "Perhaps it is better if it were never found."

Vates shook his head, an inexpressible sadness shining in his eyes. "No, my child, in spite of everything the Crystal must be restored. The Imperium teeters on the brink of anarchy. All life-bearing planets have been corrupted from their original purposes.

"Take Carcer for example. Hundreds of cycles ago it was a benevolent rehabilitation planet, a lush, friendly land set aside for the few misguided souls of the Imperium. Look at it now—a barren wasteland where vicious criminals run free, killing each other just to survive. And one can speak of equally severe degeneration on other major planets of the Imperium like Aranea, Bellator and Agrica. No, my child, we need the Knowing Crystal."

Alia struggled to rationalize this revolutionary thought with all she had been taught. "But the Crystal will only make us dependent on it again. We might regain peace, but at what price? Is there no other answer?"

A serene expression settled over Vates' features. "Only the answer the masters of the Crystal can find in their hearts. Pray the hearts are brave and true. It is our only hope."

It was all too much—the harrowing journey, her capture tosol, Vates' strange words. Masters of the Crystal? Alia buried her head in her hands, overcome with the import of it all.

"I . . . I am so weary. Let us talk no more."

The old man motioned to Teran. "Prepare a bed for her, my son. It is time we all retired. A long, hard journey awaits us on the morrow."

Alia raised sleep-heavy eyes. What did Vates mean? He spoke as if they'd all be leaving together, and she had no intention of going anywhere with them. She opened her mouth to protest, but the words would not come. It didn't matter anyway. The answers could wait until another sol.

"I am capable of making my own bed, thank you," Alia mumbled in sleepy irritation.

She gathered up her threadbare blanket. Carrying it to a spot warmed by the fire, she folded it twice in an attempt to cushion the rock floor. Immediately upon lying down, Alia was overcome with a heavy drowsiness and was soon fast asleep.

Through the fire's flickering flames, Teran watched her slumbering form for a long while. Then, with a sigh, he climbed to his feet, his own blanket in his hand, and walked over to where Alia lay. He gently covered her.

As he did this, her eyes fluttered open. The bewildered, unguarded look glistening in those brown depths stayed with Teran, long after she was once more dreaming.

A soft, soothing glow bathed Alia's face. She opened her eyes to a light that filled the entire room, radiating from a hovering, sparkling stone. At the sight of it, an expression of ineffable joy lit her face. It was so beautiful.

It called her in a voice without sound, a voice both haunting and lovely. She rose from her bed, drawn to the dancing stone, knowing it though she had never seen it before. They joined, and from deep within her soul she heard it speak. Cryptic words, yet words of hope, came forth for a people lost and hurting. She clutched them to her until the memory indelibly etched itself in her heart. She was so happy, so at peace.

Then it left her. Alia was bereft. Slowly the brilliant stone returned to its place before her, its light assuming an oddly bright gleam. It pulsated, growing larger. The once pleasant voice hummed irritatingly, a sound that rose in force and discordance. Fear sparked inside her, fanned by the increasingly harsh glare and overwhelming noise emanating from the now unfriendly rock. What had caused it to change? Why had it turned against her?

The center of the gem began to whirl wildly, until she felt dizzy from her effort to follow its flashing movement. Then, as swiftly as the radiant maelstrom had appeared, it was gone. In its place was a rough-hewn hole framing a scene of a jagged, foreboding fortress. Carved out of the rock in which it lay, the stronghold appeared impregnable. A premonition of danger and death swelled within her. She turned to run.

Her leaden limbs could not carry her to safety. She found herself slowly drawn to the eerie fortress across a boulder-strewn plain to where it lay. She opened her mouth to scream but found no voice. She struggled fiercely, but to no avail. Soon it would swallow her, engulf her in its bowels of cold, gray stone—forever lost, forever imprisoned, forever alone.

Yet in that last moment as she clung to the edge of eternity, a strong hand reached out and pulled her back. It belonged to a man, tall and powerful, his face hidden in shadows.

When she called out to him, he bent forward to reveal himself. In the next instant a curved, intricately jeweled dagger slashed between them. He was gone. She screamed, and this time it had a sound, ghastly and heartrending.

Alia awoke, the cry still fresh on her lips. She found herself in Teran's arms and heard a low, soothing voice.

"Hush, it was only a dream. You're safe."

She looked up into gray eyes warmly glowing with concern. Uttering a tiny moan, Alia crept close to him in her sleepy, bewildered state, hiding her face in the broad expanse of his chest. He had put on a tunic while she slept, a loosely tied, sleeveless garment that still managed to reveal a large portion of his upper torso. The cloth was soft, the coarsely woven fabric worn thin and smooth from hard use and numerous washings.

It comforted her, as did the warmth of the body beneath it, stirring anew her guilt. I shouldn't let him touch me like this, she thought, but just for a moment, a short time only, I need it.

Teran held her for a long while, stroking her burnished tresses. Gradually he felt her slender frame relax, the tensed muscles uncoiling. What kind of dream could have frightened her so badly? he wondered.

He looked over at Vates. The old man was busily coaxing the faltering embers back into a fire. He watched as his teacher placed a small pot of faba over the flames and finally pour some of the hot liquid into a mug. Only then did Vates raise his eyes to Teran's.

There was a look of triumph gleaming there. Teran knew Vates at last had the information he so patiently sought.

"What did you do to her?" he demanded, outraged. "And was it necessary to frighten her so badly to get it?"

"Everything has its purpose, my son, even to the simple act of holding her in your arms," Vates calmly replied. "I did no more than call forth what she so avidly sought. The dream was of her own making, or rather granted her by the Knowing Crystal. I did nothing but attend."

At Vates' words, Alia roused from Teran's embrace

and pushed herself from him. Glancing from one man to the other, she crept away until the flickering firelight barely illuminated her tortured features.

"You . . . you thief!" she cried, turning the full force of her anger on Vates. "You had no right to slip into my mind and steal my dreams. And to think I imagined you kind! You had no right, you had no right," she mumbled.

Teran turned reproachful eyes to his friend. "I hope what you gleaned was worth it, Teacher. Now she will never trust us."

"Not only will she trust us, but she will come to need us," Vates quietly assured him.

He rose and walked over to where Alia was huddled. Touching her gently on the head he crooned to her, words Teran had not heard since he was a lad.

Alia slowly raised her head, her expression wary.

"Come back to the fire, child. It is time we talked."

She followed him back. The proffered cup of faba was accepted, and Alia sipped it mechanically. There was no longer reason to fear their food. The white robe had no need of such simple artifices.

"I know what it is you seek," Vates finally said, leaping directly to the heart of the matter. "The Knowing Crystal is on Carcer, isn't it?"

He paused to pour out two more mugs of faba, one of which he handed to Teran, the other he cradled in his hands. He stared down into the liquid's murky depths.

"At last all is explained," he murmured, half to himself. "The suffering, the hardship, the cruel exile."

Vates raised eyes to Alia, eyes that glowed with some farseeing, otherworldly light. A chill prickled through her. She felt a premonition that what he had said and was about to say was a truth that would surely lead her to the Crystal. Yet the realization came not from within, this she recognized with a piercing insight, but from some place or thing outside her.

A warm joy flooded Alia. It had come from the Knowing Crystal!

"Yes, child, the Crystal is reaching out to you," the old man said, "penetrating, at last, the mental shields and emotional barriers thrown up around your heart. As proficient an instructor as she may have been, your teacher's lessons had one fatal flaw. She did not truly understand the essence of the Knowing Crystal, and I'm beginning to wonder if she would have been capable of instilling it, even if she had known.

"The Crystal requires a trusting, loving being with which to commune. That is the reason you have been unable to converse with it until I called it to you this nocte. Even then, it could only enter through the portals of your sleeping mind. Now you know the secret; the rest is up to you."

"I will do what is necessary." Alia paused to drain the contents of her mug. "For your assistance, I am grateful, but it changes nothing. I must be allowed the freedom to seek what I need—alone."

"Yours is a difficult and dangerous quest, child, this retrieval of the Knowing Crystal. You will require our help."

Alia laughed, hiding the derision in her voice with difficulty. "The help of an old man and a coward? I think not!"

Before Vates could reply, Teran interrupted, the anger in his voice barely contained. He glared over at Alia.

"Have no fear. Despite what my teacher may have offered, my services aren't included. I'll not be led around by you like some . . . some dumb equs!"

He turned to Vates. "And what has our relationship become that you no longer discuss things before committing me to the reckless quest of some half-mad femina?"

"I have not sought your help and I am not mad," Alia hissed at him.

"That's a matter of opinion!"

Vates raised his hands for silence, laughing as he did. "Please, please. The young are ever so argumentative. I only pray you can direct that same enthusiasm to the task ahead."

"There is no enthusiasm necessary for this except my own. It is my quest, not yours," Alia firmly countered.

"And how well do you know this planet, child? Or what to do, once you reach your destination?"

She stumbled momentarily over Vates' questions. "I . . . I will face that when the time comes."

It was Teran's turn to laugh. "Now I know you're mad. To refuse the help of men who have managed to survive on Carcer for over two cycles, who have traveled the length and breadth of this miserable planet. Why, you're worse than mad. You're a fool."

The truth of Teran's words stung Alia even as she struggled to find a way to refute them. But to admit she actually needed their help! She cast about for some face-saving reply, when the words of the High Priestess flashed through her mind.

Use anything or anyone who presents themselves to you, and when they are no longer of value, cast them aside.

A calculating gleam crept into Alia's eyes, and a slight smile tipped the corners of her mouth. She would yet show them they weren't dealing with a fool, and the revenge would be all the sweeter because of it.

"You are right, of course." As she spoke, Alia could not help but notice the look of stunned surprise on Teran's face. "I do need your help and most gratefully accept it."

"Good!" Vates set down his mug with a flourish. "I am glad your pride is not greater than your good sense, child. There is one more thing, however. Call it a purchase price, if you will, for our services."

Alia's eyes narrowed in renewed suspicion. Ah, here it comes! She should have known the motives of two criminals would be less than altruistic. She gave the old man a tight little smile.

"And what might that purchase price be?"

CHAPTER 3

VATES HESITATED, THEN GLANCED AT TERAN, A CURIOUS mixture of love and sadness gleaming in his dark old eyes. Alia watched him uneasily. Finally, after a moment heavy with anticipation, Vates turned back to face her.

"A simple request really, child. In return for our assistance I ask that you claim Teran and take him back to your planet."

Alia gasped in surprise.

In the next instant, Teran's cry of pained anger slashed between them. "No! I will not allow myself to be claimed. I will never subjugate myself to another!"

He rose and advanced on Vates, the older man climbing to his feet as he approached. Anguish and utter confusion burning in his eyes, Teran grasped his teacher's arms.

"How could you ask this? And why?"

The old man suffered the outraged glares of both with equanimity. "Our time together is short, my son. Your destiny now lies with her. Nothing either of us can do or say will change that."

"And I refuse to believe we are helpless pawns, manipulated by the uncaring hand of fate," Teran exclaimed, releasing his grip on Vates with a jerk.

He moved a few steps away, his head bowed in dejection. "I cast my lot with you, Teacher. I will never leave you."

Teran shot a scathing glance over his shoulder at Alia. "And certainly not for some half-mad femina on a hopeless quest!"

"I don't want you anyway." She bristled in indignation. "I don't need a slave tagging behind me like some . . . some mindless idiot."

Alia riveted her full attention on Vates. "I am sorry. As you can see, the terms are totally unacceptable to all concerned."

"But my terms, nonetheless," the white robe calmly replied. "It is enough for now that you accept them. Teran will accede in time."

"Never," the younger man muttered. "Not even for you, Vates. You ask too much."

Vates chose to ignore the outburst and continued to hold Alia with the force of his gaze. "Well, my child? It is such a small request for such a large advantage. Is it not worth it?"

Her mind raced. Truly, it was such a little thing the old man asked, requiring next to nothing of her, and it would give her total control over Teran. The thought was mildly amusing. She would be able to silence him whenever she wished. Wouldn't that drive him wild! Yes, claiming Teran could definitely have its advantages.

But what would the High Priestess say, if and when

she returned to Aranea with this brute of a man in tow? Well, Alia consoled herself, she was only utilizing whatever resources came her way. And if she returned with the Knowing Crystal, who would dare criticize?

She smiled at Vates, her decision made. "Yes, it is worth it. I will claim Teran when he is agreeable."

Vates extended his hand. They clasped, hand to elbow. Their eyes met and locked, the vow sealed.

"Good," Vates said when they parted. "In the end, you will not regret this."

As one they faced Teran, who stood his ground against them, an implacable look of defiance etched into his rugged features.

"Come, my son." Vates motioned for him to follow them to a seat beside the fire. "You will accept all this in time, but meanwhile we have plans to make. It will be dawn soon, and there is a journey to begin."

Alia and the old man sat down. The flames of the fire threw flickering tongues of shadow across their faces as they watched Teran, waiting for him. At last he came, but there was no sign of compliance in his manner. He lowered himself to the ground, across the fire from them.

"I will listen to what you say," he growled, "and I will follow you, Vates, but know I do so with great misgiving. I do not trust her, for there is much she refuses to reveal."

He laughed in wry derision. "Why, she's still afraid to share even her name. Not much of a basis for an alliance, is it?"

Vates looked at Alia. "Will you tell us your name, child?"

She sat there, her hesitation evident. What harm could it do? Her first name was not uncommon, and there appeared no need to reveal her family name.

They went by none themselves. A simple title of address could not possibly reveal she was from Aranea, and if it would placate that big, sullen lout . . .

She smiled at Vates. "My name is Alia."

"Alia." Vates rolled the name around on his tongue. "A most lovely name for a most lovely young femina."

He peered at Teran through the fire's smoky haze. "Are you satisfied now, my son?"

Teran's only answer was a snort of disgust.

Vates smiled at the younger man. Shifting into a more comfortable position, he began to speak again. "Well, now that we have that settled, it is time to talk of our journey. Where are we to seek the Knowing Crystal, Alia?"

"It is in the possession of the criminal Ferox. He is to be found in the province of Macer."

"Ferox!" Teran sputtered, nearly choking on the faba he had just swallowed. "By all the moons of Agrica, why did you have to choose Ferox for your quest? He's the deadliest, most savage felon in the Imperium!"

"I didn't *choose* him, you ignorant sandwart!" Alia snapped in exasperation. "He has the Crystal. What choice do I have?"

"No choice at all, except that of certain death."

As he turned his gaze back to the fire, time blurred for Teran until present melded into past. He was once more at the Imperial Academy, a first-level military student. Competing in the Imperium Games for the highest honor granted an Academy student, the Warrior's Medal, he had been the chosen representative of his class. The competition finals had pitted him against the finest pupil in the school, a flamboyantly popular, fiercely talented upperclassman—Ferox.

Though Teran had ultimately defeated his more experienced opponent, the rivalry hadn't ended there. Instead, the loss had festered within Ferox until it fired what was to become a lifelong enmity, an enmity, it seemed, that was once again to be fanned into a blazing conflagration.

"Well, I, for one, am not afraid," Alia defiantly asserted. "The Crystal will lead me—and certainly not to death."

Teran shook aside the long-buried memories and gave a harsh laugh. "Can it lead you through solid rock? The man's fortress lies deep in the mountains, carved out of the very substance of this planet. It is said to be impregnable."

"I know." There was a faraway look in her eyes as she spoke, as if she were seeing it.

"You know? How do you know?" Teran demanded. "Surely you've never been there?"

"Hush, my son." Vates raised a warning hand. "It is enough Alia realizes the enormity of the task she has undertaken. Besides, there is a way into the fortress. Ferox has to be able to come and go if he is to continue his interplanetary raids."

Alia blinked at them in bafflement. "I don't understand. I thought Ferox was a criminal like you, condemned to life imprisonment on Carcer."

Teran laughed wryly. "Ferox is a criminal, to be sure, but he's certainly no prisoner. He uses Carcer as his home base, probably at least partly because of the rich supply of manpower found on this planet— men with reason to kill, men with nothing to lose and everything to gain. It is from here he launches his attacks on merchant vessels that ply their trade between the planets of the Imperium."

"But what of the authorities? How can they allow this to continue?"

"They don't care," Teran replied with a shrug. "Carcer no longer tries to rehabilitate anyone. It's just a dumping ground for the living refuse of the Imperium. Ferox makes it well worth their while, not that anyone would dare go against him anyway."

He paused to appraise her. "That is, no one until you arrived."

Alia stirred uneasily. "Then no one really knows how invincible Ferox is, do they? Perhaps it is time to find out."

She looked from Teran to Vates and back again. "There's still time for you to change your mind. I will not hold you to your vow. As for me, there is no other choice. I cannot return to my planet without the Knowing Crystal."

"And what kind of a planet would send you out on a quest with no possible hope of success?" Teran demanded, his face clouding in anger. "Exactly where *are* you from, Alia?"

"Where I am from is of no import. I am the chosen one, the one destined to rescue the Knowing Crystal. That is all that matters."

She rose to her feet. "But we have already talked too long. If you are not with me, at least allow me the opportunity to try."

Teran glanced at Vates. "And you, Teacher, are you still of the same mind as before, knowing all this?"

Vates nodded. "My offer to help Alia has not changed. Will you still cast your lot with us, my son?"

Teran sighed. "I am with you while you live, Vates. You know that."

"No one can ask for any greater loyalty." The old man stood up, smiling in satisfaction. "It is time then that we begin our journey. The sols left me are precious few."

Teran's jaw tightened. That was the second reference his teacher had made to what appeared to be his impending death. He looked at Alia. She was staring back at him, a questioning light in her eyes. It was evident even she had noticed Vates' gloomy predictions.

A miserable sense of foreboding settled over Teran. His friend had always possessed the ability to see into the future and always with uncanny accuracy. But to lose Vates!

The old man had been everything to him—the warm, caring father he had never known, friend, confidant and teacher. If not for Vates, Teran felt certain he would never have survived as long as he had on Carcer. Perhaps he had misunderstood. The thought fanned the dying embers of hope. He clung to it as he packed their supplies.

As he worked, the taunting face of his old nemesis, Ferox, rose once again to fill his mind. It seemed that the youth-spawned rivalry refused to die, though both were a long way from their student sols on Bellator. Then, both had been exemplary pupils with promising military careers. Now, they were nothing more than common criminals, soon to meet again, Ferox surrounded by his army of bloodthirsty minions and he . . .

Teran paused, a self-mocking smile creasing his face. His army consisted of an elderly man, a starry-eyed femina, and the dubious powers of some legendary stone, *if* they were even fortunate enough to find it before Ferox found them. It was a hopeless, foolhardy quest at best, and he, well aware of the awesome abilities and vicious cruelty of the man they faced, was the biggest fool of all.

Alia walked over to join him. She busied herself dousing the fire while Teran finished packing in silence. It took little insight to sense his thoughts were elsewhere. Her own thoughts were also turned inward.

The rapidity with which her situation had changed filled Alia with wonder. This time a sol ago she'd been lost, alone in a vast desert. Now she was two companions richer. The quest for the Knowing Crystal was beginning to seem a little less desperate. A tiny glimmer of hope sprang to life in her breast, and she returned to her work with renewed enthusiasm.

After the cool haven of the oasis, the desert was a sweltering furnace. They trudged through the deep sand, Alia riding ahead on the equs, Teran and Vates several meters behind, all wishing the journey to the mountains of Macer was already over. Teran glanced across to Vates from time to time, a worried frown working its way across his face. They had set out at sunrise, and after just six horas the old man looked exhausted.

Teran suppressed an impulse to ask Alia to let Vates ride, since it *was* her equs. Besides, he seriously doubted she'd willingly consent to walk. Though she'd acquiesced to their offer of assistance, Teran sensed she'd just as soon be rid of them. With or without them, she'd go on. In the meantime, he strongly suspected she'd have no intention of weakening herself with a fruitless gesture of kindness to an old man.

Well, he'd never beg her for anything. If the time came, he'd carry Vates until he could no longer go on himself. Perhaps it would be better that way, better to die a quick and merciful death in the desert than to suffer the endless torments surely awaiting them at the hands of Ferox.

"He gnaws at your heart, doesn't he, my son?" Vates' low voice intruded into Teran's unpleasant thoughts. "Will you kill him this time?"

Teran glanced at the man walking beside him. "Kill Ferox? Do you seriously believe, given our current situation, the opportunity will ever present itself? Yet, if I had the chance . . ."

He slowly shook his head. "I don't know. What would my killing Ferox accomplish? Would it improve our lot or, for that matter, anyone's? I will admit, though, that I hate the man. These cycles on Carcer have cheapened the value of life for me. Who knows what will happen, if and when we meet again?"

"It saddens me to hear you say that. What of all I have taught you? What of compassion and forgiveness, of right and wrong?"

"There's no forgiving what Ferox has done, no matter how long I live or what you try to teach me," Teran growled, his eyes darkening in anger and bitter remembrance. "What has knowing the difference between right and wrong done for us anyway? Rewarded us by exile to this godforsaken planet? Perhaps in the end all that really matters is survival— whatever the means."

Vates grasped Teran's arm. "Have a care how you go about surviving, my son, or you will become little more than the like of Ferox. A living death, to my way of thinking, and one I would not wish for you."

The younger man sighed. "Nor one I would wish for, either. Truly, Vates, I don't mean to cast aside the tenets you've taught me. I just wonder what place your teachings have in an Imperium such as ours. Yours are truths that belong in a time now long past, perhaps gone forever. Why suffer needlessly for them without reason or justification?"

The old man inclined his head toward Alia, now riding far ahead. "She is the reason. Her quest is the justification for all our suffering. Have faith for yet a little longer, and all will be revealed."

Teran glanced out across the broad expanse of sand, overcome with frustration for Vates' deliberately vague words. When would his teacher cease to speak in riddles? He turned to face the older man.

"Can you at least tell me this? Why did you ask the femina to claim me? I've been your loyal friend all the cycles of my life, have followed wherever you led. Now you want to bind me over to another like . . . like some slave, someone of little import to you."

"Teran, Teran," Vates gently chided him, his expression sad. "You are the hope of our people. All I do and have ever done has been for you, to enable you to fulfill your destiny, even to the necessity of Alia's claiming you. I can say no more, except that it is vital you return with her to her planet. I have always loved you like a son, and hold you in the highest esteem. You have grown into a fine man, and I am proud."

Gazing down at his beloved teacher, words would not come to Teran's lips. They were not necessary. The long cycles shared had forged a bond between them not easily severed. They stood there, the aerlapis sand beginning to gently whirl around their feet. Love and understanding flowed from one to the other, strengthening their spirits until it finally spilled over into their tired bodies. At last they turned as one. With a lighter step, they began anew the journey.

Alia reined in the equs on a high ridge of sand. She turned in the saddle to watch Teran and Vates laboriously trudge up the hill behind her. By the time they arrived at her side, her interest was already elsewhere, scanning the rapidly darkening horizon.

Teran followed her line of vision, a grim expression

tightening his features. "A storm is brewing. From experience, I'd say it promises to be a bad one."

She looked down at him. "What do you suggest?"

With a shrug, he pointed to the base of a large sand dune about 500 meters away. "That spot's as good as any for refuge in this hellish desert. There's not much else to do but use the equs for shelter until the storm blows over."

"Then let us be on our way." Alia brushed back a wind-tossed lock of hair. "The storm will be upon us before we make camp."

She kicked the equs into a trot and began a bounding descent down the far side of the ridge. The sky blackened as fierce gusts tore at her clothing. By the time she reached the tall dune Teran had indicated, stinging nettles of sand had begun to whip through the air. Working quickly, Alia soon had the equs down, its massive legs tucked under it. She was unrolling blankets for shelter when Teran and Vates arrived.

"Here, let me have those," Teran shouted above the rising wind. He grabbed the wildly flapping blankets from her. "I know a way to fashion a tent."

After knotting two blankets together, he tied two of the ends to two points on the equs. The others, he weighed down with the saddle and saddlebags. He motioned for Alia and Vates to climb in beneath the makeshift shelter.

"What about you?" Alia cried.

Holding the other blanket and a coil of stout rope, Teran pointed to the equs' head. "Someone has to tie him down. Even I can't hold an animal of his size and strength once he's frightened, and we can't have him running off with the tent in the middle of the storm. Once that's done I'll fashion a covering over his head. We'll have to take turns staying with him."

She stood there, eyeing Teran with misgiving, until Vates grabbed her arm and pulled her toward the shelter.

"Come, child. Teran knows what he is doing. He is a seasoned warrior from his many cycles on Bellator."

They crawled in under the covering and huddled against the equs' round belly. Vates produced the last blanket and pulled it over their heads.

"The sand will leak in with the force of the wind out there," he explained. "This will at least keep it out of our eyes and mouths."

Before the words were barely uttered, the storm hit them full force. It beat on the fragile tent, tearing and ripping at it until Alia was certain it would fly away. The deafening noise rose to a shrill howl, as if they had been set upon by a pack of starving wolves. She shuddered at the similarity. The storm was hungry, too, and would mercilessly ravage the desert until it picked it clean.

As the storm grew in intensity, the equs became increasingly restless. Save for the soothing presence of Teran at its head, Alia was certain the animal would have bolted long ago. She wondered how Teran was faring out there, battered by the piercing blasts of sand. The task of tying down the beast's head was taking an unusually long time. How much longer could he stay out in that smothering sand and survive?

"He will be all right, child."

Vates' voice startled her back to the moment.

"Teran is experienced in the ways of survival. If not for him, I would certainly have perished soon after my arrival here."

"But why doesn't he join us? Surely he's tied the equs down by now."

"The equs may be giving him trouble. It would

70

explain the sporadic jerking movement we've been feeling. But have no fear. If Teran's not here in a short while, I'll check on him."

He smiled at her in the semidarkness. "It heartens me that you are concerned for him. Perhaps you are beginning to trust us, if only a little."

Alia's cheeks flushed scarlet, and she was thankful for the poor light. Whatever her inner emotions might be, it was better not to reveal them. Their advantage over her was large enough already.

"Not in the least," she murmured. "It is only because he is the physically strongest. I will need that capability if I'm to succeed in rescuing the Crystal. That is my only concern."

"As you wish," Vates said, but Alia could tell from his tone that he wasn't at all convinced.

"You said Teran was a Bellatorian warrior," she began, deciding it better to divert the conversation a little. "How is it he was convicted of cowardice?"

"The story is not mine to tell, child. It is Teran's, if ever he wishes to speak of it. You will have to ask him."

Alia laughed. "Then I doubt I will ever know. I do not think he will confide that to me, considering the low esteem he holds me in."

"Do you really think he despises you? From what I have seen, I would say differently. Quite differently."

Once again the blush crept into her cheeks. "Well, no matter," she said, suddenly angry. "I care nothing for what he thinks, save that he cooperate when I ask it of him."

Vates lapsed into silence. Alia became lost in her thoughts and after a while began to doze. They had risen quite early in an effort to gain as much distance before the heat became intolerable. Now, as she lay there with the winds whistling around her, Alia's

71

body gradually became weighted with fatigue. Finally, the desert haunted her no more.

Outside, the driving blasts of sand nearly blinded Teran as he struggled to anchor the equs' head in place. Without the use of the beast's heavy, wedge-shaped skull, Teran knew it would be impossible for the animal to lever himself to his feet. The shaggy brute was less than cooperative, however. The initially simple undertaking rapidly evolved into a major battle.

Each time he looped the rope around the equs' neck, a violent toss of its head would wrench the line from Teran's hands. His palms were soon bleeding from the rope's rough fibers. Gritting his teeth, he tried again and again, pitting his muscled brawn against that of the brutish beast.

Every breath was a guarded effort, the whirling sands nearly choking him when he inhaled. The sinews of his arms and legs strained, until he thought they would surely tear from their muscles. Sand gradually coated his sweaty body, as he was repeatedly thrown to the ground in the brutal, exhaustive battle. Still Teran struggled on, all the while knowing he would soon reach utter exhaustion. His frustration grew, as the animal's power seemed to increase in direct proportion to his own fatigue.

Finally, in a last, desperate attempt at subduing the equs, Teran threw himself onto its neck. He tried to grapple its head to the ground. The corded power of the man vied mightily with the wild force of the beast. For a long moment, Teran thought he had finally won. Then, with a huge bellow, the equs flung its ponderous skull around.

It struck Teran in the side of his head with a resounding thud. He felt a sharp pain, then a kaleidoscope of sparkling colors flashed before his eyes.

Blackness fell like a curtain. Teran toppled face first into the sand and moved no more.

Alia awoke with a start. Someone was moving beside her. It was Vates.

"What are you doing?" she asked in a voice thick with sleep.

"Teran has been out in the storm too long. I am going to see what is wrong." He crawled from the tent.

Alia sat up and attempted to arrange her tousled hair. Quickly catching herself in the instinctive feminine action, she laughed at her own vanity.

Vates' voice cut through the tumult of the storm, jolting her from her self-mockery.

"Alia, come here! I need you."

Hair arrangement forgotten, Alia slid from under the tent. Through the nearly blinding whirl of sand, she could make out the form of Vates attempting to pull Teran toward her. She crawled over to the two men.

"What happened?"

Vates shouted above the storm. "He's unconscious and nearly choked to death on the sand. Help him into the tent and give him some water. I must stay with the equs, or we'll lose him."

Alia accepted Teran from Vates' arms and struggled to drag his limp form into the shelter. Her breath, which was full of sand when she dared breathe, came in sharp gasps from the effort of moving a body nearly twice her weight. When she was finally able to pull him into the tent, she fell to the ground next to him, exhausted.

His strangled gags soon roused her to action. Feeling around her, Alia found the water flask. She worked her body under his head and shoulders to elevate them, then raised the flask to his lips.

"Drink, Teran."

The first mouthful almost choked him anew, but with each swallow his feeble efforts strengthened. His thirst finally quenched, Teran weakly fell back against Alia. He lay so still she wondered if he were conscious. It was then she first noticed the bruise on the right side of his face and the caked blood on the palms of his hands.

Biting back a cry of sympathy, Alia pulled the hem of her tunic loose and ripped it into two long strips. Pouring some of the precious water across his palms, she was able to wash most of the imbedded sand away. Then, using the long bandages, she gently wrapped the ragged wounds.

Next she turned to Teran's head. She poured more of the water into her hand and, bending over him, began to cleanse the swollen side of his face. Beneath the caked grit, the bruise appeared ugly, but no skin or bone seemed broken.

She concentrated on washing the area until gradually her attention moved to his entire face. He lay there quietly, so different from the dynamic, intimidating man she had known before. His firm, roguish lips were silent, and Alia almost wished to hear once again the deep voice, even if it meant suffering the vexation of his taunts. How she wished to see the compelling gray of those mercurial, fascinating eyes.

Alia felt a longing for something yet unknown and untried, deep inside her. In an effort to calm the disquieting desires, she forced herself to resume the nursing of Teran's bruised face.

"Ah, that feels good," he murmured, startling her.

She immediately ceased her ministrations, capping the flask and laying it aside. He turned and looked at her.

"Why did you stop? I was enjoying it."

Alia laughed nervously and leaned away from him. "You were obviously recovered, so my services were no longer needed. Now, if you would not mind getting off me . . ."

"Does my nearness make you uncomfortable, Alia?" Teran once more closed the distance between them.

"On the contrary," she lied, casting about for some plausible reply. "You do not bother me in the least. It is just that your weight is putting my leg to sleep."

He chuckled, the sound rich and warm. "In that case, I'd better move. I would hate to damage what must be very lovely legs." He rolled off Alia but in the process managed to end up wedged next to her.

"Surely there is enough room in here for you to move over a little more," Alia muttered in exasperation, attempting to scoot away from him. She gained little ground, for she was already up against the edge of the tent.

"I'm afraid not. I take up considerably more space than Vates." He didn't sound the least bit remorseful.

Curse the man! He was quite obviously making the most of a deplorable situation. Well, Alia thought, he wasn't going to rattle her composure. If he could stand such close quarters, so could she.

"As you wish," she said, trying hard to sound nonchalant. "What happened to you out there? You look like you were attacked by half the criminals on Carcer."

Teran sighed. "The equs and I couldn't seem to come to an agreement, but I must have at least tired him out. He seems quiet at last. Of course, Vates always did have a way with animals, a talent I'm afraid I sorely lack." His wicked grin gleamed in the dim light. "But enough of that miserable beast. I'd rather spend this time getting to know you better."

"You know all you are going to about me," Alia snapped, suddenly uncomfortable in his presence.

A big hand wound its way up her arm. "Really?"

"Yes!" she said, stirring uneasily under his touch. "Now, please remove your hand."

The hand reached her shoulder and stopped. "What are you afraid of, Alia? I won't hurt you, and this is hardly the time or place for me to ravish you."

She gritted her teeth, trying to quell the telltale quivering that his renewed explorations stimulated. When Teran's fingers traced a path up the side of her neck and around her ear, she jerked away.

"I . . . I am not afraid of anything. I just do not like what you're doing."

"Your body tells me otherwise. Why don't you relax and listen to it?"

His hand moved to gently cradle her chin, and he turned her face to look at him. "Are you a maiden? Is that why you're afraid?"

She turned a vivid scarlet and attempted to escape his grip, but to no avail. "That is of no import," Alia blurted, giving him his answer by her evasion. "Now will you let me go?"

Teran loosened his grasp, and Alia quickly turned her face away. For a long moment he was silent, wondering what to say next. Though he wasn't partial to maidens, having found them to be giggling and silly for the most part, that was not the case with Alia's innocence. She excited him like no femina he'd ever known, and suddenly, inexplicably, Teran wanted her to desire him as fiercely as he did her.

When he opened his mouth to speak soothing words of endearment, the storm chose that instant to increase in volume, effectively silencing him. Both became aware, once again, of the rampaging fury of sand just outside the tent. The blustering assault went on for what seemed an interminable length of time. Finally it subsided to a more sedate tirade.

"Alia, there's nothing to be embarrassed about," Teran began again in the relative quiet.

"I am not embarrassed," she cried. "I just do not know what to do, what to expect."

Teran wound a hand in her hair, pulling her down to him. His lips brushed her forehead as he spoke. "If you'd let me, I would show you."

Alia expelled a long, shuddering breath. Why not? her mind taunted. What are you afraid of? Why not experience a little of this man? It will probably be the only opportunity you'll ever have before taking vows of celibacy as a Sister of the Crystal. And it isn't as if he's unwilling. What harm could it possibly do?

"I do not know. Well, maybe . . . just a little . . ."

The moment the words left her lips, Alia regretted them. A wave of fear swept over her, a fear of losing control. This was insane! She opened her mouth to repudiate her impulsive consent. Teran's lips came down upon hers, shattering her with the hunger of his kiss.

She drew back, stunned by the surprising intimacy of his action. But the feel of his lips, warm and sweet upon hers, slowly coaxed her back to him. She found herself responding to their searching softness, instinctively returning his caresses with equally fervent ones of her own.

Caught up in the unabashed response of the woman in his arms, Teran gathered her closer. His arms encircled her, one hand snaking upward to her mass of curls, the other in the small of her back. He clasped her tightly, the long cycles without a femina suddenly flooding back with a tumultuous intensity. In that moment, Teran realized he had to have her, to possess her completely.

"Alia, I want you," he groaned.

Before she could even react, he crushed her to him, until her soft curves seemed indistinguishable from his own muscled contours. His hands began a feverish exploration, roaming over her back, cupping her buttocks, drawing her ever closer.

Alia felt heavy and warm, his very touch a drug, intoxicating her with the heady wine of awakened desire. It felt so right, so good to be in his arms. Yet suddenly an odd terror flashed through her. She heard a voice, hard and bitter, a voice that ripped through the sweet sensations, quenching the delicious heat coursing through her veins.

"... *drag you down ... don't encumber yourself ... your quest ... remember your quest ...*"

She choked back a frightened cry and struggled to free herself. "Let me go!"

Teran was beyond hearing. He knew nothing except that he wanted and needed the femina in his arms. The reality of her rejection came only by agonizingly slow degrees, wrenching him back to the harsh present.

"What's wrong, Alia? Did I hurt you?" he asked, his body as confused and anguished as his mind.

"No, you did not hurt me," Alia said, her voice shaking. "You . . . you showed me enough, that is all. I do not care to know anymore."

"Why, you little . . . !" Teran ground his teeth in frustration. "What do you think you're doing? This is not some experiment we were engaging in."

Alia pushed herself away from Teran. All the warnings about the male gender came back with a sickening rush. He was no better than the rest. And yet how much better was she? She'd allowed herself to be misled, allowed the pleasures of the body to overshadow the pure intent of her training.

78

Shame swept through her. In her anger and self-revulsion, she turned on Teran. "Calling a halt to the fulfillment of your crude animal desires, of course. I have more important things to do on this planet than become the object of your lust." She crawled toward the tent opening.

"Where do you think you're going?" Teran demanded, anchoring her by one of her ankles.

"To relieve Vates, of course. On this journey we all do our share, and it is my turn to stay with the equs. Hereafter, I expect to be treated as an equal on this quest, not just as an object suitable for the satisfaction of your physical needs."

She glanced back at the hand restraining her. "Now if you would release my foot . . ."

"With pleasure," he ground out hoarsely. "Get out of here!"

Not daring a backward glance, Alia hastily crawled out of the tent. The storm whirled around her, affording little hope of an end to it in the near future. There was no end in sight, like the turbulent emotions she felt for Teran.

With a pang she realized she'd been cruel to him just now, but what other choice had she? She had no right to allow feelings to enter into this quest; there was no time for the luxury of giving into her own desires. But why, oh why, did it have to happen this way—this strange, disturbing attraction to Teran? It only complicated an already difficult situation.

Shaking her head in dismay, Alia crawled the rest of the way to where Vates sat, his arms cradling the head of the equs.

CHAPTER 4

THE STORM WORSENED. IT LASTED SIX SOLS, UNTIL THE trio wondered if they would ever hear anything but the wind's mournful wail again. Though they were finally able to secure the equs when it went into its protective desert hibernation, the problems still continued. The food became inedible, the insidious sand working its gritty way into everything. By the end of the fifth sol even the carefully conserved water supplies were exhausted. If the storm continued much longer, they knew they would perish.

Blessedly, in the early horas of the sixth sol, the punishing assault ceased almost as quickly as it had begun. The utter silence awakened Alia first. She lay in the tent and waited for the wind to resume its melancholy lament.

Long moments passed. The heavy stillness, interrupted only by Vates' sonorous snores, remained.

Her excitement rising, Alia crawled out of the tent and glanced around her in wondering incredulity.

The bright, multifaceted stars gleamed in a darkly peaceful sky. It was true! She laughed, unable to contain her joy and intense relief a moment longer.

Teran awoke with a start. The stun gun appeared in his hand, ready for attack, as he scrambled out of the makeshift shelter. It was then he saw Alia. With an exasperated sigh, he replaced the gun at his belt.

"What are you doing awake at this hora?" he irritably demanded.

"The storm is over. Are you both blind and deaf, Teran? We have made it through the storm."

He glanced around. "It certainly is, isn't it?" A grim smile touched his lips. "But we're not out of danger yet. We've at least another sol's travel across this miserable desert before we reach the foothills of Macer. And we're out of water."

His unpleasant words reminded Alia once again how terribly thirsty she was. She licked her dry, cracked lips. Oh, to be able to drink water without care to its conservation, to wash the encrusted sand and grime from her body! Realizing how much worse they were making her feel, Alia quickly banished the fruitless desires from her mind.

She turned resolute eyes to Teran. "We *will* survive. What other choice have we?"

Teran stared back at her. "What choice indeed?"

Alia faltered for a moment under his piercing scrutiny. "I . . . I suppose it is time to go back to sleep. We need to conserve our strength for the morrow. I am sorry I disturbed your slumber."

"What you do to my sleep is the least of what disturbs me, Alia," he said, never taking his eyes off her. "You've barely spoken to me these past five sols.

Did I offend you so badly that first time in the tent?"

She swallowed hard. If only he wouldn't bring that up, if only he'd let those memories die. Yet even as she mentally cursed him for reminding her, the remembrance of his lips upon hers, the exciting feel of his body, the rough caress of his hands coursed through her like molten fire. Would it haunt her for the rest of her life?

"No, Teran, you did not offend me," she forced herself to reply. "I asked for it, so there is no blame. But it can never happen again, do you hear me? Never!"

A war of emotions raged in Teran's gray eyes, and he was unable to speak until it was mastered. "Do you think it's easy to control such things?" he huskily demanded. "The mating urge is powerful, as well it should be. Do you really have that kind of strength?"

"I must. Don't you see that?" she cried, her voice little more than a strangled whisper. "I have a destiny to fulfill, a quest to complete. There is no place for you or any man in my life."

"Then what do you call my presence on this journey?"

Alia sighed. "I will not lie to you. You are just an instrument to be used in this quest for the Crystal. No more, no less. I have never promised you anything except, if we succeed, I would claim you and take you away from here."

Teran laughed bitterly. "And where would you take me, Alia?"

"That is not mine to tell. Be content that it is a far more pleasant place than Carcer."

Yet even as the words slipped from her lips, Alia wished them back. How did she really know how he'd be received on Aranea, if life would be better for him

83

there? True, Aranean men had always appeared well cared for, the few times she'd seen any, but that strange look in their eyes . . .

Alia inwardly shuddered at the memory. A dull, hopeless, empty sadness was all there ever was. In a sense they seemed more prisoners than Teran, chained as he was to his govern collar.

"Well, be comforted in the fact you'll never have to suffer my presence on your precious planet," he growled, recalling Alia from her dismal thoughts, "for I'll never allow you to claim me."

He hesitated, wondering if it were really prudent to tell her of his decision, a decision made once he'd learned the true purpose of her quest. Yet it was important to know her mind on this for it would, by necessity, color all their interactions.

Teran inhaled a deep breath. "Since we're being so forthright this nocte, I feel compelled to say one thing more. If we succeed in rescuing the Knowing Crystal I will not stand in your way—as long as you promise to return it to its rightful home."

"And if I deem its rightful home to be other than your choice, if I choose to take it elsewhere?" she challenged.

"Then I'll have to stop you."

Alia stared at Teran. Were his words just a ruse to throw her off guard, to lull her into a false sense of security? Did he indeed covet the Knowing Crystal and its power for himself? In light of the High Priestess' warnings, that question should be well considered.

"Well, at the present moment that's the least of our problems." She laughed, her uncertainty making the sound harsh and brittle. "Let us first deal with recovering the Crystal."

"Of course, Alia," Teran agreed quietly, his eyes

still glittering with the light of battle. "Be assured, though, no matter what happens, the Crystal will be returned to where it belongs. You have my word on that."

"I have no doubt of your intentions." It's your motives I'm worried about, Alia silently added. She was tempted to ask him where he considered the Crystal's rightful place to be. The impulse, however, quickly passed. Whatever his answer, dare she believe him?

"Never doubt, however," she said as she squarely met his gaze, "that I can ever be swayed from the completion of my quest."

"Then we understand each other?" He met her bold look with a hard one of his own.

For an instant Alia quailed before the onslaught of Teran's fierce countenance, then, with an inward effort, she returned his glare. It matters not what he thinks of me. It will take more than the likes of him to sway me from this task.

She nodded. "Yes, we understand each other. Now, no more of it. It is time we rested. The morrow is soon enough to face the difficulties before us."

Alia walked back to the tent. She felt Teran's eyes boring into her, but though she waited for him to speak, he remained silent. She crawled back in the tent and over to her spot near Vates. Drawing her legs into a protective fetal position, Alia lay there, waiting for a blessed oblivion that never came.

The smothering heat weighed her down, tugging at her arms and dragging at her legs, until Alia believed each step to be her last. She raised weary eyes to scan the horizon one more time. Where, by all that was sacred, were the mountains of Macer? She looked back at the equs she now led. At least the beast was tolerating the heat and lack of water. Alia fervently wished for just a little of its desert adaptability.

She wearily moved to its side. At least one of us should avail ourselves of the animal's strength, she thought, now that it had had an opportunity to rest without any weight on its back. With a lithe motion, she swung herself up onto the equs and nudged it back into a plodding walk.

They had traveled for nearly a sol without even the faintest sign of a mountain range in the shimmering distance. The ill-fated loss of the locator compass during the storm had been a severe setback. Fortunately, Teran had been able to reorient them by means of the stars into what hopefully was the right direction. Yet as the horas passed without even a glimmer of a familiar landmark on the map, Alia's confidence in his abilities began to wane.

"That storm must have rearranged the face of the entire desert," Teran muttered, as if he sensed her rising doubts.

He turned to gaze up at Alia. Looking as haggard as she felt, Teran's face, through the layer of aerlapis dust, was a reddish bronze from the sun, his lips cracked and bleeding. Compassion flashed through Alia. Suddenly she wanted to reach down and stroke his face.

At that moment, Vates, walking on the other side of the equs, staggered and fell. Plummeting face down into the sand he lay there, unmoving.

Teran ran to the old man's side. "Vates, are you all right?"

"I . . . I can no longer go on," Vates mumbled weakly, when Teran knelt and turned him over. "Leave me. Save Alia and yourself."

"No, never will I forsake you. You're coming with us, one way or another."

Teran gathered the old man into his arms. The effort necessary to stand with his burden cost him dearly, but he said nothing.

Alia silently watched Teran as he started off once again, stumbling awkwardly through the shifting sands. Confused emotions assailed her. Why did he weaken himself by continuing to sustain a dying old man? Was not his life of more import?

A twinge of guilt wended its way through her consciousness. Vates had been kind to her. Though her training told her it was time to leave the old man behind, that Teran's gesture was but a stupid, futile one that could only lead to all their deaths, still Alia hesitated. The clear delineation between right and wrong, as taught to her on Aranea, was suddenly very hazy.

As she paused in her moral dilemma a harder side, honed by her cycles of indoctrination, gradually asserted itself past her fledgling conscience. It must still be considered that Vates could be of use; he still possessed valuable knowledge of the Crystal, knowledge she desperately needed. It was too great a possibility to toss aside, Alia realized, at least not for the present.

She urged the equs forward a little more forcefully this time. Startled into action, the animal broke into a feeble semblance of a trot. Well, Alia thought, if Teran lacked the sense to protect his waning energy, she would have to do it for him. There was definitely no doubt of his value in terms of brute strength and a sure knowledge of Carcer.

Reaching his side, she placed a restraining hand on his shoulder. "Teran, stop this. You'll kill yourself."

Alia stopped short, stunned by the look of anguished determination in his upraised eyes. He loves the old man, she realized with an aching wonder. Nothing she could say or do would ever sway him. If Teran were to survive, she had to give up the equs to Vates. With a resigned groan, Alia swung down from the animal.

Teran shook his head to clear his bleary eyes. "What are you doing?" he asked in a ragged voice. "Get back on the equs."

"No. It is better if Vates rides."

A look of utter confusion clouded Teran's face, then the expression altered. Without another word, he lifted the old man onto the equs' broad back. Gathering the reins in one hand, Teran tugged the animal forward and began again the difficult trek through the deep sand.

Alia followed, his tall form throwing a refreshing shadow upon her. She puzzled over the look in Teran's eyes just before he placed Vates on the equs. What had it meant—that warm scrutiny, that melting silver stare? It unnerved Alia to the depths of her being, sending a strange sense of foreboding rocketing through her. Never had she met anyone like him; never had she faced an opponent quite so formidable. For a brief instant she allowed herself to wonder what would happen, how they would settle the differences between them, if they were successful in finding the Crystal.

"Alia, you're not much stronger than Vates," Teran suddenly rasped from over his shoulder, breaking into her reverie. "What am I to do when you can no longer walk?"

"Don't worry about me. I can walk a long while yet, and when I can't, you can carry me. I am lighter than Vates and will not weaken you as quickly."

He glanced back at her. The vestiges of a smile weakly teased the corners of his mouth. "Have a care, Alia. That's a temptation I can hardly resist."

At his words Alia tossed her head and snorted in mock disdain. Despite the burning rays of the sun, she felt herself grow even warmer. The man was incorrigible! Still, she felt heartened. If he yet had the strength to joke, there was hope. With renewed determination she forced her parched body onward.

The rosy glow of the setting sun signaled a halt for the nocte. They set up camp beside two huge boulders that rose out of the desert floor like eerie sentinels. But what was there to guard out here in this wilderness of sand? Alia wondered with a shudder.

Try as she might, she found herself unable to shake off the sensation of being watched. Perhaps it was a case of dehydrated hallucinations, she wearily comforted herself, as she slid to the ground next to one of the stone guardians. It felt cool against her feverish flesh. For that, at least, she was grateful.

Teran gently pulled Vates from the back of the equs and carried him over to where Alia sat. Squatting with his living burden, Teran propped the old man against the rock. His silver eyes dark with concern, he made Vates as comfortable as possible.

Vates slowly opened his eyes. "Are we at the mountains yet, my son?" he asked in a cracked voice. "I knew you would lead us there. You were always the best of Bellator's sons."

Teran sadly smiled down at him. "No, Teacher, we're not quite there, but soon, very soon . . ."

He turned to Alia. "Can you find the strength to walk a ways with me? We need to talk."

She opened her mouth to protest that she was too exhausted to humor his need for a stroll, then stopped. The look in Teran's eyes was pleading, and Alia realized he didn't want Vates to overhear. With a groan, she pushed herself up to a kneeling position, everything a hazy blur. Teran's hand appeared before her. Without thinking, she accepted his aid. They walked for a short distance from the rocks, Teran's hand still tightly clasping hers.

The rapidly darkening sky was clear, and Alia picked out several familiar star clusters. Aranea was up there in one of them, she thought with a surging sense of homesickness. Would she ever see that beloved planet again?

"Alia, we cannot survive much longer without water." Teran's voice interrupted her poignant distraction. "The mountains aren't much further. I am almost certain I caught a glimpse of them just before the sun set. I want to take the equs and try to reach them."

"But what of Vates?" she asked, startled by the abruptness of his plan. "Surely he cannot travel further. It might kill him."

"I know that. I want you to stay with him." He raised a hand to silence her protests. "You aren't strong enough to travel much further yourself. Time is of the essence. The equs and I can travel with greater speed if not burdened by the encumbrance of another on foot. Without the heat of the sun to drain me, there's a good chance I can reach the foothills and water before sunrise."

"You . . . you would leave us out here in this desert?" Her mind raced, attempting to ascertain Teran's chances of success. In the chaotic edges of her consciousness, a tiny suspicion grew. What if Teran never came back and left them here to die? He would have everything he needed—the equs, the stun gun, and the knowledge of where to find the Knowing Crystal. What further need did he have of them, a feeble old man and a quest-crazed femina?

Teran sensed her doubts and the sudden withdrawal. In an attempt to dispel her distrust, he grabbed

Alia by the arms and shook her.

"I will come back for you and Vates. I swear, Alia!"

She shrugged her way out of his grasp and moved a few steps from him. "What choice have we? Your plan is sound. You are the strongest of us. I have no choice but to trust you," she sighed, "as difficult as that is for me. Go, Teran. Now, before I change my mind. We'll be here when you return."

For a heartrending instant, Teran battled with the impulse to gather Alia into his arms. All the emotions rose with even greater force, intensified by the realization he might never see her alive again. She stared back at him with her parched lips parted and a luminous glow in her eyes and said nothing.

With a low, tormented groan Teran wrenched himself from the heady spell her nearness cast upon him. He rapidly strode over to the equs. Flinging himself onto its massive bulk, he gathered up the reins and rode back to where she stood.

Their gazes met and melded. An ardor, unspoken yet palpably intense, arced between them, the air crackling with the electric discharge of their emotions.

"I will come back for you, Alia," he said in a hoarse whisper. "I swear it!"

He wheeled the equs around, the forceful action punctuating his vow, and rode away into the nocte. She stood there watching him until the darkness swallowed his mighty form. Then, more alone than ever, she returned to where Vates lay.

Alia awoke to the sun glaring on her face. For a moment she was confused and disoriented in the unfamiliar surroundings. The unyielding hardness of the rock, pressing into her spine, wrenched her back to the reality of her situation.

Teran was gone. She and Vates were alone in the desert. She edged over to the crumpled form of the old man. In his fragile state, had he survived the nocte?

With the utmost care Alia pulled him to a sitting position and into the last vestiges of shade that this side of the stone afforded. "Vates, are you awake?"

After what seemed an eternity, Vates' eyelids fluttered open. He moved slightly. "Yes, child, I am alive."

He chuckled weakly. "Isn't that what you really meant to ask? Any sign of Teran yet?"

"How did you know . . . ?"

Alia cut off her words in midsentence. She smiled. Why should she be surprised? Vates always seemed to know what would happen before it even occurred.

"No, he hasn't returned."

"He will, child. Have no doubt of that." Vates took her hand. "Teran has never failed. He is strong, his spirit indomitable. He'll come back for us."

Strange words of praise for a coward, Alia thought wryly, but then Teran had never struck her as fainthearted. It was all very mystifying, just like the feelings he stirred within her.

"He cares for you, too, child."

Vates' statement caught her off guard. Then, remembering his mind seek, Alia gave an exasperated shake of her head.

"Really, this prying into my head is quite immoral. Please stop it."

The old man smiled. "I am sorry, child. It is just that time is short, and there's much I still need to know. I am heartened by what I see in you, though."

"And what do you think you see?" Alia challenged, half afraid to hear or know the truth about herself.

"I see a very frightened yet very brave young

femina, afraid of the enormity of her quest and even more afraid of her virgin emotions."

He paused to smile tenderly at her suddenly lowered head. "I know of your training and can guess at the real purpose of the one who taught you. I tell you this, my child. Beware. One's actions eventually reveal one's true motives."

Alia raised puzzled eyes. "I do not understand."

He sighed. "Much I cannot tell you, much you must work through yourself, but this much I will say. Your quest is not just for the Knowing Crystal. It is also the search for your true self, long buried under cycles of intentional misdirection. Without that inner knowledge and self-acceptance the Crystal, even when you find it, will be more than useless. It will be dangerous."

"You speak in such riddles," Alia said, her mind spinning with bafflement. "It is more than I can bear. You and Teran, each in your own way, are trying to wear me down, to confuse me. Why won't you leave me alone and cease your hammering at me?"

"We only want to help you, child." Vates stroked her hair, gently smoothing the tangled, matted curls. "I wish there was time enough to teach you the mind seek. Then you could discover for yourself what is truly in our hearts."

He sighed. "I know how difficult it must be for you to trust us, raised as you were, but trust this much, if you can. We wish for the rescue of the Knowing Crystal as much as you do. In the giant tapestry of fate, it is for this very purpose that Teran and I were exiled here and have waited all these cycles for your arrival. Our lives have been interwoven since the beginning, destined from all eternity to finally cross."

Alia's eyes widened. "No!" she cried, yet even as

she uttered the denial, she sensed the truth of his words.

As much as she hated to admit it, Alia now realized she had never been alone on this quest, even from its onset. She knew it, as surely as the High Priestess did that sol in her chambers. Strangely, the knowledge offered no comfort, as if a presentiment warned her of the great pain to come.

To shake off the disquieting thoughts, Alia unsteadily rose to her feet. She walked around the far side of the tall rock and smiled when she found her expectations fulfilled. It was rapidly becoming shaded and would soon provide some semblance of coolness. For a while, until her inner turmoil abated, Alia sat there.

Finally, her mental defenses once again strong, she returned to the old man's side and knelt beside him. "Come, Vates. You will rest more comfortably on the shaded side. We need any respite from the heat we can get."

"Yes, child." He smiled up at her, realizing the time for openness with her had passed. "It is a good spot to watch for Teran's return."

If he returns, Alia thought sardonically, as she bent to the difficult task of moving Vates.

The horas passed. Once the torrid red sun reached its zenith, the stones offered no further shelter. Realizing they would not survive in the blistering heat without some protection, Alia dug a hole at the base of the monolith, just large enough for the two of them. When the exhausting task was complete she helped Vates into it, then pulled a blanket over them.

Periodically, as the afternoon passed, she would peek out to search the horizon for sign of Teran but no movement or hint of life penetrated the billowing haze. He's not coming back, she thought in growing despair. He lied to me.

Curiously, the idea didn't upset her anymore. It took too much energy to be angry. That was one thing she could no longer spare.

She glanced at Vates, who had lost consciousness several horas before. Poor old man. Well, at least he no longer suffered. Alia prayed for the mercy of that oblivion herself. Oh, at last to be free of the gut-twisting pain of thirst!

The warmth rising off the desert floor shimmered in an airy dance, catching Alia's bleary gaze. She took to watching it, fascinated by the distorted forms behind the undulating waves. It reminded her of the movement of water.

Alia's mind began to drift back to a more pleasant time. She was swimming naked in a cool, invigorating spring. The feel of the silky fluid drifting over her body filled her with a curious elation. It called to her, beckoning her to swim deeper into its dark, bottomless depths.

She hesitated, instinctively realizing there was no hope of return. But what held her to life, anyway? She was being baked alive on a parched wasteland, exiled from her home, betrayed by the one man she had dared begin to trust. It was too much to endure. Better to blot it out, to forget, to die.

Yet just as she turned her back on the living, a white light filled her mind, blotting out the tantalizing waters. It glittered with a celestial resplendence, pervading every fiber of her being. It sang to her, calling her back to life, to the completion of her sacred quest. She gathered strength from it and struggled back up, out of the black void. The bright stone at the heart of the radiant light faded from view.

Alia opened her eyes to the harsh reality of the desert. There, far beyond the surging heat waves, was the powerful figure of a man on a massive equs. With the last vestiges of strength she threw off the blanket and raised herself. The man must have seen the movement, for he urged his beast to an even faster pace. For just one, lingering instant more, Alia willed her quivering muscles to obey. Then she fell to the ground in sweet, blessed unconsciousness.

Strong, comforting arms encircled Alia, rocking her to and fro. She snuggled contentedly against a muscular chest and slept the dream-filled sleep of delirium. It was so good to be held like that, to be loved. Her vision took her back to a time when she was quite small and the eyes that smiled down upon her were as brown as her own.

"Hush, child," her mother crooned. "Mama is here, and nothing can hurt you." Gazing up at the beloved face, Alia felt safe and happy. It had been so long since her mother had held her.

As she contemplated the beloved visage, slowly assuaging the hunger of their long cycles apart, a shadow fell across them. It was the form of the High Priestess. Her mother sighed, a terrible sorrow etching the smooth planes of her pretty face.

"I must leave you, sweetest child," she said, laying Alia down. "Never forget me, and that you were always loved."

Before Alia could protest, her mother was gone, like so many cycles before. She cried out, begging her not to leave. Her pleas were to no avail. The pain of parting knifed through her heart, and the tears began, welling up to join the sobs. There was no controlling either, and the intensity of both finally woke Alia from her dream.

She was in Teran's arms. Confused, feverish eyes peered up into tender gray ones.

"Alia, I am here, and nothing can hurt you," he murmured, his voice like rough velvet as he wiped her tears away. "You have been ill but will soon recover."

"Where . . . where am I?" she whispered, her own words sounding strangely foreign.

"In the foothills of Macer."

She smiled then, a weak upturning of the corners of her mouth. "Good."

For a long while she was silent, the terrors of her dream slowly soothed by the solace of Teran's body. "Vates!" Alia finally blurted out, remembering the old man. "How is Vates?"

A form angled into her vision. "I am fine, child." He smiled down at her. "My mind sleep protected me from the full effects of our ordeal."

Alia stirred weakly in Teran's clasp. "Then we must continue on our way to Ferox's fortress. We have lost so much time."

Teran and Vates both laughed, the relief evident in their voices.

"She will most definitely recover," Teran chuckled. "Her stubborn determination has returned in full force."

Vates nodded in agreement. "There is time enough for you to regain your strength, child," he said, affectionately gazing down at Alia. "We have ample food, water and shelter here. Now, sleep, my child. Rest is the best healer."

He touched her forehead. A heavy curtain of drowsiness fell, enveloping her mind once more.

Alia awoke as the earliest rays of sun filtered through the trees. The morning was gilded with reddish gold, peacefully silent except for the chirping of birds high overhead. She tried to rise, only to find

Teran's sinewy arm flung across her waist, anchoring her down. He lay close to her, barechested, his head pillowed on his other arm.

A feeling of irritation swept through her. How dare he sleep so close to her, like . . . like she was some wanton! There was no excuse for it now; they were no longer constrained by the close confines of the tent. No one on Aranea slept together. Once the ritual of sanctioned mating was accomplished, both sexes always separated to their own beds.

She grasped the masculine arm that lay across her to fling it aside, when something caused her to hesitate. She looked more closely at Teran. Lines of deep fatigue etched his bearded face. With a pang, Alia realized he must have been awake with her through most of her illness.

The recollection of his image, floating in and out of her fevered dreams, and the comforting feel of his strong arms about her came rushing back. She wondered how many sols she'd been ill. Several, at least, from the look of the dark smudges under Teran's eyes.

Gently lifting the sleep-heavy arm, Alia carefully replaced it at Teran's side. She gingerly sat up, waiting for the dizziness to clear. After a while, when she felt her strength adequate, Alia climbed to her feet. Swaying precariously, only the assistance of a nearby tree saved her from unceremoniously toppling to the ground.

Lurching from one tree to the other, Alia made her way toward the sound of running water. She wanted a bath. Her breaths coming in shallow gasps, she finally arrived at the water's edge.

There, rising high above, a waterfall cascaded into a turbulent little lake. A warm breeze gently wafted by, tipping the cobalt blue waters with glinting silver waves. The temptation was too great. Lowering herself to the fern-strewn bank, she pulled off her boots. Her disrobing, despite her eagerness to sink into the lake, took a painfully long time.

At last, she inched her way into the water. As the cool liquid slowly lapped its way up her body, Alia heaved a deep, contented sigh. She pushed off a little from the shore and floated blissfully in the shallow water. If she died now, she'd die—

"By the ken of the Crystal!" Teran's angry voice slashed across the peaceful lake. "What do you think you're doing out there?"

Alia hastily pushed herself back into the more veiling depths of the lake. "I was taking a bath, of course. You and Vates were still asleep, and I did not want to wake you."

Her voice trailed off. "What . . . what are you doing?"

"Coming in to get you before you drown," Teran said matter-of-factly as he sat down and began to pull off his boots.

"Don't you dare! I am quite capable of getting out under my own power," Alia cried, raising a hand as if to stop him.

Teran laughed. "You thwarted me once before, but not this time. It's for your own good. You're in no condition to be swimming around a lake yet, bath or no bath."

She watched in helpless horror as Teran rose and slowly advanced on her. Casting about for some avenue of escape, she realized her strength wasn't equal to the task. She put out her arms to keep him from her.

"Teran, please. Don't!"

He ignored her plea and gathered her slim, water-slick body to his. "Don't be afraid," he muttered, his voice husky. "I won't take advantage of you in your weakened state. I meant what I said. I've come to take you out of the water and back to your bed."

Teran lifted her from the lake, sliding one arm under her thighs and the other across her upper back. He looked down at her with a cold, impersonal stare, but an involuntary shudder, as her bare flesh met his, betrayed him, nonetheless.

The expression of anguished longing that passed across Teran's face was lost on Alia. Embarassed, yet oddly comfortable at the same time, she hid her face in the furry strength of his chest. As the movement of his powerful body announced his progress out of the water, she relaxed against him, her nakedness suddenly of no concern. There was safety in the muscled haven of Teran's arms.

The morning air suddenly felt cool, and Alia began to shiver, unconsciously moving even closer to the attractive warmth of the hard body pressed against hers. At her artless gesture he smiled and tenderly kissed the top of her head.

The forceful action of Teran's body relaxed as they finally cleared the water. He strode over to the small pile of clothing Alia had left, yet many secundae passed before he finally lowered her feet to the ground. Slowly, almost reluctantly, Alia raised her eyes to his.

He gazed down at her, his eyes dark with emotion. The look shook Alia to the depths of her being, for never in her life had she seen such intense longing. And it's for me, she reflected wonderingly. He wants me! The thought filled her with a heady elation, her own primitive urges floating to the surface of her consciousness. He wants me!

"Alia . . . ," Teran groaned, his hands caressing her bare shoulders. "I need you so badly. If you only knew how much . . ."

"I . . . I think I am beginning to understand, if only a little," she ventured. "Is this some spell you have cast to make me feel this way?"

Teran stared at her, his dark brows knit in confusion. Then he tossed back his head and laughed, the sound full and masculine.

"A spell? No, Alia, I'm no sorcerer. My talents are not those of Vates, however benign they be."

His expression turned serious. "What is growing between us is the true mating urge, not just the desire for a moment's easing but something that is meant to endure. It's been so long since I've felt this way, and yet, at the same time, I've never felt this way before. It frightens me."

"Frightens you? Why does it frighten you, Teran?"

He hesitated, reluctant to reveal much of his heart, not knowing how she would accept it or even if she were ready. Then he sighed. "Have you ever loved someone and then lost them?"

At his question the memories of her mother stirred in her mind, filling her with a heavy pain. It took all her strength to hold back the tears that threatened to flood her eyes.

"Yes, Teran, I have lost a loved one."

"Then perhaps you can begin to understand." He released her, though his body remained close, and exhaled a shuddering breath. "It is enough for now to say I want you. If you feel the same, you must come to me of your own accord or not at all."

He picked up his boots and rapidly strode off through the trees. Alia stood there in wondering silence, watching until his brawny form disappeared from view. Then, with a sigh, she turned back to her clothing and dressed.

CHAPTER 5

TERAN WAS NOT IN CAMP WHEN ALIA RETURNED.

"He has gone off to explore, child," Vates said, answering her unspoken question. "What did you do to him to make him bolt out of here like that?"

Alia turned dazed eyes to the old man. "What . . . what did you say?"

Vates laughed. "Never mind, child. You've answered my question."

He paused to study her intently. "You look worn. Here, drink this," he said, handing her a mug of fragrantly scented, amber liquid. "It is a healing draught and will give you strength."

She took the cup and drank deeply of the potion. It was not long before she was overcome with a heavy sense of weariness, but whether of mind or body, it was difficult to discern.

"Sleep now, child," the old man urged, "and when you awake, you will be strong again."

"Yes, perhaps that would be wise," Alia murmured, as she walked over to her bedding and lay down. Almost before her head touched the blanket she was asleep, wrapped in the dark comfort of her dreams.

"Vates! Alia!"

Teran's excited voice startled Alia out of her slumber. She rose on one elbow, drowsily wondering how long she'd been sleeping.

"What's wrong, Teran?" she called, groggily glancing around.

He was nowhere to be seen. Climbing to her feet, Alia was momentarily surprised at how refreshed Vates' draught and the nap had made her feel.

Teran's tall form broke through the trees. An instant later, he stood before them, his gray eyes sparkling, his rugged face flushed. "Equs! There's a herd of wild equs in a valley just two hills away. Come on!"

Not awaiting an answer, he grabbed the coil of rope and the saddle and bridle. His long strides carried him away almost as fast as he'd arrived. Alia and Vates exchanged a bemused glance, then followed, barely managing to keep Teran in view from one moment to the next.

They finally caught up with him at the top of the second hill. He lay on his belly, intently peering down into a small valley. Teran raised a silencing finger to his lips, then motioned for them to drop down beside him.

Alia crawled over to Teran's side and inched her body forward until she could scan the scene below. A large band of equs, mostly bays and chestnuts, grazed peacefully in the little valley. Led by a powerfully

104

built, black stallion, the shaggy, bearded herd appeared savage and untamable.

"Very nice, Teran." Alia turned to face the man beside her. "And, pray tell, what do you propose we do with them? Eat them for supper?"

Teran snorted in disdain. "Actually, I'd something more like riding them in mind. Two of us are without transportation. A few extra equs would ease our journey considerably."

"Are you mad? These are wild animals. We don't have the time it takes to tame them."

"There are quicker ways." Teran smiled as he pulled the stungun from his belt.

Standing up, he took careful aim. A bright chestnut mare fell to her knees at the first blast of the gun. With the second, the black stallion toppled forward. Shoving the gun into Alia's hand, Teran quickly gathered up the equipment he had brought with him.

She looked down at the gun. "And what exactly am I to do with this? Put you out of your misery if one of the equs stomps on you?"

"Hopefully you'll take care of the equs before he has that delightful opportunity."

He started down the hillside, then stopped to look up at her. "Well, are you coming or not?"

"Coming?" she squeaked in surprise. "What exactly did you have in mind?"

"You're going to make sure they stay stunned until I can saddle and bridle them." He grinned. "Then, my dear femina, we're going to tame those two particular equs as fast as we can."

Teran continued down the hill toward the two unconscious animals. Alia watched him for a long moment, then turned to Vates, who chuckled. "He seems quite determined, child. Perhaps you'd better see to his aid. He may have need of it. In the meantime, I will return to camp and begin preparing our noon meal."

"That man is intent on killing himself before we even get to Ferox," Alia muttered disgustedly. Shaking her head, she left Vates standing on the hill and began her descent.

Teran knelt at the black's head, fastening the bridle in place. "Good," he said, glancing up when Alia halted beside him. "I was hoping you'd see the wisdom of assisting me. First, I'll break the stallion for me, then the chestnut mare for you. It's better if Vates rides your equs, if you've no objections," he finished, arching a challenging brow.

"None at all. I can handle the mare."

"I thought as much." Teran glanced back over his shoulder. "Why don't you hand me the saddle? This beast is beginning to recover. We'll have to hurry if I'm to be mounted when he wakens."

Shoving the stun gun into her pocket, Alia quickly returned with the saddle. "Perhaps I could be of help," she began, as she handed it to him. "I noticed some familiar bushes growing near that stand of trees. They could be of use."

"Not now, Alia." Teran peeled off his tunic in a quick, fluid motion and flung it aside. "The equs has almost revived."

A few secundae later the saddle was on the equs' back. Working the cinch under its belly to the other side took longer, considering the animal was lying down, but at last the task was complete.

As the increasingly restive beast climbed to its feet, Teran swung onto its back. "As soon as we're out of the way, see to the mare. Tie her feet together and bind her eyes. She'll be more than docile in that condition," he ordered.

The equs lurched upright. For a brief instant, the huge animal stood rigidly still, as if trying to fathom the new weight on his back. Then, as the significance finally filtered through to its brain, he gave a loud bellow. Lowering his head, he began a series of bone-jarring bucks. Teran grimly held on, the muscles of his arms and legs bulging with the effort to remain on the wildly agitated equs.

Alia watched the battle of man against beast. Teran was a skilled rider, despite his former self-deprecations as to his abilities with animals. When she finally saw that he was in control, she turned her attention to the mare.

That animal, too, was beginning to stir. Alia hastily set herself to the task of securing its feet. Next, she wrapped an old rag around the equs' eyes. The mare now subdued, Alia returned her gaze to Teran.

The black equs appeared to decide on a new plan of attack. He reared on his hind legs until Teran clung to him in an almost vertical angle. Alia's breath caught in her throat as she watched the pawing, cloven hooves slash the air. She saw the equs teeter precariously and realized he was losing his balance.

"Get off, Teran!" she cried. "He's going over!"

In a horrified slow motion, the beast toppled over, Teran still clinging to him. Before its massive weight crushed the man beneath it, Teran flung himself aside. Almost before the stallion hit ground, he was rolling over and climbing to his feet.

"Stun him!" Teran shouted. "Stun him before we lose him!"

Jerked out of her astonished paralysis by Teran's words, Alia pulled the stungun from her pocket. Swiftly taking aim, she fired. The equs sank to his knees and remained there, unmoving. Alia ran to Teran's side.

"Are you all right?" she asked, her voice breathless with concern.

Teran paused from brushing off the dirt clinging to his breeches and glanced over at Alia. The merest hint of a smile grazed his lips.

"Yes, Alia. Aside from feeling like that beast dislocated every joint in my body, I'm quite intact."

Unmasked by the piercing scrutiny of Teran's gaze, Alia felt the heat rise to her cheeks. She hid her discomfiture by turning to inspect the downed equs.

"So what do you plan to do now? Your opponent seems intent on killing you, even at the risk of its own life."

"I don't have much choice. I'll have to convince him life with me is more pleasant than life without me." As he spoke, Teran grasped Alia's shoulder, the gesture adding yet an extra meaning to his words.

Her pulse quickened, the sudden warmth of his fingers scorching her through the thin fabric of her tunic. She wheeled around and found herself in his arms, gazing up into gray eyes as heated as the blood that pounded through her body.

"Alia . . ." Teran murmured huskily, gathering her to him.

This time there was no fight, no internal battle. Alia came to him willingly, needing him and wanting to feel his body against hers. Just then, a movement caught the corner of her eye.

"Teran," she mumbled from a place deep within his arms, "the equs. The equs is waking."

He immediately released her and turned to face the restless animal. "Your timing is perfect," he growled. Striding back, he resignedly remounted and waited for the equs to rise.

This time the black was hardly on its feet when it bolted down the valley. Crouched low on its back, the black mane whipping his face, Teran rode the equs with a fierce resolve.

Alia watched the two forms disappear from view. What if the animal tried to fall on Teran again and succeeded? And even if he evaded the brute's attempts, she was now too far away to use the stun gun. At the very least, all their riding equipment would be lost.

Time passed as Alia's eyes strained for sight of the pair. Finally, she saw the black once more, the form of a man firmly upon its back. She let out a sigh of relief. Teran still rode the animal, but what a change! Lathered, his sides heaving, the massive stallion docilely trotted along, no longer fighting the powerful man upon his back.

She waited for them, her heart beating furiously. His black, wavy hair windswept, a light sheen of sweat glistening on the broad planes of his muscled arms and torso, Teran rode as if part of the animal itself. Yet it was the boyishly proud grin on his bearded face that seared her with a poignant sweetness. It was all Alia could do to keep from running to him.

Teran reined in the equs beside her. "Well, what do you think? Has the beast learned his lesson?"

"It appears so," Alia agreed smilingly. "Your technique is quite effective, if a little crude."

"Crude!" Teran's grin quickly darkened into an angry scowl. "By the Crystal, how else do you propose to tame an equs? You're one of the most unappreciative feminas I've ever had the misfortune . . ."

His voice trailed off as Alia turned and headed toward a nearby stand of trees. Once there, she began to pick leaves off a silver-green, lacy-leafed bush. His irritation mounting, Teran was about to urge his mount toward her when she started back to him.

"Has anyone ever informed you you're also quite rude?" he demanded, when she finally reached his side.

Alia smiled sweetly up at him. In her hands she clutched the strange leaves. "You wouldn't listen to me before, so I decided to let my actions speak for me."

She walked over to the chestnut mare. Once there she knelt and slowly fed bits of the foliage to the animal.

Teran slid off the black and led him over to where Alia knelt. "What are you doing?" he asked, barely containing his exasperation.

"You'll see soon enough."

She finished feeding the rest of the leaves to the equs, then raised her eyes to him. "Now, if you would be so kind as to assist me in untying this animal, I would like to ride her."

"Are you mad?" Teran sputtered. "How can you hope to stay on? Wait until I tie up my black, then I'll ride her for you."

"Your services will not be necessary, but if it makes you feel any better, here is the stun gun. If I need help, you always have that—not that I will be needing any assistance."

Teran snorted in derision. "Don't be so sure."

Nonetheless, he bent down and helped free the equs' legs. The mare rose to her feet but didn't move away, the rag still wrapped around her eyes making her uncertain.

Alia stepped to her side. Grasping a handful of mane, she swung up onto the animal's back and smiled down at a dubious Teran.

"Remove the blindfold, please."

Teran hesitated. "But you've no tack on the beast.

110

This is very dangerous. Are you sure you want to do this, Alia? I'd rather it was I who risked injury."

"Quite sure. If this is to be my equs, I should be the one to tame it."

He dubiously stared at her for a moment longer, then sighed. "As you wish." The cloth covering the beast's eyes fluttered to the ground.

The mare stood there, calmly munching the last of the leaves Alia had fed her. As the secundae passed and nothing happened, Teran's tension increased proportionately. The animal was sure to blow up any moment now, sending Alia sailing through the air. He clutched the gun in his hand, poised for instant use—but nothing happened.

"What's wrong with that equs?" he finally asked, his brows knit in puzzlement. The light of realization slowly brightened his eyes. "It was those leaves, wasn't it?"

"Yes, it was. They grow quite abundantly on my planet and are commonly used to tame an equs."

Teran's face transformed into a glowering mask. "Then why, by the five moons of Bellator, didn't you tell me about them before? I could have broken my neck on that black monster of mine."

Alia gave a nonchalant shrug. "If you recall I tried. I assumed, when you refused to listen, you preferred doing things your way. And who am I, but a weak, stupid little femina, to question the great warrior Teran?"

"Fine," he choked out the word through clenched teeth. "From now on, however, please share any specialized knowledge you may have. I will be certain to give it my undivided attention."

"As you wish. Now that I know I have an appreciative ear, you can be sure I will." She glanced up at the red sun hovering above them in the sky. "Well, if you are quite through with equs training, perhaps it is time we were getting back to camp. It is noon. Vates has our meal ready by now."

A wicked gleam flared in Teran's eyes. "Care for a race?"

Alia eyed the powerful stallion who could easily outdistance her mare. Oh well, let Teran have his tiny victory. It wouldn't change who had really won. With a laugh she nudged her equs forward, the race begun before Teran even had a chance to mount.

Early the next morning the trio packed up camp and left the verdant forest at the foot of the mountains. They climbed the rocky path to the summit of the foremost peak, arriving late that afternoon. The evening meal was started just as the red sun set far in the distance, beyond several more jagged mountain ranges.

As they ate, Alia suddenly lay down her platter, a curious expression on her face. The action immediately drew the attention of Teran and Vates. Her features assumed an intent, almost listening appearance. Then, woodenly, she rose to her feet. Without comment, Alia walked a distance away to silently gaze at the rose-lavender hue settling over the mountains.

Teran made a move to follow, but Vates lay a restraining hand on his arm. "No, my son," he said, shaking his head. "Give her peace. The Crystal calls her. Let them commune."

Grudgingly, the younger man sank down across from his friend. He picked up a twig and idly drew on the ground.

"This power she has," he said, without looking up. "It grows in strength the closer we get to the Crystal."

"Yes, my son. Why does that trouble you?"

Teran was quiet, seemingly intent on etching swirls

in the dirt. "I fear," he finally began again, "the Crystal will call her away to a place I can never go."

He raised tortured gray eyes to Vates. "Is that, too, part of our destiny? Must I lose her?"

Vates smiled, a distant look hovering in his dark eyes. "This much I can tell you, Teran. You will most certainly lose her unless you follow her—in every way."

A shudder coursed through Teran's big body. Vates' sight had once more foretold the future, and suddenly it was a future Teran feared. It asked too much of him, required a sacrifice he was loathe to give.

"You still insist I let Alia claim me, don't you?" he muttered bitterly. "Is that the price I must pay to be with her?"

"That and much more, my son. Though Alia doesn't realize it yet, she needs you even more than you need her. The Crystal can never regain its full powers without you."

"What?" He leaned toward Vates, visibly shaken. "What do you mean? This is no time to speak in riddles, teacher!"

"And this time I shan't. You, too, have the ability to key the Crystal, my son. The gift is yet not as strong nor well-developed as Alia's, but it is there, nonetheless."

"But how can that be? Everyone knows only those of a certain royal line can commune with the Knowing Crystal."

Vates sighed. "It is time you heard the truth, a truth your family has tried to hide all these many cycles."

He gave a dry laugh. "For some reason they always found it a disgrace that your great-grandmother was not Bellatorian. Though distantly related, you and Alia are of the same blood."

Teran sat there, the import of the old man's words slowly seeping into his stunned mind. It was all so confusing.

"You've known this all along, haven't you?" He suddenly spat the words out, frustrated anger rising within him. "Is that all I've ever been to you, Vates? A pawn in the great scheme to regain the Knowing Crystal? And is it now necessary to complete your intricately woven web by coercing me into being claimed, tied to another like some mindless slave? Is that, perhaps, how I'm meant to serve the Crystal— as some resource unit Alia can draw additional power from?"

Vates said nothing. He returned the angry glare of the man before him with a calm one of his own.

Unable to bear the sense of betrayal he felt in the presence of a man he thought loved him, Teran rose and strode into the gathering darkness.

Alia returned to the camp a short while later and glanced about her. "Where is Teran?"

"Gone off to think about things." Vates raised sad, penetrating eyes to her. "So, child, what have you learned from the Crystal?"

"It showed me the way to Ferox's fortress. The journey will be difficult."

"Then we will need our rest. Come, let us sleep."

Their beds were made in silence, and they lay their exhausted bodies down. Sleep quickly claimed its due.

In the early horas Teran returned to camp, but not to sleep.

Vates never stirred, but Alia noted Teran's return. She watched him lower himself to sit on his blanket, his corded arms wrapping around his drawn up legs, and saw him blankly stare out into the darkness. His face in the dim light was grim, his mouth tight, his eyes unreadable in the shadowed recesses of his face.

She lay there for a long while wondering what troubled Teran, wanting yet afraid to approach him. At last, weariness beckoned her back to oblivion.

The next sol dawned, gray and cold. Scanning the horizon, Alia suspected it would rain before the sol ended. Combined with the vision she'd had last nocte, the tone of the whole quest had suddenly turned as dreary as the weather. She rose and walked over to where her equs was tethered. The only antidote to feelings like this was action. She began to secure the animal with the rope bridle Teran had fashioned.

The mood of the two men was just as somber. They hardly spoke except to relay some vital bit of information as they packed up camp. Alia wondered what had transpired while she had been away last nocte. She almost asked Teran about it once. As if guessing her intent, he quickly silenced her with a hard, angry look.

She shook off the curious sense of exclusion their enforced silence made her feel, but the hurt lingered. Were they angry with her? Was she the cause of their apparent dissention?

At last all were mounted. Alia turned to Vates. "I will lead from here on. The Crystal will guide me."

"No!" Teran's voice sliced between them. "I'm not having some trail-ignorant femina leading me through these mountains. There's no telling what disaster you'd blunder into. *I'll* lead."

"Why, you . . . you arrogant . . ." Further words momentarily escaped Alia as she turned to face Teran. "How much do you really know about my expertise? Have you ever cared enough to ask?"

"And how could anyone possibly get anything out of you?" Teran growled, his gray eyes flashing. As much as he hated to admit it, he was burning for a fight, an outlet for the growing pain and frustration. "You're the most secretive, cold-hearted—"

"Cold-hearted! And who are you to—"

"Teran. Alia." Vates held up a hand for silence. "When will you two stop squabbling and begin to work together? The solution is simple. The quest is both of yours now. Ride together."

Harking back to last nocte's conversation, Teran shot Vates a raw glance. He said nothing, though, when Alia urged her equs into place beside him. Except when forced to ask for directions, he seldom spoke to her for the next several horas.

As the sol progressed, the trail became steeper and more hazardous. They were frequently forced to dismount and lead their equs past piles of boulders that nearly blocked the increasingly narrow path.

As the trail's summit came into view a few hundred meters ahead, an eerie sensation wended its way through Alia—a feeling of being observed. As unobtrusively as possible, she glanced around her.

Closely studying the mountainside, all Alia could see was stone. The huge rocks, thrusting themselves from the sides of the mountain, mocked her by their very ungainliness. She felt mildly ridiculous, but the impression lingered. Someone was watching them.

"Is something the matter?"

Teran's low, deep voice jolted her from her thoughts. "What would make you think that?" she nervously asked.

"The look on your face, combined with my own feeling that something's not right."

She shook her head. "I don't know. It could just be my anxieties assuming tangible shape, but I think we are being watched."

A wry grin twitched the corner of his mouth. "It may be of small comfort, but I feel the same way. Our

116

stalkers are skilled. Try as I might, I've seen no sign, heard no movement, but they are up there, nonetheless." With a casual motion of his head, Teran surreptitiously indicated the ledge above them.

As if the movement triggered it, the mountain started to shake. They halted their mounts in stunned horror. The swaying mass of stone groaned and quaked, and the equs shied in terror. Bits and pieces of rock loosened and fell around them, the debris increasing in size and speed as the tremors continued.

"Let's get out of here!" Teran shouted above the growing din. "Now!"

He gave Alia's mare a sharp swat on its rump. As the animal sprang forward, he rode back to grab the reins of Vates' mount. Kicking his black fiercely in the side, the pair of equs and their riders bolted up the path behind Alia.

The trio quickly reached the summit and began to recklessly career down a precipitously angled road. More time seemed to be spent in the air, sailing over dead trees and boulders, than on the ground. Still, the barrage continued, only now the missiles seemed to have a deliberately aimed direction.

Glancing behind her Alia saw a large stone strike Teran on the shoulder, nearly knocking him from his equs. Only the powerful pressure of his thighs, clamped around the stallion's side, kept him astride. He wavered, then regained his upright position. Urging the animal on, Teran continued to lead Vates' mount behind him.

The flinty shards rained on them until Alia wondered if it would ever end, if they'd ever outrun the attack. She crouched low on the mare's back and rode, her eyes riveted upon the road before her. Several times rocks struck her equs. The animal squealed in pain yet never broke stride. On and on they fled, the roar of falling stone finally diminishing. The torrent of jagged projectiles ceased.

Though apparently out of immediate danger Teran moved ahead to take the lead. He continued their mad escape, drawing ahead to lead them over seemingly impossible obstacles, sliding down steep slopes when the path was impassable, but always, unerringly, taking them ever closer to Ferox and the Crystal. Alia briefly wondered how he knew the way without her to lead but swiftly brushed the question aside. There was little time for the luxury of thought, as Teran pushed them through the maze of rock.

He abruptly reined his equs in. With a huge sigh, Alia pulled her mare to a stop and twisted in the saddle to look back at Vates. Though pale and windblown, he appeared none the worse for their fearsome ride.

She turned back to face Teran. "I'm glad you finally found us safety. The equs couldn't have kept up that mad pace much longer."

"We're not out of danger yet," he muttered grimly. "I stopped because of those." As he spoke, he gestured upward.

Alia's vision, jaded by the multitude of stone that surrounded her, had failed to notice the particular rocks Teran now indicated. She let out an involuntary gasp as her eyes traveled heavenward. Two huge boulders jutted out of the ground like eerie sentinels, just like the ones at the edge of the desert.

A sickening sense of foreboding flooded her. "What do you think they mean?" Alia asked, desperately trying to quell the dread that threatened to overwhelm her.

"They mark the outer boundaries of Ferox's stronghold," Vates said from behind her. "The rockslide

118

was but a gentle warning. Beyond these stones lie the real dangers."

"Somehow I thought you'd say something like that," Teran growled sardonically.

He swung down from his black steed. "We can spare little time; we may be pursued. The equs need a short rest, though. Then we must push onward."

For a weary moment Alia remained on the equs, her battered body too weak to move. She watched as Vates dismounted and walked over to the base of one of the monoliths, then she blearily turned her gaze in Teran's direction. He leaned against his equs, his head bowed in fatigue, rubbing his bruised shoulder.

At the sight of him, she immediately forgot her own troubles. Alia slipped off her animal and hurried to Teran's side. His back was to her. When she hesitantly touched him, he responded with a jerk. When he turned to face her, pain, exhaustion and doubt darkened his eyes.

He wonders if we should go on. Well, at least he has a choice, she thought with a sudden pang of envy.

"How is your shoulder?" She lightly touched the area.

"Badly bruised, but nothing broken." He paused, as if trying to frame his next words. "Alia, surely by now you realize this quest is hopeless. These mountains are teeming with Ferox's men, and we have only one weapon between the three of us. Turn back with us now. Vates and I have learned how to survive on this miserable planet. We can protect you."

She looked up into silver eyes now warm with hope, eyes that tugged at her heart, eyes that urged her to come with him. It would be so easy to forget everything, to turn her back on the horrors still before her and follow him. Who would care? Who would miss her on Aranea? Certainly not the High

Priestess, she thought, remembering the glowering hostility on the femina's face that sol in Aranea's transport chamber.

Yet almost before the name escaped the hidden sanctuary of her mind, the High Priestess' words rose to torment her, to pull her back to the true reality.

"You are our last hope."

Alia drew back from the heady closeness of Teran's body, a sad, wistful smile on her lips. "I am sorry. I cannot. There is no other destiny for me."

Her heart twisted within her at the hurt she saw well up in his eyes. "You are free to turn back, Teran. I would not hold you to this."

He pulled her to him. All of Vates' words and all the emotion he felt for the flame-haired femina washed over Teran, threatening to drown him in a flood tide of sharp revelation. Though the admission was dredged from a place beyond reason, he could deny his fate no longer. They were bound, one to the other, until victory or death claimed them.

"Alia," Teran said, "don't you understand? I'm no longer free to leave. We are joined by more than words. My fate now lies with you."

"Then you will go with me?"

"Yes."

A sudden surge of tenderness coursed through Alia. Impulsively, she reached up to stroke Teran's face. The beard felt strange beneath her hand, yet surprisingly soft and stimulating, too. Her lips parted in wonder at the sensuous feel of him. For a moment, she was lost to everything but the sweet presence of the man before her. She saw him move toward her, his silver eyes glinting fiercely.

"Teran. Alia." Vates' voice ripped into their private world. "Come. I must talk with you."

Turning as one, they walked toward the old man,

each step draining some of the fever from their brains. By the time they reached Vates, both were again nearly lucid.

"What is it, teacher?" Teran inquired. "Are you rested enough to continue our journey?"

A pensive light glimmered in Vates' eyes. "Ah, yes, our journey. The exact subject I wish to discuss."

He paused. "I can travel no further with you. It is time for you and Alia to go on alone."

The shock of Vates' words hit Teran full force. "Have you been hurt? I saw no rock strike you, no wound," he demanded, the long-suppressed fears making his voice husky. "Or have you perhaps lost faith in the quest?"

"No, my son," the old man replied, shaking his head. "On the contrary, I have all the faith in the world. But the simple fact is that my purpose has been served. I am no longer needed. The torch has been passed. The fate of the Imperium now rests in younger hands."

Teran fought down the nauseating dread surging through him. Vates' past predictions of his death rose to haunt him once more. This time, however, Teran couldn't still the impending sense of inevitability.

"The choice is not mine to make, my son," the old man gently explained, grasping his young friend's arm. "I am but a servant of the Crystal. You two," he gestured from Alia back to Teran, "will be much more. You will be its masters."

"But I don't want anything to do with that cursed stone. *You* are what I care about, not some elusive glory or some nebulous power."

He wrenched his arm from the old man's clasp and stepped back, the raw anguish sharply etched into his features. "You've been my father, my friend. I don't want to lose you."

"Nor I you, my son. But the decision is not ours and has never been."

Teran violently shook his head, backing away from them all the while. "No, I won't accept it. I can't," he cried, the anguished sounds dredged from some deep, private place.

Turning, he strode a short distance from them as if his physical flight also assured escape from the reality of the situation. He stood there, his back to them, his head bowed in dejection.

Vates watched for countless moments, an expression of sorrow creasing his wise old face. Then, with a heavy sigh, he turned to Alia. He stared at her intently, as if trying, for one last time, to see into her mind.

She felt the mental probing, and this time allowed him entry. A benign warmth pervaded her. For an instant they merged, his essence gladdening her, filling her like one fills an empty vessel with the mellow brilliance of its spirit.

The old man smiled. "Thank you, child. My life fade will be all the sweeter, because you have finally come to trust me. I know now the Crystal will be in safe hands."

His expression saddened. "Be kind to Teran. He will greatly mourn my passing. Trust him as you have come to trust me. He is the best of my pupils, the greatest hope for the future of our people. All the good I have learned, I have tried to instill in him. More than you realize now, you need him—and he needs you."

"I will do as you ask," Alia whispered, her eyes bright with unshed tears. "This much I can do for you . . ." Her voice broke. With a soft cry, she threw herself into his arms.

Vates gathered her to him and crooned an old song,

all the while stroking her burnished red tresses. "Hush, child," he finally said. "Teran will not fail you; the Crystal will be yours. But beware Aranea. The hardest test is yet to come when you return to your home. Remember who you are, the proud blood that flows in your veins. Your house was truly a great one, no matter what you may have been told. It was not your ancestors who betrayed the Crystal."

"Then who?"

He gently disengaged himself. "All will be revealed in time. This much I see for you, this small comfort I can offer. All will be well, if only you trust your heart. Now go, child. My life force rapidly fades. I must say my farewells to Teran."

She nodded and stepped back from him. The old man wearily made his way over to Teran.

"My son," Vates began, "there is little time left. Do not shut me out when such pain is still between us. Listen to your teacher one last time and trust me."

Teran's rigid form relaxed. He turned to face his friend. A look of wild grief lay heavily upon him, the suffering in his eyes almost blinding him.

"What more is there to say?" he rasped. "You are leaving, and I must stay. Your task is done, and mine is just beginning. That I will live should be of some comfort, but I find none in it. All I know is you will be gone, and that I love you."

"Then do this final thing for me, as one last proof of your love." Even as he spoke Vates' form began to softly glow, the outlines of his body blurring. "Allow Alia to claim you. Once the Crystal is recovered, return with her to her planet. Then have faith that all will be well."

The old man raised a hand, a hand that no longer had substance. "Farewell, my son, my friend. I have loved no other as dearly as you."

As Teran watched in utter helplessness, the being known as Vates faded. For a long while afterwards, he stood frozen to the spot, a look of tortured disbelief twisting his face.

A light drizzle began to fall. At last, the shock of the chill, splattering rain roused him back to the present. Teran looked about in stunned confusion, his glance alighting upon Alia.

She stared back at him, uncertain what to do or how to approach him.

"Well, what are you waiting for?" he growled. "Mount up. We've already tarried too long. This is no sanctuary. We're still in the gravest danger."

She opened her mouth to speak, then thought better of it. Instead, she forced herself to walk toward her equs. He was right. It wasn't safe here. Her words of consolation weren't meant for this moment. The time for talking and comforting would have to wait.

CHAPTER 6

THE LIGHT RAIN FELL ALL SOL. DARK GRAY CLOUDS scudded across the sky, blotting out any hope of sun. Wet to the skin, Alia and Teran's clothing clung heavily to bodies weary and cold. The wind, at first warm and blustery, gradually turned bitingly sharp. It gnawed through the soaked garments of the two riders, chilling them with icy fangs of air.

Still, the outward misery of the weather could do little to worsen their spirits, spirits already deeply immersed in a sodden lethargy. Only once before had Alia felt so bereft and desolate. Vates was gone, and in her innermost of hearts, she feared she also had lost Teran.

An aching despair welled inside her. He would never forgive her for Vates' passing; he would blame her for setting into motion the events that had led to that inevitable conclusion. She'd irrevocably destroyed the fragile link building between them, and though she knew she shouldn't allow it to matter, it did. It mattered more than she'd ever realized.

Dusk settled over the dismal, barren terrain. Alia wondered how much longer Teran would force the pace. To travel the steep, narrow paths in the dark and attempt to navigate courses that fell off so precipitously into nothingness was foolhardy. But Teran, always the precise, careful warrior, wasn't in the most level-headed state of mind.

Except for a few terse commands, Teran had not spoken since Vates' life fade. Shoulders slumped and head bowed, he rode on, seemingly unaware of his surroundings. Though the evident lack of his old friend was an excruciating reminder of his life's passage, Teran's mind seemed unable to broach the expanse to final acceptance.

He felt bleak with sorrow, the huge lump of pain in his chest beyond tears. How could he go on without Vates? With his teacher at his side, there had been hope of eventually leaving Carcer, hope for a new life and a new beginning. Now, instead of the hope of winning his freedom, he faced a future even more desperate, more harrowing than before.

It was all so futile—this quest for the Knowing Crystal. Even if they managed to find their way through the pitfalls and deathtraps sure to lay before them, the dream of Ferox willingly giving up the Crystal was insane. The only possible outcome would be to find themselves in an endless noctemare.

At the contemplation of what Ferox would do to Alia, a cold chill ran through Teran. Memories of another time and another femina rose to haunt him. With a mental wrench, he thrust the old heartache aside. If only he could dissuade her from the quest . . .

A hopeless gloom settled over him. Once more his thoughts took on an empty rawness. There was no way to stop Alia, no way but death. And now there was no way for him, either.

Watching the dispirited appearance of the once proud, vibrant man, Alia's heart went out to Teran. She yearned to help him, to afford him some measure of comfort, but didn't know how.

The thought of her inadequacy filled her with frustration. Never had she been trained to handle the pain of emotions, nor how to offer solace. Perhaps it was better to deal with Teran in a purely objective manner and confront him with the fact he was endangering them and their quest with his self-centered mourning. She had to do something. Teran was rapidly becoming useless in this condition.

Yet when she opened her mouth to chastise him, all the gut-twisting feelings of loss rushed back, engulfing Alia in her own private anguish. Further attempts at cold rationalization failed miserably, as the emotions broke through the poorly erected barriers of her heart. She, too, had come to love Vates. That admission, coupled with the lingering pain of her own mother's death, filled her with a curious empathy. She found she hurt *for* Teran. She wanted to hold him and whisper soothingly that all would be well, to cradle him in her arms, to press his head to her breast.

With a start, Alia returned to the present. None of this was of practical use to them, she chided herself. First, they must find shelter for camp. The meager light was fading, and soon it would be too dark to see. If Teran was incapable of coherent thought, then it was time for her to take charge.

He suddenly reined his equs in and turned to look back at her. "We'll stop here for the nocte. The cave up there appears as good as any for shelter."

Alia's eyes followed the direction of his finger. Halfway up one rubble-strewn mountain was a gaping black hole. A tiny path that appeared little more than an animal track wound its way to the cave entrance.

"As you wish," she murmured, grateful for any respite from the bone-chilling drizzle.

Turning her mare, Alia angled the animal toward the crude road. Teran followed, pulling the gray equs they now used as a pack animal behind him.

The cave opening was tall enough to lead the equs through once Alia and Teran dismounted. She halted when Teran and the two beasts he led were safely inside.

"It's black as the pits of Fodina in here," Alia muttered, turning to confront her companion. "How far into this hole did you want to go?"

Teran didn't answer. Instead, he stared up at the ceiling, then walked over to one of the stone walls. Pulling out his tinderbox, he propped a small wad of tinder on a rock ledge. After several secundae of striking steel against flint and a few good puffs of breath, Teran had the beginnings of a tiny fire. He found a stout branch lying near the cave entrance and applied one of its ends to the growing flame. The torch quickly flared, illuminating the darkness.

He walked back to the stone wall he had been trying to examine. After a moment of careful inspection he rubbed his free hand over the rough surface, then paused to taste a bit of the dust that clung to his fingers. His morose mood lifted for a moment.

"Just as I thought," he said, half to himself.

Teran wheeled around to face Alia. "This cave's made of aerlapis, the same porous stone as our underground chamber at the oasis. It's ideal for absorbing smoke. We'll set up camp well into its depths. It'll be warmer there and less likely to announce our presence."

"I will agree to anything you say, Teran, just as long as I don't have to go out again into that miserable rain."

At the tone of utter weariness in Alia's voice, Teran raised the torch high enough to shed some of its meager light on her. Alia's once bright hair was dark with dampness, tangled and matted from the wind. Her tunic and breeches hung limply, weighted with moisture. She looked pale, haggard and exhausted.

Guilt sliced through him. Immersed in his own grief, he had nearly forgotten about her. And not once had she complained or asked for assistance, but had followed faithfully on.

"Hobble the equs near the entrance. They can warn us of any intruders," he said, his gruffness hiding his sudden surge of remorse.

He shoved the torch into a nearby wall crevice and untied the bedrolls he took from the gray equs. "Here." He tossed a blanket to Alia. "When you're done with the equs, get out of those wet clothes. Wrap yourself in that. I'll be outside gathering firewood."

Too tired to argue, Alia mutely nodded. Still, the thought of only the thin protection of a blanket between her and nakedness was disturbing. She shoved down the stimulating thoughts, a little exasperated with herself. The man meant nothing by it; he was only being practical.

With a rueful sigh, Alia grabbed the reins of the three equs and led them to a spot out of the wind. She quickly hobbled them and measured out the last of the dried grass they had gathered in the foothills. As the great beasts hungrily munched the hay, she removed their tack and rubbed them down.

The equs finally tended to, Alia picked up one of the blankets. Stepping back into the shadows, she undressed. Her tunic and boots were off when Teran returned. Instinctively, Alia moved to cover herself, then realized he couldn't see her in the comparative gloom of the cave's depths. Nonetheless, she made no sound and, from the haven of the darkness, watched him.

He stood there for a moment, looking around for her. From the glow of the torch near him, Alia saw the faintest hint of a smile flicker on his lips as his sweeping gaze passed over the spot where she stood. For an instant, she almost thought his glance had pierced the shrouding blackness. What he actually saw, he never revealed. Tossing an armload of wood to the ground, Teran left.

Alia began to shiver, but whether it was from the coolness of the air on her bare skin or from the tension of Teran's presence, she didn't know. She forced her trembling limbs back into action, hastily peeling off the sodden breeches. Wrapping the blanket around her, she stepped back into the dim light and sat down to await Teran's return. Little by little, as the chill gradually left her body, Alia nodded off.

She woke with a start. There was something hovering over her. In the growing darkness of the dying torch, her sleep-clouded vision could only make out a hulking form. Her hand moved against a large stone. In one quick motion she grasped it and flung it at her adversary. He deftly dodged it, then grabbed her upraised hand.

"Hold on, Alia! It's me. Teran."

"Teran?" she gasped. "I . . . I'm sorry. I must have fallen asleep and you startled me, standing over me like that. Please forgive me."

Teran's eyes narrowed, and a muscle twitched in

his jaw. "There's nothing to forgive. I would have reacted the same way."

He wheeled away from her. "Cover yourself, then come help me with the firewood," he muttered from over his rapidly retreating shoulder.

Alia looked down and gasped. In her fright she had allowed the blanket to fall away, exposing herself from the waist up. Curse him! she thought. That man always seemed to be catching her in one form of undress or another. She was lucky to still have her maidenhood.

Gathering the blanket around her, Alia firmly knotted two of the ends above her breasts, then slid the open length around to her side. Clutching the fabric closed, she rose and walked over to Teran. He knelt by a large pile of firewood. From the size of it, Alia realized he had made several trips outside. How long had she been dozing?

He glanced up at her. "Bring as much wood as you can carry. I'll relight the torch, and we'll go further into the cave and find a warm sleeping spot."

Using his tinderbox Teran quickly ignited the torch, then gathered a load of wood under the other arm. Raising the torch, he led the way deeper into the cave.

They walked for a short while, the flickering brand throwing agitated shadows against the wall of blackness. Just after the cave seemed to sharply curve to the left, Teran halted.

"This looks as good as any. The bend in the cave will deflect any wind that may blow through. Drop your load. We'll go back and get our supplies and more firewood."

Several trips and an hora later, Alia and Teran sat before a noisily crackling fire. As she stirred the soup she had made, Alia's spirits lifted. She felt warm and comfortable at last. Glancing over at a nearby rock,

Alia noted that her clothes were slowly drying. In the rapidly warming air, small wisps of steam rose from the fabric. It would take many horas more to get them thoroughly dry, so she would probably have to spend the entire nocte wrapped in her blanket.

The soup bubbled in the small pot, its savory aroma langorously wafting to Alia's nose. She hoped Teran would find it acceptable, knowing how much he always liked Vates' cooking. She shot him a furtive glance.

He sat there, unmoving. The activity of getting settled in the cave had distracted Teran only fleetingly. Now there was nothing left to him but thought, no further escape from the painful memories. He stared into the fire, his eyes fixed, a look of utter grief and despair carved into his rugged features.

Even as Teran sat there, immersed in his agonizing reminiscences, Alia still saw the inner strength of the man. He mourned like a wild animal, privately and in silence. Though his head was bent and his shoulders slumped, the proud carriage of his body could not be denied. His damp clothing clung to his muscular frame, accentuating his powerful physique. Yet despite the impressive physical presence of the man, it was his moment of loss, his vulnerability, that captured Alia's heart.

"Teran," she hesitantly murmured, "the soup is ready. Won't you have some?"

He turned to her with a slow pivot of his head, as if the effort to return from some faraway place cost him dearly. His silver eyes were dull, drained of the flashing fire Alia had come to associate with him.

"No, I'm not hungry," he mumbled thickly, turning his gaze back to the undulating tongues of flame before him.

A frustrating sense of helplessness swelled inside Alia. He needed to eat, to get some warmth into his belly, to take off those wet clothes before he became ill, but he wouldn't listen to her. There was nothing between them anymore, no further lines of communication, save what Vates had formerly directed.

Oh, Vates! How could you leave us at a time like this? Alia cried out to some inward place. Teran is hurting, and I don't know how to help him.

Yet still she struggled on, driven by the promise she had made the old man. "Teran, please," she forced herself to begin again. "You need to take care of yourself. Just eat a little to keep up your strength."

"No, I said. Leave me alone!" Teran suddenly raged at her. "You don't really care what happens to me, save how it affects the outcome of your quest. So don't concern yourself. Just leave me alone."

The last words were muted from a place deep within his hands.

A sob rose to Alia's lips. It wasn't true. It just wasn't true, at least not anymore. Somewhere in the midst of all the turmoil and all the mixed emotions, she had come to care for Teran. Ironically, though he now had no use for her, she teetered on the brink of betraying everything for him.

"You are wrong," she whispered. "I do care, and I trust you. It is you, so eaten up by your hatred for me, who twists what lies between us."

His head jerked up, his silver eyes narrowing to smoky slits. "And why," he asked in a voice of deadly calm, "would I hate you, Alia?"

"Because you blame me for Vates' death," she cried, the tears simultaneously spilling forth.

Teran stared at her in amazement. He had never seen her, at least in her waking moments, quite like

133

this—so vulnerable, so needing. If only he dared hope some of it was meant for him. It would almost make everything worth it.

With a low groan he was at her side, gathering her to him. "Alia," he murmured into the soft halo of her hair, "I don't blame you. You came into this as innocently as I. Only Vates truely knew what lay ahead, and still he felt it worth the sacrifice. Can we do less?"

She raised tear-filled eyes to a face only a breath away. He stared back at her, his expression piercing to the very depths of her being. A small, hesitant smile touched her lips.

"No, Teran, we can truly do no less. It would dishonor all that Vates stood for."

Teran released her. He took a long shuddering breath, as if to steel himself for the effort that lay ahead. Reaching up to his neck, he freed the key that hung from his govern collar.

"Will you claim me then, Alia?" he asked, as he offered it to her in his outstretched palm. "It was my teacher's last request, though I have yet to understand its significance. But honor it I will, if you'll accept me."

The words shocked her, shattering her prior assessment of the man. Never had she thought Teran would bow to claiming, not one as proud and as fiercely independent as he. Yet here was his key, glinting dully before her in the firelight. She covered his hand with hers. Their eyes met and locked, their hearts and minds joining in mutual commitment. When she finally pulled away, the key was gone. Teran was bound to her now—for the rest of his life.

Suddenly, Alia couldn't meet the searing intensity of his gaze. Lowering her eyes, she busily attempted to add the new key to the one she already wore around her neck. She fumbled ineffectually, her fingers awkward with emotion.

Two strong hands closed around hers. She glanced up, startled. Gray eyes smoldered with an intense heat, setting ablaze an answering fire within Alia. She caught her breath as the flame coursed through her veins and stared at Teran with stunned, brown eyes.

"Let me help you," he simply said, taking the key.

As he worked, his fingers lightly grazed the hollow of her throat, sending bursts of excitement tingling throughout her body. Her pulse quickened, and her breathing turned erratic. The nearness of him and the familiar masculine scent emanating from his body drove her toward him, impelling her into a headlong spiral of desire.

Yet just when Alia could almost feel his inner walls come crashing down, Teran pulled back from her. Rising, he walked away to the far side of the chamber. She watched him, his tall form partly hidden in the shadows, and wondered why he had left. Had she misinterpreted his feelings, the things he had said? She had to know.

Alia climbed to her feet and slowly walked over to Teran. She halted a little ways from him, almost afraid to get too close. "Have I offended you in some manner that you would flee my presence like that?"

At her words, his powerful body tensed. "No," he answered her at last, the fight ebbing from him, "you have not offended me. On the contrary. If I'd stayed with you a second longer, I might have offended you."

Emboldened by his words, Alia slipped closer to him and lightly touched his shoulder. He wheeled around to face her.

"Nothing you could do would offend me," she said, forcing the statement through a throat suddenly gone dry. "Now come back to the fire. You need to take off those damp clothes and eat."

He followed her without protest and sank down at his place near the fireside. She knelt in front of him and tugged the ends of his tunic loose from his belt.

His hands came down upon hers. "You don't have to do this," he said, his voice husky.

"I want to. Won't you allow me?"

Teran's hands fell away.

A mounting tension built within Alia. Slowly, ever so carefully, she spread the front of Teran's tunic apart and slid it off his shoulders. Though she had seen his bare chest many times, this time it stirred her like never before. The broad expanse, covered with a tangle of black hair, held an irresistible fascination. Her hands left the shirt still hanging on his lower arms and sought out the matted planes of his chest.

Tentatively, savoring the delicious feel of him, Alia ran her fingers over Teran. It was an exquisite sensual feast—the rough feel of his hair, the velvet softness of his dark nipples, the hard strength of his muscular torso. She lost herself in admiration of the virile body beneath her hands and felt the desire for him flame into an intense longing.

Did he feel the same? Was she, in her unseasoned maidenhood, pleasing him as much as he pleased her? Hesitant brown eyes raised to search his face for the answer.

The smoldering fire and savage hunger in those silver orbs startled her—but only for an instant. From a place deep within, Alia felt a curious swooping pull, followed closely by a breathless joy.

"I . . . I please you, don't I?" she asked in shy wonder, as if she barely believed the truth herself.

"Yes, Alia, you please me. Even in your tender maidenhood you have a provocative way of touching a man," Teran growled, his glance roaming over her blanket-clad figure with intense hunger. "If we're not careful, I may lose my sanity before I get out of these wet clothes."

Alia's dark lashes fluttered on her downcast cheeks. "Oh, I am sorry," she murmured in embarrassment. "How thoughtless of me. Here, let me help you."

She hurriedly slipped Teran's tunic from him and laid it aside. Next, Alia turned her attention to his boots and began tugging on them. It proved to be a difficult task, considering the necessity of keeping her blanket intact around her at the same time.

Laughingly, Teran finally came to her aid. He removed her hands. A few secundae later, the tall, leather boots were sitting alongside his tunic. His hands then bent behind him to unlace his wide, studded belt.

"Please, let me do that." Before he could reply, she was leaning toward him, her arms encircling his body, her slender fingers deftly disentangling the ties.

As she worked, her attention intently directed to the intricate task, Teran forced himself to remain rigidly still. The effort became more difficult with each passing secundae.

One arm around either side of his taut, narrow waist, her body drawing close and reaching for the back of his belt, Alia unconsciously brushed against him each time she moved. Her fragrance, like some exotic flower, drifted to Teran. Delicate arms and shoulders gleamed with a reddish gold luster in the firelight, beckoning to him and taunting him, until he thought he'd go insane.

Yet just when Teran thought he'd explode from the effort necessary to control his burgeoning arousal, Alia freed the last lace of his belt. She leaned away and laid the studded length of leather next to his growing pile of clothing. Reaching over beside Teran, she handed a blanket to him.

Dark brows arched in amusement. "And what is that for?"

"To cover yourself, once you get your breeches off," she replied, coloring fiercely.

"But aren't you going to finish undressing me? You said you wanted to." A wicked grin stole across Teran's bearded face. "Unless, of course, you're afraid . . .?"

Eyes, now the shade of amber, flashed at him. "I am not afraid. It is just . . . just that I . . ."

She threw up her hands in defeat. "Yes, curse you, I *am* afraid. Everytime I am near you, I get confused. Emotions like I have never known swallow me up, until I am little more than a trembling fool. And the hardest, most frightening part of all is that I don't know what to do about it. I don't know anything at all."

He reached out to her then and grasped her slender shoulders in his large hands. Almost of their own accord, his fingers caressed the soft, white flesh. A curious, half-smile lifted the corners of his mouth.

"I would teach you, Alia, if you could find it in your heart to trust me in this. I've wanted you since that first sol, when I saw you in the water. But you must decide now, for I cannot continue like this much longer."

He took a deep, shuddering breath. "Do you want me, Alia? Will you let me join with you?"

The implication of his question sent waves of excitement surging through her. She felt as if she were teetering on a precipice, leaning over a dark chasm that promised a glimpse of the mysteries of life. Yes, she was afraid, but the need to taste the secrets and the pleasures of Teran's body was stronger still.

Even before she spoke, the answer glowed in Alia's eyes. "Yes, Teran," she whispered, "I want you."

"Alia," he groaned, pulling her to him.

His kiss was surprisingly gentle, in spite of the coiled tension of his body. Sensuously slow, it sent delicious shivers through her, filling her with the heady wine of desire. She responded to him on some primitive level, her soft lips parting under the insistent pressure of his mouth. He devoured her offering, gently forcing them yet further apart until, at last, his tongue entered the sweet portal.

The intensity of his ardor increased with each passing moment, mounting in its fiery need for possession. He felt her succumbing to the forceful domination of his lips. The realization only stoked the raging fires of his body, yet he forced himself to slowly pace himself to her inexperience. His own fulfillment was of little consequence if it cost him her trust. He hoped for more than one passionate nocte with her. Even a lifetime wouldn't seem long enough.

Wrapped in the protective cocoon of Teran's arms, Alia eagerly pressed into his hard body. Her hands moved to caress his chest, then traveled upward, until with a start she touched his govern collar. Their eyes met, and their mouths parted. Teran's expression was suddenly guarded, and she felt the tension of impending rejection stiffen his body.

Staring up at him, Alia's features clouded over for a brief instant in remembrance. Yet the recollection of why she was here, in the arms of a condemned criminal of Carcer, suddenly seemed of little import. Who he really was and what his crime had been mattered not in the searing heat of their passion. It was enough that she wanted and trusted him.

139

The moment of hesitation quickly passed, and Alia ardently returned to her tactile explorations. Sensing his doubts, his fear of her rejection, she tenderly pulled him down to her.

With a tortured moan he returned, this time more fiercely than before. His hands began their own investigation, moving over her body to skim her hips and thighs, then back up again, retracing the burning path he seared on her flesh. At long last Teran's fingers traveled across her chest to the knot of her blanket.

He untied the coarse material with slow, deliberate movements, all the while kissing Alia's lips and face and hair. Hypnotized by the sensuous touch of his mouth, her head fell back in utter submission. Even the moment of disrobing, when the blanket fell away from her body, mattered little. She felt unashamed, proud of the feminine form that could excite a man like Teran and drive him to such wild passion.

"You're so beautiful," Teran rasped between ragged breaths. "I'm almost afraid to touch you, afraid you're some lovely vision my hands might defile."

"How can you possibly defile me, when we both want and need this joining?" Alia whispered in a voice throaty with emotion. "My only wish is that I knew what to do, how to please you. That is my fear—that you'll find me lacking."

She took up his hands and tenderly kissed each calloused palm in turn. "Show me how, Teran. Show me what to do."

His tormented groan was muffled, as Teran lowered his head to nuzzle the lush fullness of her breasts. Large, bronzed hands gently outlined the soft mounds, his strong fingers circling the sensitive, swollen nipples. The rosy buds quickly grew taut and hard, sending delicious jolts through her loins.

140

"Teran, oh, Teran," she moaned in delight. "You make me feel so strange, so . . . wonderful!"

He moved then, his mouth capturing the crested peaks, as his hands spread her open blanket on the ground. His tongue flicked first one then the other of her breasts, until Alia lost herself in a quivering delight. She felt a heat rise from deep within her belly. Suddenly, she wanted the moment of joining with all her heart.

Her hands were captured by his and guided down to the ties of his breeches. "Finish what you started," he commanded, though the sound of his uneven breathing belied the control he struggled to convey.

Movements made jerky by the urgency of her own need, Alia unlaced the last of his clothing. There was no shame in her hunger to have him naked, only an anticipation that the pleasure of him would be well worth it. At last the fabric parted. Driven by her curiosity, Alia tugged the cloth down, away from the hard, flat belly and narrow hips, dragging the breeches across his thighs.

It was then she first noticed the swollen evidence of his arousal. She gasped at the sight of his blood-engorged shaft, a self-protective jolt of fear spasming her body. Though she knew little of the actual technique of mating, Alia had heard enough of the whispered gigglings of the other novices to envision how the sexes joined. But with a man as large as Teran! In spite of herself, she shrank from him.

Noting the terror in her eyes and realizing its probable cause, Teran quickly reached out to capture Alia. He gathered her to him once again, crooning softly to her.

"Alia, don't be afraid. Trust me. I swear I will not harm you."

"But . . . but you are so . . . so . . ."

"Large?" Teran finished the sentence, the amusement in his voice barely veiled. "It may seem so to your maiden's eyes, but believe me, we can mate without difficulty. Our bodies were meant to join and meant for the experience to be pleasurable for both."

She hid her face in his hairy chest. "Then let us do so—now, before my foolish fears overcome me."

Gently, Teran raised her chin until their eyes met. "Do you truly want this, Alia? Do you realize what we'll unleash this nocte?"

A look of confusion spread across her face. "I . . . I don't understand."

"Once I've taken your maidenhood, I'll not cease to desire you. Quite the contrary. Do you understand what I'm telling you?"

Gazing up into gray eyes glinting like silver lightning, all the doubts and fears faded, swept away by the burgeoning passion for the man who held her. Nothing mattered at that moment—nothing except to possess and be possessed. There was no fire he could not quench, no hunger he could not satisfy. Even for but a twinkling in life's vast eternity, it was enough to be his.

"Yes, Teran," she murmured, her gaze strong and sure. "I could bear it no other way. I want you, with all the strength of my being and with all my heart."

A look of ineffable tenderness lit Teran's face. Softly moaning her name, he gently drew her down onto the blanket. As one, they crept into each other's arms to cling mutely to the other.

After a time, he moved, his mouth eagerly seeking out hers, hungrily demanding, possessing, devouring. His kiss became increasingly urgent as the hot tide within threatened to overpower him, as he gave himself over to the savage cravings so long denied.

The caress of his lips set Alia aflame, until she felt

she'd explode with the taste and smell of him. Never, in all the cycles of her life, had she wanted anything as much as she wanted Teran.

In spite of her former resolve to hold back and never allow herself to open up to another, Alia found herself surrendering all—her lips, her body and, without even realizing it, her heart. Her mind was in a swirling delirium, as Teran's mouth branded his possession on her, each kiss more rapturous than the last. It was impossible, inconceivable, to think of anything but this glorious, passionate man.

With the lightest of touches his hands began once again to explore her body. Each stroke of his fingers sent currents of pleasure shooting through her. She squirmed against him in the primal dance of mating, her hands snaking around to cup his taut, muscled buttocks. He felt so good, so magnificent. It was all she could do to keep from yielding to the burning sweetness that grew within her.

Driven to the brink of control by her unabashed writhing, Teran gritted his teeth as he desperately fought for the last vestiges of restraint. His eyes, glittering like smoldering embers, swept over her with deep longing, yet he still held himself back, denying the ultimate union.

Before he claimed her he had to know she was ready, her body loose and willing. If not, he feared what he would do to her in his unbridled passion. She was so innocent, so unseasoned. If he hurt or frightened her, she might turn from him forever, and that was more than he could ever endure.

His hand left her breast, tracing a blazing path across her chest and flat belly until it reached the triangle of curls between her thighs. Wedging his way between her unconsciously clenched legs, he slowly, tenderly spread them apart.

"Don't be afraid," Teran whispered, as his lips nuzzled the silky hollow of her throat. "Let me touch you, and you'll discover even greater pleasure."

Trusting him, Alia gave a small sigh and relaxed. As his fingers gently insinuated their way into her velvet depths, sudden waves of heat converged in her loins, threatening to shatter what little control remained.

As he worked her tender female core, Alia's excitement ascended in ever increasing spirals. Teran slowly and thoroughly explored her, prolonging the exquisite torture until she was a quivering, boneless being in his arms. Her intoxication pounded through her until the need for release grew to explosive proportions. She could bear no more.

"Teran, please join with me, or . . . or I'll surely die!" she begged, her voice hoarse with need.

He held himself back no longer. Teran quickly positioned his body between her open legs. Gripping her hips tightly he at last entered her, the movement long and exquisitely slow.

Alia felt a sharp, stretching pain, then he was inside. The dull, throbbing ache that burned in her belly exploded into a myriad of sharp, delicious sensations, coursing through her body like a molten fire. He felt so good, his fullness filling her and completing her.

With every thrust of Teran's taut, straining form, her breath came in surrendering moans. There was nothing in the universe but the hard, hungry man who possessed her—body and soul. It was a sad joy, a sweet pain, a dying and rebirth, all in one divine instant. Deeper and deeper she fell into an abyss of shuddering ecstasy until, faraway in the darkness, she heard a voice crying out, mingled with her own.

CHAPTER 7

IN THE DIM LIGHT OF A DYING FIRE, ALIA AWOKE TO THE awareness of a large, warm body next to hers. For an instant, disorientation swirled through her mind, then the movement of Teran, snuggling close, calmed her sense of confusion. She turned in his arms to face him, the memory of last nocte's tempestuous union flooding back with an exciting clarity.

He slept on, his rakishly bearded face serene in the blessed freedom of slumber. A wave of tenderness washed over her. At least, for a short while longer, he would be spared the pain and uncertainty of the past few sols.

Her eyes lowered to his govern collar. Save for it, he lay there naked, yet its message marked him more indelibly than any chains or prison garb—criminal, exile, coward. The stigma would remain with him the rest of his life, and now there was the added burden of slave as her claimee.

145

It was a frightening thought, this ability for total power over another. She fingered the twin keys dangling from her neck. Exactly how did the govern collar work to control a recalcitrant felon? A mood change, a mind purge or an instrument of torture?

Alia shuddered at the latter. Gazing down at the sleeping form of the man who had so tenderly held her last nocte, who had so passionately initiated her into the exquisite pleasures of mating, the thought of causing him pain sickened her.

Still, an insidious little voice clawed its way into her consciousness. He was a danger to her quest, for in his arms all resolutions dissolved; all thoughts of the Knowing Crystal scattered before the seductive onslaught of his virile body.

But she needed him, Alia protested to that cold, inner voice, if she were to successfully complete her mission and regain the Crystal. She needed his brute strength and his warrior's skills, the voice agreed, but not his affection or his loyalty. The govern keys now commanded all the obedience she would ever require.

The bitter voice assumed a hard, familiar tone. *Control or be controlled. Use, then discard. The quest is the salvation of your people.*

As the repetitious phrases whirled through her tortured mind, it was all Alia could do to choke down a sob of bitter frustration. She had nearly sacrificed the humanity of an entire planet for a transient pleasure in the arms of a man. Yet he had made her so happy, and that was more than life on Aranea had ever done.

But wasn't duty a higher calling than carnal delights, honor more glorious than love? Hadn't her cycles with the Sisterhood inculcated those beliefs, if nothing else? Gazing down at Teran's sleeping form, Alia was no longer so certain.

She brushed away the single, traitorous tear that trickled down her cheek. There was no choice, had never been one. Her budding relationship with Teran must be sacrificed. The quest for the Knowing Crystal was all that truly mattered.

Harking back to Vates, Alia ruefully shook her head. He had said she and Teran would be masters of the Crystal. At this moment all she felt was its servant, the unwilling chattel of a heartless stone, bound to a path she loathed, a cruelty she dreaded.

A smothering sensation rose in her throat. It was all too much, this conflict between duty and her feelings for Teran. She had to get away and breathe some fresh mountain air before she suffocated under the weight and pain of it all.

Slipping from Teran's side, Alia rose and hurriedly dressed. She added a few sticks to the fire and, taking up a freshly flamed torch, walked to the cave's entrance.

The rain and wind had ceased, but the sol was no more cheerful than before. The sky was a heavy gray, silence pressing on the mountains as if held there by some giant hand. Alia repressed a shudder. The sensation of being watched struck her more forcefully than ever before.

She turned, drawn in the direction of Ferox's fortress. Only two sol's journey and they would be there. Whatever the pitfalls that still lay in their path, whatever the nameless horrors, Alia refused to dwell upon them. None of it mattered. There was no turning back.

With a sigh of ineffable sadness she turned to walk back into the cave, her decision as to what to do about Teran no clearer than before. Perhaps there was yet a way to still have both—the Crystal and her lover.

A melodious sound reached her ears. Whirling around, Alia intently scanned the area, searching for the origin of the strange noise. She found nothing, the tone coming from nowhere, yet everywhere. Stronger, more insistent than it had ever been before, its voice was both haunting and lovely. In rising joy, Alia recognized it for what it was—the Knowing Crystal.

In her mind's eye the glowing rock took form, calling her in a voice without sound. It drew near, merging with her. From deep within her soul, she heard it speak.

The pain, the hopes, the sacrifices of those who had devoted their lives to the Crystal's service passed before her. All had been directed to her quest. The knowledge of her part in the glorious scheme, to return it after all these hundreds of cycles to its rightful home, filled her with a dazzling determination. And before the brilliance of that realization all else, by comparison, had to pale—even human love.

As unexpectedly as it had appeared, the vision of the Knowing Crystal vanished. Alia found herself alone again, more desolate than before. The dream she had cherished for her and Teran was shattered and destroyed beyond any hope of revival. All that was left was the will of the Crystal and the consolation of her noble destiny. But why now? Why did the Crystal speak to her so directly, so forcefully, when heretofore it had communed largely through her dreams in vague, cryptic ways?

The answer filled Alia with a poignant, bittersweet pang. She forced down the sob that welled up from the depths of her heart. Once more, she heard the kind, gentle voice of Vates.

"The Crystal needs a trusting, loving being with which to commune. Now you know, the rest is up to you."

After the past nocte, she was indeed more open to the Crystal than she had ever been. Except as a small child with her mother, when had she ever been more trusting and loving than in the arms of Teran? But the same emotions that provided the opportunity for true dialogue with the Crystal were the same emotions that must now be denied to Teran, the man who had fanned them back to a full, flaming intensity.

There was nothing to be decided. The choice was beyond hers to make. Alia turned to the cave, resolutely heading back to Teran and a painful confrontation that would surely wrench apart both their hearts.

He was awake, already dressed in breeches and boots. When she entered, Teran rose from the pot of water he was tending on the fire and strode over to her. Pulling Alia to him, he attempted to reclaim her, crushing her soft, rosy lips to his searching mouth. For a delicious instant Alia instinctively responded, then catching herself, she froze in his arms.

She tore her mouth from his. "Teran, don't. Let me go."

A scowl of puzzlement wrinkled his brow. Teran released his grip and stepped back. "What's wrong, Alia?"

The wary look she knew so well returned to his eyes. Forgive me, she inwardly moaned.

"What happened between us last nocte must never happen again," she blurted without further preamble. "Considering the circumstances, it was quite

149

understandable and I tender no blame, but as my claimee, you have overstepped your bounds. Do you understand my meaning?"

His eyes turned a thunderous gray, and a muscle clenched violently in his bearded jaw. "With painful clarity, Domina," he muttered through gritted teeth, bending low as he spoke. "Who am I to protest if my claimant uses me in any fashion she desires. My life is yours."

Alia winced at the exaggerated subservience in Teran's manner. It was ample proof of the pain she had caused, the humiliation she had exacted. She feared he would never forgive her.

"It . . . it is not my choice alone," she hastened to explain, all the while wondering what good the explanation would do. "The Crystal spoke to me while you slept. It told me what I must do. Please try to understand."

"You owe me no explanation for your actions. The Crystal, it seems, rules us both now."

She moved to gather the bedding and roll up the blankets. "Then let us talk of it no further. There are more important things to concern ourselves with," she said, hesitantly raising her eyes to his.

With an angry growl Teran snatched up the leather saddlebags, packed their meager supplies and then stomped out of the chamber. Alia silently finished her task, her heart an anguished weight in her chest.

Finally she rose. Gathering up the bedrolls and the tunic Teran had left behind, she paused for a moment to pour the pot of boiling water on the fire. Then she turned, leaving behind the cave of bittersweet memories.

The trail became even more difficult. Strewn with large rocks, the footing was precarious, and they were soon forced to lead the equs. It was tiring,

150

tedious work. By the time the sun was at its zenith, Teran called for a rest.

High up on a windy ledge overlooking a large valley, they ate a silent lunch, the anguish between them too deep for words. The fruit nearly choked Alia, the dried meat they had prepared in the foothills of Macer almost impossible to swallow, but she forced them down. Food would give precious strength to her body for the arduous trials ahead. If only it could serve as well to sustain her heart.

"It's time to move on," Teran finally ordered, his voice terse and cold. "We're too vulnerable out here in the open. I'll feel better once we reach that forest." He indicated a mass of trees covering the valley below them.

Alia looked in the direction of his pointing finger. Yes, the forest would give them shelter from detection, but it could also hold ambush and other pitfalls, dangers far worse than the ones they'd already passed. She tried to shake off the disturbing thought, but it returned with nagging insistence. What was it about that forest?

"Is something the matter?" Teran asked, noting her uneasy expression. "Has the Crystal spoken?"

She gazed up into hard, distant eyes. "I am not sure. There is just something about that forest. Is there no way around it?"

"None. It covers almost the entire valley. From what I've heard from some very reliable sources, the only way to the next range of mountains is the road through that forest."

Alia sighed. "Then we must use the utmost caution. It is filled with danger."

"Considering the nature of our quest, is it any wonder?"

She stared up at him. What words could possibly soften the harsh reality of their situation? What could

she say that would ease the naked longing and raw
pain she saw burning in those gray eyes? Though he
tried to veil his true emotions beneath a mask of cold
indifference, there were moments, like the one just
now, when their gazes melded and the truth was
plain to see.

Unable to bear the visual recriminations, Alia
hurried over to her equs. Swinging onto the animal's
broad back, she urged the beast forward, down the
trail that led to the valley.

As she rode along she fought back the strange,
moist burning in her eyes. Had it come to this then?
Was her control so weakened that she could barely
look at or think of him without weeping? Oh, Teran,
Alia silently mourned, if only things could be different.

Two horas later, they reached the forest's edge.
Teran reined in his equs and turned to Alia. "With
your permission, I'll take the lead."

He held up a silencing hand when she opened her
mouth to protest. "By your leave, Domina. Unless
you've been holding something back, I'd guess my
skills in this situation are better than yours. Besides,
if you ride behind me and we're attacked, you at least
have a chance of escape."

He grimly smiled at her, a bleak, empty look.
"After all, that is my primary purpose on this quest—
to insure *your* success."

Alia defiantly tossed her head. For a second she
nearly released her growing sense of guilt and frustration, nearly raged at him to relieve her own
overwrought nerves, but Alia bit back the treacherous impulse. Above all, she must maintain control.

"As you wish. Let us be on with this, then," she
snapped irritably.

Teran wheeled his equs around. Without a backward glance, he led the way into the dark forest. Alia's first perception was one of fetid dampness and ancient, musty decay. Though the silence was complete, not a chirp of a bird nor buzz of an insect to break the quiet, eerie sensations seeped through her.

An icy fear twisted around her heart, and she shivered. Urging her beast forward, she closed the widening gap between her and Teran. If anything were to happen, Crystal or no, let them face it together.

In an attempt to quell the unsettling emotions, she forced her attention to the flora of the gloomy forest. Trees of various size and shapes, many varieties Alia had never seen before, grew in dense profusion along the tiny trail. Strange ferns and bushes crowded together on the woodland floor, some displaying hauntingly lovely flowers, flowers that seemed to almost speak to her.

Perfect places for ambush, Alia thought, fiercely calling back her wandering attention. She nervously glanced around.

"Stop!" Teran's low-pitched voice jerked her from her anxious survey.

Alia reined in her equs. "What's wrong?"

Teran dismounted and carefully walked over to an overgrown patch of yellow-green bracken directly in front of him. He stood there for several secundae, intently examining the foliage. Finally, picking up a large stone, he paused to heave it into the mass of greenery. With a crash and cracking of breaking branches, the middle of the road caved in.

He walked back to his equs. Looking up at Alia, Teran smiled thinly.

"If it's any comfort, your instincts about this place were correct. That wasn't one of the most cleverly

153

hidden pits I've ever come upon, but I'm sure Ferox only meant to tease us with it. The traps will only get worse from now on."

Alia swallowed hard, her face pale. "What can I do to help?"

Teran swung onto his beast. "Keep your eyes and ears open. Never let your guard down for an instant. The moment you get even the slightest inkling of something amiss, alert me."

She nodded and nudged her mare forward. Skirting the gaping hole, they resumed their careful journey. They rode in silence, the tension of straining senses making the forest come alive with sound. Every breath of wind rustling the leaves, every twig that fell to the ground caused Alia to pause. She began to see movements among the trees and suspected every pile of windswept debris on the trail. When and where would the next trap be sprung?

It wasn't long in coming. Once again Teran halted and stared fixedly at a jumbled stand of trees on their right. Dismounting, he cautiously approached the trees from the edge of the path. A few meters away, he bent down and intently studied the ground.

At last he rose and turned to Alia. "Get down and hold the equs. I'm going to spring this trap. It might startle them."

Alia hastily slid to the ground. Leading her equs and the pack animal forward, she grabbed hold of Teran's skittish stallion. With baited breath she watched Teran squat and run his fingers along the ground, as if searching for something hidden in the dirt. At last his movements stopped.

He gingerly freed a fine wire from its hiding place under the leaves. Taking a firm grip Teran jerked hard, pulling in the direction of the trail.

A tall sapling, bent nearly double in the clump of trees, snapped forward with such force that it swung across the trail. From its trajectory and the timing of the recovery, Alia could tell the first rider would have been severely struck by the young tree.

Teran rode on. As she passed the offending clump of trees, Alia slowed her mare to take a closer look. She gasped in horror. There, imbedded in the upper trunk and branches of the culpable sapling, were hundreds of tiny metal spikes. An unwary rider would have been impaled on that seemingly innocuous tree.

Teran had been right. Ferox's traps were indeed getting more sophisticated and deadly. She repressed a shudder and hastily urged her equs to catch up with Teran's.

Their pace slowed even more after that. By the time early dusk fingered its shadowy way through the trees, Alia and Teran were but halfway through the giant forest. Only by painstaking vigilance were they able to avoid three more traps, each one more deceptive than the last.

The strain of constant wariness began to tell on Teran. His face creased with fatigue, his eyes dulled. He finally turned to her.

"We need to make camp for the nocte. It'll soon be too dark to discover more pitfalls, and my ability to continue to do so has been sorely taxed."

Alia glanced around. "Where do you suggest we camp? I see no secure spot in these trees."

"There's no refuge in Ferox's domain. We'll have to do without a fire and take turns at watch throughout the nocte." He swung down from his equs. Grabbing the reins, Teran headed into the trees just off to the right.

155

The thought of spending a cold nocte awake in this alien, most unfriendly of woods was far from pleasant, but what else could be done? With a dejected sigh Alia dismounted and led her mare in the direction Teran had gone.

They finished their supper in the same heavy silence as their noon meal, the food just as tasteless and just as difficult to swallow. Finally, throwing the last morsel of dried fruit aside, Teran glanced over at her.

"We'll divide the watch into two shifts, so we can each get several horas of unbroken sleep. Which do you prefer, the first or the second?"

Alia looked at him. He appeared exhausted from the intense strain of the sol's journey through the trap-infested forest.

"I'll take first watch."

Teran studied her, then, with an indifferent shrug, got up and walked over to the bedrolls. He made his bed and lay down. Pulling the threadbare blanket over him, he turned his back to Alia. It was not long before she heard the deep, even breathing of slumber. Must be some warrior talent, she thought wryly, to be able to fall asleep so easily in any situation.

Rising to her feet, Alia walked over to where the equs were tethered. She carefully checked their hobbles and saw that they still had an adequate amount of forage. At least the miserable forest had been good for something.

She stood there for a long while, listening to the silent woods. The twin moons of Carcer, Albus and Nigrus, shone clear and bright in the black sky peeking through the treetops. A light breeze barely rustled the leaves but, aside from that, the nocte was quiet. She realized it had been that way all sol, no movement of animals, no birdsong. The thought sent an icy shiver down her spine. The forest was lifeless, little more than a haven for horrible traps and possible death.

The nocte loomed before Alia, bleak, cold and filled with nameless terrors. Hugging herself tightly, as much to comfort as to protect herself against the creeping chill, she walked back to where Teran lay. She crouched across from him. Wrapping the other blanket around her, Alia leaned against a tree.

The trunk's bark was rough and jagged through the thin fabric of her tunic, but it was also real and familiar in this place of unreality. Needing the slight discomfort, she pressed even closer.

A lilting, hauntingly lovely melody slowly filled the air, caressing the shrouding gloom with a compelling harmony. She listened for what seemed but the span of a few secundae until a strange compulsion filled her. Drawn by a force outside herself, her limbs suddenly heavy with an unusual lethargy, Alia rose. Yes, a dream, she thought drowsily as she moved in the direction of the hypnotic music. This is all but a dream.

As she passed where Teran lay, wrapped in his blanket, she turned slumberous eyes to him. His drawn, haggard features were relaxed, the strain of the past sol at last erased from his face. Good, she thought in drowsy satisfaction. He, too, needs to rest and dream of happy things. Slowly Alia turned from him, back toward the beckoning, mesmerizing tones.

In and out of the closely spaced trees she walked, following a path illuminated by silver moonlight. Her mind was beguiled, drawn by the beautiful sounds that seemed to emanate from a small, glowing area up ahead. A fragrant perfume wafted by, filling her nostrils with its heady scent. Tantalized by the aroma, Alia quickened her pace. Something was calling her. Was it the Knowing Crystal?

The compulsion to follow the moonlit path grew the nearer she came to the clearing. The forest, once so foreboding, now seemed benign, almost friendly. It pervaded her with the certainty that ahead lay sanctuary.

At last, she entered the open area. There, in the middle of the clearing, grew a giant flower, vaguely reminiscent of the blossoms of other plants along the trail. Delicately shaded in ever deepening hues of crimson, its huge petals waved languidly in the nocte's gentle breeze. Surrounded by a soft light, the blooming plant possessed an irresistible attraction. She moved toward it, hypnotized by its beauty.

Her heavily lidded eyes caught the sight of bones, picked clean and white, lying in grotesque disarray around the base of the plant. A tremor of danger coursed through her. The dreamlike state vanished. She must get away!

She wheeled about to flee when a slim tendril snaked from the flowering plant, entwining itself around her foot. With a gasp of horror, Alia was jerked to the ground. Millimeter by millimeter, the now sinister bloom dragged her ever forward.

Though she viciously kicked at the vine, the frantic blows did little more than mar its green surface. Clawing at the ground as it passed beneath her, Alia dug at the damp earth for a handhold, for anything to break the inexorable progress backward.

Yet each time she was able to grab at something, a powerful tug by the plant's tentacle would break her grip. It was hopeless, Alia thought as her muscles slowly spasmed in exhaustion.

She glanced behind her. In but a few secundae she would be at the very maws of that awful flower, its center now spread wide, a thick, sticky liquid copiously dripping from the opening.

"Teran!" she cried with all the strength left in her. "Teran, help me. Please!"

The scream instantly woke him. He leapt to his feet, poised in a fighter's stance, the stun gun in his hand. Where, by the ken of the Crystal, had the cry come? He glanced around for Alia. She wasn't there.

The forest lay dark and silent. Which way had she gone? He closed his eyes and opened his mind to any sound, any voice from without or within. Vates had said that he, too, could commune with the Crystal. Let it be now, before the quest ended with Alia's death. The secundae passed with excrutiating slowness.

Teran! Help me!

He turned in the direction of the sound. It was so faint he wasn't sure if it had been his ears that had heard it. He ran toward the call, weaving in and out of the trees at a dangerous pace. It was so dark. How could she have possibly found her way?

Sounds of a struggle and a choking cry reached him. A fierce elation filled Teran. Alia was up ahead!

A soft light glowed faintly from a small clearing through the trees. Teran quickened his pace, heedless of the stinging branches that slapped at him. He broke into the clearing. There, almost at the very mouth of a huge cantare flower, was Alia, one of her legs captured by the plant's vine. He raised the gun and fired.

Emitting an animalistic shriek, the cantare released its intended victim. Folding in on itself, the flower disappeared into the ground.

159

Teran ran to Alia. Turning her over, he pulled her to him. "Alia," he anxiously murmured into her fragrant hair, "are you all right?"

She moaned and stirred in his arms. "Teran, you came. Thank the Crystal. You came."

He held her tightly. Had it indeed been the Crystal that had spoken to him, leading him to her through the blackened woods? It didn't matter; she was safe. Gathering her into his arms, Teran rose to his feet.

She looked up at him, her eyes wide with confusion. "I . . . I can walk. Please put me down."

Ignoring her request, he began to return through the forest. With a small sigh Alia relaxed against him, burrowing into the strong haven of his arms. Let him hold me for a few, all too brief moments, she thought. It feels so good, and how I need the physical solace of him after the horrors of this sol.

All too soon the swaying motion of Teran's body halted. After a long pause, he put her down. She looked around and found they were back in camp. She raised eyes full of gratitude to him.

"Thank you once again, Teran." Alia hesitated, revulsion spreading across her face at the sudden memory. "What *was* that awful flower?"

"It's known as a cantare or singing flower. It calls to its intended victims with a hypnotizing song. Once the prey is close enough the plant captures it with powerful tentacles and consumes the unfortunate captive. The process is slow and intensely painful for the victim, as the flower must digest the flesh in order to assimilate it."

Alia shuddered. "Why did its song affect only me?"

He gave a dry laugh. "Vates saved me from the cantare only a few monates after we arrived on Carcer. Once you've heard its song and survived, it

160

loses its ability to ever affect you again. At least that flower is one less danger to us."

"A small comfort." She glanced up at the sky. The twin moons had barely shifted their positions. "There are still a few horas left of my shift. If you can, why don't you rest? After what just happened I'm hardly sleepy."

"Are you sure?" His eyes narrowed as he studied her.

"Quite sure. Go back to bed, Teran."

He walked to his blanket and lay down. As before, he was soon fast asleep.

The long horas passed. The time for the end of her watch came and went, but Alia let Teran slumber on. Tormented by the memories of her harrowing experience with the cantare, she realized she would not sleep anyway. He had been so tired. At least she could give him the gift of a good nocte's slumber. It wasn't much and wasn't what he really wanted, but it was all she had left.

She shivered uncontrollably, the cold seeping into her very bones as the horas slipped by. A wild impulse to crawl over and huddle against Teran assailed her. It was quickly followed by a sharp longing at the memory of the brief, precious moments spent earlier in his arms and of last nocte's tender union. Oh, to be warm again and cradled next to the protective strength of his body.

Alia stifled a sob. It was so hard to be alone after having known the heartwarming, sensual touch of another. Perhaps this was the ultimate test—continued dedication to her quest even when her frail emotions tugged her so painfully in another direction.

For the first time since receiving her mission, Alia

found little consolation in the thought. Honor and duty paled before her overwhelming need for the man sleeping near her. The thought ripped to the depths of her soul, filling her with an aching desolation, yet she continued to fight against the traitorous feelings that threatened to overcome her. And as she battled, the nocte slipped away.

Teran awoke with a start. It was sunrise. He sat up, mentally cursing Alia for having fallen asleep on her watch. Turning, with words of recrimination on his lips, his glance found her sitting across from him, wide awake.

"By the ken of the Crystal, Alia!" he rasped hoarsely. "Why didn't you wake me for my watch?"

She slowly turned her gaze to him. "You were so tired, and I wasn't."

"Well, you will be later. What use do you think you'll be to me half asleep? Did you even think about that?"

"I will manage," she said defensively, on the verge of tears. "I will do my part."

He snorted in disgust, but noting her emotional state, he let the matter drop. That femina could be impossible when she wanted, which was quite often lately, and yet she could be so . . . so wonderful. With an angry shake of his head, Teran threw off that painful memory and turned to the task of preparing a cold breakfast.

They rode out a half hora later, both dreading the rest of the journey through the forest, but with renewed determination. A full nocte's sleep had completely refreshed Teran, and he seemed to discover the next several traps with ease.

After several horas the glimmer of light at the end of the trees beckoned. Alia was never so glad to be through a forest in her life. It was almost over.

"Teran . . ." she began.

At the sound of her voice he glanced over his shoulder. "Yes? What is it?"

In that brief instant of distraction, Teran let down his guard. His equs stepped forward toward the end of the trees—and into the last trap.

CHAPTER 8

METAL CLAWS ROSE FROM THE GROUND, LOOMING UP ON both sides of Teran's equs like the fangs of some subterranean predator. Alia pulled her mare to a halt and screamed.

"Teran!"

He wheeled around on his mount. As he did, Teran saw the huge trap yawning up about him. Its jaws closed, with a swift, sickening snap into the equs' soft belly.

Only his lightning-quick reflexes saved him from impalement along with that of the animal. As it was, the metal claws tore bloody gouges into his thighs, the tough hide of his knee-high boots the only thing that saved his lower legs. The mortally wounded animal writhed and bellowed in agony, his frenzied movements flinging Teran to safety on the ground.

Swiftly regaining his footing, he watched the monstrous contraption slowly sink back from whence it came, taking his steed with it. He ran to where Alia still sat in dazed horror on her equs.

"Give me the stun gun. Then dismount and bring the rope."

She opened her mouth but couldn't speak. Instead, Alia handed him the gun, then slid off her mare. She grabbed the coil of rope from the pack animal and ran after Teran.

He knelt at the edge of the gaping hole. From far below, Alia could hear the agonized squeals of the unfortunate equs. As she watched, Teran aimed the stun gun into the pit and fired. With a startled grunt, the animal was rendered unconscious.

"Give me the rope," he said, his voice calmer now.

"What are you going to do?"

"The gun's effect will only last a short time. I'm going down to put the beast out of its misery before it awakens."

He rose. Walking over to a nearby tree, Teran knotted one end around its gnarled trunk. Returning to the pit, he threw the other end into it.

"Teran, don't!" Alia cried. "You can't know what else is down there. What if there's another trap, or even worse?"

He didn't answer her. Instead, Teran methodically looped the line around one forearm. He finally glanced up, his piercing gray eyes knifing through her.

"I don't want that animal to suffer. I can't leave him here like this. Have no fear, though. I'll return to serve you."

His mouth twisted into a sardonic grin. "That is your true concern, isn't it, my femina?"

She glared at him with burning, reproachful eyes. "What would you like me to do?"

"Hold onto the rope and keep it taut. This won't

take long. Here, take the gun. You'll need it for protection if I don't come back."

With that, he pulled the knife out of his boot sheath and slid it under his belt. Then, with a small jump backward, he entered the black abyss.

Alia leaned over as far as she dared, trying vainly to peer into the murky depths. As she did, she pulled back hard to keep the rope taut. The secundae passed. Finally, the line slackened. Teran must have reached the equs.

After a few more secundae she felt the tension on the rope again. She pulled hard once more to keep it taut. Eventually, Teran emerged from the hole.

He climbed out and brushed off the dirt clinging to his clothing. "It's done," he said, squatting to wipe the crimson-stained blade on the grass.

As he did so, the torn breeches and bloodied, raw flesh beneath them caught Alia's attention. She motioned toward the ground.

"Sit down, Teran. I need to care for your wounds." She walked back to the pack equs to grab a water flask and some clean rags.

He glanced down at his legs. At the sight of the ragged wounds, the realization of how narrowly he'd escaped death struck him with a dizzying clarity, and the lacerations began to throb and burn fiercely. He sat down.

Curse it all! he thought. This was neither the time nor place to be even the least bit debilitated. The task before them was difficult enough without his being weakened by pain and blood loss.

Alia returned, distracting him from his impotent ragings. He glanced up at her. "Just wrap some bandages around my legs to staunch the bleeding. We must be out of this forest."

She knelt and opened the water flask. "It will only

take a moment more to flush the dirt from your wounds. We can't afford to have you further weakened by an infection, can we?"

He shot her a sharp glance as she poured the fluid across his gaping lacerations, but whether it was from the pain or her words, Alia couldn't tell. Once satisfied that the wounds were clean, she quickly wrapped the rags around his thighs and knotted the ends.

As soon as the task was complete, Teran rose. Alia looked up at him as she busied herself gathering the supplies, guilt for her contribution in his falling prey to the last trap lancing through her.

"I . . . I am sorry, Teran," she hesitantly began, as she climbed to her feet. "If I hadn't distracted you . . ."

Teran replaced his knife in its sheath, his eyes never meeting hers. "It was my fault as much as yours. I grew overconfident, so close to the edge of the forest. That trap was meant for me. Ferox hasn't lost any of his knowledge of human nature or how to exploit it."

"You sound as if you know him."

"I do—or rather did. Though he is of another planet, we trained together on Bellator for many cycles. Then our paths diverged." His expression darkened in grim anger. "It seems, though, they may soon cross again."

"Were you friends?"

He regarded her with impassive coldness. "No, never friends. Bitter experience teaches one to trust few others. Now, no more of this. It is time we leave this wretched place. I'll ride the pack equs, if you've no objections."

Alia shook her head. "No objections," she murmured, avoiding the meaningful glance he had shot her way with his words.

He hadn't spoken just of Ferox but of her, too, when he'd mentioned trust. Oh, if only the quest were at its end! If only she no longer had to face him and bear the unending recrimination in his eyes. She silently walked to her equs and mounted.

Teran finished recoiling the line. After retying the rope on the saddle, he mounted the equs. Urging the beast around Alia's mare, he led the way out of the forest.

They were soon clear of the last of the trees and climbing a trail that led back into the mountains. Like the previous sols, this one was also windy and clouded. Alia began to wonder if the mountains of Macer ever saw the sun.

The horas passed in a wearying repetition of their previous journey through the mountains, until she couldn't identify one path from the other. Yet each time they came to a fork in the trail, she always seemed to intuitively know which one to choose.

The lack of sleep last nocte began to tell on her. The effort to keep her eyes open, much less stay upright on her equs, became increasingly difficult. She prayed for the sol's end and watched with burning, bleary eyes as the cloud-covered sun gradually inched its hazy way toward the distant peaks.

Finally, Teran called a halt near a sheltered outcropping of rocks. "This will do as good as any for camp," he said, dismounting. "This nocte, however, *I* will take first watch. Have no fear, though. I won't hesitate to wake you for your turn."

Too weary to argue, Alia untied her bedroll and threw it to the ground under the low overhang of stone. She proceeded to get out the hobbles for the equs, when a strong hand came down on hers. She raised tired eyes to Teran's, too exhausted to even be surprised at his unexpected action.

169

"Let me take care of the equs," he said, the gentleness of his voice belying his stern expression. "Go, get some rest."

Alia started to protest she'd do her share, then realized it was pointless, if she'd even had the strength. Stumbling over to her bedroll, she wearily unwound it. She was soon wrapped in it, fast asleep.

It was pitch black when Teran woke her. She struggled to a sitting position and rubbed her eyes.

"How long have I been sleeping?"

"About seven, eight horas, I'd guess. But since you fell asleep so early, you haven't impinged on my time. Here's some meat and dried fruit," he said, handing her the food. "You slept right through supper."

She took the rations from him, her hands brushing his in the dark. Both froze. Her heart began to thud so loudly Alia was certain Teran must have heard it. The electricity between them surged back and forth, until the very air crackled. At that moment, if Teran had taken her into his arms, Alia knew that all her brave words and noble resolutions would have melted before the fiery onslaught of their passion.

Instead, he turned from her. Crawling a few meters away, he wrapped himself in his blanket and lay down. "Wake me at sunrise," were his last words before he fell fast asleep.

Morning came quickly. After another cold breakfast, they were soon on the trail. By now Alia was used to the gloomy weather and took no further notice of it. Higher and higher they climbed, until the altitude made them short of breath and their ears ache from the pressure change.

Though there was no sun to guide them, Alia knew when noon came. Still, Teran pushed on. At last they reached the craggy, windswept summit of a high mountain pass. For a long while they gazed down on a panorama of lesser peaks that gradually flattened to a high plateau. There, nearly hidden by the gray rocks around it, was a jagged, grim-looking fortress.

"Ferox!" Alia whispered, her pulse racing. "At last!"

Yes, Ferox, Teran thought fiercely. Soon we'll meet again, and at last Darla shall be avenged. The memory of a lovely, blue-eyed blonde flashed, unbidden, through his mind. Strange, but he hadn't allowed himself to think of her in so very many cycles. His hands clenched into rock-hard fists as he recalled her death.

"Ferox!" he muttered hoarsely, the name acquiring the sound of a curse.

Alia glanced over at him in surprise. "Teran?" she murmured, her voice tinged with concern.

He glowered at her for a moment, then turned away to stare back at the fortress, his features hardened into an impassive mask.

What is the source of their enmity? Alia wondered. Never had she seen such frank hatred mixed with such raw anguish on another being's face. And to discover it on Teran's, above all, truly frightened her.

She gingerly touched his arm. Whatever he was thinking and feeling, it was better he be drawn from it before the emotions consumed him in their destructive intensity.

"Teran, it is time we were going."

For one long moment more, Teran stared down at the scene below him. Then, with a violent shudder, he turned and walked back to his equs.

Their pace increased with the anticipation of drawing close to the long-sought goal—the man who possessed the Knowing Crystal. The downward path was steep and unstable. They were soon forced to dismount and lead the equs, carefully picking their way through rubble. It was over two long, difficult horas later before they found themselves viewing the castle from a much closer perspective, high atop a cliff.

"Finally," Alia breathed, her voice trembling with triumph, as they lay on their bellies, staring down at the sight. "Finally the Crystal is almost within my grasp. How I have dreamed of this sol, yet I hardly dared hope I would actually see it."

She crawled back from the view and rose to her feet. "Come. There's no time to lose."

Teran rolled over to stare up at her. "What do you mean 'come'? Surely you're not considering riding down there without taking time to observe the area?"

"That is exactly what I plan to do. The Crystal will guide me."

"Are you mad?" he demanded, his anger rising. "We barely escaped the traps in that cursed forest. Do you seriously think Ferox would protect his own lair any less well? Give me time to watch the comings and goings of the fortress. There are bound to be safe ways in and out of there."

Alia vigorously shook her head. "No, Teran. The time to go is now, before they suspect we have arrived. The element of surprise will be to our advantage. The Crystal calls me."

The muscles in his bearded jaw spasmed furiously as he lifted himself up on his elbows. "You know nothing of the ways of battle. How can you presume to tell me how to do this?"

Teran scooted back to where she stood and climbed to his feet. He turned to confront her, his tall, powerful frame towering over her.

172

She had to lean back to look into his eyes, yet she refused to be intimidated by his formidable stance. "I presume because this is *my* quest and because . . ." she paused to swallow hard before continuing, "because you are now foresworn to obey me in everything."

A hard look glittered in his silver eyes. "You would command me to do this, even knowing how insane and how dangerous I feel this to be?"

"Yes," Alia replied defiantly. "It is my right. I do command it!"

He considered her for a long moment, as if trying to fathom the depth of her resolve. A tight, cold smile slowly spread across his face.

"Then do as you wish. I refuse to obey such a foolhardy request."

She stared at him, aghast at his outright rebellion. "You have no choice—and you know it! I can force you to go."

He shrugged. "Then force me—if you dare."

Wheeling about, Teran walked away from her. "*If* you have the nerve," he taunted from over his retreating shoulder.

As she watched him stride away, Alia's shock veered to sharp anger, and her anger quickly became a scalding fury. How dare he defy her? He had sworn to help her, and now, when they were at last so close, he suddenly refused to cooperate. She needed him desperately—his skills and his strength—and just when she required them the most, he'd become obstinate. Curse him!

Her hand went to the keys that dangled around her neck. Should she use them and teach him a little lesson? But what if the key-joining harmed Teran or even killed him? She chided herself for her foolish fears. That would never happen. The purpose of the govern collar was to control not destroy a valuable slave.

She removed the keys from her chain and took one in each hand. "I am warning you one last time, Teran," she called to him. "Accede to my wishes or suffer the consequences!"

If Teran heard, he gave no visible indication. He continued to walk away toward the tethered equs.

"Teran!" Alia cried, the anger in her voice mixed with a wild entreaty.

She watched his retreating form for a moment longer. He never wavered. Then, in a burst of rage and frustration, she joined the ends of the two keys.

174

CHAPTER 9

FOR AN INSTANT, ALIA WONDERED IF THE KEYS ACTUALly worked. Then Teran stopped and turned to glance back at her. An expression of surprise, then pain, slashed across his face. Small, rhythmic tremors, starting at his fingertips, inexorably worked their way throughout his body.

The tremors became jerking spasms. With a guttural cry, Teran collapsed on the ground. He lay there as the secundae passed, a helpless pawn in the clutches of the agonizing neural impulses of the now-activated govern collar.

Horror rose within Alia. She hadn't meant for such terrible retribution or torment to occur. She had only meant to frighten Teran into obedience. Frantically, Alia tried to disconnect the two keys and terminate the govern sequence. They couldn't be separated.

In growing alarm, she realized once the sequence

175

had begun there was no way to stop it until it had run its course. A sense of futility overpowered her. She flung the keys to the ground and ran to where Teran lay.

His body convulsing under the collar's wracking impulses, his face contorting in agony, Teran struggled to regain his footing. Each time he reached his knees the overstimulated muscles would fail him, and he'd crash to the ground. Still Teran fought on with the same heartbreaking results, until at last he lay there, unable to summon forth any more strength.

Alia knelt at his side and reached out to pull him to her.

"No!" gasped Teran. "Don't . . . don't touch . . . the collar . . . would bind you . . . to me!"

She jerked back. There was nothing she could do to help him, not even hold him in her arms. The govern sequence would have retained both in its torturous impulses, if she had but touched him. Yet Teran, in the midst of his excrutiating pain, had protected her.

"Oh, Teran," Alia whispered miserably. "How long will this go on?"

He was unable to answer her, his back arched, his muscles frozen in what seemed a particularly painful neural jolt. Sweat bathed his pale face, and he ground his teeth in silent agony. Finally, for a blessed moment, the impulses ceased, and his powerful form relaxed. Weakly, he turned his head to her.

"Horas . . . Alia. It can go on . . . for horas," he said, his breath coming in ragged pants.

"No! Oh, no, Teran!" she cried and covered her face with her hands. When she finally lowered them to gaze down at him, her eyes glistened with tears. "I didn't know. I swear, I didn't know."

Teran managed a wan smile. "Stay with me."

As the govern sequence began again, a low groan escaped his clenched lips. The painful neural inductions allowed him only brief moments of respite. As time passed and he gradually weakened under the body-wracking torture, Teran ceased to fight. His face assumed the same flaccid appearance as his body. Gradually, he became unresponsive except to the periodic jolts that convulsed him.

Alia stayed there, never leaving his side through the long horas of his torment. She yearned to touch him, to soothe him, yet she could do nothing but watch. The horas dragged by with painful slowness. Finally, the collar appeared to cease its cruel domination. Teran fell into an exhausted stupor, while Alia remained there beside him, staring, unable to move even her own mind or body to action.

Thunder crashed overhead. Glancing up at the rapidly darkening sky, Alia felt the first raindrops splash on her face. She turned her gaze back to Teran, who was still unconscious. It's up to me to take command, she firmly told herself. The resolve roused her from her lethargy.

She tentatively touched him. He was felt moist and cool, but no shock jolted her. Climbing to her feet, Alia grasped Teran under both arms and dragged his limp, unwieldy body toward a shallow, cavelike opening in the mountainside.

Once Teran was deposited safely inside, Alia ran out to grab the supplies and blankets off the equs. She quickly hobbled the animals, then hurried back to the cave through the now-heavy downpour. Teran lay there, motionless, his skin clammy and pale, his clothing damply molded to his body. She'd have to get him warm and dry as soon as possible, Alia realized, if he were to avoid taking a chill.

With a sigh, she undressed him, spreading his

clothes over a large, flat rock to dry. The boots were her greatest trial but, after much tugging, she was at last able to remove them. Once Teran was naked, Alia vigorously rubbed him with one of the blankets, then covered him with the other. She cleansed and re-dressed his leg wounds, applying a rank smelling ointment she'd found in her rummagings through the saddlebags. Then, having done all she could for him, Alia sat down beside his inert body and stared out at the torrential rainfall.

The sheets of frigid water fell from an ominously gray sky, the early evening light assuming a sickening yellow cast. As if to wring the very last, most misera-ble drops out of this most wretched of sols, Alia thought morosely. Had she at last fallen to such depths that it had come to this? Turning on the one person left who'd always shown her kindness, whose intent had always been to help her? And what more would he suffer because of her? Perhaps it would be better to leave him and take her chances on her own, rather than further risk his life.

The image of a wise, gray-bearded face rose in her mind's eye. Only with the greatest of efforts did she repress the sob the memory called to her lips. One life too many had already been lost on this quest, yet if she were to believe Vates' words . . .

As the horas passed, Teran roused from his lethar-gic state. He tossed and turned, occasionally mum-bling an incoherent phrase. A few times he bolted upright and, save for Alia's restraining hands, would have flung himself into the rain. She held him to her, stroking his head and murmuring soothing words, until he finally calmed down and drifted back to sleep. Tenderly laying him down and pulling the blanket up around him, Alia once again returned to her pensive thoughts.

Dusk slowly filtered through the craggy rocks. Finally, the rain ceased. A fresh breeze, clean and sweet, blew through the mountains. Assuring herself that Teran was still asleep, Alia rose and went out to check on the equs.

They appeared calm, albeit wet, and she quickly turned back to the cave. On the way she stepped on something hard. Kicking it from her, she heard it strike a rock with a metallic cling. The govern keys.

She searched for them in the rapidly waning light and found them lying in a puddle of water. Alia picked them up. For a long moment she studied the metallic objects, filled with loathing.

Then, with a firm resolve, she separated them and buried them in different spots. Though even the thought of retaining symbols of her domination over Teran sickened her, there was always the possibility the keys were important in other ways. Later, if it were necessary, she could always retrieve them. But no matter what happened, Alia silently vowed, the keys would never be used against Teran again. With a small sigh, she continued her trek back to the cave.

Gray eyes gleamed at her in the dim light. Alia's heart leapt in her chest. "How do you feel?"

He managed a weak smile. "Awful. Water?"

She grabbed the water flask. Slipping an arm under his head, Alia helped him drink. He took a few swallows, then fell back, exhausted by the effort.

"That was good," he murmured. "Thank you."

Alia's heart twisted at the sight of him lying there, so weak and helpless—and then to have him thank her! She turned from him, biting down hard on her lip to keep from weeping.

"Alia?" Teran whispered uncertainly. "Are you all right?"

"Yes . . . No!" She wheeled around, her face a

tortured mask. "How could I be all right after what I did to you? Oh, Teran, I am so sorry. Can you ever forgive me?"

"Forgive you? I purposely forced you into using the collar. It was the only way to prevent you from that foolhardy attempt on Ferox's Fortress." He paused to smile up at her, the old, familiar gleam flaring in his eyes. "It worked, didn't it?"

A tumble of confused thoughts and feelings assailed her. He would bring such suffering upon himself, just to keep her from danger? Yet, on the other hand, how dare he manipulate her like that. She swung from one realization to another, uncertain whether to be mad or glad.

"Teran, Teran," Alia finally said, "you risk too much for me. I never asked for your life."

His gray eyes studied her with a curious intensity. "You've claimed me, Alia. That grants you my life. It's your right to punish me as you see fit."

"No. Not anymore." She vehemently shook her head. "I have hidden the keys. I will never use them against you again." Alia smiled at him. "So, you see, you are free of me, if that is your wish."

"And what will you do?"

"Go on. My quest lies in the fortress at the end of this trail. That much is unchanged."

He took her hand. "Then I will ride with you. Keys or no, I am bound to you."

She placed her other hand over his. "Even if we succeed, I can promise you little. You must know that."

"It is worth the risk."

Is it, Teran? Alia thought. How can you be so certain when you know so little about me, my life, my training? What do you see that makes you so sure, when all I see is uncertainty and hopelessness?

"Come," she said, shying away from the disconcerting subject. "Drink some water, then try to sleep. You'll need your strength for the morrow."

Teran obediently raised his head and took several swallows of water. "You *will* wake me for my turn at watch, won't you?"

"Perhaps."

He pulled her to him. "Promise me."

Alia tossed her head and laughed. "You are beginning to act like your old self, bullying me again. The only difference is, I am not afraid of you anymore."

"I never meant to frighten you, Alia. That was the furthest thing from my mind, even that very first sol."

She trembled at the deeper meaning to his words. "Hush, Teran. If you promise to stop talking and go to sleep, I will hold you for a while."

"I'd like that." His eyes burned into hers.

"But just hold you and only for this nocte. Is that understood?"

Teran rolled his eyes toward the ceiling and sighed. "Yes, my Domina."

"And stop calling me that!"

"Yes, my Domina."

"Oh, you're incorrigible!" Alia muttered, as she gathered him into her arms.

"Yes, Alia."

It was late morning before Teran awoke. The sun, for a change, was burning brightly, rapidly evaporating the dampness of the previous nocte. He rolled over to where he had last seen Alia, ready to reprimand her for letting him again sleep through his watch, but she wasn't there.

Teran jerked upright, almost striking his head on the cave's low ceiling. He peered out in the direction of the hobbled equs. The chestnut mare was gone. Uttering a curse, Teran hastily pulled on his clothing and boots. Instinctively, he knew what she'd done. Alia had gone on alone to Ferox's stronghold.

He crawled out of the shelter, dragging the blanket and supply bags behind him. For a moment, as he climbed to his feet, his head whirled giddily. Curse it! Though the long rest had repaired most of the damage to his nerve-tortured body, it'd still be a few sols before the effects of the collar completely wore off.

That knowledge had been indelibly imprinted the time the keys were first used, that sol now so long ago when the collar was initially implanted. He shrugged the unpleasant memory aside. He hadn't the luxury of further rest; Alia was in the gravest of danger. He must go to her.

She had left him everything, even the stun gun. The thought only served to intensify his anguish. *Alia, Alia, why did you do this?* Teran inwardly raged. *I told you I would help you. Why didn't you wait for me?* The agonized questions constricted like a steel band around his heart. Would he ever see her alive again?

Quickly saddling up the remaining equs, Teran mounted and headed down the trail. It was difficult to pinpoint exactly how long ago she had left. From the condition of her tracks in the rapidly drying mud, he guessed it to be at least three or four horas.

Aching frustration welled up inside him. To make up that much time and catch her before she reached the fortress would be impossible. Still he urged his animal on with reckless abandon, until they were careening down the rocky path at breakneck speed.

Horas passed as the faithful animal negotiated the trail as best he could. The red sun passed its zenith, blazingly hot in the heat-whitened sky. The equs' shaggy coat became sleek with sweat. Still, Teran drove him on. He knew he dared not push the beast much longer, but if he could just catch a glimpse of Alia up ahead . . .

The strain of last nocte's torture began to tell on him. Curse that femina! Teran thought, mentally vanquishing his fatigue. She seemed bound and determined to get them both killed in this misguided attempt at sparing him. They had succeeded so far because of his extreme care and vigilance. Why did she throw all that aside now, when they were at last so close? If anything happened, if Ferox laid one hand on her . . . ! A raw and primitive rage overwhelmed him. He pushed his equs on to an even faster pace.

Despite the ground gained, Teran was finally forced to rest the exhausted animal. He slipped off and led the equs down the steep, winding trail. When the beast was cool, Teran offered him the last of the water from the flask. Over an hora was lost before he felt safe to remount and ride again. This time he maintained a slower pace, realizing the animal hadn't much more to give.

Deep lavender twilight settled on the peaks before Teran finally quit the mountain trail to head across the boulder-strewn plateau. In the last stand of trees before the desolate wilderness began, Teran found Alia's equs. At least she had used a little caution, he thought. Her approach would be less obvious on foot, and hiding the animal here gave her a remote chance of escape. Teran hobbled his equs beside hers and set out on foot, taking only the coil of rope as extra baggage.

Far in the distance, he could make out the dark, jagged form of Ferox's fortress. Strange that no one had opposed his progress so far. Perhaps Ferox was so sure of his impregnability that he needed no guards.

Harking back to the sols of their Academy training, he recalled how careful and devious the young Ferox had been. Never one to take a chance, Ferox had seen to it that all eventualities were planned for and protected against. No, Teran realized, the worst obstacles and greatest dangers lay within the fortress itself.

What unkind fate had destined them to be lifelong rivals? he mused as he jogged along. Even as young warriors-at-arms they had constantly vied for the honors of battle, the most beautiful feminas, the respect of the other men. It had been an equal contest until Ferox, obsessed with the lust for power, had turned to more sinister pursuits.

Eventually caught cheating, he was unceremoniously dismissed from the Academy, all the while cursing Teran for his downfall. If Ferox captured him now, Teran knew the long-awaited revenge would not be pleasant, nor would death be cleanly given. Yet death, though not willingly sought, would indeed be willingly embraced if he could but take his bitterest enemy with him.

The journey across the rocky land became more difficult as the sol dwindled. It would be much wiser to wait until sunrise and better light, Teran realized, but the thought of Alia spending even one nocte in Ferox's clutches was more than he could bear. He stumbled on, the eerie lights of the castle guiding him ever onward.

At long last he reached the foreboding structure. A huge, notched mass of stone in the blackness of the nocte, its size and shape were barely discernible even in contrast to the relative lightness of the star-studded sky. Rectangular in outline, its length ran for at least 500 meters before blending into the rock from which it was carved. At each end were twin towers, angular in construction, seemingly without windows or light source of any kind.

A wide moat of foul-smelling black liquid surrounded its high walls, walls that at first glance appeared without entry. Teran stepped forward to the very edge of the bubbling, stinking moat to catch a closer look at the fortification.

Behind the high, crenelated walls, a movement caught his eye. A hulking form, not quite human, passed by. It had to be the guard on his rounds. Was the beast alone in his duties?

Teran resumed his intent inspection of the walls. The outline of a carefully hidden drawbridge gradually became apparent. Cleverly constructed to telescope in upon itself, its closure, combined with the great expanse of the moat, presented a daunting picture to anyone desirous of entry.

Removing his belt, Teran reached into one of its many inner pouches and drew out a mini grappling hook. There were always less simple ways of getting in, he grimly reminded himself. Taking his coil of rope, he secured one end to the grapple's ring. With a quick twist of his wrist, he swung it about his head. When the rope fed out to the appropriate length and proper speed, he hurled it upward toward the castle wall.

The grapple caught behind one of the crenelated edges. With a practiced tug, Teran settled the hooks more securely. Then, with an easily loosened reverse knot, he quickly tied the other end of the rope to a ring on the bailey pilings. Getting a running start, he jumped toward the highest part of the rope within reach. Hand over hand, Teran swiftly worked his way upward. Now, if only he could reach the top of the wall before the guard returned or the grappling hook gave way . . .

The grating tread of footsteps, drawing near on the catwalk, urged Teran on with even greater speed. The guard was returning sooner than he'd anticipated. Only another few meters, he thought. If only he could reach the wall in time . . .

A gruesome, wolfish head appeared at the point where Teran's grappling hook was imbedded. With a sinister grin, the mutant guard began to work at loosening the hook. The taut line reverberated with every movement to dislodge it. Another few secundae and Teran knew he'd be free of the wall, tumbling toward a horrible death in the moat below. He grabbed the stun gun from his belt and fired at the ugly, contorted face of the guard.

The rope stopped shaking. Teran heard a loud thud as the guard's body disappeared. Then his hands grasped the rough stone wall. Pulling himself up and over, Teran landed beside the still form of the guard. The mutant would rouse soon and alert the fortress of his arrival.

Without a moment's hesitation, Teran lifted the body and dropped it over the side. There was the sound of a splash. Then, with a sickening gurgle, the moat greedily devoured the offering.

Teran untied his grappling hook and replaced it in his belt. With a sharp jerk, he loosened the knot on the bailey piling. Recoiling the rope back to him, he slung it over his shoulder. There was no point in leaving any evidence of his arrival, not to mention the possibility of always needing the rope later.

He looked around. Far down the narrow catwalk on his right was one of the towers, where a dimly lit passageway beckoned. Turning, Teran quickly surveyed the other direction. The walk on his left stretched on endlessly, finally disappearing into the gloom.

Faced with the fact that he needed a place to hide from detection, Teran chose the most expedient alternative—the tower on his right. Stealthily running over to it, he peered into its open doorway. The structure contained a stone stairway, dizzily winding downward.

With swift care, Teran descended the steps, coming out onto an empty inner courtyard. Across the cobblestone area loomed the hulking mass of the main building, its windows mere sinister slits in the rough, gray mass of stone.

Inexplicably, Teran sensed that was where he must go. Alia was in there, somewhere.

Hiding in the shadows as much as possible, he worked his way over to the arched entry. Slipping back into the protective shadows, Teran was confronted with three dark portals, all of them open, their door handles only on the exterior side. He hesitated, realizing that once through, there was no turning back.

Teran chose the door on the far right. It swung closed behind him with a heavy clang, instantly enshrouding him in blackness. At the unexpected sound he jumped, his hand reaching out to find the wall.

It was damp with slime.

He instinctively jerked away from the distasteful sensation, then, with a resigned sigh, Teran forced himself to touch the clammy wall again. Repulsive as the slippery, oozing wall was, it was the only way to maintain some sense of direction in the total darkness.

The passageway wound on for what seemed an eternity, sometimes taking such sharp turns that Teran stumbled into the wall before realizing his error. His hands and forearms were soon cut and abraded from the attempt to shield his face from the unexpected outcroppings of rock, obstructions he had no way of seeing. The stone floor was slippery from dripping water that noisily splattered and plopped from the ceiling. Teran slid, almost losing his balance several times. Debris lay scattered in his way, tripping him as he stepped through the blackness. Rank, musty scents assailed his nostrils, some of which he recognized as those of scavengers known to lurk in subterranean depths.

He gripped the knife at his belt. In the darkness the stun gun would be ineffective. At any moment, Teran fully expected to fall upon some trap or other hideous surprise. Yet he staggered on. Alia needed him, and he must do his best to reach her, if only he survived the pitfalls Ferox had laid.

At the thought of his old nemesis, a sense of futility welled up inside Teran. How could he ever hope to successfully traverse the myriad ensnarements the man surely had built into this fortress? Even now, he was forced to rely on little more than base instincts and raw courage. With no information to ground his decisions upon, all his cycles of warrior training were useless—his strength, his physical prowess, his skills. Even intelligence seemed ineffectual. He felt powerless, a mere pawn in the vengeful hands of the Imperium's most vicious criminal.

Still, Teran stumbled on, driven by the vow he had made Alia. He was bound to her, in heart as well as body. He could not, would not, rest until she was free. If it meant his life, he was willing to give it. His love for her could do no less.

Why now, in this blackest of moments when death hovered on every rasping breath, did he finally admit that he loved her? Perhaps it was the danger, the uncertainty of life from one moment to the next, that made emotional defenses no longer so important. Yet how ironic, too, that once again he risked losing the femina he loved to the same man—Ferox.

A growl of pure animal rage swelled in Teran's throat. Not this time, not ever again! Alia was his. Though she had yet to admit it, yet to even realize it herself, since that nocte of Vates' death they were bound by more than the keys of the govern collar. The Knowing Crystal had joined their fate long before they met or were even born. Their nocte of mating had sealed it. Just as surely as their flesh had melded, their two hearts had become one.

He trudged on, his determination to reach Alia all the stronger. Finally, a dim light appeared up ahead. He quickened his pace, though he dreaded what he knew would be Ferox's next test.

Entering what seemed a long, narrow hall, Teran noted that the only escape from it was the door at its other end. He took a step forward when something on the ceiling caught his eye. There, suspended overhead, were hundreds of long spikes. Teran froze, edging backward. A grim smile touched his lips. So, Ferox, you've borrowed an idea from our sols of training. From all appearances the spikes were designed to fall if one took a false step on the walkway below, and therein lay the problem—how to traverse the area without stepping in the wrong spot. There was no way to know.

Teran inhaled a deep breath and shut his eyes. If Alia had made it into the castle, it could only have been with the help of the Crystal. It was also the only way he would be able to travel through in safety. He opened his mind to any voice that might whisper to him and prayed it would guide him through the danger.

For what seemed an eternity, Teran heard and felt

nothing. Then a sound, faint yet lovely, wafted through his mind. The fleeting sensation was so brief that in the next instant he wasn't certain he hadn't imagined. Was this his reply, the answer he must entrust his life to? He opened his eyes and stepped forward.

The spikes remained on the ceiling. Teran slowly exhaled, not certain he believed what he saw. Was it just a lucky guess, or had his feet been directed? There was no way to know save continue and test the strange biddings once more. With a heart pounding in his throat, Teran again listened for the sound. Once more he strode out as indicated. The spikes didn't fall. On and on he went, his confidence growing. At last, he reached the door at the other end.

Teran swung the portal open and edged through. It closed behind him with a dull thud. Another of Ferox's one-way doors, he thought dryly. The light in this passage, though dim, was enough for Teran to make his way. He set out cautiously, expecting a deathtrap at every turn. The tunnel wound around in a zigzag course with openings at various intervals. With a growing sense of frustration Teran finally recognized it for what it was—a labyrinth.

Again, he called upon the Crystal for assistance. This time the voice was stronger, and Teran followed it without hesitation. As he progressed through the maze a terrible, high-pitched wailing drew near.

An icy chill ran down his spine. It was the cry of a rapax, half-bird, half-wolf. Wildly ravenous with huge claws and teeth, the monster was usually found on barren, windswept mountain peaks, blindly attacking whatever it came upon.

It was strange that it roamed this subterranean labyrinth. Ferox must have had it captured and imprisoned here. There was little hope of fighting off an animal such as that, especially out of its natural habitat where it was even more dangerous in its rage and frustration. Teran cherished no illusions what such an outcome would be. A wrong turn now would most certainly lead right to the voracious beast.

He traveled on, trusting the inner voice. The wails swiftly changed to excited howls as the rapax appeared to catch Teran's scent. From the increasingly louder sounds of scratching and snuffling on the other side of the labyrinth's many walls, it was evident the distance between them was narrowing.

The rank stench of the beast settled heavily on the air, nearly choking Teran with its acrid, suffocating weight. The creature had to be very close. Perhaps on the other side of this wall? And would the next turn at last bring them face to face?

A terrifying thought struck him. What if the Crystal wasn't leading him? What if his successful progress had been the result of warrior training and instincts, mixed with a little luck? After all, he still had no concrete proof of his ability to commune with the Knowing Crystal. All he'd experienced so far was the faint sound in the forest and now a few pretty tones.

A fine sweat broke out on his brow, beading until it trickled down the sides of his face. Teran's hands clenched into unconscious fists, and he tasted the acrid bitterness of fear. Suddenly unsure of himself, of whether to go on or turn back, he halted. It was too much—the uncertainty, the traps, traps that were more like tests. But of what? His abilities, his courage?

Teran shook his head in frustration. It couldn't be that; these pitfalls required more than normal human talents. They required something outside oneself, like the powers of the Knowing Crystal.

A smile of growing realization spread across his

face. Ferox had devised the path to him to more than discourage and frighten. Each danger overcome, each trap survived, had only been a stepping stone to a higher, even more difficult test, tests that ultimately required the ability to commune with the Knowing Crystal. That was why Alia had passed through unscathed, and why he, too, had managed to succeed so far.

The finely strung tension slowly ebbed, and his taut muscles relaxed. He only had to continue in his trust of the Crystal. Teran forced himself to go on.

He met no predator. With each successive turn, the gruesome sounds grew weaker. He willed his mind to prepare for the next test. The Crystal would lead him, of this he was finally certain. Now, if only he could reach Alia in time.

The horas in the dark tunnels blended, one into the other, until Teran eventually lost count of the time. Trap after trap he successfully traversed, thanks to the Crystal's faithful guidance.

At last, near physical and mental exhaustion, he arrived at one more door, a door even more massive than the others. Heedless of what lay beyond, he leaned a bruised, weary shoulder against the rough wood and shoved. It took all of his remaining strength to wedge it open. In one last, desperate lunge, Teran stumbled into a blinding brightness.

CHAPTER 10

"STRANGE. VERY STRANGE."

The blond, devilishly handsome man intently peered at the projection while, at the same time, he absentmindedly toyed with the govern collar around his neck. "How has he been able to survive so long without you?"

Alia tore her gaze from the hazy holograph of Teran, just passing out of the labyrinth. She glanced up at Ferox. Once again her breath caught in unwilling admiration.

He was flawless, from the clear-cut lines of his strong, intelligent profile to the massively powerful, black leather-clad physique. If not for what she knew of the man and those eyes . . .

The eyes were dead, empty save for the sinister gleam of greed, obsessive power and unspeakable cruelty. As outwardly beautiful as Ferox was, it still wasn't enough to mask the hideous malevolence of the man within.

"Well, what do you know about Teran's unusual fortune in negotiating my traps?" he prodded, his mouth twisting into a savage, strangely unsettling smile.

Alia repressed a shudder at the speculative look he sent her way. "Nothing," she forced herself to reply. "I know nothing except that Teran is a brave and resourceful warrior. Perhaps your traps aren't as difficult as you imagined. After all, I traversed them without problem."

He languidly ran his finger up her bare arm. "But you, my lovely femina, were helped by an outside power, weren't you?"

Alia recoiled, just as his tactile trail reached the shoulder of her gown of shimmering gold. The dress, draped low across her full breasts, had been forced on her by what she hoped were female slaves. The fabric lovingly clung to her torso before softly flaring to her feet, which were clad in sandals of delicate spun gold. This beautiful gown, more exquisite than any she'd ever worn, filled her with the same revulsion as the man who'd given it to her.

"I . . . I don't know what you mean," she murmured, frantically hedging for time, for some way out of the tension-fraught situation. Did he suspect she'd come for the Crystal?

"Don't you?" He arched a sensuous brow. "It is past the point of games, you know. Despite your disparaging remarks about my fortress, no ordinary being could ever hope to pass through it and live. It takes a special talent, one I suspect you possess. And one," he muttered, turning his gaze back to the holograph, "I'm beginning to wonder if Teran might also have."

Too startled by his unexpected statement to dare offer any reply, Alia joined Ferox in his observation of Teran. As she watched, Teran hesitated on the edge of a steaming river of red. The only way across it was by way of a path of floating rocks. She questioningly looked over at Ferox.

He graced her with a sly, assessing glance. "So, the femina does care what I have in store for her companion. It's one of my favorites. I've a very active part in this particular test. To successfully cross the river of flesh-melting lava, Teran must guess which stone is stable and which will sink.

"Of course," Ferox chuckled, "since I don't know from one moment to the next which stone I'll chose to lower or which to maintain, neither will Teran. How much luck do you think this little test will take?"

She shot him an angry look. He knew, as well as she, that Teran needed more than instinct and luck to get across the river, with such outside interference as Ferox planned. If only there were some way to help—

"Forget about communing with him," the blond man harshly said, interrupting her. "Nothing human, physically or mentally, can penetrate these walls. I was most careful to attend to that."

"You would let him die there?" Alia cried, rising to her feet. "Well, I won't stand by and watch." She hurried down the steps of the raised platform, her gown swirling airly about her.

"Stop her!" Ferox shouted.

Two hulking Simians lurched forward, their curved, razor-sharp pikes blocking Alia's progress.

"Chain her to my throne!"

He leaned back in his chair as one guard held the now struggling Alia while the other roughly clamped a shackle around one of her ankles. A heavy chain was quickly attached to the iron band, and the other end was fastened to a ring at the base of Ferox's ornately gilded, stone seat.

He beckoned to her. "Come closer, and watch with me. Surely you want to know what becomes of Teran."

She walked back to him, her heart as reluctant as her steps. Though she dreaded watching what was certain to be Teran's death, Alia couldn't desert him. Even as only a spectator, she'd stay with him to the end.

A large, powerful hand settled upon her shoulder, forcing her to a position at the foot of the throne. Sad, hopeless, honey-brown eyes turned to the holograph of Teran. He was making the first motion forward toward the floating stones.

"Let's see how good you really are now, my old classmate." Ferox snarled at the projection. "Can you guess which of those first two stones is safe, which one fatal?"

Ferox's choice for the secure stone flashed through Alia's mind. It startled her in its unexpectedness. She looked up to see if he had spoken. His face, set in a gloating look of hatred, was still, his lips motionless. The message hadn't come from him, she realized, but from the Knowing Crystal. If only she could send that same communication to Teran!

In that split secundae those same thoughts were still whirling through Alia's mind, Teran seemed to make his decision. He stepped out, his foot choosing the safe path. Wild hope flared in Alia's breast. Had he possibly heard her? But how could that be? Ferox had said his walls were impenetrable to mental messages.

A foul curse reverberated through the hall.

"So, Teran, you were fortunate this time," Ferox growled. "Let's see how you fare with the next choice of stones."

Before the words left his lips, a confused jumble of messages assailed Alia. First one stone, then the next was chosen, as if Ferox's thoughts were jumping back and forth between the two rocks. She watched Teran hesitate, a look of puzzlement spread across his face. Was it possible he was hearing the same information as she?

Elation filled Alia. With clenched fists and baited breath, she gazed at the holograph. After a moment, Ferox's thoughts settled and fixated on one stone. Teran stepped out toward it.

Another fiercely angry curse rang through the giant assembly hall. He knows, he communes with the Crystal, Alia realized, her thoughts simultaneously joining with Ferox's shout of rage. Teran will live, will traverse all the traps as successfully as I, for the Crystal leads him.

The joy and relief surged through her until she felt almost giddy. It is true then, what Vates said. We are both Crystal Masters.

That final understanding froze in her mind. Both masters? But the Crystal could have only one master, one home. And which would that be, with both of them from different planets, both of which desperately needed the Crystal's guidance?

An uneasy feeling filtered through Alia, its unsettling tendrils ensnaring her heart. Had Teran known of his powers all along and hidden them? It would have been so easy to allow her to regain the Crystal, risk the greatest dangers, and then take the stone from her back to Bellator. Perhaps that explained the reason for even his mystifying exile on Carcer, a heretofore unheard of Bellatorian punishment.

Had that been the extent of their friendship then? To curry her trust and affection? An icy sensation, beginning at the pit of Alia's stomach, insinuated itself throughout her body. She felt weak and nauseated, yet still the doubts relentlessly pounded at her heart and mind.

Indeed, had that even been the ultimate motive for their mating that nocte and his continued masculine attention toward her? To use her, to lull her into some pliant, lovesick femina easily manipulated into doing his slightest bidding? Perhaps into betraying the Crystal?

She had always wondered at his kindness and his disturbing effect upon her. Though it hurt to consider the possibility, it answered so many questions she'd always had about Teran. Perhaps the High Priestess had been right all along—better to suspect everyone as a danger to the quest and discard them as soon as their usefulness was served. It seemed the only safe way.

As Alia watched, her eyes dulled with grief and confusion. Teran carefully but successfully crossed the molten river. Ferox's rage grew more impotent by the moment. With one final curse, he switched off the holograph projector. He grabbed Alia, yanking her up and backward to fall against him.

"So, my lovely femina, I find I've two of the Power in my grasp," Ferox said, his handsomely cruel face only millimeters from hers. "And which of you shall I keep, which destroy? Even you must realize one of you must die if the other is to have ultimate power. Would you wish it Teran?"

Yes, I wish it Teran! she silently cried, the floodgate of her doubts and deepest fears bursting asunder to churn wildly in the confusion of her mind. He used me and betrayed my trust and love. I want him dead!

"You choose, as you will anyway," Alia replied instead, her voice deceptively calm, the ebb tide of high emotions numbing her. "It matters not to me."

He arched a brow. "So you say, but we shall learn the real truth, won't we, when Teran arrives? Have patience. He will soon be here."

Yes, he will soon be here, Alia thought miserably. He will traverse all of Ferox's traps, and the two, lifelong enemies will finally meet again. Yet his deadliest foe will still be me, for now I know his secret, the power we both share, and it is a power one of us must surely take to the grave.

Teran staggered out into the brightly lit assembly hall. He blinked in the intense glare until his vision readjusted. His glance scanned the huge chamber, taking in the assortment of armed guards lining the walls and the two large rings that marred the center of the room. Finally, his eyes came to rest upon an ornately decorated platform far across the hall.

There, chained to Ferox's gilded stone chair, was Alia. Their eyes met and locked. An expression of what seemed to be pain, then bitterness, swept across Alia's face.

"Alia," Teran whispered, his voice hoarse with a weary longing.

A triumphantly evil laugh reverberated through the hall. "Pray, come closer, Teran." Ferox motioned to a point about ten meters in front of his throne. "I've been watching your progress through my humble abode with great interest. You have remembered the lessons of the Academy well. Come closer."

Ferox watched as Teran strode to the indicated spot, his handsome face twisting into a feral grin. "It's an honor to have an old classmate in my presence again—or should I say in my clutches? I cannot begin to tell you of my delight when I discovered it was you who led the femina there by my stone guardians in the desert of Mors. A sweet sol indeed, now that I at last have the pleasure of repaying you for ruining my career. Our paths meet once again—for the last time!"

"You ruined your own career because you were too weak to bear honest competition. I see you have chosen to surround yourself with men of your same ilk," Teran observed dryly, glancing around him. He took another step forward.

When the guards made a threatening movement toward him, Ferox held up a restraining hand. "Let him come closer. I have no fear of any man within my own fortress."

Striding forward, Teran halted at the base of the platform. Once more his glance sought out Alia. For a fleeting instant he saw his own feelings mirrored in the brown depths of her eyes, before she closed them against him. Puzzled by her response, he wrenched his gaze from her. If they were fortunate, perhaps there'd be a time to delve into her strange withdrawal, but not now, not when they were in the midst of the worst danger of their quest, indeed, their very lives.

Teran confronted Ferox, his gray eyes burning into that of his foe's. "Whatever the basis for our quarrel, it doesn't involve her. Deal with me as you will, but set her free."

Ferox howled in derisive laughter. "And who are you to demand anything? You have succeeded in escaping all my traps, but you will never escape me. You are nothing but my helpless pawn, and this nocte, my hated rival, our enmity will at last end—in your death!"

Teran's fists clenched. The muscles of his arms bulged with the effort it took to restrain himself from going for Ferox, but he didn't dare use the stun gun, not with Alia in the line of fire. He'd never endanger her because of his hatred for Ferox. One innocent femina had already suffered because of their lifelong enmity.

"Then come down from there," Teran cried, "and I'll fight you. If I win, she and I must be granted safe passage out of here."

The howling began again, more vociferous than before. "You forget yourself, Teran. This is my lair, and I set the terms of the agreements," Ferox finally snarled. "And I plan to have it all, your death *and* the lovely femina."

He motioned to his henchmen. "Bring him to me."

Teran was barely able to lunge forward before the guards were upon him. He managed to disable four or five soldiers before the rest overran him, wrestling his powerful form to the floor. Though Teran struggled mightily, almost succeeding in breaking free several times, in the end their massive numbers overpowered him.

His arms bent high behind his back, his head forced backwards at a choking angle, he was dragged over to face Ferox. Despite his dogged resistance, they forced him to kneel before the throne and held his head to the floor.

For the moment, Ferox chose to ignore the man before him. He pulled a horrified Alia to his side. Taking her pale face in his hands he spoke as if to her, but his voice easily carried to Teran.

"See how easily he's brought to his knees before me? You are too lovely to be wasted on the vanquished. I assure you, the pleasure you'll find in my arms will soon wipe out all memory of him."

"Never!" Alia spat at him, her voice low and hard as she wrenched her face from his painful grip. "I want neither of you. You are both less than the lowest vermin of this foul planet. I would rather mate with

201

a . . . a rapax than with either of you."

An ugly expression twisted Ferox's face. "We shall see how soon you beg me to take you, pretty one. You're not the first of Teran's feminas I'll have had, you know. Of course," he smiled, his expression assuming an evil leer, "the other one hadn't your fire or strength. She was far, far too fragile for a man of my appetites. You'll suit me better, I think."

At his words, a cry of animal rage burst from Teran's lips. He wrenched himself almost free of his captors, heedless of the pain as he twisted his pinned arms into grotesque angles in his efforts to escape. Dragging three guards with him, he staggered half-way up the platform's steps.

"Curse you, you vile, murdering fiend! Lay one hand on her and I'll kill you! I swear it!"

Before he could make another move, an onslaught of soldiers overran him, burying him in a mass of bodies. Ferox watched them beat Teran to the floor. A hard, lethal expression spread across his face.

"Chain him to the floor rings. It's time we see how deep his courage runs."

Through a haze of pain and blood, Teran felt himself hauled bodily across the rough stone floor to where two thick, iron rings awaited him. Unceremoniously dropped face down, a booted foot pinned his head while his wrists were encased in broad, metal shackles. Heavy chains were attached, then his arms jerked out, away from his body.

Suddenly, he was alone in the midst of the hall. Teran lifted his head and looked around. The guards were back at their posts, Ferox still on his throne with Alia beside him. Awkwardly, agonizingly, he climbed to his feet. He glanced down at the chains that bound him to the floor, his arms stretched out tautly, far from his sides. An anticipatory hush spread through the gathering.

The grating of stone rolling across stone filled the large chamber. The focus of the sound seemed to emanate from behind him but, try as he might, the tightly extended chains allowed Teran little movement. Still, a sense of evil and impending doom wafted over him, permeating him with its numbing breath.

Alia's sharp gasp was the first warning of the monster's arrival. Teran wrenched his head around. Out of the corner of his eye, he saw the serpent. Huge, a mottled brownish-green color, its slitted, yellow eyes gleamed maliciously. A forked tongue flicked in and out of wide, powerfully fanged jaws.

Ever so slowly, it rose out of the pit and began its slithering, slippery approach. Teran struggled wildly to free himself, to turn and face the scaly reptile. The chains held fast, the shackles gouging into his wrists until they tore his flesh into bloody wounds. On and on the snake came, relentlessly winding its slimy way, its scales rasping harshly across the great stone floor.

As Alia watched the dreadful scene unfold, her emotions waged an equally frightening battle. Cold intellect whispered that she shouldn't care, that she should instead be glad to be rid of Teran. Hadn't he served his purpose by getting her to the Crystal? His continued presence would only be a hindrance, especially now, in light of the recent knowledge of his own Crystal abilities. Far better to accept the inevitability of his imminent death and be glad she hadn't been forced to kill him herself.

Yet, as she gazed at his virtually helpless form, bound as he was to the floor, the huge viper inexorably advancing, Alia found it hard to remain unmoved.

His tunic hanging in tatters about him, his arms and torso bruised and bloodied by his recent struggles with the guards, the strain of the past few sols lay heavily upon him. She wondered how long he'd be able to fight off the serpent, before he finally succumbed to its overwhelming advantage and it at last killed him.

No matter how she struggled to remember his deception and cruel manipulation of her, the memories of him holding her during her illness, saving her from the cantare flower and, most of all, that nocte of their mating would not be stilled. They warred with her anguish until she thought she'd scream from the torment.

She clasped Ferox's arm, her face mirroring her horrible conflict. No matter what Teran had done, he didn't deserve to die like this.

"If you haven't the courage to fight him yourself, at least set him free so he'll have a chance against that creature."

Lifeless blue eyes looked down at her. "Ah, sweet femina, when will you learn? *I* choose the form my entertainment will take. Besides, I don't fancy letting Teran damage my pet. Now be silent and watch."

Teran glimpsed the serpent drawing near. He took a deep, steadying breath. There was no hope, none whatsoever, of surviving an attack from behind. If only the creature would move to his front . . . He closed his eyes and called on the only thing that could help him—the Crystal.

Nothing happened. The snake continued to advance, drawing ever near. From the sound of its sibilant hissing and the harsh noise of its scales sliding across the floor, Teran knew it was almost upon him.

He tensed, anticipating the attack. If there were a

merciful fate, perhaps his life would be ended at the reptile's first strike. It was all the hope he had left. The Crystal couldn't, or wouldn't, help him.

Teran waited, his body prickling with the tension of certain death, and nothing happened. Suddenly, he felt a movement between his legs. Looking down, Teran saw the head of the serpent glide past, followed by its wide body. It slithered through until he straddled the snake's midsection, the head of the monster rising before him, slowly swaying.

It arched in the air, its head dancing to and fro, preparing to strike. And strike it did, its fangs aimed directly for Teran's head. At the last possible second he dodged, his booted right foot coming up to side kick the snake in the head. His blow opened a deep cut near the creature's left eye, and the reptile reared back in pain.

"Curse the man!" Ferox snarled. "He's hurt my pet."

He pointed a small, flat, rectangular box in the direction of the snake. "Time to end this before it's damaged further."

The monster struck again, this time with lightning quickness, aiming for Teran's broad chest. He evaded the attack as best he could, attempting to jerk his body out of the way. The chains, however, limited much movement. The serpent's fangs sank into the muscles of Teran's left upper arm.

Alia watched his face contort in agony as he wrenched himself free, the fangs tearing a long, deep wound. At the sight, something within her snapped.

"I beg of you. Stop this!" she cried, her honey-brown eyes wide and beseeching. "You'll kill him. I'll do anything, even give myself to you, if only you'll spare his life."

Ferox leaned toward her, his eyes suddenly as

slitted as his reptile's. Alia swallowed hard against her revulsion.

"But," he whispered, his words toneless and chilling, "I already have your body, willing or not. Have you nothing else of value to bargain with?"

The color drained from her face. She forced herself to return his gaze. His dead eyes glittered with an evil anticipation, as if he already knew what he wanted. But what? she wondered frantically.

The Crystal! Of course, it had to be the Crystal's power he desired. Though he physically possessed it, up until now it had been useless to him, and he was clever enough to know the only way to control it was through the manipulation of a willing Crystal Master. But how terrible to give over its power to one such as he!

A choking sound caught Alia's attention. Her vision swiveled back to an appalling scene. The serpent's tail had wound itself around Teran's neck and was slowly strangling him. He struggled mightily, attempting to wrench free of the encircling bonds. Bloodied and torn, he fought back as best he could, but Alia realized his death was but a few moments away.

She grabbed Ferox's arm, her nails digging into his flesh. "Just tell me what you want," she cried, loathe to willingly reveal her Crystal abilities to him. "Whatever I have, I will give you!"

He grimly smiled down at her. "If you're unaware of it, it's not yours to give, and if that's the case, you've nothing to offer. Such a shame," Ferox sighed melodramatically, his glance turning to Teran. "A terrible way to die, strangling to death."

The cruel words burned into Alia's brain. Her knees buckled, and she sank to the floor. Death—

how she hated it. First her beloved mother, then Vates—and now Teran. She was surrounded by death, its gnarled, grasping hands dragging her down, stealing between her and everyone she'd ever come to love.

It couldn't end this way again. It just couldn't. She was the chosen one, her destiny entwined with that of the Crystal. And the Crystal was now so near. Why wouldn't it help her? Why couldn't it save Teran?

A white light appeared in her mind, blinding in its flashing brilliance. The Crystal! The realization surged through Alia, filling her with a fierce joy. It *would* help her, no matter what her decision.

She rose to her feet beside Ferox's throne. "Spare Teran," she cried, "and I'll show you the Crystal's power!"

An exultant smile leaped to the man's brutal lips. "If you can truely do as you say, Teran's life will be spared. You will do more than show me its power, though. You will harness it to my eternal bidding. Agreed?"

Alia wet her dry lips. The Crystal forgive me, she thought. "Agreed."

"Take care you don't disappoint me. I can be quite savage when crossed."

She met his warning glance with a defiant one of her own. "I care not for your threats. Call off the serpent. Now! If Teran dies, no amount of coercion will make me activate the Crystal."

"As you wish."

He pointed his small box toward the monstrous snake. It froze for an instant in its relentless throttling of Teran. Then, with a terrible hiss, it released its grip. Teran fell limply to the floor and lay there, unmoving. The serpent slithered away, back to its pit in the floor.

A look of respect gleamed in Ferox's eyes. "We'll make quite a team, you and I. Perhaps joint rulers of the Imperium some sol."

He signaled to a servant, who hurried over with a golden box shaped like a geode. On it was engraved an intricate design of the mutant weaving spider, emblem of Aranea. He carefully opened the box and removed a clear, multifaceted stone.

"Now, show me the Knowing Crystal's power."

For an instant Alia stared at it, nearly overcome with the impulse to snatch the Crystal from Ferox's hand. Control yourself, she firmly thought, marshalling her iron discipline back around her.

She looked up at him. "Have the guards bring Teran to me. I must be certain he lives."

"You test my patience," her captor growled. "Have care not to push me too far."

Ferox motioned for his guards. "Bring him to me." He pointed to where Teran lay.

Alia watched as the guards removed the chains and roughly dragged Teran toward them. They halted a few meters from the platform, awaiting further orders.

She turned to the man beside her. "Unchain me."

With an impatient grimace, Ferox did as she asked. Alia ran down the steps to where the guards still held Teran's limp form between them. She knelt in front of him and gently raised his drooping head. Tenderly, she brushed away a lock of hair that had fallen into his eyes. His face was bloody, one eye almost swollen shut. Alia stroked his cheek, his beard soft beneath her palm.

"Teran?" she whispered, her voice choked by unshed tears burning at the back of her throat. "Teran, can you hear me?"

His eyes flickered open. "Alia?" he said, so low and

hoarse she could scarcely hear him. "I know . . . what you promised. I . . . I beg you. Don't sacrifice yourself and the Crystal . . . for me. What is my life . . . to that of the Imperium?"

Tears glistened in her eyes. All her doubts about him faded in the poignancy of that moment. "The Crystal forgive me, Teran," Alia murmured brokenly, "but all I care about is you—and that you live."

"Enough!" Ferox bellowed from behind them. "You have what you wanted. You have ascertained that he is alive. Now it's time for the commencement of your vow. Come here."

"Farewell, Teran." *My love,* her heart added before she let him go. She climbed the steps back to Ferox.

The guards began to drag Teran away. He fought to free himself, but his wounds had weakened him to the point of exhaustion. He felt the heavy fog of unconsciousness enfold him. With one last effort he half-turned to see Alia draw near to Ferox. A powerful, black-clad arm possessively encircled her shoulders.

"Alia . . ." Teran moaned. Then everything went dark.

CHAPTER 11

A HEAVY FEELING OF DESOLATION SETTLED OVER ALIA, as she watched Teran forcibly hauled away. Would he survive his wounds with no one to care for him? Could she truely trust Ferox to spare his life?

Alia turned to her captor. "Where are they taking him?"

"He is being seen to the front door, so to speak." Ferox smiled thinly. "My guards will deposit him on the other side of the moat. Without his rope, I doubt he'll be able to get back in. Even if he does, it'll be too late. You and the Crystal will be mine." As he spoke, he ran a possessive hand up Alia's arm.

She controlled the urge to pull back, though she was unable to suppress the wave of nausea that rolled over her. She had offered the Crystal and herself to this man. If Teran were to live, she must keep that promise.

Ferox's hand tightened painfully around Alia's

arm. "You've wasted enough time. Show me your powers." In his palm, Ferox once more revealed the Knowing Crystal.

Unable to tear her gaze from it, Alia stared in wonder. Hardly larger than her fist, its many-faceted surface appeared dark and lackluster. Could this be the same bright stone she had seen in her visions? Confronted with the task of publicly communing with the famous Crystal, Alia's courage suddenly dissipated.

What if she failed to key it? Glancing up at Ferox's foreboding face, she instinctively knew the answer. Well, at the very least, she consoled herself, she'd guaranteed Teran's escape.

"Know first that you cannot betray me and kill Teran," Alia began. "The Crystal will tell me. I'll see to it you then lose its power—forever."

"Yes, yes," Ferox interrupted, his irritation growing. "My revenge against Teran is of little import, when compared to the unlimited power of the Crystal. Now show me. I grow weary of your games."

Closing her eyes, Alia uttered a fervent prayer to any benevolent god who might be listening. Then, inhaling a shaky breath, she turned her mind inward, to that deep place where she had learned to find the Crystal.

There was nothing, except the dark emptiness of her own soul. She felt alone. Had the Crystal deserted her? Was it angry with her for binding its powers over to Ferox? She begged its forgiveness and beseeched it to understand. If she had done wrong, let it show her the proper path, for she had acted with the same heart that had finally enabled her to commune with it.

A faint light began to glow. Alia's heart swelled with gladness. The Crystal was still hers. As she watched, the light strengthened, casting aside the dark shadows in her soul. A sparkling stone appeared, its flashing brilliance filling her with peace.

A gasp spread through the assembly hall. Alia opened her eyes to see the same bright light emanating from the crystal in Ferox's hand. Fear, stark and vivid, glittered in his eyes, the harsh lines of terror marring his flawless face. He appeared on the verge of dropping the stone or flinging it from him.

With a beckoning gesture she called it. The Crystal rose from Ferox's trembling hand. Dancing through the air, its facets hurling shining rays as it turned, the Crystal came to Alia.

A luminous splendor bathed her features. She closed her eyes, and from deep within her soul, she heard it speak.

It whispered of a quest fulfilled, of special powers, of unexpected fruitfulness. As the knowledge seeped through her, Alia felt a curious sense of release and a renewed purpose.

"Give it back. Return the Crystal!"

Startled from her vision, Alia reluctantly opened her eyes. Ferox's face was contorted like some wild, cornered animal. "No," was her simple reply. "The Crystal chooses its own master. That has never been you. I was wrong to promise you something I had no right to give. The choice was never mine."

"You would play false with me? Think again, femina. I will have your life before I allow that to happen!" With a cry of rage, Ferox sprang at Alia, a dagger in his hand.

Alia watched the man approach. For an instant, as her eyes followed the dagger in its trajectory toward her heart, she imagined it the awful weapon of her dreams, but as her mesmerized eyes examined the knife more closely, she realized it wasn't the same at all. There were no jewels in its intricately carved handle, no tiny spiders engraved along the curve of the blade.

She previously hadn't remembered the spiders, but now, in this flashing moment between life and death, Alia knew they'd always been there. It had been an Aranean dagger. Her dream had warned of death on her home planet.

Wrenching herself from her trancelike state, Alia lifted a hand to ward off the fatal blow. Before his blade could strike, her outstretched fingers touched him. She heard a strangled cry, and Ferox plummeted to the floor, unconscious.

Alia stared down at the crumpled form of her attacker, then her eyes raised to scan the room. When she saw the guards make a threatening move toward her, she wheeled about, the Crystal gleaming brightly in her hand.

"Touch me and suffer the same fate as your master," she cried to the onrushing mass of soliders.

They hesitated but a secundae in their mad charge, then fled, their weapons clattering to the floor behind them. Alia turned back to Ferox, silently examining his unmoving form. He was not dead, of this she was instinctively certain. Perhaps it would be better for her and Teran if he were. She moved toward Ferox, when the warning voice of the Crystal halted her.

With a sigh, Alia stopped. A Crystal Master was forbidden to take another's life, she heard the stone say, no matter what the personal consequences. To do so would banish one from the Crystal's presence for all eternity. Even as it spoke, its light flickered erratically and dimmed.

With a strange sense of foreboding, Alia placed the now fading stone into the pouch hanging from her belt and securely fastened it. Turning from the body at her feet, she walked toward the doors that led out of the fortress.

The further Alia drew away from the presence of the disturbing lord of the castle, the more her steps and heart lightened. She had what she'd come for. The past sols of doubt and hardship were over. Ahead lay a new beginning, a future once more bright.

Alia's steps quickened. She was eager to leave this place of dark despair and be free once more, unfettered by confining walls and hostile threats. And, most of all, eager to rejoin Teran.

As Teran regained consciousness, he became aware of a feeling of restraint. Thinking he was still in the grasp of the guards, he struggled, striking out blindly.

A soft voice pierced the haze. It was Alia. The realization calmed him, and he relaxed in her arms. Though only a dream, they were together at last. That was all that mattered.

Teran felt something wet and cool trickle down the side of his face. He brushed at it, irritated at the intrusion into his comforting fantasy. His hand touched soft, smooth flesh, and he opened his eyes.

Alia smiled down at him. "Welcome back to the land of the living. How do you feel?"

Teran stared at her, struggling to focus his vision and clear the lingering cobwebs of confusion from his mind. She really was here, holding him. But how could that be?

"I . . . I don't know," he said, through a throat raw and dry. "Do you have any water? I'm thirsty."

She laughed, the sound light and girlish. How good it was to hear her happy again, Teran thought. With Alia's help, he raised his head to drink from her cupped hand. The icy water soothed his parched throat. With a sigh of pleasure, he sank back against her.

His immediate physical needs satisfied, his attention was drawn to the tantalizing sight of Alia's full cleavage, bending over him. "Nice dress."

She looked down at herself and flushed. "You're incorrigible," she sputtered in exasperation. "Wounded and flat on your back, and the first thing you notice is my dress. Or should I say, the noticeable lack of it?"

"What did you expect, with your bosom flashing in front of my face?" Teran grinned wickedly. "I may be hurt, but I'm not blind."

With a snort of disgust, Alia pushed him away and stood up. "It doesn't sound like you're as weak as you pretend to be, either. See if you can get to your feet. We need to leave this place as soon as possible."

For the first time, Teran glanced around. It was dawn and they were outside Ferox's fortress, just clear of the drawbridge. Thinking back, all he could remember was being unceremoniously dumped here by the guards. After that, everything was a blank.

Yet Alia was now at his side, apparently unharmed. How had she escaped? Where were Ferox and his men? He opened his mouth to ask her, then quickly clamped it shut. It wasn't the time. The danger was too acute to waste in asking questions that were easily answered at a later, much safer moment.

"I see your point." He crawled to his knees. Even that effort left him dizzy and weak. Teran looked up at Alia. "Nonetheless, I won't be going anywhere without your help. Would you lend me your hand?"

"Only if you promise not to look."

Teran sighed in mock dismay. "The things I sacrifice to please you." He grudgingly closed his eyes, however, and lifted his hand.

With Alia's assistance, he struggled to his feet. For a few secundae he swayed precariously, his throbbing skull causing bright lights to dance before his eyes. The light-headed sensation gradually dissipated. Finally, Teran was able to take a tentative step forward.

"Good," Alia encouraged him. "We'll take it slow and easy. We've got at least a couple of horas before we make it back to my equs. Just tell me when you need to rest."

They started out, their journey awkward as they stumbled through the rock-strewn valley. Several times, Teran almost lost his balance. Save for the support of Alia's arms he would have fallen. Between his weakness and the effort it took for Alia to brace him, their rest stops were frequent.

The coolness of the early sol rapidly warmed, as the red sun ascended in the wakening sky. Soon, it was blazingly hot, and the scattered stones offered little shelter from the harsh rays.

Still, they staggered on. Finally, Alia glimpsed a dark mass of trees far ahead. She stopped and turned to Teran. "My equs is not far. Rest here. I'll soon return."

He struggled to hide his utter exhaustion and tried to dissemble the taut look of pain, but he was too weary to mask any of it successfully. "I . . . I can go on. My equs is hidden there with yours. Once I am on its back, I'll be able to travel for many more horas. Besides, what if Ferox's men await you there?"

"I have the Crystal," she said. "I am safer than you. Now, let me help you lie down so you can rest while I'm gone. Alone, I can be back with the equs before we could ever reach it together."

Knowing she was right, Teran reluctantly allowed Alia to assist him to the ground next to a large boulder. She stared down at him for a few secundae, then turned to go.

"Alia," Teran called to her. "You never did tell me how you managed to escape Ferox."

She smiled over her shoulder. "That's a long story. One that can wait until we're well out of reach of his fortress. Now rest until I return." As if to forestall any further protest, she turned from him and resolutely set out.

Her slim form, clad in the clinging gold dress, slowly disappeared into the hazy heat waves rising from the plateau floor. Teran watched for a long while. He saw Alia stumble repeatedly and cursed the fragile sandals that provided her such poor footing.

The dress, however comely, was definitely not suited for riding either. It would provide little protection against the sun's rays. Perhaps they could fashion something out of one of the lighter blankets.

Lulled by the warmth of the sun, Teran dozed. The next thing he knew, Alia was bending over him.

"Teran, I've returned with the equs. Do you feel able to ride?"

He struggled to his feet. "Most certainly," he mumbled groggily. His stance was unsteady, but with Alia's aid he was finally able to mount his animal.

For a long while, as they once again treked up to the mountains, Teran seriously doubted his ability to persevere. His wounds throbbed painfully, and the jarring gait of the equs rapidly drained his waning strength. It took all he could do to grimly hold on. At last, the passing horas mercifully drugged him into numbness.

A little after noon Alia turned to look back at him. Teran clung to the gray equs' mane, his head resting wearily on the animal's massive neck for support. Though all of his wounds had clotted, he still looked a bloody mess. He desperately needed tending.

"Let's rest a while," she said, in what she hoped was a nonchalant voice.

He shook his head. "No. As you said, the further we remove ourselves from that fortress the better. The sol is still young. If you lead my equs, I can sleep as we ride. That's all I need—just a little sleep."

Alia scrutinized Teran. He looked so pale and exhausted. His tunic hung from him in shreds, revealing jagged red wounds from his combat with the serpent. She really needed to cleanse and dress them. But if they could just put a little more distance between them and Ferox . . .

She sighed. Turning her equs, Alia rode back to Teran. "Give me your reins. We'll go on for a while longer, but if you show any signs of falling off, we stop."

"Have no fear of that," he said, a weak smile tipping the corners of his mouth. "Sleeping on an equs is an old warrior's trick, one at which I've become quite adept."

They rode on. Teran, true to his word, managed to stay on his beast, and Alia decided to ride on as long as he slept. Surprisingly, that consumed the rest of the sol.

Just before dusk, they reached the overlook of the fortress and the spot where they had rested that last nocte in the small cave. *This was where I used the govern keys on Teran,* Alia recalled, as she glanced around at the now familiar scene. A sharp pang shot through her. He had suffered so much on her account.

She halted her equs and, dismounting, walked back to Teran. He opened his eyes, awakened by the sudden cessation of movement. "Why did you stop?"

he mumbled sleepily. "I can ride for several horas more."

"Maybe you can, but I can't." She raised her hands to him. "It will be dark soon, and we have finally reached shelter. Come down."

He glanced around him, recognizing the area. "Ah, yes, I remember this place," he said, his eyes glinting with tired amusement. "Should I expect to find you here in the morning?"

"Only if you promise to stop teasing me." Suddenly, Alia felt uncomfortable. The intensity of his gaze now echoed his question, as if asking for reassurance of a more permanent nature—some committment perhaps?

Her heart melted at his glance. It was becoming increasingly difficult to deny him anything, but now was definitely not the time.

"Are you going to stay up there all nocte?" she asked, trying to make herself sound stern. "There is camp to set up, and your wounds need tending."

Teran sighed in defeat, realizing the moment had passed. He awkwardly swung down from the equs. For an instant, he teetered with an attack of severe dizziness. Only Alia's quick support prevented him from unceremoniously toppling to the ground.

"Just as I thought," she murmured in his ear. "You have pushed yourself far too hard. If I help you, can you make it to the cave?"

"Yes, I . . . I think so."

They made their halting way toward the little hollow in the rock. Once there, Alia assisted Teran to sit down against the wall. She ran back to the equs and quickly unlashed the bedrolls. Returning to his side, she made a bed under the low overhang of stone.

"Climb in," she ordered.

For once Teran did not argue. He slowly crawled to

his blanket and lowered himself onto the makeshift pallet. Almost immediately, his eyes closed.

He's more weary than even he will admit, thought Alia. She stroked his face, and his eyes opened.

"Rest for a while." She tenderly smiled down at him. "I will care for the equs and bring in the supplies. Then I will cleanse and dress your wounds."

She returned to the animals, hobbled them and removed their tack. Some tall grass grew nearby, and Alia picked several handfuls which she used to rub their sweaty coats. Finally finished, she gathered up the saddlebags and water flask and headed back to Teran.

He was asleep. As much as Alia hated to wake him, she knew it wasn't wise to put off tending his wounds any longer. She only hoped they weren't already infected.

"Teran," she said, hesitantly touching him, "forgive me, but your wounds need tending."

Alia paused to rummage through the bags until she found some clean rags and the jar of foul smelling ointment. She held it up to Teran. "Are you sure Vates said this was a medicinal ointment?" Her pretty nose wrinkled in distaste. "Smells more like rotted dung."

He smiled at her. "It's definitely for wounds. I'd forgotten we still had it. Its healing properties are next to miraculous."

"Good," Alia muttered, as she twisted open the water flask and moistened a clean rag. "A few miracles at this point would be more than welcome."

Teran's eyes narrowed speculatively. "Speaking of miracles, are you ever going to tell me how you escaped from the fortress?"

She glanced up at him, the indecision apparent in her eyes. "I suppose I owe you some explanation, but

I am still confused about it myself. I hope it will make sense."

"Just tell me what happened," he quietly urged her. "If I get lost, I'll let you know."

Alia felt for the Crystal, secured in the small pouch dangling from a cord attached to her belt. Reassured it was still there, she began to speak.

"After they took you away, Ferox demanded I key the Crystal. It spoke to me, telling me of many things, some of which I have yet to understand. But most importantly, it told me of a power all mature feminas of my planet possess—the ability to paralyze. That's what happened to Ferox, when he attempted to get the Crystal back from me."

Dark brows knitted into a puzzled frown. "But what happened to the guards?" Teran asked. "And why haven't you used this power of yours before?"

"The guards all fled when they saw what happened to Ferox." Alia lowered her eyes, a becoming flush spreading across her face. "In answer to your second question, the power to stun was not mine until it was brought to maturity."

"And exactly how was it brought to maturity, Alia?" he asked, raising himself up on one elbow. From her growing discomfiture, Teran sensed her reply would be well worth hearing.

"By . . . by mating with you," she said, finally lifting her eyes to his. "The first act of joining frees the stun power locked inside each femina."

There was a long silence. "And what is the significance of this singular power?" Teran finally asked.

Alia shook her head. "I do not know. It has yet to be explained to me."

Try as she might, Alia couldn't wrench her gaze from his. Teran's gray eyes bore into hers, probing to her very soul yet revealing nothing of his own. The enigmatic expression on his bearded face confused her. What was he thinking? Had she offended him?

His low laugh suddenly shattered the heavy quiet. "It seems I've been useful to you in ways one would never have expected. Do you have any more surprises in store for me?"

Alia stiffened. Had he guessed the rest? Should she tell him?

"None that I care to discuss at the moment," she murmured, her courage fleeing her. "Now be still. I need to clean your wounds."

And please don't ask me any more, she silently begged him. I don't want to lie to you, but I just can't talk about it. First, I need time to sort it all out myself.

Teran obediently lowered himself back onto the blanket. Alia spread the torn tunic apart to bare his chest and slipped it off his shoulders. She stared at the tattered garment, trying to decide if it was worth saving. It wasn't. With an exasperated shake of her head, she tossed it aside.

Alia winced when she more closely inspected the wound in Teran's left arm and the deep slash across his abdomen. Ever so gently, she cleansed them, steeling herself to continue even when the pain caused Teran to gasp. Finally, Alia applied the soothing, smelly ointment and bandaged the wounds with fresh strips of cloth.

The gash on Teran's left thigh was less severe and was quickly cared for. As she next turned to the scratches and bruises on his face, she frowned.

"Do I look that bad?" Teran's bemusement intruded into her intense focus on the task.

"What?" she asked. "Oh, no, you look fine, underneath all the blood and swelling. I was just trying to keep from hurting you. There!" she said, throwing down the blood-stained rag. "All done."

"Thank you, Alia."

"There's no need to thank me. I could never begin to repay you for all you've done for me. Who would have thought I'd have to come to a prison planet to find a man of your courage and loyalty?"

"Perhaps you just inspire others with your own courage." The words were spoken with a quiet emphasis.

Alia shook her head, embarrassed. "No, no. I am not brave. I would never have willingly set out on this quest if it had been up to me. There was no other choice; no one else was . . ."

"Worthy?" Teran provided his opinion. "Courage, Alia, doesn't consist of brave deeds of your own choosing. It's found in summoning the heart to attempt tasks and right wrongs that appear beyond one's abilities or one's strength. Sometimes," he sighed, "even against one's people."

"To turn against one's people?" Alia shuddered. "That would ask more of me than I could ever give. Betray my own kind? Never!"

Teran shrugged. "There is much to be said for loyalty, but the first thought should always be for your own heart. Now," he said, deciding to change the subject, "have we anything left to eat in those bags? I'm starved."

Alia dug through the leather pouches and triumphantly produced some dried cerasa fruit. "It's all we have, but we should make it to the forest by tomorrow. I think I remember a few fruit trees growing just outside it, and there's always the possibility of catching game." She handed him half the fruit.

Teran laughed as he bit off a hunk of dried cerasa. "Ah, yes, the forest. Well, at least this time there'll be no traps to slow us—unless, of course, Ferox has managed to slip ahead and is waiting there."

"No," Alia said, a faraway look in her eyes. "The Crystal says Ferox is still within his fortress. We are safe—at least for this nocte."

"Yes, you're right, of course," Teran muttered dryly. He bit into another piece of dried cerasa fruit.

At his nonchalant admission of his Crystal abilities, Alia tensed, her face clouding with a wary uneasiness. She laid aside her own portion of food, her appetite gone. Turning from him, she began stuffing her supplies back into the saddlebags.

Teran immediately noticed the change, the sudden heaviness to the atmosphere that had, only secundae ago, been warm and happy. Once again she was withdrawing from him, cold and aloof. Just like . . . in Ferox's assembly hall!

He lay down the remaining portion of his meal. "Alia, what is it?" Teran touched her. "Have I offended you in some way? Tell me what it is. Let us talk about it."

She shook his hand away. "There is nothing for us to talk about. Go to sleep. You'll need your rest for the next few sols of travel ahead of us."

"No!"

As swift and hard as his reply, Teran's hand shot out to grasp her arm. He roughly pulled Alia to him. Rolling atop her, he pinned her to the ground, his face only a warm breath away.

"No," he repeated, his voice more controlled this time. "Neither of us will sleep until I know the reason for your anger. Tell me, Alia. Please."

Alia gazed up into eyes burning with confused pain. She fought against the surge of longing that flamed within her, but he was too close, too warm, too stimulating. She smoldered with a heat that quickly grew to suffocating proportions. The hard, muscular planes of his body pressed into hers, until

225

she felt as if they were fusing into one.

"Let me go," Alia cried. "I command it!"

"No."

"You forget yourself, Teran. You're my claimee, and as such, I can expect unquestioning obedience. Now release me this instant!"

His eyes gleamed in the dimming light, narrowing until they were mere slits of icy blackness. She saw his jaws tighten, the muscles spasming furiously as he fought to control himself.

In one sharp moment of insight, Alia also saw the pain beneath the anger, raw and deep. She had hurt him. Her voice softened, and the block of ice around her heart began to melt.

"Please, Teran."

With a shuddering sigh, he released her. Rolling away, Teran crawled back to his bed.

Alia watched the uneven rise and fall of the broad back turned toward her, wondering what to do, what to say. She had hurt him, but it shouldn't matter what he wanted. Yet it did. Would there never be an end to it then? The barriers between them, the eternal misunderstandings, the pain?

"Why didn't you tell me, Teran?" she forced herself to begin. "Why did you hide the secret of your Crystal abilities from me all this time? I can forgive much, but not that, never that."

Teran slowly turned to face her, his expression guarded. "Is that what this is about? My Crystal powers? You think I've known of them all along and been hiding them to use against you when the time was right? Is that it?"

"Yes."

He exhaled a deep breath. "I'll admit I have known for some time now, since Vates told me that I, too, would be a Crystal Master, but I didn't believe it then.

I thought my old friend was talking in another of his many riddles. It wasn't until I entered Ferox's keep that I realized his words were true. It was only then I truly knew it was the Crystal that spoke to me."

He paused to shake his head, his expression bewildered. "The thought of it still fills me with wonder and a strange joy. But as for hiding the truth from you, that was never my intent. There just hasn't been an opportunity to speak of such things—at least not until now, anyway."

"Perhaps I misjudged too quickly," she said. "A truce then, if you will. The morrow is another sol and time enough for us to work through the problems between us." Alia offered him her hand.

After a moment's hesitation Teran grasped her small hand in his. "A truce—until we've the luxury of time to talk again."

She withdrew her hand and busied herself with laying out her bedroll next to his. Her glance caught his, intently studying her efforts.

"The nocte in these mountains will be cold. There's no wood to be gathered here. Without the warmth of a fire, it is better if we lie close to conserve body heat."

"As you wish, Domina."

"Teran!" Alia lay down and pulled her blanket over her.

He stifled a chuckle as he moved over to lay beside her. "Doubts or no about me, I'm glad we're both alive and able to share another camp. This time last nocte I doubted I'd ever see you again, much less survive the next sunrise. At this moment, it is enough we are alive—and together."

"Rest well, Teran," she replied, unable to find any other words that wouldn't betray the burgeoning emotions of her heart.

He sighed, pulling her close, his lips moving to tenderly kiss the top of her head. "Rest well, Alia."

After a while, both fell into a deep sleep. Gradually, in the freedom of slumber, they found their way into each other's arms, at long last gaining the solace both desperately needed.

CHAPTER 12

"THERE IS A QUESTION I HAVE OF YOU, IF YOU CARE TO speak of it," Alia said, as she cleansed Teran's wounds the next morning.

"And what might that be?" He glanced up from his fascinated preoccupation with Alia's soft, delicate hands, so gently tending his slashed arm. Though slightly inflamed, the wound appeared to be healing rapidly. That, combined with a good nocte's rest, had greatly renewed Teran's vigor.

When she hesitated and instead busied herself applying the healing ointment, he prodded her, his curiosity rising. "What is it? You know you're free to ask me anything."

"That nocte in Ferox's fortress, he spoke of my not being the first of your feminas. What did he mean, Teran?"

He didn't reply. Alia finished wrapping the bandage around his arm and tied it in place. When she glanced up at him, she was startled at the depth of anguish burning in his eyes. Alia realized the reason for his pain, and suddenly her heart felt heavy. *He loved, perhaps even still loves, that femina.* The thought filled her with despair. *How can I ever hope to compete with a beautiful memory?*

"Teran?" Alia took his hand. "It is of no import. Please forget I even asked it."

He shook his head. "No, you have a right to hear the tale. Perhaps it'll help you understand the extent of my hatred for Ferox and help you accept what I must now do."

He paused to inhale a deep breath before continuing. "Darla and I were betrothed. She was beautiful, with long golden hair, the bluest eyes and the most delicate and feminine of bodies. When I held her in my arms, it was as if I engulfed her, hiding her away from the world and all its ugliness."

His features hardened into a cold mask of rage. "But even I couldn't protect her forever. While I was away on a Bellatorian mission, Ferox raided Moraca, Darla's home planet. He and his men massacred over half the capital's inhabitants. Most of the rest were easily captured and sold into slavery. He took Darla for his own."

Teran's breath caught. For a secundae he couldn't go on. Even now, after all these cycles, the memories ripped at him, tearing afresh the agonizing wounds of his heart. He bowed his head, struggling against the pain, his hands knotted into fists.

"He took her against her will, again and again, until she fled from him in the only way she could—into the deepest recesses of her mind. My men and I were finally able to overcome the stronghold where he'd imprisoned her. Ferox, unfortunately, eluded capture, but he left behind Darla—or what was left of her."

Alia's grip on his hand tightened. "That is enough, Teran. You need not tell me more." She couldn't bear to see him like this, so twisted and suffering.

"No, Alia, you must hear it all and know the depth of my hatred and why I hunger so for revenge," he said, his voice muffled and strangely hoarse. "I brought Darla home with me, back to Bellator. I hoped, in time, to ease her horrible memories and regain what we'd had before, but it was never to be. She remained terrified of all men and, inexplicably, of me most of all. Even my slightest touch set off hysterical screams.

"As time went on, Darla couldn't even bear the sight of me. She had to be kept in protective seclusion in a locked, darkened room, allowing only the presence of her old nursemaid near her." His mouth quirked into a sad smile. "Fortunately, for her at least, Darla's time of suffering was short. She died only six monates after I'd rescued her, leaping to her death from her bedroom window during one of her frequent noctemares. They say she thought she was running from me."

Teran fell silent then, his head bowed. Alia stared at him, unshed tears burning the back of her eyes, wondering what to say and how to comfort him. But there was nothing that could be said, nothing that could ease the torment of that lost love. All she could give him was her presence and the comfort of her touch.

They sat there for a long while, as the searing freshness of Teran's renewed sorrow burned out. At last he squared his shoulders and looked up, his glance turning to boldly meet Alia's.

"Now you know. Now do you understand my hatred for Ferox?"

She silently nodded. The basis for his long-standing enmity was more than clear, yet still it bothered her. To bear such hatred and allow it to fester for so long without surcease was not healthy.

Alia couldn't help the small shudder that shot through her. She had thought she'd known the man and understood all his motivations however different they may have been from hers, but now she was no longer certain. Such hatred for another must have eaten away at a part of him, leaving a rotting emptiness within. Was there enough heart left to ever love again?

"I'm going back, Alia."

"What did you say?" His totally unexpected statement startled her. "Going back where, and for what reason?"

"To lay in wait for Ferox. He is sure to pursue us, for the Crystal as well as for vengeance. I'll be waiting for him. He'll not escape me this time."

The words were uttered in a flat, calm voice, sending a spine-tingling chill through Alia. So this is what the feud had finally come to, an all-out fight to the finish in which neither would probably survive. It was his right, perhaps even the inevitable end to the soul-corroding hatred. Yet to lose him!

"No, I cannot allow it," Alia cried, her love refusing to allow such senseless self-destruction.

A look of implacable determination settled over Teran's features. "But you can no longer stop me, can you, Alia?"

No, she couldn't, she realized, now that she'd forever spurned the use of the govern keys. They were still buried here. It would be easy to get to them, yet the painfully fresh memory of Teran, writhing for endless horas in agony, was more than Alia could bear. No matter what, she could never use the keys again.

She raised honey-brown eyes to him. "You are correct, Teran. I cannot stop you."

"And better for both of us that you don't try. Your primary purpose must be the return of the Knowing Crystal. If I stay behind and stop Ferox, my efforts almost assure the success of your quest."

He gave her a wry smile. "A small price to pay, wouldn't you say? My life for that of the entire Imperium? In the end, we'd both get what we wanted—I, my long-desired revenge, and you, the power and glory of being the sole Crystal Master."

He was right, Alia grudgingly admitted. His plan solved so many problems all at once. There was no further need to worry about the inevitable rivalry over mastery of the Knowing Crystal, no more fear of betrayal—and no hope for a life together. But that was a weak, selfish reason. What really mattered, in the light of eternity, was the Knowing Crystal rather than their puny, personal desires.

A spark of hope flared within her. Didn't the Knowing Crystal rightfully have a voice in this decision? Indeed, what *would* it say?

Teran thoughtfully studied Alia, a look of longing flashing across his face, before his expression once more resumed its masklike facade. He forced himself to turn from her, before his weakening resolve crumbled. By all the moons of Agrica, it was hard to leave her! Yet if he didn't, she possibly faced the same fate as his first love—and he'd never risk losing Alia in that way.

A small hand reached out to stop him.

"Wait, Teran. This is a decision too colored by outside influences for us to make. We risk choosing the wrong course, as mired as both of us are in past experiences. It is a choice best made by the Crystal. Agreed?"

He hesitated. To leave the decision up to the Knowing Crystal? Considering its renowned capabilities, it seemed the wisest course. Yet what if the Crystal ordered him to refrain from killing Ferox? Could he obey? Could he ignore the gnawing, nearly intolerable need for revenge that haunted every waking and sleeping moment?

He was so very tired of continually sacrificing his own desires on the exalted altar of moral responsibility, yet the lessons of his old teacher could not be denied. The sense of right and justice ran too deep. With a weary sigh, Teran turned back to face Alia.

"Agreed."

"Then let us ask the Crystal together, so there'll be no doubt." Alia opened the pouch at her waist.

Teran's only answer was a nod, as he watched her reach into the little bag and draw out the Crystal. Holding it up between them, Alia closed her eyes. An intent look of concentration spread across her face. He felt a warmth flow through him and knew it for what it was. Closing his eyes, Teran listened.

It was a long while later before the Crystal's light faded. Teran was the first to return to the present. He slowly, almost reluctantly, opened his eyes. Tears streamed down Alia's pale face. He took the now dull stone from her outstretched palm and replaced it in her pouch.

The movement drew Alia from her trance. Brown eyes flickered open, eyes that gleamed with a joy that belied the moisture still coursing down her cheeks. As he finished the task of securing the Crystal she stood there, momentarily weak in her relief.

Teran finally looked up at her. "Why do you cry?"

He stifled an impulse to wipe away her tears. A mixture of angry frustration and affection warred within, both directed at the femina standing before him.

"Because I am glad the Crystal forbade you to take Ferox's life. You will obey its decree, won't you?"

He shot her a wrathful glance. "Only because it made me see that for now it's the wiser course. But I'm not the Crystal's slave, Alia, nor anyone's anymore. Don't ever forget that."

"We should all be slave to reason, Teran. It is the wiser course." She took his hand. "Come, it is time I finish tending your wounds. The sol is fast slipping away, and we must be going."

He resisted her gentle tug. "There is yet one thing more. The govern keys. Show me where you hid them."

The shock of his words halted her. Had the Crystal told him about the keys? It must have. "Why?"

"You cannot leave them here. They must be in your possession when we arrive at the transport station. If not, I cannot leave Carcer. It isn't the policy of the Imperium to release claimees without some evident means of control."

He smiled tightly. "In the meantime, however, they'll remain in *my* possession."

"As you wish. Come, I'll show you where I buried them."

They covered a good distance that sol, thanks to Teran's renewed vigor. Just before twilight they reached the edge of the sinister forest. Camp was set up outside it. With the fruit they were able to gather and the long-eared lepus Teran trapped, a simple but adequate supper was eaten. After dividing the watch, the nocte settled into one of heavy quiet.

The morrow dawned, hot and bright. After passing through the forest without difficulty, they began the climb back into the mountains. The trail was tedious and anything but pleasant. Near noon, they passed by the cave high on the mountainside. Gazing at it as she rode along, Alia wondered if that nocte in Teran's arms had been nothing more than a beautiful dream. With a poignant pain in her heart, she mourned for what would never be again.

At that moment, Teran turned and caught her eye. Something intense flared between them. With a fleeting surge of joy, Alia knew that he still longed for her. A stray rock careening down the mountainside distracted their attention. The spell was broken. The reality of their situation, of the seemingly insurmountable barriers between them, rose once again as a taunting reminder of what could never be.

Soon afterwards they stopped for a short lunch, the meal including little conversation. Both were too immersed in their own personal pain to have much to say to the other. They mounted up and continued the now difficult, steeply winding path toward the next summit.

By dusk, they arrived at the stone monoliths marking the boundaries of Ferox's domain. A strange air of leave-taking permeated the eerie spot. Teran refused the supper meal and walked off some distance to be alone.

As she watched from camp Alia saw him slowly focus inward; the battle against the pain of losing Vates began anew. Sensing his need for privacy and the completion of a mourning long denied, she didn't press him.

In the early horas of the morning, Teran finally returned to camp, waking Alia from a restless sleep. The sol dawned far too soon for the both of them, and their tense, irritable mood did not improve with time.

In midafternoon they arrived at the oasis at the foot of the mountains. Using the remainder of the sol to rest, bathe and replenish their food supplies, they set off the next morning across the great desert of Mors. This time no sandstorms blew to hamper their progress. By the end of the third sol of travel, they had reached the last oasis.

"Well, Alia," Teran said as he removed the tack from his equs, "only three sols more and we'll be at the transport station."

He bent down and hobbled the animal. "Do you want to stay here and rest a few sols or head out on the morrow?"

Alia paused from the task of removing her mare's bridle. "I'd prefer to ride on, if you don't mind. I won't really be able to relax until I'm safe, back on Ara—." She stopped, catching herself in the act of revealing the name of her home.

Teran's brow rose a fraction. He stood up. It was obvious he'd noted her hesitation and the reason for it. He waited. When she didn't continue he finally spoke, his expression tight and grim. "And where would that be, Alia? Your planet, I mean?"

The old tentacles of suspicion slowly wound their way around her heart. "It is not yours to ask," she finally replied.

"You can say that, after all we've been through?" he asked, in a voice harsh with disbelief.

He took a step toward her. "I must know, Alia— and I mean to."

She held out a warning hand. "Don't, Teran. Don't force me to choose between you and my quest. Ask me anything, but not that."

"And why not? Haven't I earned the right to know?

Hasn't the hardship and suffering I've endured for the Crystal and you gained me at least that much?"

His words were bitter, filled with angry contempt. They elicited a comparable rage in her. "Then ask the Crystal," she taunted. "You're an admitted Crystal Master now. Discover what you need yourself."

"It won't tell me, and you know it," he growled. "It's for you to reveal, and I demand it. Can you deny me what I ask, Alia? What will you do to stop me? Stun me like you did Ferox?"

His eyes glinted like hard bits of glacial ice. "You've no other choice, now that I've your stun gun and the govern keys. Is it at last time to turn your terrible powers upon me?" As he spoke, Teran continued his inexorable advance until he towered over her, his body only millimeters away.

She cringed, her misery so acute it felt like physical pain. How could she raise a hand against him, after all he'd already been through because of her? Yet how could he demand the one thing she didn't dare give?

Alia threw back her head, her own anger rising to his challenge. "And what would you do to me, even if I didn't stun you?" she asked, her voice low. "Would you harm me to obtain the information you seem so determined to possess?"

A shudder ran through Teran's big body, as if jolted with the realization of the course their argument was taking. His breath came in ragged gasps, fueled by his suddenly impotent anger. What, indeed, would he do? Hurt the femina he loved? With a defeated groan, he strode off into the trees.

She watched until he disappeared from view. With an effort, Alia tried to calm the trembling that unexpectedly shook her body. Why, oh, why had he insisted on forcing that particular issue? What had that shattering moment of conflict gained either of them?

Lowering her hands, she turned in the opposite direction and wandered aimlessly through the trees. After a while, she reached the spring. Alia sat down on a large rock and stared, unseeing, into the deep, blue water.

Gradually, her mind grew heavy, weary from the sols of endless turmoil. Nothing mattered anymore; thinking took too much effort. A strange lethargy stole into her limbs, weighing them until even breathing required more than she could give. Alia shook her head to clear the haze that threatened to crowd out her consciousness. What, in all the heavens, was the matter with her?

A primitive urge to flee rose within. Something was wrong. Alia struggled to climb to her feet, but her body wouldn't obey. Instead, she flopped helplessly to the ground, unable to move. The sense of terrible danger grew so strong she could almost taste it. Teran, she called wordlessly. Teran, help me!

The snapping of branches caught Alia's rapidly waning awareness. With the last of her strength, she forced her head to turn in the direction of the sound.

Teran must have heard her and was coming. As her gaze fell upon the tall form of the man standing across the calm, blue expanse of the spring, the spark of hope that had so quickly flared in her breast just as cruelly extinguished.

Ferox, his men crowding around him, smiled triumphantly over at her. "So, we meet again," he chuckled wickedly. "Did you really think you could escape me?"

CHAPTER 13

SHEER FRIGHT SWEPT THROUGH ALIA. THE ENCROACH-
ing mists evaporated from her mind. If only she
could reach the Crystal, she thought, she could more
than adequately protect herself from Ferox and his
men.

Muscles strained in an effort to move her hand to
the pouch that hung at her belt. Perspiration beaded
her brow as she willed her arm to comply, yet despite
repeatedly frustrated attempts, all Alia could managed was a slight tremor of her fingers.

Curse it all! What had Ferox used on her to disable
her so? An inhalant? A neuromuscular blocking
gas?

Oh, but he was clever. Acutely aware of the danger
of her ability to stun, not to mention the power of the
Crystal in her hands, Ferox had effectively paralyzed
her. Held in the throes of the disabling drug, she was
at his mercy.

241

And what of Teran? Once she was gone and the Crystal was back in Ferox's clutches, what hope had he?

A sickening wave of impotence rolled over Alia. Teran would once again be dragged into her problems. How many more times could he hope to survive? A silent sob rose in her throat. Oh, Teran, forgive me—if you can.

"The Crystal, pretty one," Ferox prodded, aiming a lethal blaster gun at her. "Where is the Knowing Crystal? Do you have it, or does Teran?"

Alia opened her mouth to speak, unsure if any words would issue forth. "It is hidden," she rasped hoarsely. "Release me from this paralysis, and I'll take you to it."

The now familiar howl filled the air. "And let you get close enough to disable me again? I am not that stupid. All I want is the Crystal. I can wait to find someone else to key it for me, someone a little more cooperative."

"There are no others. I am the last of my line, and Teran is without issue."

Ferox snorted in derision. "Don't delude yourself. You may be the last of the line on *your* planet, but after the Crystal was lost, the royal blood was intentionally seeded throughout the other planets of the Imperium. There are sure to be others of your ability. Teran is but one example of the truth of my words. Even if neither of you cooperate, all I have to do is find another potential Crystal Master. Promises of untold wealth can do wonders for corrupting most hearts."

He paused to casually wave the gun at her, as if to add further emphasis to his next words. "Now, shall I kill you on the spot, or will you tell me where to find the Crystal? One way or another, I mean to have it."

He *would* kill her whether she answered him or not, Alia realized.

"Then try and find it," she defiantly cried, "for I—"

With a crash of breaking foliage, Teran sprang onto the bank next to Alia. In his hand he held the stun gun, a savage look of battle on his face. "Keep your distance, Ferox," he growled. "You'll have neither Alia nor the Crystal."

A deadly quiet settled over the little spring. For a brief moment, the conflict between the two men seemed deadlocked, then Ferox threw back his head and laughed, the malevolent sound reverberating throughout the clearing.

"Teran, Teran, once again you mistake yourself. You have no advantage here, if you value the femina's life. You are outnumbered. Even if it were possible to stun some of us, one of my men would still manage to take her out. Is it your wish then that yet another femina lose her life because of you?"

He grinned evilly. "That's why Darla died, you know, because I knew you cared for her. Everytime I had her, I manipulated her mind to think it was you. She came back to you terrified, didn't she? So terrified she finally took her own life. I could just as easily do the same to Alia."

A muscle twitched violently in Teran's jaw as he tried to control his fury, but Alia also saw the look of defeat creep into his eyes.

"What would it take to spare her life, then?" he finally muttered through clenched teeth. He replaced the gun back at his belt.

Ferox shrugged coldly. "Perhaps it's not possible to spare her life. I haven't quite decided. But I *have* come for the Crystal, and I mean to regain it. Perhaps if you give it to me, my temper might ease a bit."

Teran turned to Alia. "Where is the Crystal?"

"I will not give it to that animal," she protested. "It would not save my life anyway."

"Alia, where is the Crystal?" he repeated, his words taking on a quiet emphasis.

It was too much. She couldn't fight Teran as well as Ferox. Her strength rapidly ebbed in the numbing cold of her despair. "In the pouch at my waist," she whispered, her voice barely carrying to him.

Teran bent and untied the little bag from her belt. He rose to his feet. "Here it is," he shouted across the water. "What would you have me do with it?"

"Why, bring it to me, of course," Ferox cried. "It is time you learned to do my bidding. I have a mind to take you back as my personal slave."

"Neither of us will live to see that sol," Teran muttered under his breath, as he began his trek around the edge of the spring.

The unpleasant churning in his mind slowly gave way to a soft, soothing hum. The easy mental tones gradually changed, assuming the sharp clarity of words. With a start, Teran realized the Crystal was speaking. An indescribable sense of peace pervaded him. The merest hint of a smile touched his lips. So, he thought, once again we learn a little more of the vast powers of the Crystal.

His stride lengthened, until he at last reached Ferox. He positioned himself in front of his hated opponent, effectively blocking Alia's view. For a long moment the life-long adversaries glared at each other, their enmity creating a tangible, heated aura.

"Your cause was lost from the beginning, old classmate," Ferox snarled, as he extended a hand toward Teran. "No matter the outcome, I am destined to be the ultimate victor. Give me the Crystal."

With a grim smile, Teran slid his hand inside the

pouch and removed the stone. "Is this what you want?"

Uttering a frightened cry, Ferox stepped back. Before him, the Crystal glowed, blindingly bright. "Stop . . . now . . . before I order my men to kill the femina!"

"What men?" Teran replied, the tone of his voice almost pitying. "You are alone, Ferox. Once again, you've erred."

Ferox glanced wildly around him, seeing the forms of his guards blur and fade. An instant later he stood before Teran, the sole remainder of his small army. Fear etched sharply into the handsome planes of his face, Ferox aimed his blaster at Teran.

Before he could fire, Teran dropped the still glowing stone and slammed the full force of his body into Ferox. Both men fell heavily to the ground, the gun flying through the air in a spiraling arc and landing in the spring. Alia watched it sink from view, then turned her attention to the scene across the water.

Ferox had managed to extricate himself from Teran's grasp. Rising to his feet with a surprising agility, he viciously kicked out at his opponent, catching him in the chest. With a grunt of pain, Teran fell backward and lay there, stunned.

His opponent grabbed a stout tree branch. Running forward, he swung it at Teran. In the split secundae before wood made contact with flesh, Teran rolled out of the way, swiftly regaining his footing.

They faced each other. Ferox circled around, swinging his weapon, a malevolent grin on his face; Teran crouched low, ready to dodge the inevitable blows. They were evenly matched, Alia realized, these two boyhood adversaries. Both were powerful, expertly trained warriors, equal in intelligence, strength and cunning.

Growing apprehension filled her. It was quite possible Teran might not emerge victorious in this battle, no matter how dearly he desired his final revenge. She must get to the Crystal before Ferox had the opportunity to reach it. Alia felt some sensation returning, spreading down her arms to her fingertips like a river of molten fire. Ah, the pain, but one she forced herself to endure, if only it would hasten the return of her strength.

Gritting her teeth against the burning agony in her limbs, she grasped at a nearby tree root. Her fingers obeyed, clenching awkwardly around the protruding wood. Summoning forth all her effort, Alia commanded still half-numb muscles to pull her forward. She was rewarded with a small movement. Digging her nails into the soft earth, she tried again. Once more, she was compensated by a heartening advance.

Alia glanced over the spring's water to where the two men struggled, locked in mortal combat. Sweat glistened heavily on them, as both fought to gain the advantage. His face contorted in a fierce mask of hatred, Teran accepted blows as damaging as he delivered, his expression never changing.

An icy fear twisted Alia's heart. Gripped in a prison of mindless rage, Teran fought without thought to pain or injury, an unthinking automaton. He was in the throes of a blood lust, that swiftly spreading malignancy of hatred that would completely and permanently corrode the mind and soul of a person.

With a small cry, Alia renewed her crawling, her progress more coordinated as more sensation returned to her arms. She had to get to Teran before it was too late or risk losing the man she'd grown to know—and love.

Her eyes never left the men fighting before her.

They appeared on the verge of exhaustion now, their movements slow and heavy, reflexes weighted by muscles aching with fatigue. Still they battled on, both acutely aware that only one could emerge victorious—and live.

Up ahead, the sunlight caught and held the glint of something hard and shiny. The Crystal! Alia's heart gave a wild leap. If only she could get to the Crystal, perhaps she could save Teran.

The secundae dragged by as she worked her way toward the stone, half-hidden in the grass. At last she reached out to draw it near. Its small bag lay nearby. Alia pulled it to her, refastening it at her waist.

The stone held tightly in her fist, Alia awkwardly climbed to her knees. Shutting her eyes to the scene of vicious battle, she concentrated on achieving union. Make Teran stop, she begged her inward light. It will destroy him, even if he should emerge victorious. Oh, please, break through the barriers of his all-consuming hatred. Save him!

Alia waited for what seemed an eternity for the Crystal's reply. Finally, it came.

He has blocked out my voice, came the soft, gentle tones. *His heart is devoured by his death feud and will not be touched. Teran is lost to us. Forget him.*

The words of implacable logic echoed in Alia's mind, reverberating along her jangled nerves until she shook with the reality of it. Forget Teran? Give up on him? How was it possible the Crystal would ask such a thing?

She looked over at Teran with imploring eyes. He was in the spring now, the water lapping about his thighs as he grappled with Ferox. Alia saw the blond man slip and, losing his balance, fall. In a split secundae Teran was upon him, his hands throttling Ferox's neck. Black-clad arms and legs flailed wildly in an attempt to knock his attacker loose, but to no avail.

Heedless of the nerve-tingling pain, Alia struggled to her feet. She must stop him—now, before it was too late. The Crystal once more found its home in the pouch at her waist. Tying it tightly shut, she moved forward.

"Teran!" Alia screamed, as awkward legs propelled her into the water. "Teran, stop before you destroy yourself! Think of your destiny, your Crystal powers!"

Her hands grasped his shoulders, trying to wrench him from his deadly purpose. He was as if carved from stone, his body hard and immovable. She clawed at him in the hope of pain eliciting some response. He remained fixated, his face set in an expression of mindless fury. Her frantic efforts turned to blows, falling heedlessly on his body.

The cries became choking sobs. "Teran, Teran, listen to me," Alia cried. "To take another's life will . . . will negate your Crystal powers. Would you sacrifice the welfare of the entire Imperium for that? Would you deny all that Vates stood for, the sacrifice he made? If you care not for your own life, at least honor the purpose of his."

From a place faraway Teran heard a sound, sweet and tearful, calling him from his blood frenzy. Alia. Ah, Alia! He ached to go to her, but the searing hunger to choke out the life of his vilest enemy was too potent, anesthetizing him to pain, reason and honor. Far, far too long had he dreamed of this sol to so easily toss it aside, to deny himself this final satisfaction.

At dizzying speed the past rose to confront him, faces flashing before him in his mind's eye—his sweet, gentle Darla. Her memory cried out for—nay, demanded—retribution, however inadequate it ultimately might be. To spare Ferox now would be to betray her and deny the love they'd once shared. Did he not owe her the death of her violator?

The face of an old man shimmered before him, gradually replacing that of Darla's. Vates. He seemed to stand before Teran, his white robes softly glowing.

Teacher, Teran inwardly cried, help me. Understand me, and what I must do.

And what must you do, my son? the beloved specter seemed to ask. *Forever abdicate your sense of morality? Satisfy your blood lust for one brief moment in time?* The white-robed vision sadly shook his head. *No, my son. Ask me not what you must do. You already know the path to be taken.*

As the final words were spoken, Vates' apparition faded. The torment began again, more intense than before, for now Teran felt as if he were being drawn in two directions at once, his limbs torn assunder in his agonizing dilemma. He must choose—now, before the choice was no longer his.

A clamor of sounds rose in volume and intensity, until it acquired the semblance of voices. Their vibrations resonated within his skull, pounding and pulsating, until Teran thought he'd go mad. Then, from out of the chaotic din, a familiar, sweet voice rose above the rest. Teran . . . Teran . . . I love you. Come back . . . come back to me.

Was it Alia? Oh, how he wanted and needed her! Yet she could not be his until this final, most bitter of choices had been made. He glanced down at the form that lay below him.

What had Ferox meant about being the ultimate victor, no matter the outcome? That look of savage triumph that flashed across his brutal face as he spoke—what was its significance? In a piercing moment of insight, the truth loomed before Teran. To kill Ferox would be his own destruction, whether he physically died in the act or not.

The realization filled him with a curious, soaring sense of release. The consequences were too great, the loss of his soul too horrifying, to risk the chance. Not for Ferox. Indeed, not for anyone!

By slow, painful degrees, Teran wrenched himself toward the beloved voice that called him. The dark mists of anger cleared. From out of the haziness, Alia's slender form appeared. He gazed up at her standing before him, his expression confused and tormented.

"Alia . . .?"

Unashamed of the tears streaming from her eyes, Alia tenderly stroked his face. He has returned, still the man he was—and more, she thought. Gently taking his hands, she pried his fingers loose from the throat of the now limp Ferox. Groping about in the murky spring, Alia pulled the half-drowned man's head out of the water.

"Help me!" she gasped, raising beseeching eyes to Teran. "For the Crystal, for Vates!"

He wavered but an instant, the old rage momentarily flashing across his face. Then, with a low groan, Teran grasped the inert form under its arms. Flinging Ferox over his shoulder, he strode out of the spring.

Alia followed, still uncertain as to the extent of Teran's cooperation. They reached the bank. After walking a few more meters, Teran halted. Unceremoniously dumping his human burden on the ground, he turned to confront her, his silver eyes glinting like shards of glass.

"Though I chose to spare his wretched life, the problem of Ferox is not yet resolved. Something must be done with him. He cannot be allowed to remain here, or he will yet endanger the quest. What do you propose, Alia?"

She studied him for a moment. "What did you and the Crystal do with his men?"

The hard tenseness to his face gradually eased. A brief flicker of humor warmed his gray eyes. "We sent them far into Mors, a good two sols travel to the nearest oasis and at least six sols away from even the foothills of Macer. Far too kind a fate even at that, but the best I could convince the Crystal to perform."

"Then send Ferox there."

The line of his mouth tightened a fraction. For an instant, Alia thought he would refuse. Then the tenseness disappeared, as if an amusing thought had suddenly flashed across his mind. His mouth twisted into a wry grin.

"As you wish." He extended a hand. "Give me the Crystal."

Pulling it out of her pouch, she wordlessly handed it to him. Their fingers touched as the stone passed from one to the other, their eyes meeting in a silent affirmation of trust.

Alia realized, in that moment of piercing clarity, that Teran's intentions were indeed honorable. He had come through perhaps the greatest test of his life, his spirit purged in the white hot fires of an unyielding conscience. He, at least, was now worthy to be called a Crystal Master.

Ferox was beginning to stir, his uneven breaths interspersed with gagging coughs as he attempted to expell the water he'd inhaled. Teran held the Crystal out before him and closed his eyes.

The stone began to glow, the whirling light within sending out radiant beams. As Alia watched, Ferox's form blurred and faded.

She turned her gaze to Teran. His face was set in an expression of firm resolve, the clenched fist at his side the only evidence of the effort it took for him to carry out this task. She tore her eyes from him, back to the spot where Ferox lay. It was empty.

The intense emotions of the last hora drained out of Alia in one gushing wave. She began to shiver, her wet gown clinging heavily, chilling her despite the relative warmth of the rapidly ebbing sol. "Teran . . ." she weakly whispered.

Teran turned to find her standing there, pale and blue-lipped. Quickly shoving the stone into his belt, he gathered Alia into his arms. Glancing down as he bore her through the trees to where they'd left their supplies, he smiled.

She said nothing, only stared up at him, her slender body wracked with tremors Teran knew were from more than cold. He clasped her tightly to him and was heartened when her shivering seemed to abate a little.

Hurriedly bearing her to the supplies, Teran removed the sodden gown from her unprotesting body, tenderly wrapping her in one of the blankets. Stripping off his own wet clothes, he pulled her chilled form to him. Enfolding her blanket around the both of them, he lowered their bodies to a sitting position against a nearby tree. Slowly his warmth, combined with the cover of the blanket, eased Alia's jerking spasms.

It felt so good to have her pliant young body next to his again. Pressed against him as she was, Teran could feel the soft mounds of her breasts crush into his upper abdomen and the velvet skin of her belly brush across his groin.

He choked down a moan as the hot blood shot through him, his arousal swelling to a throbbing hardness. How he wanted to caress the curving lines of her body, to kiss the sweet, rosy lips, to join with

252

her again. The consuming flame of his desire soared higher and higher, fueled by the memory of their first mating. Would she refuse him now, if he made an overture?

Teran brushed his lips across her forehead as he slipped a hand under the blanket and up a smooth arm. She stirred, her face lifting to his. Wide, wondering, brown eyes stared up at him. His fingers skimmed the silky curve of her shoulder and up the line of her graceful neck, to finally cup her chin in his palm.

Alia said nothing, watching him through thickly lashed, languorous eyes. Teran's head lowered, his heart pounding in his chest. He touched his lips to hers, coaxing them apart. When they did, his tongue slid gently between them. Slowly, ever so tenderly, he deepened the kiss, teasing and tormenting her as he plunged in, then retreated.

Heated tendrils of desire curled down Alia's spine, banishing the lingering terrors at the spring and the hardships of the past sols. She had almost lost Teran, and the touch of his body now, so warm and powerful, was a reassurance she desperately craved. It felt so good. She quivered with pleasure, exquisite to the point of painfulness. The tips of her breasts, where they touched his hairy skin, tingled. Sensuously, greedily, she rubbed against him to intensify the sensation.

At the provocative movement, Teran's breath sucked in through clenched teeth. His hands moved down Alia's back, molding her tighter and tighter to his hard length. His mouth opened hungrily over hers now, slanting fiercely back and forth. When she responded in kind, Teran went wild. He shifted his weight atop her, wedging his knee between her legs.

The urgent hardness of his desire pressed against her most sensitive place, probing for her hot, snug wetness.

At the touch of him Alia tensed, reality flooding back. No matter how much she wanted to, she couldn't join with him—not now, not ever again. It would only make things worse and hurt them both in the end. She wrenched her mouth from the heady pleasure of Teran's plunging tongue.

"Stop!" she gasped. "Please, Teran. We . . . must . . . stop!"

Teran groaned softly, a harsh masculine sound that filled her with equal portions of pain and longing. "No. I love you, Alia. I need you. After all we've been through, can you deny me this? We are meant to be together. I beg you. Don't turn from me now. Don't deny me your body and your love."

Before she could reply, his mouth came down hard on hers, silencing her objections, taking her lips in a fierce, devouring kiss. His hand moved to fondle a breast, pushing it upward, teasing the sensitive nipple until it stood, erect and proud, against his palm. His warmth and maleness enveloped her, as did the joyous realization that he loved her.

She supposed she'd known for a long while now that his affection for her ran deep, as did hers for him, but to finally hear his admission of love was both heady and terrifying. Though she held back from whispering those same words to him, fearing the consequences such an act would set into motion, Alia suddenly knew she couldn't turn from Teran's ardent plea. It might be wrong—their mating but a bittersweet futility—but she could no more resist these sweet primal urges than to cease to breathe.

Helplessly, delightedly, Alia surrendered to the inflaming demands of Teran's hands and mouth.

"Yes," she sighed, her voice husky with desire. "Oh, yes! Touch me, love me!"

A thick, sensual haze engulfed Teran. He heard Alia whisper his name again and again, urging him to come to her. Shuddering with the effort it took to hold back his burgeoning excitement, Teran's powerful thighs spread her wide. Then, with one final glance to confirm her continued willingness, he rammed himself into her.

She arched to meet him, clawing at his back to draw him ever closer, her hips thrusting upward in savage abandon. A wildly exciting rhythm pounded through Alia as their two young, healthy bodies met, then fell away, only to plunge together again and again. Fierce delight carried them higher and higher in a churning maelstrom of passion until, with a choking cry, Alia was lost in a searing, soaring ecstasy.

Head thrown back, his body straining to savor the fullest depth of her, Teran fought to contain the ravaging need building within him. It could not long be controlled. With a guttural cry, he found his release, his muscular frame shuddering above her in taut gratification.

Then, as quickly as the passion had built and peaked, it was over. Teran lowered himself to lay beside her, gathering Alia into the warm haven of his arms. She went to him with a blissful sigh. They lay there for a time, until sleep claimed their damp, sated bodies.

Several horas later, Teran awoke, a soft smile on his lips at the memory of their frenzied coupling. Their first joining, when he'd taken her maidenhood, had been sweetly satisfying, but this time there had been nothing gentle about it. Both had been driven by a hot, savage need, lost in an instinctive mating urge. And it had been one of the most exquisite experiences of his life.

But now, she lay in his arms, limp and nearly lifeless save for the soft sound of her breathing. Had he hurt her or frightened her in the savagery of his passion? He thought not, but still he needed to hear it from her lips.

Teran stroked the damp tangle of her hair. "Alia, are you awake? Are you all right?" The wave of sudden concern made his voice sound harsh.

She gave a tiny moan and shifted in his arms to look up at him. "Yes, Teran, I am all right. Just don't let go."

Teran pulled her even tighter, until they molded, one into the other. "Sweet femina," he said, his voice suddenly husky with emotion, "I never want to let you go. You are my heart, my life. Do you realize how afraid I was for you, seeing you once again in Ferox's clutches? I thought I'd go mad."

She snuggled closer to him. "And I was so worried for you, terrified you would appear and be killed. And then, even worse, when I saw you about to murder Ferox . . ." Alia gave a small sob. "I can't believe it is all over, almost as quickly as it began."

Teran's brows knit in concentration. "They did arrive here rather suddenly, didn't they? When we've had a time to rest, I think I'll take a little walk around the oasis. They might have brought along a more sophisticated form of transportation. If that's the case, the Crystal's insistence on sparing their lives would almost be worth it."

His mention of his Crystal powers wrenched Alia from the satisfying comfort she'd found in Teran's arms. Why, at the most inopportune of moments, did the memory of that potential conflict have to intrude so cruelly? Yet why was she surprised? Their passionate coupling had been but a brief respite from the reality of their situation. The Crystal and the pitiless demands of her quest remained as before. Still, she didn't begrudge the wondrous moments she'd just shared with Teran. With a sigh, Alia gently pushed herself away and sat up.

He intently stared at her. "What is it? Do you regret our joining?"

She shook her head, a soft, sad smile on her lips. "No. It should never have been, but no, I don't regret it. It . . . it's something else."

As if sensing her thoughts, Teran slowly levered himself to an elbow. "It has to do with my Crystal powers, does it not?"

Alia wet her dry lips. "Yes, Teran. I need to know your true intentions for the Crystal."

"My intentions are as they have always been, Alia. To help you rescue it, then return it to its rightful home."

"And where do you deem its rightful home to be?" she asked, her heart thundering in her chest. *Whatever hope we have for a life together lies in this answer,* she silently cried. *Choose your words well.*

The old wariness flared in Teran's eyes, then he smiled, as a look of trust wound its way into the gray depths. "I thought that was obvious, but apparently not. The Knowing Crystal's rightful place is as it has always been—on the mother planet, Aranea."

She laughed joyously. "Then we are in agreement —have always been it now seems." Alia hugged him fiercely. "Aranea is my home. If you only knew how much I feared we were at odds in this, and now I find we were always in accord. Oh, Teran, I am so glad."

He wrapped his arms back around her. "Are you, Alia?" he asked, pressing his lips to the top of her head. "I had hoped you were beginning to feel something for me, and our joining lends but further credence to that dream. Am I presumptuous in imagining that meaning in your words?"

At his tender question, she swallowed the despair that rose in her throat. Teran loved her and was asking, hoping, for the same depth of feeling from her. Though the realization filled Alia with a bitter-sweet pang, she couldn't allow it to sway her from her chosen path. She was bound to her people, to the service of the Crystal through the Sisterhood. Was there a place in it all for him? Perhaps, but until she was certain, it was kinder not to encourage him.

Alia raised glistening eyes. "What you think you hear matters not, Teran. My life is not my own. I am destined to serve the Knowing Crystal."

"But that is also my fate. Why can't we serve it together?"

She sadly shook her head and lowered her gaze, unable to bear the sudden, eager hope in his eyes. "Because I am committed to the Sisterhood of the Crystal. My entire life, my training, even my outlook has been constantly directed to that end. There is little choice for me."

"There's always a choice, if you really want to make it," Teran cried in a hoarse voice.

He rose to tower over her, magnificient in his nakedness. "At least find the courage to face me without the safety of weak excuses." He gathered his clothes and dressed, his movements quick and jerky with anger.

Alia tugged the blanket around her, as if marshalling her remaining defenses. "Where . . . where are you going?"

"To find Ferox's transportation," he growled. "If he brought some faster means, we may be able to use it.

The sooner we get to the transport station, the better I'll like it."

And the faster you'll be free of me, Alia thought. That's what you really mean, isn't it, Teran? With a growing sense of desolation, she watched him stomp off through the trees.

Gathering the blanket around her, Alia rose and slowly walked to where Teran had draped her gown across a bush to dry. Twilight was falling. It was time to dress and prepare camp for the nocte. The mundane, sol-to-sol routine of life was all she had left to comfort her.

CHAPTER 14

ABOUT AN HORA LATER, TERAN RETURNED. ALIA glanced up from the pot of faba she was tending over the campfire. She was relieved to find the tense, angry expression gone from his face. Maybe they would have a pleasant meal and nocte after all.

He sat down across the fire from her. Pouring a mug of the rich, sweet liquid, Alia handed it to him. "Did you find anything interesting in your explorations?"

Teran took a sip of the drink, his glance carefully blank. "Yes, as a matter of fact. Ferox was kind enough to leave several skim craft behind. If we get an early start, we should be able to reach the transport station by noon."

Alia forced a wooden smile to her lips. "How nice. That would save us over two sols of travel. I must admit that thought doesn't displease me."

"Nor I," he said, taking a long swallow of faba.

"The desert has never been one of my favorite places." A smile of sudden remembrance touched his lips. "I doubt Ferox and his cohorts will find it to their liking, either."

Alia looked up at him, her brown eyes sparkling in sudden interest. "Why do you say that?"

Teran's smile tightened grimly. "As great as the Knowing Crystal's powers are, even it has its limitations. Though the stone can apparently transport life forms for certain finite distances, it's unable to send along inert objects."

Alia's eyes clouded with puzzlement. "I don't understand. How is that to Ferox's disadvantage?"

"I'd wager he and his men are finding the desert particularly uncomfortable by now. Unprotected skin will burn to a crisp in this cauldron. The Crystal was only able to transport their bodies, not their clothing." A malicious gleam danced in his eyes. "Poor, poor Ferox."

Watching him, it was all Alia could do to keep from laughing out loud. "Exactly how far can the Crystal transport? Perhaps it could send us directly to Aranea?"

"Apparently not. I thought to ask how far, but it stated it wasn't programed for such distances. Probably could be, if one found the right pattern."

He shot her a sideways glance. "Of course, there's also the problem of its other limitations to consider. One wouldn't want to arrive naked, would one?"

She unsuccessfully tried to suppress the flush that rose to her cheeks. "I don't think I fully realized until now what a deviously wicked mind you have. Well, no matter. Spending one more nocte in this pleasant spot is certainly no hardship. We can free the equs here, too. This will certainly be a more pleasant existence than returning them to the claiming station to serve new masters."

Teran lowered his eyes and swirled the remaining faba in his mug, as if fascinated with the interplay of the brown hues. "And what are your plans for me?" he suddenly asked. "In light of your holy quest, even the use of my body is now of little value. Assuming you know how to operate a skim craft, I am of no further service."

She hesitated, trying to comprehend what Teran was really asking. Did he seek reassurance of her feelings for him, that the future wasn't really as bleak as it seemed? Or was it his uncertainty if she still meant to take him back with her to Aranea? Surely he knew he had earned that right.

Or did he? A sad little smile found its way to her lips. He was as unsure of her and her true motivations as she had been of his.

"Your body is of great value to me," Alia said, "as is your heart and mind, but I will not argue over that anymore. Only time will give us those answers. In the meanwhile, the choice is yours, Teran. If you so desire, you may come with me to Aranea. It was the oath we took at claiming, and I will keep that vow. I will do what I can for you there."

His steely glance probed at her, and gradually his tense muscles relaxed. Teran sighed. "What is it like? Aranea, I mean? I have heard its climate is similar to Bellator's. But what are your customs, your industries? How could a warrior such as myself fit in on your planet?"

She faltered, unexpectedly at a loss for words. What could she say to ease his concerns? How much did she really know about Aranea herself, considering her formerly cloistered existence? Looking back now, Alia suspected the High Priestess had always shared only information she deemed important, and that had been very little. How much more was there, and of what significance?

Alia glanced across at Teran. He was silently scrutinizing her, awaiting a reply. Well, she thought, all she could do was be as honest as possible with the knowledge she had.

"Some of our customs will probably appear strange to you," Alia began. "For one, we segregate the sexes. As far as I can tell, they are allowed to come together only for mating. I could be mistaken, though," she added hastily, noting the look of horrified dismay on Teran's face. "That was part of my training yet to come, so perhaps I've misunderstood."

"I hardly think so. In fact," he paused to eye her closely, "I've heard tales that Aranean feminas indulge in the practice of post-coital murder. Isn't that taking the mutant spider worship of yours a little too far?"

Alia's eyes flared. "How dare you accuse us of such . . . such depravities! Just because we've learned to adapt to the evolutionary necessities of our planet is no reason to fabricate lies about us. We protect our men because they have become weak, degenerating over the cycles into little more than objects of species propagation. It is our greatest tragedy, but we have never treated them harshly and certainly never disposed of them in the manner you speak of."

Teran shrugged. "Perhaps not; I only know what I've heard. Rumors can be misleading. But what of your weaving spiders? Do you deny that you don't worship them?"

"We don't worship them in the sense of deities.

They are admired for their untiring productivity and the beautiful gold threads they spin, but that is all. It's difficult not to feel gratitude for a thing that provides the most important export product of our planet."

A thoughtful expression flitted across her face. "Strange, isn't it, though, how closely our lives have come to mirror the life of the Aranean spider? We feminas have attained the dominant role, as our males gradually weakened to little more than sexual objects—just like the mates of the weaving spider."

She glanced up at Teran, her chin raised in defiance. "But that is where the similarity ends. We are not insects but civilized, intelligent beings who don't turn on our mates. They are protected in their weakness; we deeply mourn the loss of their former strength and manhood."

His gray eyes darkened with some strong emotion. "Is that why you turned from me? Was I perhaps not to your liking, my lovemaking not submissive enough for your refined tastes? Strange, though, that you responded as you did. I could have sworn you found me satisfying."

"Once again you overstep your bounds," Alia snapped. "I've already told you why we could not continue in that fashion. Besides, as I've said before, you ask the wrong person. I've yet to learn all the teachings of my people. That is a lifelong undertaking of a Sister of the Crystal."

Teran snorted in disgust. "Your training may have been somewhat rudimentary in your customs of mating, but I doubt you could have misunderstood the basic tenets. Even growing up in the sheltered existence of your Sisterhood, you must have absorbed the subtle nuances of your culture."

He frowned. "Tell me more of this Sisterhood of yours. Perhaps if I had a better understanding of it, I could appreciate the problems you face."

"I . . . I have no problems." The tone of Alia's voice was once more defensive.

"Don't you, Alia?" Teran retorted, his gray eyes piercing to the very depths of her soul.

Finally, with a deep sigh, Alia answered him. "I do what I must and give what I can, Teran. If you wish to be my friend, you'll have to accept that."

"I want more than your friendship, Alia," he said quietly. "Surely you realize that by now."

A look of tired sadness settled over her features. "But friendship is all I can give, Teran. The rest is not mine to share."

"We shall see," he muttered. "Now, will you tell me of your order?"

"I can reveal little, only as much as the common Aranean knows," Alia said, relieved he had changed the subject. "The rest is privileged to members of the Sisterhood."

"Then tell me what you can. If I am to live on your planet, it would be wise to begin learning about it."

Alia took a deep breath. "The Sisterhood of the Crystal was originally formed to serve the Knowing Crystal. Its members consisted of a High Priest or Priestess of the royal blood, who was the conduit of communication to the Crystal, and several sub-priestesses to serve the Priest or Priestess' needs. As time went on and the Crystal gained greater and greater importance to the Imperium, the size of the order gradually increased."

"But the Crystal has been lost to Aranea for hundreds of cycles. What has been the Sisterhood's function in that interim? What services does it perform to justify its existence?"

"The Sisterhood of the Crystal doesn't need to justify its existence to the Aranean people," Alia retorted, once again finding herself compelled to defend her beliefs. Why did Teran always make her feel so unsure of all she had formerly accepted as truth?

She mentally forced herself to relax. "We have always known the Knowing Crystal would some sol be returned to us. The Sisterhood, ever faithful and vigilant, has also waited. It has striven to preserve the heritage of the Knowing Crystal, preparing for the sol of its return."

"Sounds like an assemblage of power-hungry old feminas, sitting around at the people's expense," Teran muttered sarcastically.

"That is not true," Alia cried. "They earn their way in many forms of labor. The Sisters are responsible for the annual matings, are highly trained midwives and manage the nurseries. Hardly what one would call 'sitting around.'"

"Hold on, hold on." Teran forced a laugh, raising his hands in mock defeat. "Perhaps my judgement was a bit premature. This supervising of the Aranean matings interests me, though. Exactly what do the Sisters do?"

Alia colored fiercely. "Not what you assume, I am sure. They merely choose mates for feminas of breeding age, monitor them for signs of fertility and then pregnancy, and finally assure a healthy prenatal course. The genetic improvement of the race is not considered an obscene endeavor on our planet."

"Nor on mine," Teran said, his expression wryly amused. "We expend particular enthusiasm in devoting our efforts to that pleasurable enterprise."

Teran hesitated a moment, his gaze measuring her. Then, shifting into a more comfortable position, he asked, "What of this breeding program? I find the subject very intriguing."

"You know far too much as it is," Alia said, firmly shaking her head. "It is time we moved on to other aspects of Aranean culture."

Teran raised a dubious eyebrow. "Why do I get the impression you're holding back something important? I think you owe me an answer, Alia."

She lowered her head to avoid the probing gray eyes. Yes, she did indeed owe him an answer, a fuller understanding of what a male's life on Aranea would be like. But did she truly know what it was? His questions had stirred long-suppressed doubts and seeming contradictions of Aranean culture that until now she'd chosen not to examine too closely.

Alia raised her gaze to his. In an effort to calm the sudden jangling of her nerves, she expelled a long breath. "What more do you wish to know, Teran?"

He stared back at her. "What function does the male serve on your planet, Alia? Aside from propagating the species, I mean?"

She remained silent, her eyes seemingly fascinated with the hands in her lap.

"Alia," Teran cried, his fear and frustration growing, "am I to serve no other role on Aranea but as a stud to your feminas—a breeding animal? Is that what you want for me?"

"No," she whispered, stung by the harsh accusation and the pain in his voice.

She raised despairing eyes to him. "I want nothing, save for you to be received and treated with honor. You have earned that right. I intend to demand it for you."

"Considering the high opinion males are held in, do you seriously think it will be granted?" There was skepticism in his arched brow and a sardonic twist to his mouth.

"Why not?" An edge of exasperation threaded

Alia's voice. "Am I not the Chosen One, a Crystal Master, as are you? And did you not help me rescue it?"

Teran nodded. "Under normal circumstances one would think there would be little problem. However, the Imperium is in chaos. Rational thought is in short supply. I truly don't know what to think or expect."

"Nor do I, Teran," Alia admitted sadly. "Nor do I. I am sorry."

He sighed. Picking up a small twig, Teran tossed it into the campfire and watched it burn as if mesmerized, before raising his eyes back to her.

"Just tell me the truth, no matter how unpleasant it may be. You do me no kindness by trying to protect me. Only with knowledge can I defend myself and learn to adapt."

She flinched at the harsh reality of his words. "You are right, of course. I have been unfair. There is scant more to reveal on that particular subject, however."

Alia paused, the hesitation evident. "This much more I will tell you, though ask me not what it means. Aranean males are not allowed to freely roam the planet. Instead, they are confined in compounds all their lives. Though apparently well cared for, they do not appear content."

"How do you know this?" Teran demanded, his strong frame suddenly tense and wary.

"Only from my infrequent observations, when we novices of the Sisterhood were allowed out on our chaperoned excursions. I was never permitted to speak to the males, but I could see it in their eyes and their manner."

With a muttered oath, Teran rose to his feet. "Where are you leading me?" he cried. "Must I leave one living death only to find another?"

"And what do you want of me?" She choked the

words out, the tears welling in her eyes. "It is your choice."

At the sight of her pain, the anger in Teran dissolved. "Perhaps that is exactly what frustrates me. There really is no choice; indeed, there has never been one. Vates was adamant I go with you. Do you know how that makes me feel? Helpless, out of control. To place my life and trust in another is one of the hardest things for a man like me to do. Even," he smiled sadly, "others as trustworthy as you and my old teacher."

"It is a hard thing for many to do, Teran," Alia whispered. "Myself, included. I will try to be worthy of that trust. Truly I will."

His smile slowly broadened into one of genuine happiness. "That is all I or anyone can ask, Alia. I've the feeling I'll be needing your friendship in the sols to come. Now," he said, "tell me more of Aranea. Surely some of its practices won't seem so foreign to me."

She answered Teran's multitude of questions for the next several horas, but eventually fatigue claimed their minds and bodies. When Alia awoke, she walked to the edge of the oasis to silently watch the sun climb over the distant horizon.

Mauve washed the early sky, gradually blended by ever brightening shades of magenta. At last the sun emerged from its slumber behind the sand dunes and cast its golden light over the land. A new sol and a new life, Alia mused. There's always hope of a fresh beginning, as long as the sun rises each morrow.

Two strong hands settled onto her shoulders. "Come back to camp, Alia," Teran rasped, in a voice still heavy with sleep. "We both need to eat if we're to adequately prepare for the sol ahead."

She turned under his hands and gazed up at him.

In the glowing light of the new sol, Teran's handsome face seemed ablaze with a passionate beauty. A warm euphoria swept through her. Their life together was just as fresh, just as new as the radiant sol before them.

"Yes," she murmured. Wrapping her arm around his tautly muscled waist, Alia ambled back to camp.

The bleak, aerlapis stone outline of the transport station, marking the end of the desert of Mors, loomed closer as the skim craft sped along. As they rapidly neared the portals of the complex, Alia glanced down at the time dial in the instrument console. Had it been but four horas since they'd left the oasis?

"Here, take this."

Alia turned her attention to the man beside her flying the aircraft. In his free hand, he held out the govern keys. "What . . . what are you doing, Teran?"

"Returning the keys to you. Only temporarily, of course. The station wardens would frown at the criminal possessing them, wouldn't you say?"

With a small shudder, Alia took the set of keys from him. "I suppose so."

She raised troubled eyes to Teran. "But just as soon as we arrive back on Aranea . . ."

"Have no fear. I plan on reclaiming them even before then, once we've passed the warden's processing."

He paused to scrutinize her. "That is, if you've no objection?"

"No objection," Alia murmured, "no objection at all."

"Unidentified skim craft," a clipped, metallic voice interrupted, "transmit ID code and purpose of mission."

271

Teran's attention immediately focused on the station controller. After circling while completing required contact with flight control, they finally landed at the hoverpad atop one of the buildings.

Quickly disembarking, Alia and Teran followed a long, winding corridor to a portal marked PROCESSING. The pair exchanged a meaningful glance, then passed through the opening.

Inside a large room, crowded with computer terminals and disk storage boxes, was a rotund little man in the uniform of a station warden. He was bent over one of the desks that lined the walls, immersed in data displayed on one of the terminals.

Teran and Alia waited patiently for the man to notice their arrival. Alia had to finally clear her throat to gain his attention. "Your pardon," she began. "Is this where one comes to complete final processing of a claimee?"

The squat little man wheeled around in his chair and squinted up at them. "Wha . . . ? Oh yes, certainly." He paused to eye Alia admiringly. "How may I serve you?"

"I am prepared to return to my planet with this claimee," she said, indicating Teran. "I was told to report here."

"Yes, yes," the warden muttered impatiently. "It is necessary to make official notation of where the prisoner is being taken, the new owner's name, etcetera, etcetera."

He glared over at Teran. "What is your name and planet of origin, claimee?" he demanded.

"Teran, House Ardane, of the planet Bellator," Teran muttered, a fierce scowl clouding his brow.

The warden turned to the blank screen and punched in a code. Amber letters flashed across the black void. Finally the man turned again to face them, a smug, oily grin on his face.

"Well, *Lord* Ardane of Bellator, it seems you've found a way to buy your freedom after all. Did you ply this femina with your arrogant manner, or was it something as basic as providing royal stud services?"

With an angry growl, Teran advanced on the man, his fists clenched as if to strike. The warden's eyes grew round. He hurriedly retreated behind his chair.

"Stop him! Use the govern keys," he blubbered, looking past Teran's powerful form to Alia.

Alia smiled, allowing herself the momentary pleasure of enjoying the man's discomfiture. "And take the chance of damaging a valuable slave because of your insolence? I think not."

"What?" the warden cried. "You would spare a common criminal over me? I warn you, he is not yours until the processing is complete. Have you no other means of control over this . . . this animal?"

"None except my voice. Shall I ask him to stop?"

"Yes, yes," he whimpered, cowering before the presence of Teran towering over him. "Please!"

She laughed. "Teran, let him be."

Teran snorted in disgust. Wheeling around, he walked back to stand at Alia's side. She smiled up at him, then returned her attention to the still very much shaken little man. "Take care to watch your tongue henceforth. I might not be able to control him next time."

"Yes, Domina. My apologies to you," he said, continuing to nervously eye the tall man beside her. "Now, if you wouldn't mind answering a few questions about yourself, I can expedite this."

"I would be more than happy to comply," Alia replied. "We are eager to depart Carcer."

The warden hurriedly fired off a string of questions, the responses to which he typed into the computer. At last he pushed back his chair and rose.

"The requirements have all been met. Is there anything else I may do to serve you? If not, your next stop will be the transport chamber."

"Only one," Alia said, a grim determination settling over her features. "I'd like my claimee's govern collar removed."

As one, Teran and the warden riveted their gaze on her in shocked surprise.

"But . . . but . . ." the station warden sputtered, "that is unheard of, inconceivable. No one has ever made such a request. It is unprecedented!"

"Nonetheless, it is what I request," Alia calmly replied. "Why should there be a problem? He is mine to do with as I wish. And I wish for his collar to be removed."

"But that's completely out of the question, not to mention impossible," the warden huffed in indignation. "There is no way to remove the collar once it is applied. When they condemned him for life, that was exactly what they meant. There is no method known to man for removing an Imperium govern collar."

Alia frowned in dismay. "Are you certain? Surely the one who designed the collar knows how to remove it."

The man sighed wearily. "If it were possible to dismantle the collar, don't you think some criminal mastermind would have discovered it by now? That was the whole point. Make the collar impregnable so there would never be any doubt of complete control. It's out of my hands."

Alia turned to Teran. "I'm sorry," she whispered, as she fought back tears of frustration and disappointment. "I had hoped . . . There's so little else I can do for you."

Teran grasped her by the shoulders. For a long moment, there was no one in the room but them. "That you cared enough to even try is sufficient for me, Alia. If you're not ashamed to be seen with me wearing it, why should I be bothered?"

She reached out to touch the collar, then wound her hand up to rest alongside his face. "How could I ever be ashamed to know a man like you, Teran? I am proud to call you my friend."

"Er, excuse me," the warden hesitantly interrupted, his eagerness to be rid of them more than evident. "If there is nothing else . . .?"

Alia smiled. "No, nothing else. Which corridor do we take to the transport chamber?"

"The first one on your left," the little man said. "It'll be the fifth door on your right. It's marked. You can't miss it."

"Thank you for your trouble."

Grabbing hold of Teran's arm, she pulled him toward the exit. Behind them, they heard the warden's baffled mutterings.

"What a strange pair . . . sure to be problems when she gets that one home . . . thank the red sun of Carcer we're free of those two."

Alia and Teran grinned at each other as they turned down the appropriate hallway and headed toward the transport chamber. As they walked along Alia glanced up at him, a look of curiosity flaring in her eyes.

"Why didn't you ever tell me of your standing in the royal house of Ardane? How are you related to King Falkan?"

"He's my uncle," Teran muttered, making no effort to hide the bitterness. "But that is of little import. The king stood with the others in condemning me. Only my younger brother rose in my defense. Essentially, I no longer have a family nor home, no matter what my title may be."

Alia clasped his arm, effectively halting their progress down the hall. "Perhaps you can begin anew on Aranea. Even though you must wear the collar, once the people realize your contribution to the rescue of the Crystal—"

"I ask for nothing except to be allowed to live as a free man without further threat of the govern collar," Teran gruffly interrupted her.

He extended a hand. "Will you return the keys to me now, so I may insure at least that much?"

Cold metal filled his palm as her hand brushed over his. "Most gladly, Teran."

For a moment they stared at each other, the wary, proud look in Teran's eyes gradually melting into one of wonder and hope. He made a move toward her, then, as if remembering himself and the task still before them, he turned and resumed his journey down the hall. With a small sigh, Alia followed.

They halted in front of the door prominently marked INTERPLANETARY TRANSPORT. Alia paused with her hand beside the control panel. "This is the last chance to change your mind. Once you're on Aranea, there is no turning back."

A spark of some indefinable emotion flickered in his silver eyes. "Since I first met you, Alia, I don't think there's ever been a choice. My life and heart are now in your hands."

She struggled to swallow the lump that rose in her throat. "So be it, then," she murmured. Sweeping her hand over the control panel, Alia opened the door to the transport chamber.

His words remained with her, reverberating through Alia's mind as they checked themselves in, registered their destination and mounted the transport platform.

Her gaze nervously flicked around the large room, as they waited for the technician to complete the preliminary settings. Though of the same cool green hues as the room where she'd first arrived on Carcer, this one possessed, besides the raised transport platform, a console consisting of an impressive array of levers, buttons and lights. As she stared at it in fascination, a transparent, circular shield lowered around them, effectively separating Alia and Teran from the rest of the chamber.

The transport technician shoved the power lever forward on the control panel. Multicolored lights flashed on the console. A curious buzzing once again filled Alia's ears.

Suddenly, she was overcome with an awful premonition, an impulse to cry out. The procedure must be halted. Something was wrong. Something hideous awaited them at the other end of transport.

Alia turned in drugged slow motion toward Teran, her mouth moving wordlessly. He was already fading, the disembodiment having begun. She reached out to him with a hand that blurred and disappeared.

It was too late, her mind sobbed, too late.

CHAPTER 15

THROUGH A SPARKLING BLUR, ALIA DISCERNED THE forms of somberly clad feminas. As the faces gained clarity, the unsmiling countenance of the High Priestess came into view. Garbed in the black gown striped with red piping, she stood at the head of a group of Sisters. Her cold eyes flickered briefly from Alia to Teran as the pair stepped down from the transport platform.

"So, you return at last, child," the High Priestess rasped, her thin mouth contorted in her version of a smile. "Have you the Knowing Crystal?"

Alia bowed in deference to the femina's rank before answering. "Yes, Domina Magna," she said, rising to face her. "The Crystal has at last come home to Aranea."

"Then give it to me, child." The claw of a hand, the jeweled ring of sovereignty sparkling brightly upon it, extended toward Alia.

Alia and Teran exchanged glances.

"No," Alia replied, turning serene but determined eyes back to the High Priestess. "The Crystal will remain with me until its safe return to the pedestal of power."

A flicker of rage passed across the older femina's face. Silently accusing eyes rested on Teran for an instant, before her countenance was quickly covered with a veil of seeming indifference.

"So be it, child," she murmured. "The ceremony of Crystal Reinstatement will be held at the next full rising of the Weaver's moon, in but ten sols' time."

The pale, brittle eyes moved again to scrutinize Teran. "And who is this male?" The tone of her voice was ample evidence she'd noted the govern collar.

"He is my friend." Alia sidled closer to Teran. "Without his aid, I would never have succeeded. I promised him sanctuary here."

A murmur rose from behind the High Priestess, like the clucking of excited hens. "She promised him sanctuary? And who does she think she is?"

The voices of the Sisters rose in volume and hysteria as they talked among themselves. "Look, he wears a govern collar. Why, he's nothing more than a common criminal. We could be in danger of our very lives, with a male like that in our midst."

Alia struggled to hide the rising tide of annoyance that surged through her. How dare they utter one word against Teran, eternally secure in their insular little world here on Aranea. She glanced up at him, at a face beginning to darken with anger. Impulsively, Alia grasped his hand, giving it a reassuring squeeze. He looked down at her, a faint smile slowly replacing his tense expression.

Alia wheeled about to face the feminas assembled before them. "Have we sunk so low we no longer honor our promises? I gave this man my word he would be safe here and welcomed. Will any of you deny him that or disavow my oath?" Alia demanded, the challenge ringing in her voice, defiance burning brightly in her eyes.

The excited chattering stilled, and the Sisters exchanged nervous glances. The High Priestess raised a conciliatory hand, though the look in her eyes was anything but reassuring.

"Not I, nor any of your Sister, will ask such a thing. The male is welcome, for your sake, as well as for his efforts in our behalf." She turned her gaze upon Teran, who was dressed only in boots, belt and torn breeches. "You appear in need of new clothes and a good meal. If you would, please follow Sister Myrna."

The High Priestess motioned a white-robed novice forward. "She will escort you to your chambers where you may rest and refresh yourself. Alia will join you later."

Teran arched a dark brow in amused skepticism. "And what if I choose to remain with Alia?"

The High Priestess' face tightened, the skin stretching taut in a pale mask. "It is your prerogative, of course," she finally purred, "but there is really no need for your presence just now. Alia and I have matters of the Sisterhood to discuss. I must assume you'd rather spend the time recuperating from your long journey. Aranea is renown for its invigorating hot mineral baths, one of which you will find in your chamber."

Teran grimly smiled at the High Priestess, not at all deceived by the smooth courtesy of her words. "What is your wish, Alia?" he asked, turning his gaze to her. "I will go or stay on your word alone."

Alia shot a furtive glance at the older femina. "She is right. We need time to talk. You can better spend it refreshing yourself." She squeezed his hand one more time before reluctantly releasing it. "I will join you later."

"As you wish." Teran looked over at the little white-gowned femina hesitantly standing behind the spare form of the High Priestess. "I am at your command, Sister," he said, smiling reassuringly at her. "Lead the way."

Sister Myrna scurried forward. After a perfunctory bow that was little more than a slight bobbing movement, she motioned for Teran to follow. Alia watched his tall, powerful form move across the room and out the door.

For a wrenching instant, she was nearly overcome with the impulse to run after him, to beg him to stay. She repressed the foolish thought and turned her gaze back to the High Priestess. This was ridiculous! She was in no danger from her own Sisters on her beloved planet of Aranea.

"I pray Teran has not offended you, Domina Magna," she said. "We have suffered many trials together and he is still quite protective of me. It will pass, when we have had a time to rest in safety."

"It is a natural response, my child," the High Priestess replied. "One that we expect from a male." She emphasized the last word. "However, members of our order are expected to rise above such base responses. You *are*, of course, able to set aside any primitive urges you may have experienced with this male, aren't you?"

Resentment surged through Alia, but the cycles of training prevented her from a hasty retort. It was all she could do to offer a lame reply. "He . . . he was very useful to me. His loyalty deserves a like loyalty in return, does it not?"

"In most cases." A black-gowned hand grasped

Alia's shoulder. "But we can talk of that another time." The High Priestess hesitated, as if a sudden thought had crossed her mind. "The govern keys. Where are the keys that control the male?"

Alia winced. What could she say that would make her answer more acceptable? The attempt to stall was pointless. They wouldn't like the truth no matter how it was couched. Alia lifted her chin and boldly met the High Priestess' gaze.

"Teran has the keys."

A murmur of horror rose from the covey of Sisters standing behind their leader, but, for a slight widening of her eyes and an immediate clamping of her lips, the High Priestess remained unmoved. "An unwise act, to be sure. You bring a condemned criminal to us with no means to control him?"

"He is an honorable man." Alia's impassioned response resounded throughout the chamber. "There is no danger to any of us."

The older femina arched a dubious brow. "That remains to be seen. Do you even know what his crime was, the one that condemned him to Carcer?"

Alia glanced away for a secundae. Why hadn't she ever asked him? Was it perhaps a fear of hearing the truth?

"No, I don't know his crime." She turned her gaze back to the femina standing before her. "But it is of no import. I know the man. I say again—he is honorable."

The pale eyes hardened for but an instant. The High Priestess gave a dramatic sigh. "Your Sisters and I must trust in your judgment, child. I pray your trust is not misplaced. Now, come, it is time you bathed and donned again the robes of our order."

Her cool glance appraised Alia's torn and dirty gown. "It must have been particularly humiliating, having to wear such a revealing dress."

Alia lowered her head, suddenly embarrassed by the unaccustomed exposure of her body. "The criminal Ferox made me wear it. It was not of Teran's doing."

A grim look stole across the High Priestess' face. "He is a male, child. In the end, they are all alike."

Alia opened her mouth to defend Teran, but the proper words eluded her. What would it accomplish anyway? Gazing at the hostile faces she realized, at least for the present, their minds were closed against him. And knowing Teran as little as they did, who could blame them? All they saw was a condemned criminal, apparently uncontrollable without the use of the govern keys.

It would take time, on both sides, to allay the fears and mutual suspicion. She must be the bridge between them, the common ground upon which Teran and her Sisters could come to trust and finally respect each other. Yes, Alia reassured herself, all it would take was patience and a little time.

"Come, come, child," the impersonal voice of the femina before her cut through Alia's musings. "Go with Sister Zayla. It is time you rejoin us and throw off the temporary trappings of a life that was never yours. Go, wash away the memories of your sols on Carcer. A new era of the Crystal will soon begin. You must prepare to assume your part."

Alia obediently followed Sister Zayla down the old, familiar corridors. They passed through a door that led outside into the arched cloisters enclosing a charming little garden of meditation. Fragrant scents assailed her nostrils as her eyes feasted on the spectrum of colors of the flowers and bushes growing there. Oh, how she had missed this beloved place!

As she walked across the red cobblestone path, a soothing peace settled over her. She was truly home again, the terrible quest at last over. There was nothing left to stand in the way of her profession. Nothing, except the Final Test of Worthiness.

A fleeting stab of fear slashed through her, but she quickly controlled it. After what she had been through on Carcer, the last test would surely prove of little difficulty. No, Alia comforted herself, all the real trials were over.

They silently climbed the winding, stone staircase to the dormitory. At last they halted in front of Alia's cell. She thanked Sister Zayla, then eagerly stepped inside.

Everything was how she had left it, the sheer, white-curtained bed, the songbirds chirping in their gilded cage in the corner, the flower-bedecked balcony overlooking the courtyard garden. With a deep sigh of contentment, Alia sank down on the edge of her bed and began to undress.

The ragged gown slid to the floor, forming an iridescent puddle of fabric around her feet. She stepped out of it and ran to the bathing room. Warm, mineral-scented water bubbled invitingly from the large stone tub. She climbed in and sank deeply into the churning liquid. Bliss. Pure bliss. She only hoped Teran had found the same pleasure.

Indeed, what *was* Teran thinking and feeling at this very moment? The image of a strong, bearded face rose to mentally confront her. Guilt surged through her.

Oh, Teran, Alia inwardly cried, what is the matter with me? How could I have let myself begin to dream of Final Profession? To become a Sister of the Crystal now would be to separate us forever, and I'll never let that happen.

She hurriedly scrubbed herself clean and rose, albeit reluctantly, from the bath. The sooner she discussed the issue of Teran with the High Priestess, the better. Before the femina had a chance to make elaborate plans for her life, she had to make it very clear what her own desires were. No, her hopes and dreams for a life with Teran could not wait a moment longer.

Less than a half hora later, Alia was gliding down the stone corridor to the High Priestess' chambers. Her burnished red curls, still damp from her bath, were twisted into a long, smooth braid down her back. She had donned a white gown piped with a narrow black stripe, the distinctive garb of the order's novices. High-necked, with full, long sleeves, it covered every bit of flesh save for Alia's face and the tips of her fingers.

She felt strangely confined in it but tossed the sensation aside as a transient notion. After all, the desert tunic and breeches had been unfamiliar at first. All it would take was time.

Her passage along the smooth stone corridor reminded Alia of that sol the High Priestess had first summoned her to her quest. It seemed so long ago now, she yet a child, a mere girl unversed in the ways of courage and danger and—love.

The dark wooden portal with its familiar ornate handle came into view. Alia's hand grasped the carved metal spider, her resolve firm. This time there was no hesitation as she shoved the door open.

"Come in, child."

The High Priestess motioned her to a small stool next to the large wooden throne. She watched Alia walk across the room and lower herself onto the seat. Then, and only then, did the femina reclaim her own regal chair, carefully arranging the dark folds of her robe to drape the arms.

Gazing up at the femina, Alia imagined she encompassed not only her chair, but the entire room as well. Calculating eyes peered down at her.

"Now, child, tell me of your quest. My thoughts have been with you this past month. I wish to hear everything."

"I don't know where to begin or what will be of interest, Domina Magna," Alia murmured, "but by your leave, I will attempt an accurate accounting."

She retold the story of Teran and Vates, their adventures, her growing trust and dependence on them. She sadly noted Vates' life fade, the journey into the mountains of Macer and finally the confrontation with Ferox and the retrieval of the Crystal. Inexplicably, Alia withheld the nocte of mating and Teran's own powers with the Crystal. Somehow, though it was vital information, it was too personal, too special to share without reason.

The High Priestess leaned back in her chair and studied the femina before her, a hard, speculative look burning in her eyes. "A very interesting story, child," she finally said. "I sense, however, you have left out a few important details. For example, that you and Teran were lovers."

A small gasp escaped Alia. "How . . . how did you know?"

"Quite easily, child," the femina purred. "For one of our race, the signs of pregnancy are evident quite early, especially to a practiced eye such as mine. Surely you knew?"

Alia's head lowered. "Yes, Domina Magna, the Crystal told me."

"Does the male know?"

"Teran? No, I did not know how to tell him or find the right moment."

"Good." The High Priestess paused to stroke her chin thoughtfully. "There will be no need for him to ever know. You must promise me not to tell him."

Alia's head jerked up in surprise. "Why would it matter? It is his right, is it not?"

"Not in this instance. He is an exile, a stranger to us. Our laws need not apply to him."

"There is one that could tell him besides myself," Alia hesitantly offered. Perhaps it *was* better to reveal it all. Maybe then the femina would understand why it was so important for her and Teran to remain together.

The black-garbed femina's eyes narrowed. "And who would tell him, if you are sworn to secrecy?"

"The Knowing Crystal. Teran also has the gift."

"What?" The High Priestess' eyes widened in horror. "How can that be? There should be no one, save yourself. I have most carefully seen to that."

"Perhaps no one else on Aranea, but Teran is of the planet Bellator, of the Royal House Ardane. He told me we are somehow related."

"Ardane!" A fist slammed down on the arm of the chair. "Curse that great-grand aunt of yours! I had forgotten about her." She rose and began to pace the room, her agitated steps carrying her back and forth across the small chamber. "There is no time for hesitation," she muttered to herself distractedly. "This very sol would be best, but the morrow will have to do."

With a swirl of lustrous black robes, she turned to once more face Alia. "Crystal Reinstatement is a high ceremony, one that demands the purest of intent and the utmost preparation. You must not see the male until after it is completed. You must devote your heart and soul to the preparation of this ritual, if the new reign of the Knowing Crystal is to begin providentially. Do you understand me, Alia?"

"But *you* don't understand," the younger femina protested. "Teran and I—"

"The separation will be for ten sols. Surely the male's devotion is equal to such a short parting. I would not ask it, if it were not of the greatest import."

Alia expelled a small, frustrated breath. Teran would understand, if only she could have a moment to explain it to him. But when? How?

"Alia!"

The harsh tone of the High Priestess' voice wrenched her back. She raised troubled eyes to stare at the older femina.

"I will have my answer."

"As you wish, Domina Magna. When must I begin my purification?"

"On the morrow." She paused. "One thing more. Though the Crystal remains in your possession it must not be used again for any reason until after the ceremony. It is not safe. Do you understand?"

"Not safe? How can that be? I found no impediment to its use on Carcer."

The High Priestess sucked in an exasperated breath. "Only by the fairest of fortunes have you managed to avoid the pitfalls of untutored usage. There is also the instability of Crystal transmission when it is not in its pedestal to consider. Bring the two into play simultaneously, and an inaccurate command could be the death of us all."

"I . . . I had no idea," Alia murmured. "Why wasn't I told this before being sent to Carcer?"

"There was no time to prepare you. We had only just discovered the whereabouts of the Crystal ourselves. But no matter. After your sols of purification and the ceremony, you will see the astounding difference in your abilities. Have I your word then, child?"

"Yes, Domina Magna."

The High Priestess' arm raised to indicate the door. "Good. Now go. The nocte draws on and you'll need your rest. The next ten sols will be ones of holy purpose. Your people—and the Knowing Crystal— will be depending on you."

There was nothing to do but obey. Alia walked from the room. What had happened to the high hopes with which she'd entered but a little while ago? Would her life be forever controlled by her sense of duty, her heartfelt need to serve her people? Would she never have a chance to fulfill her own dreams?

A firm determination welled up inside her. She would yet resolve the issue of Teran. It had only been delayed a few sols and only for the most consequential of events—Crystal Reinstatement. Teran might be angry with her and might not understand, but his pain would only last a short while. She would make it up to him afterwards, when they could at last be together—this time forever.

Teran restlessly paced his room. As the sun set somewhere behind the monastery, the lengthening shadows of twilight insinuated their way through the balcony doorway of his sleeping chamber. Soon, the room was shrouded in darkness. He pounded his fists in frustration. Where was Alia? What had they done to her?

A timid knock roused him from his fruitless questions. Alia! He ran to the door, a door he'd earlier discovered opened only from the outside, just as it slid apart. "Alia," he cried in relief. "What has kept you?"

The small, hesitant form of Sister Myrna stood before him, bearing a tray of food. "Not Alia, but I, Myrna," she quavered, noting the dark look he sent her way. "I . . . I bring your supper."

Expelling an angry breath, Teran took the tray from her. "Then perhaps you would be so kind as to tell me where Alia is and when I am to see her. It has been horas since we parted. I'm concerned."

"She . . . she has been detained." Myrna alternately bobbed and backed away at the same time. "I am not at liberty to say where. You will meet her eventually. Of that you can be sure." The femina fled, her escape as swift as a frightened bird.

"By the five moons!" Teran cursed as he watched the partition silently slide closed again. He looked down at the tray. With a heavy sigh, he carried it to a nearby table.

Horas later, the meal still untouched, Teran finally undressed for bed. He smiled to himself in brief amusement as he once more examined the fresh garments Sister Myrna had provided earlier. In style, the tunic was similar to the one Alia had worn on Carcer, from the high neck to the full sleeves gathered into tailored cuffs. But it was white, accompanied by a bright red sash!

Teran suppressed a laugh. What a sight he would make in such effeminate colors. Did the men of Aranea normally dress this way? Well, his own garments were ragged beyond repair. He had no choice but to utilize the proffered clothing. He would continue to substitute his own belt, however. To be expected to don that red sash was asking too much, no matter how firm his resolve to adapt as painlessly as possible to Aranean customs.

Naked, Teran flung himself upon the bed. Though his body was weary, his mind would not let him sleep. He tossed and turned on the large bed, alternately pounding on the cylindrical pillows, then bunching them beneath his head.

Where was Alia? He yearned to talk with her, to hold her in his arms and hear her words of assurance that all would be well. Yet even as he did, Teran struggled to fight down a growing sense of unease, a fear that he may have already lost her.

Curse it all! All he needed was just a little more time, if he were to cut through the entangling web this vile Sisterhood had spun around Alia's heart. But time, so generously bestowed when one took it for granted, was now so painfully dear. In his innermost of hearts, Teran feared there might not be any time left.

After a while, he fell into a fitful slumber. Strange dreams haunted him, as relentlessly as his conscious mind had while awake. He found himself in Alia's arms, his hands caressing her body until she moaned in rapturous delight. As they lay together, distant voices edged their way into the room, until the sounds surrounded them with an eerie chanting. Over and over the voices repeated the same words and phrases, until the chamber filled with a discordant roar. They clung to each other, Alia and he, until suddenly all was once again silent.

Teran found himself alone in a cold, dark room, the only illumination a light glaring brightly upon the stone slab on which he lay. He discovered, with a growing horror, that he couldn't move.

Glancing wildly around, the terror built inside him. What was wrong with him? Why was he here? Where was Alia?

A hand appeared out of a full black sleeve. Slender fingers grasped a dagger, curved and lethally sharp. Teran watched as it lowered toward him, its glinting tip aimed directly at his heart. Gripped in his prison of unmoving flesh, he stared at it in fascinated horror.

Alia! his mind cried. Alia!

He woke with a hoarse cry, his body bathed in sweat, his heart hammering in his chest. Jerking upright, Teran cradled his head in his hands. What had it all meant, that dreadful dream? Was it just a culmination of the past sol's doubts and the difficulty adjusting to this new planet and its strange customs? Or was it the Knowing Crystal speaking to him, warning him of danger?

The door to his room slid open. There, backlit by the brighter light of the corridor, was a slim, feminine form, hair and sheer sleeping gown billowing around her in the sudden draft from the balcony window.

"Alia!"

She came to him then, her face luminous in the dim light, an ethereal vision gliding across the room. Sitting down next to him on the bed, she stroked his face with a tremulous hand.

"Are . . . are you all right?" she whispered. "I heard you cry out and call my name."

"A bad dream, no more. Now that you're here, it doesn't matter." Teran turned his head into the palm still cradling his face.

He kissed it tenderly before taking it into his own. "Where have you been? I've waited for you all sol, not knowing where to find you or what was happening to you. Are you all right?"

"Yes, Teran, I am fine, quite fine."

Alia's reply was stiff, as she attempted to withdraw her hand from his grasp. What in the heavens above had come over her in that moment she'd heard him call her name? She had promised the High Priestess she would not see him, and now here she was, in his room.

He noticed her emotional withdrawal and tightened his grip. "Why do you pull back from me?"

293

"I . . . I must be returning to my chambers. It is late and not proper that I be found in your room."

"We are past the need for formality between us, I think," Teran growled, his face darkening in anger. "Or are you suddenly ashamed to call me friend and admit to what we've meant to each other?"

Alia's breath caught in a sharp, choking sob. "No, never! I will never be ashamed of you. I cherish the time we had and hope for it again, but not now. Before we can be together, there are still obligations to fulfill."

"This talk of yours distresses me. You can't seriously believe I would so easily let you go, can you? What is the matter, Alia? Tell me."

She sighed. "We must part for the next ten sols."

At his look of protest, she placed a silencing finger on his lips. "Try to understand. Please. Before I can participate in the high ceremony of Crystal Reinstatement, I must spend time in seclusion. It is tradition."

"And who told you that? The High Priestess?" he angrily demanded. "I don't trust her, Alia. She is evil and does not have your best interests at heart. I fear she'll do all within her power to separate us—and I don't mean just for a few sols, either."

"You are being unfair. Because she insists I adhere to a time-honored custom is no reason to doubt her motives. We will only be apart for ten sols. I swear it!"

"In the right hands, ten sols can be the opportunity of a lifetime," he muttered darkly.

"And you forget we are both Crystal Masters. What are her powers in light of that stone?"

"As nothing, one would think, yet still I wonder." Teran pulled her even more closely to him. "It is not the separation that galls me, Alia. Though the time apart will be painful, I could bear it, if only I were

294

certain that afterwards we'd be together. My heart is bound to you by bonds stronger than life. If I were to lose you . . ."

At his words, a pain squeezed Alia's chest, leaving an aching, empty space around it. "You won't lose me," she cried, at the same time struggling to move away from him. If she didn't leave now . . .

"You must let me go for a time. Even now, I am forbidden to see you."

"I care not for the rules of others," Teran said, his voice husky. "You are mine and I am yours. The morrow is soon enough to part."

His mouth came down on hers then, hungry and hard, as if to reclaim what she'd so willingly given before. Though Alia fought him, beating futilely against his broad, naked chest, Teran's kiss soon ignited arcing bursts of fire through her veins.

She slowly succumbed to the passionate possession of his mouth and the ardent feel of his body against hers. Melting into him, Alia found herself merging so totally there was nothing in the world except the man in her arms and the heady sensations rising from deep within her.

He pulled her down on top of him. Their legs entangled in the sheet that covered him as he rolled over onto her. Through the thin fabric, Alia could feel the urgent hardness of his desire pressing into her soft flesh.

The tangible evidence of his need kindled an answering conflagration in her. She wanted him, had to have him, needed again the fullness of his manhood inside her. High Priestess' command or not, she would have him one more time before beginning the ensuing sols of enforced chastity and separation.

Alia wrenched her mouth from his, her lips swollen from the aftermath of his fiery possession. "I want you so badly," she gasped. "For this nocte, then, let us forget the desires of others. If only you knew how I have longed for you, for the joining of our bodies!"

A strange look passed across Teran's face. He raised himself from her, the muscles of his arms and chest straining with the effort it took to hold himself back from her.

"Answer me this, Alia. Am I just a physical release for you, nothing more than a male to father your children?"

"No, Teran, no," she whispered, the truth seeking its way to her eyes. "You are not just a momentary pleasure and have never been so. I love you."

She stared into bottomless gray eyes, trying to fathom the effects of her words. "Teran?" she hesitantly began.

With a low groan, he gently lowered himself back onto her. "Alia, forgive me. Though your love gladdens my heart, I've no right to demand such answers, but for some reason, it seemed imperative you begin to understand your true feelings for me. My dream must have disturbed me more than I realized."

"Hush, hush," Alia crooned. "I found no offense in your questions. On the contrary. It is past time I share what I feel for you. I only wish I'd more to offer. Even my love seems so little, when there's such uncertainty of a life together."

She kissed him on the forehead, her hands encircling his neck. A tiny frown etched itself on her smooth brow. "You spoke of a dream. Would you care to talk of it?"

He stirred in her arms, his hands moving to lightly stroke her body. "No," he muttered thickly. "There'll be time to talk later. We've already squandered enough on words."

"Good," she giggled, releasing her grip to fall back onto the bed. "I also find myself preferring more physical pursuits." As if to emphasize her eagerness, she levered herself up for an instant to playfully nip a flat, brown nipple.

Teran leaned down, his lips gliding across the silky length of her shoulder until his mouth met her neck. Searing a path of scorching kisses up the slim column, he paused when his lips reached her ear. He gently bit her earlobe, then lightly outlined the delicate shell with the tip of his tongue. The grazing sensation sent jolting shivers down Alia's spine, leaving her weak and pliant in his arms.

Ever so slowly, Teran edged the gown further and further down Alia's body, until she lay half-exposed to him. With a sharp intake of breath, he paused to view the delectable sight of her full, white breasts. They lay there like ivory mounds, glinting in the moonlight.

The sight was too much to bear. In one eager motion, he grasped Alia's hips and rolled her back over on top of him. Pulling her further up along his body, his hands didn't stop until her breasts dangled tantalizingly over his mouth.

With a hungry growl, he flicked his tongue against one rosy peak until it hardened with excitement. As he mercilessly worked the firm bud with his mouth, his hand gently caressed Alia's other breast. She whimpered softly above him, her hips writhing in ardent abandon over his muscular abdomen. The sleeping gown slipped lower until it finally caught in the depression between Teran's legs and her straddling form. Frustrated by even its sheer barrier to her total nakedness, he reached up from his roving exploration of her buttocks to tear away the garment. Rolling Alia onto her back once more, he wedged himself between her thighs. Then, firmly grasping her hips, a bold thrust plunged him into her.

She gasped at the searing pleasure, at the joy of total possession of the powerful man in her arms. Hearing his breath suck in, Alia knew he, too, had found the same delicious gratification.

"Alia," he rasped hoarsely, his body beginning its primitive dance against hers.

Carried away by a spiraling excitement and drawn to a height of passion she'd never known before, Alia joined in the rhythmic thrusting. Smooth and languid, the strokes gradually escalated to a savage hysteria. She clasped at Teran, clawing at the bulging muscles of his back, grasping in wild abandon at his straining body.

Higher and higher rose the consuming passion, the effort to restrain the ultimate release becoming a bittersweet agony. Still, Alia fought it until at long last she was hurtled past the point of caring. A burning sweetness captivated her, transporting her on waves of whirling delight to a place of joy and unfettered freedom.

They dozed for a long while afterward, entwined in each other's arms. It felt so good to lie with him and feel the hard strength of his chest and the rough springy hairs that caressed her cheek. Alia burrowed even closer, her kisses alternating with teasing little bites.

"Keep that up and you'll suffer the consequences," Teran gruffly warned her. As if to emphasize his point, he cupped a round, female buttock in his hand.

"I may just hold you to that," she purred contentedly, "but for now, it is enough to lie in your arms."

"All that I have is yours, my love, to do with as you wish." His deep voice was heavy with suggestion.

She raised on one elbow to stare down at him, her fingers playing with his dark whorls of chest hair. Could this be the moment to finally ask him about the crime that had sent him to Carcer? The unspoken question had haunted her since that first sol together. Alia took a deep breath. "Does that offer include telling me about your past?"

"Yes," he laughed, "if that would please you."

"Well, then, I'd like to hear why you were exiled to Carcer." As she spoke, her glance never wavered from his. "All you've told me is that it was for some act of cowardice. After coming to know you, I find that totally absurd. You're the bravest, most valiant person I've ever known."

Teran stared into her eyes for a long moment, his expression sad but accepting. "Thank you for the compliment. Your high regard means more than I can say."

He pulled her down to him. His kiss was gentle and searching, yet thrilled her to her innermost being.

Then with a deep sigh, Teran released her. "There are many forms of cowardice," he began. "Bellator has developed its own code of conduct, as have all Imperium planets since the loss of the Crystal. My crime was to lack the courage to follow what my people considered a lawful order."

"I don't understand. Vates said you were one of Bellator's finest warriors. What could you have possibly done to merit such punishment?"

"Do you remember that nocte when you cared for my wounds, after we escaped Ferox's fortress?"

Alia nodded.

"We talked of faithfulness to one's heart and innermost beliefs. Sometimes, Alia, that can clash headlong with one's traditions and people. On Bellator we hold strict, unthinking discipline, in my case military discipline, in the highest regard. A warrior can do no wrong as long as he faithfully carries out a lawful order, no matter how cruel or unjust. At any rate, you asked about my crime and by necessity will receive only my version."

Her fingers traced a line up Teran's chest to his neck, then along his square, bearded jaw until it stopped at the corner of his mouth. "Your version will more than satisfy me. I care only for the reasons of the man I know and love, not for that of a planet I know nothing of and care even less about."

He shot her a sudden, arresting smile, the relief evident in his silver eyes. "I'm glad your trust in me is so boundless. I only hope the rest of my tale won't disillusion you."

Inhaling a deep breath, Teran continued. "Six monates before my exile to Carcer I was on a routine assignment on the planet Agrica. The natives are a gentle, primitive people for the most part, but due to some unfortunate circumstances, they'd attacked one of our outposts. My men and I were ordered against them and told to destroy a nearby village in retribution—an entire village, Alia!"

"And what did you do?" Even as she asked, a hard knot of apprehension rose in her throat.

"I had my men gather all the people and herd them into one of their animal pens. I gave the order to fire into them upon my signal, leaving no one alive. As I raised my hand to give the command, I happened to glance down at the villagers. The face of an old man caught my eye. I was struck at how much he resembled Vates. Suddenly, I didn't see an enemy anymore but a fellow being, albeit a few hundred cycles behind us in progress.

"Realizing what was happening to me, I forced my gaze from his, only to next have it captured by that of a young femina's. To wrench my eyes from her was even harder, yet nowhere in that crowd of pitiful faces could I find peace after that."

Teran paused to inhale a ragged breath. "I finally called off my men, though several protested mightily. I ordered them to free the villagers. True sons of Bellator, they obeyed me. Though I couldn't find it within myself to submit to a higher command, my men would still serve me. A few, however, were more than eager to report my infraction when we returned to the main outpost. I was immediately jailed to await execution for my act of cowardice."

Alia frowned in confusion. "But you weren't executed."

He gave a bitter, mocking laugh. "I was of royal birth, the son of a lord only second in line to the High King of Bellator. There was a great debate in Council over my fate, many insisting I should be made an example in order to reaffirm the law to the common people.

"After monate's of discussion, it was finally decided I was victim of my teacher's corrupting influence and hadn't known my own mind. In their great mercy, the Council decided to spare my life. Realizing, however, there was little hope of rehabilitation after cycles of Vates' dominance, they decided it safer to banish me to Carcer. For his part in my crime, Vates was, of course, exiled with me."

"That was quite a show of compassion for your Council."

Teran snorted in derision. "Do you think so, Alia? With an average Carcerian life expectancy of less than six monates, the Council thought they were sending me to certain death, albeit a bit delayed. Sometimes the only thing that kept me going, when I hurt so badly I wanted to die, was the memory of their sneering faces that sol of my sentencing. That and the fact I refused to give up, to admit that all Vates had taught me had been for naught."

He stroked her red tresses. "Who would have thought I'd live to hold you in my arms, free once more? I see now Carcer was only one of many steps in the path of my destiny, the happy fate that finally brought me to you. For that much at least, I am thankful."

Inexplicably, the image of a curved, bejeweled dagger flashed through Alia's mind. A tremor shook her. She turned to hide her face in the comforting brawn of his chest.

"What is it?" he asked in concern, noting the sudden change in her. "Is it something I said? Did I offend you in some way?"

"No, of course not," she mumbled, her voice muffled from her place at his chest. "I only wondered what has your wonderful destiny really gained you. You are but on another alien planet fraught with strange customs, and even I can offer no certainty of what the next sol will bring. How can you find peace in that?"

"Because of you," Teran replied, gathering her even closer to him. "Because a life with you at my side would be enough, no matter where I am. And after this nocte, I now know you're as truly mine as I am yours."

He cradled her chin in his large hand, lifting her face to gaze into her eyes. "Come with me, Alia. Be my life mate. If your Sisters won't allow us to remain here together, let us find our own way on Aranea. We need nothing but each other to make our happiness."

"Yes," Alia murmured drowsily, the warmth of Teran's masculine body gradually lulling her toward sleep. "It will be as you ask in but ten sols . . ."

302

She stifled a yawn with the back of her hand. "I am so weary. Let us talk no more. The morrow is time enough for . . ."

Alia was asleep before she could finish. Teran bent to lightly brush his lips across hers. "As you wish," he whispered tenderly. "I can wait. Your feelings for me won't have changed with a few hora's sleep. The morrow is time enough."

CHAPTER 16

TERAN AWOKE TO BRIGHT SUNSHINE, STREAMING INTO the room from the open balcony. A playful breeze teased the long draperies on either side of the doorway, sending the heavy fabric weaving in and out of the golden pool on the floor. He watched the interplay of light and shadow, content to lie in bed with the femina he loved.

At last he turned, his body stirring hotly with thoughts of last nocte's mating. The spot where Alia had slept was empty, the wrinkled imprint of a body and her lingering fragrance the only evidence she'd ever been there. With a frustrated groan, Teran climbed out of bed and strode toward the bathing room. Perhaps she was enjoying the hot mineral bath. He could almost feel the warm, churning waters bubbling up around him, as he envisioned himself sliding into the large tub to join her.

Alia wasn't in the bathing room, either. A low curse

escaped Teran's lips. Where had she gone off to now? An inexplicable sense of foreboding crept into his mind. It wasn't like her to slip away without a farewell, especially after the nocte they'd just shared.

He quickly washed, rejecting the bath for the more expedient standing basin. As he did, a small, metallic panel on the wall next to the basin caught his eye. Flipping it open, Teran found it contained an acid bath disposal system. Similar to a design used on Bellator, it consisted of an acid-impervious container in which to place trash. Once the panel was closed, a powerful caustic dissolved nearly any kind of waste.

Teran returned to the sleeping chamber and pulled the two govern keys from their hiding place in his belt. Walking back into the bathing room, he opened the waste panel and tossed the keys inside. The hissing sound of acid eating through metal permeated the small chamber. After several secundae he lifted the panel to peer inside.

It was empty. Good, he thought. Further possession of the keys was only to his disadvantage, especially if the High Priestess managed to obtain them.

His ablutions completed, Teran returned to the sleeping chamber and pulled on his breeches and boots. The outer door, reflected in the mirror of the dressing stand, slid open just as he reached for his tunic.

A small group of dark-robed feminas, led by the High Priestess, stood there. Teran turned to face them, his expression as guarded as his stance. "What may I do for you, Domina?" he tersely asked the High Priestess.

Her glance appreciatively slid up his body before coming to rest on his broad, muscular chest. With an unconscious sweep of her tongue, she licked her lips as if savoring a secret thought. She was like a rapax about to attack, Teran realized with sudden insight. The thought sent his heart to pounding, and he tensed, ready for battle.

"Alia asked me to explain her absence for the next ten sols," the High Priestess finally said, the cold, hard expression settling once again over her features. "She will be in seclusion for the purification rites prior to the ceremony of Crysal Reinstatement. In the meantime, she asked me to see to your needs." She arched an inquisitive brow. "Would you perhaps be interested in visiting our male compound?"

Teran studied the femina's face as he gave her suggestion serious consideration. Was there an ulterior motive behind the offer? If so, what could it be? And what would be her reaction if he refused?

His glance scanned the assemblage of Sisters. All could possess the ability to force him through their stunning powers, and without the presence of the Crystal, he was virtually helpless. It might be the wiser course to acquiesce, at least until he was surer of the situation.

"That would be most interesting," he forced himself to reply, a tight smile hovering on his lips. "There is much I wish to learn about Aranea, if I'm to now call it home."

"To be sure." The High Priestess turned to go, then stopped, looking back at Teran. "Finish dressing, then follow us. We will take you to the compound."

He watched the spare, unfriendly form glide away, as if fully expecting him to obediently follow. His barely suppressed anger heated to a scalding fury. For a secundae Teran was tempted to rescind his compliance, then sanity returned. If he could bear with the femina for ten sols, Alia would once more be his. In the end, that was all that mattered.

Contenting himself with a dark scowl, Teran quick-

ly slipped on his tunic and grabbed his studded belt.
Fastening it around his waist, he strode out after the
High Priestess and her bevy of agitated little atten-
dants. Along the maze of hallways and winding
passages he followed, unknowingly drawing further
and further from Alia toward the male compound.

The male compound seemed benign enough, a
scattering of long, low-slung, stone dwellings that
were evidently the sleeping quarters, all joined like
the spokes of a wheel to a much larger, round, central
building. Encompassed by a bountiful orchard of
various fruit trees and a large vegetable garden, the
setting reminded Teran of the bucolic villages of
Agrica. Perhaps his doubts as to the treatment of the
Aranean men had been wrong. Maybe they were as
Alia had said—nothing more than cherished, protected weaklings.

"If your survey of the compound is complete," the
black-gowned femina beside him said, "it is time to
take a closer look."

Teran turned from the stone parapet of the
monastery's outer wall and once more followed the
assemblage down the steps and out the main gate. In
but a few moments they were on the actual grounds
of the male compound. As they walked along Teran
noted men working, hoeing the garden for weeds,
climbing down ladders with fruit-laden baskets on
their backs, slowly but purposefully moving to and
fro.

He intently studied the men as some passed near,
hoping to catch their eye. Yet despite the presence of
the High Priestess and her entourage, the men
showed no interest, instead keeping their glances
firmly fixed on the task at hand. Teran thought it

strange, but maybe they had more important things to do than stare. Still shaking his head at their singular lack of curiosity, he turned his gaze back to the Sisters, already awaiting him at the main building.

A pale, twisted hand reached out as he halted in front of them. "Your belt."

Teran shot the High Priestess a suspicious look. "And what do you want with my belt, Domina?"

"The quarters are built of magnes stone. Are you familiar with its properties?"

"The rock laced with magnetic lodestone? Yes, I've heard of it."

She gave him a tight little smile. "Then perhaps you can understand why nothing of metal is allowed within. We long ago tired of having to remove eating utensils and the like from the walls and ceilings. Have no fear, your belt will be returned when you leave."

If I leave, Teran mentally echoed what he suspected she must be thinking. He reached behind him to untie the laces that bound his belt. "As you wish, Domina."

He reluctantly handed her the wide length of leather. Without the belt and the various implements contained therein, he was weaponless. A tiny needle of doubt pricked at him. Was the High Priestess by gradual degrees leading him into a trap?

She wordlessly accepted it and handed it to a Sister. Then, with a swirl of her heavy black robe, she walked through the door that slid open before her. Teran followed but not without noting that this door, too, opened only from the outside.

They headed down a brightly lit corridor lined with glass-paned doors. Teran glanced into each room through the viewing portals as they passed until, with an irritated sigh, the High Priestess turned to him. "I have every intention of showing you a representative room, if you would restrain your curiosity a few secundae longer."

A slight bow of a dark, wavy head of hair was her only acknowledgement.

Two doors up the hall the High Priestess paused, then entered through the portal that opened before her. Teran followed, stopping short as his glance took in the surprisingly high-ceilinged room. Around him, suspended from various loomlike frames, were delicate, intricately woven webs glinting like spun gold in the sunlight streaming in from high windows.

"The famed weaving spiders," Teran murmured, his gaze scanning the room in awe.

"Yes, the principal industry of Aranea, and one for which the gentle natures of our males seem particularly well-suited. Though not possessing the aggressive natures of males of certain other planets," she paused to stare pointedly at Teran, "our men, nonetheless, serve our people well."

"So it seems." Teran returned her look with an unwavering one of his own. "There are many forms of aggression, however. Some are not so negative, like defending oneself and one's mate or standing up for one's beliefs."

The implied challenge was not lost on the High Priestess, and her eyes frosted over in a glacial stare. "A luxury denied most of us until just recently. Perhaps the new reign of the Knowing Crystal will remedy that."

"It will, Domina. Of that you can be sure."

Cold fury flashed in the High Priestess' eyes. "We shall see. Now, enough of this. It is time to show you your new quarters."

"My new quarters?" A dark brow arched. "That

won't be necessary, Domina. I'm quite content where I am."

"It is not proper for you to remain in the monastery, the only male among so many females. Surely you can appreciate the impropriety of that. And it will only be for ten sols. Once the ceremony of Crystal Reinstatement is completed, I gather you and Alia will be making other arrangements."

Teran said nothing, his mind whirling with possible motives for this new, unexpected turn of events. On the surface what she said was quite plausible, yet it would distance him further from Alia, even if only physically. For some inexplicable reason, he didn't like the idea at all. A look of implacable determination spread across his face, etching the rugged planes in stubborn lines.

"It is a perfect opportunity to observe the ways of Aranean life, wouldn't you say?" the High Priestess cut in, cleverly throwing back Teran's own words at him. "These ten sols can be spent to your greatest profit here, learning about your new home."

A muscle worked in Teran's jaw as he forced down the growing frustration. She had backed him into a verbal corner, and they both knew it. The sense of a trap closing in on him was now almost tangible. Yet how, by the five moons of Bellator, was he going to get out of this?

His glance strayed toward the door. It was closed, as was most certainly the door to the outside of the building. A feeling of impotence, sickening in its intensity, welled up inside Teran. He, a highly skilled warrior of Bellator, the unlikely survivor of two grueling cycles on Carcer, was now the helpless pawn in the manipulative hands of the High Priestess of Aranea.

He choked down the bitter gall that rose in his

throat. Only time could now provide the opportunity for escape. He must bide his time. Teran gave the femina a bitter smile.

"Your suggestion has merit, Domina. Lead on."

A sound woke Teran from a fitful sleep. It was the portal of his room sliding open. A tray of food was swiftly placed on the table next to the door, then the panel once more closed. For a long while he lay there, feeling oddly lethargic. What time was it anyway?

Last nocte, after a hungrily devoured supper, he'd passed many horas in angry pacing, minutely examining the windowless room for any possibility of escape. He had found none. When the room finally darkened, the recessed ceiling light turned off by some unknown hand, Teran had sat there in the blackness, futilely rehashing the events that had led up to the miserable circumstances he was now in.

Teran wondered how Alia was faring. Was the High Priestess even now working on her, attempting to drive a wedge between them? Would Alia's love for him be equal to the onslaught of that evil femina? If only he could be at her side, if only they'd had more time! The horas, haunted by agonizing possibilities, dragged on. Finally, Teran slept.

It must be breakfast, he told himself, forcing his thoughts back to the present. Teran rose and stumbled toward the food. By the ken of the Crystal, but he was weak! Perhaps some nourishment was all he needed. Carrying the tray back, he sat down on the bed and uncovered the various dishes.

A short while later, the partition slid open again. Quickly throwing a blanket across his lap to cover his nakedness, Teran set down the cup he'd only managed to take a sip from.

The black-garbed form of a Sister he'd never seen before stepped into the room. "It is late. The High Priestess thought you'd like some outdoor exercise."

He pondered that for a moment. The High Priestess might possess some devious purpose for the offer, but it also suited his needs. There was always the possibility of allies in the other men. "A moment to dress myself, then I'll gladly accompany you."

She nodded and backed out of the room. As soon as he was alone Teran, immediately forgetting about food, jumped to his feet. The sudden effort sent his head to whirling giddily. He was forced to sit back on the bed for a few secundae. Finally, the dizziness cleared, and he rose, more carefully this time.

Teran slowly dressed. Fresh air was all he needed to sweep clean the cobwebs of weakness ensnaring his mind—just a little sunshine and fresh air.

There were several men in the exercise yard, aimlessly wandering about the grounds. Teran walked over to the nearest one. "Greetings, brother," he began in the common tongue. "My name is Teran Ardane, originally of the planet Bellator." He held out a hand as he spoke. "I'm a stranger to your planet. Would you talk with me?"

The man, dressed in the same garb as he, raised heavy-lidded eyes to Teran's. His mouth moved wordlessly for the span of a few sentences, then, head down, he shuffled away. Teran regarded his retreating form quizzically, then strode over to another man. His efforts were rewarded with the same response.

By the end of the third hora, when the noon meal was wheeled out into the yard, Teran was fighting a seething fury. What was the matter with these men? He couldn't believe they were a true representative of the males of Aranea. They were little more than mindless idiots or drugged slaves!

Drugs! The thought flashed through his brain. Was it possible they were drugged? But how—and more importantly, why?

Teran watched the men crowd around, crawling over each other in their efforts to get to the food. If nothing else, they were certainly well-fed. He felt a rising hunger, strangely intense in its onset and strength. Well, after all, he hadn't eaten breakfast, Teran reminded himself. Maybe he'd better get over there before all the food was taken. There was no predicting when the next meal might be served.

They came for him shortly thereafter, two solemn-faced Sisters. "It is time to return to your chambers."

Teran shook his head. "I'd prefer to stay with the others."

"It is not your choice. Do not make us use force."

He eyed them coldly. Force was it now? How quickly the superficial civilities had disappeared. The High Priestess must think he was already entrapped, without hope of escape or rescue. She was mistaken.

There was still the problem of the two Sisters, though. They could easily exert restraint by reaching out and stunning him. If he forced the issue he knew they'd not hesitate. Yet here he was, out in the open, the opportunity for flight never more available. In their long gowns, the two feminas would never be able to catch him.

Still, Teran hesitated. If he stayed, there might yet be a way to help these childlike men and discover the true cause of their passivity. And there was Alia. To run now would be to desert her in her hora of greatest need. With a sigh of resignation, Teran bowed to the two black-clad feminas. "As you wish. Lead the way."

By suppertime Teran could barely move from his

bed. His limbs felt heavy and numb, his mind muddled. From a place faraway he watched the tray with the covered dishes placed inside the door, then the panel slide shut once again.

Any interest in rising and walking over to it seemed to elude him. What was the matter with him? He felt like . . . like the way the men in the exercise yard looked this morning.

He was drugged, just like he'd guessed those Aranean men to be. It had to be the food. He'd felt almost as bad this morning after eating that first meal last nocte. The lethargic feeling had slowly dissipated when he'd skipped breakfast, then began all over again after he'd eaten the noon meal. No wonder there was never a need for walls or guards to control the men. Drugs worked even more effectively and without the outwardly distressing signs of coercion.

An angry, frustrated groan slipped from Teran's lips. Eight more sols before Alia completed her seclusion. It would be difficult to go eight sols without food. He didn't dare let himself weaken too severely; it would place him at the High Priestess' mercy.

Better to eat a little every sol or two. If he were careful he'd be able to minimize the effects of the drug that way. And maybe, just maybe, find the opportunity to convince some of the men to cut down their intake of the drug-laced food.

With a grim, triumphant smile, Teran closed his eyes. There were still ways to subvert the High Priestess. She hadn't won yet.

The lines on the page of ancient vellum blurred. Lulled by the warmth of the enclosed garden and the soothing sounds of the chirping birds, Alia's head nodded drowsily. The leather-bound book slowly slid down her lap, until it hovered precariously on the edge of her knees.

A loud *splat* woke Alia from her dreaming. The book lay, spine up, on the ground before her. With a small, horrified cry she grabbed it, hastily brushing the dirt and bits of debris from its thick, yellowed pages.

How could she? she cried in silent self-recrimination. It was one of the few volumes left on all of Aranea, their sacred Book of Readings, and she had treated it with such flagrant disrespect.

She shook her head, to clear the last wisps of fuzziness from her mind, and dutifully resumed the required reading. So beautiful, these phrases recounting life under Crystal Rule. Along with all that had transpired in the past five sols of her seclusion, they served to further intensify her desire for the Crystal's new reign. With each passing hora the utter rightness of her contribution, the intricacy with which her destiny was interwoven with that of the shining stone, was brought even more forcefully home.

Alia glanced around her, her senses greedily absorbing the beauty of the little garden—the vibrant colors of the flowers, their delicate, fragrant scents wafting to her flared nostrils, the drugging warmth of the sun beating down from a sky of blue, the gentle caress of the breeze so like the feel of Teran's lips on her body.

Teran! The mere mention of his name filled her with a heady warmth. Had it truly been only five sols since they'd parted? Strange, but it already seemed so long ago, the memory of their nocte of mating already acquiring a hazy unreality. Now the only reality, it seemed, was the present—this monastery, her well-earned place in the Sisterhood, and the Knowing Crystal.

She tried to visualize Teran's beloved features and was rewarded by a vague outline of a bearded face. A shiver of panic coursed through Alia. She could hardly remember his face! Her cheeks flushed hot with the rush of guilt that rose within her. Had she forgotten him—their love—so easily?

The hand lying upon the ancient tome clenched knuckle-white. No matter what her final choice and her eventual course in life, she owed Teran the loyalty of seeing to his safety and assuring his peaceful assimilation into Aranean ways. Even if she wasn't allowed to speak to him, surely the High Priestess would share some knowledge of his progress, perhaps even allow her to view him from afar.

And if she didn't? Then Teran's warnings would have more than a kernel of truth to them. Then it would be necessary to rethink her plans, to perhaps even rescue Teran and escape the monastery.

Carefully tucking the revered volume under her arm, Alia rose and walked out of the garden. Yes, she thought, as she strode along, first she must confront the High Priestess. Why worry about events that might never happen?

"No, child, it would not be in your best interests."

"But why, Domina Magna?" Even as she spoke, Alia felt the frustration twist her stomach into tight knots. "I'm not asking to talk to Teran, only to have a glimpse of him. How can that possibly be against my best interests?"

"This time of seclusion and purification is meant to be one of emotional as well as physical distance. You are only halfway through your time. Seeing the male now might set you back. I cannot allow it."

"And what will the endless worrying and the sleepless noctes spent thinking of him do to me?" Alia demanded, her eyes flashing. "I cannot find inner peace if I'm not assured Teran is safe and happy. I wonder at the real intent of keeping me from him."

Hard eyes narrowed, thin lips tightening in barely repressed anger. "You dare doubt me?" the High Priestess snarled. "You dare . . . ?"

With an effort the femina restrained herself, a mask of pleasant concern slipping over her formerly incensed features. "If I seem harsh in my attempts to keep you from the male," she began again, her voice low and honeyed, "it is with good reason, child. To my dismay, these past sols have revealed aspects of him that are, shall we say, far from pleasant. I thought only to protect you, to shield you from them until at least after Crystal Reinstatement."

She grasped Alia's arm. "Can you not wait until then?"

Disengaging herself from the older femina's clasp, Alia firmly shook her head. "Allow me to judge Teran for myself."

The High Priestess sighed. "Very well, child. Come with me. You may see what I would have spared you."

The tall, gaunt frame turned in an impatient whirl of black and strode out of her chambers. After a secundae's hesitation Alia followed after her, down stone corridors, out through the inner courtyard, and up steep steps that led to the walkway of the outer wall. High on the windswept parapets, the High Priestess finally halted.

"Why . . . why are we here, Domina Magna?" Alia panted as she tried to catch her breath. "Where, in all the heavens, have you sent Teran?"

"I have sent the male nowhere. He is where he wished to be." As she spoke, a black-swathed arm pointed downward toward the male compound.

Wide, honey-brown eyes followed the path of the arm, until Alia's gaze came to rest on a gathering in the compound's exercise yard. There, standing in the midst of a group of males, was Teran.

Her breath caught in her throat at the sight of him, tall and strong, his muscular body clad in loose white tunic and breeches and dark boots. Teran, her heart cried. She made an unconscious move toward him.

A hand snaked out to clasp one of her arms, the pressure hard and painful. Wrenched back, Alia turned to the High Priestess.

"Why is Teran in the male compound? He is no prisoner. He is our honored guest."

"He could not remain within our holy cloisters. Like our own, the male is best cared for under supervision. Look at him. Do you see any sign of maltreatment, though his conduct has been less than exemplary?"

Puzzlement clouded Alia's brow. "I don't understand. What has Teran done that you speak of him so?"

"The male is uncooperative and argumentative. We've been forced to restrain him several times already, before he harmed some of our males. He is dangerous and unpredictable, child. I am deeply concerned."

"No." Alia shook her head in disbelief. "I don't believe it. Teran isn't like that at all. There must be some problem, some terrible misunderstanding. Let me talk to him."

"That was not part of our agreement."

The words dashed any hope Alia had of convincing the High Priestess to let her meet with Teran. Her shoulders sagged momentarily before she once more raised her eyes to gaze down at Teran. As she

319

watched, the serving cart for the noon meal was wheeled into the yard. The men hungrily crowded around it, grasping out for the food.

Teran stood there, suddenly alone in the middle of the exercise yard. Then, with a cry too faraway for Alia to hear clearly, he sprang forward, shoving his way through the milling throng of men. Tearing the food from their hands and mouths as he went, he left a wake of dumbfounded bodies behind. At last he reached the cart. Grasping hold of one of its wooden sides, he began to rock it to and fro.

"You see? You see?" a triumphant voice hissed in Alia's ear. "He has gone mad, attacking our males, wreaking havoc during meals. He is an animal—and you so foolishly forfeited the govern keys to control him!"

Stunned by the scene below, Alia's face went deathly pale. Her hands balled into fists at her sides. Teran, oh, Teran, what has happened to you? she silently cried.

The confusion swelled inside until it nearly choked the breath from her. She wanted to turn away from the man attempting, in a mindless rage, to overturn the food cart while the others stood there in what seemed passive acceptance. At last he succeeded, the long, corded muscles of his arms and back straining as he pulled the wagon over. Its contents spilled onto the ground. Three Sisters, stun guns in hand, came running out of the building. As Alia watched, they all raised their weapons and fired.

In horrible slow motion, she saw Teran jerk, his powerful form spasming from the neural impulses bombarding him. He wheeled around to face his tormentors, his face contorted in agony. Then he fell, his body violently convulsing even before it hit the ground.

Alia could bear no more. She turned from the vision of him lying there in the dust, his body twisted into some unnatural position. Her breath escaped in shuddering gasps. What had she brought him to that he now lay there in the dirt, crippled and suffering?

A hand, cold and comfortless, briefly touched her head before sliding down to rest on her arm. "Did I not try to spare you this, child?" the High Priestess asked. "Perhaps next time you will heed my words more carefully."

She tightened her clasp on Alia's arm. "Come. Your Sisters will care for the male. It is time to forget him. He was never what you imagined him to be. Time you return to where you truly belong, to the life you were reared for. Come back to the monastery, where your true destiny lies."

Eyes that were little more than pools of misery looked at the older femina. Was it true what she said of Teran? Had he indeed degenerated into the animal all males were ultimately purported to be?

No, she could not, would not believe it of him. The memory of their loving, his strong brown arms clasped around her, was still too potent. He had not hurt her then, at a moment when one's most primitive urges rose to nearly overwhelming intensity. If he could control himself even then, in that most vulnerable of times, he could never be an animal.

Still the doubts assailed her, as she walked back toward the monastery. The words of the High Priestess returned again and again to hound her, baying at the gates of her heart in a mournful, maddening wail.

He was never what you imagined him to be.

321

CHAPTER 17

THE TENTH SOL HAD ARRIVED AT LAST.

The thought slashed across Teran's sleep-freshened consciousness with a searing, soaring elation. He had beaten the High Priestess. Alia would come for him this sol.

Opening his eyes, he made a move to rise when the dull clink of metal followed by a rough jerk on both wrists reminded him of the cursed chains.

For five sols now, since that incident in the exercise yard, he had been confined in his chamber, chained to the wall. As if he could have escaped from the room anyway, Teran thought wryly.

But soon none of it would matter—the self-induced fasting, the long sols spent alone in his eternally darkened chamber, the tormenting doubts. Soon Alia would be here.

The rasping sound of his door sliding open distracted Teran. Raising silver eyes to stare toward the form backlit by the doorway, his heart thundered in his chest. Was it Alia? Had she come at last?

Before he could discern if it were indeed she, a bright, blinding light filled the room. His eyes clenched shut as a reflex, his head lowering in an attempt to shield his face from the painful brilliance after what seemed an eternity spent in total darkness.

"It will do you no good, you know."

With an angry jerk Teran's head snapped up. In the dazzling overhead light, his narrowed gaze found the High Priestess, standing but a few meters out of reach. "What do you want?" he growled.

She shrugged nonchalantly. "A last opportunity, perhaps, to gloat over my vanquished foe? You really were quite disappointing as an opponent." A wistful sigh escaped her lips. "And I'd expected so much more of a presumed Crystal Master."

"My purpose here was never to entertain you. Though perhaps the real drama will soon occur, once Alia joins us."

The femina gave a brittle laugh. "And what, my handsome male, do you think Alia can do to help you? Or for that matter, what would she want to do once she finally sees you again?"

"You're a fool, if you think you can change her feelings for me." Teran's temper flared, fueled by the long sols and noctes of worry about just that. With an effort, he regained a semblance of outward control, the muscle twitching furiously in his bearded jaw the only evidence of his inner turmoil.

He could not, would not, let that femina gain the upper hand. "Even you cannot prevent her from coming to me, not with the Knowing Crystal in her possession," he continued in a calmer, more measured voice.

"Hardly my intention, to be sure. Perceptions can

be altered, however. Fertile soil for the seeds of doubt to grow into a change of heart, wouldn't you say?"

"And how do you plan to do that? Your attempts to drug me into one of your mindless idiots have failed. You couldn't force me to eat, and now it's too late. You've won nothing."

A thin, bitter smile touched the High Priestess' mouth. "The contest for Alia is not over—and that is what it truly is, isn't it? A battle between you and me for control of Alia and the power she possesses. Well, have no doubt, criminal of Carcer. I *will* triumph. Too many cycles have I waited for Alia's powers to mature to allow you to snatch them from me."

"And that is exactly why you'll fail." Teran ground the words out through tightly gritted teeth. "Alia is not an object to be manipulated. She's an intelligent, courageous, loving femina and has learned to heed the call of her heart. Your cycles of influence are over, your cold-blooded reign of Aranea at an end!"

The High Priestess stared at Teran, the murderous look in her eyes sending an ominous chill down his spine. "We shall soon see, won't we? I sincerely doubt Alia's tastes run to savage, rutting beasts."

Teran smiled grimly, the challenge glinting in his silver eyes. "Your opinion of all men, I presume?"

"An opinion soon to be shared by Alia."

Something in the tone of her voice set off a skin-prickling response in Teran. He should have known she wouldn't relinquish control without a fight. "What are you planning?"

"We have many drugs," came the malevolent reply, "even one to stimulate the, ah, mating urge in our males. It is quite effective. The drug encourages our reluctant males to assist in the procreation of the race and, because of their behavior in the process, sickens our feminas against them. Haven't you wondered why Aranean feminas never protest the imprisonment of their males? After just one mating, they never want to be touched by a male again."

She turned and walked toward the door, then paused, as if remembering one last, infinitely amusing thing. "After this nocte Alia won't care what happens to you. I promise it." With a low, mocking laugh, she stalked out of the room.

Teran sprang at the High Priestess, a hoarse, furious cry on his lips. His effort was futile, for he quickly reached the limits of the chains. The shackles dug into his wrists, roughly wrenching him backward.

Curse the femina! he inwardly raged. Curse the fate that delivered him into her hands! Curse his own stupidity!

With a frustrated groan, he fell back onto the bed and buried his head in his hands. What was he about to do to Alia? He had seen too much of the High Priestess' powers to doubt the evil truth of her words. The heels of his hands gouged into his eye sockets in total, frightening helplessness. He could bear anything except to hurt Alia, to destroy her love and faith in him.

A faint odor wafted by, acrid and mildly irritating. Teran lifted his head. An unusual fizzing sound permeated the tormented chaos of his mind. Where was it coming from?

Teran strained to look behind him. There, billowing out of the air vent, was a sickeningly yellow cloud. Was this the drug the High Priestess spoke of?

He grabbed the blanket, wadding it up to cover his nose and mouth. The vapor gradually spread throughout the room, enveloping its contents in a yellow fog.

Despite the thickness of the material protecting his face, Teran began to smell and taste the bitter, drug-laced gas. His eyes watered, then blurred. The room swam before his bleary gaze until it whirled dizzily, seeming to draw him into a spinning vortex. He felt as if he were floating, his limbs losing all sensation.

A black pit rushed toward him. He was falling into a yawning maw of unconsciousness. In that last, terrifying instant before it swallowed him, a wild, heartrending cry flashed through his mind. It grew, burgeoning inside him until it ripped its way free.

"Alia," he groaned, each breath sending him further into the awful chasm of oblivion. "Forgive me . . . Forgive me for what I do . . ."

Through the deepening twilight before moonrise, the nocte of the Weaver's moon, two figures slowly made their way across the darkened monastery. Robes shimmered in the faint light of wall-recessed torches, one gown the luminous color of moonstone, the other the midnocte hues of ebony. The sound of low voices, hardly more than the murmur of the gentle evening wind, floated by to rapidly dissipate in the air.

"Two horas, child. That is all you have until the ceremony of Crystal Reinstatement. A time better spent in meditation and soul-soothing preparation than in dialogue with the male."

Alia glanced over as they walked along. "My mind is at peace with the Crystal, Domina Magna. I am ready. I'll not tarry long with Teran, just a few moments to assure him that all is well. Then I'll return without protest."

The High Priestess sighed. "Child, child, when will you cease to doubt my counsel? I wish only to protect you from the harsh reality of what the male truly is. Will you not allow me to spare you this pain?"

327

"And what exactly is he?" Alia stopped short, to confront the High Priestess. "He has been alone these ten sols, struggling to adapt to the customs of a strange planet, among people suspicious and hostile to him. Who can blame him for some frustration, some anger?"

"Allowances, more than you could imagine, have been made, but he persists in fighting us, his behavior becoming more and more bizarre as the sols pass. If the truth be known, child, I fear for your safety. He is not the same male you brought with you from Carcer."

"Then it's time I discovered that for myself." Alia struggled to make her mind feel as calm and steady as her voice sounded. "Permit me that much."

"As you wish," came the terse reply.

They continued their journey to the male compound, neither speaking as they walked along. Finally, the two feminas halted in front of a windowless portal. Alia turned questioning eyes to the High Priestess.

"The male's chamber," the older femina replied, stepping back as the panel slid open. "Have a care, child, and remember my words."

Taking a deep breath to steady her finely strung nerves, Alia stepped into the room. As the door closed behind her, she stifled the impulse to turn and run. There, at the far end, was Teran, his head down, hands clenching and unclenching in rapid repetition, agitatedly pacing the floor. For an instant she watched him, her heart swelling at the sight, all her anxiety melting in the intense reawakening of her love.

"Teran," she finally whispered. "It is I, Alia."

He froze at the sound of her voice and slowly turned to confront her. At the sight of his face, a cold knot formed in Alia's stomach.

Gray eyes stared back at her without sign of recognition, eyes that flicked over her body with a feral, hungry look. The white tunic and breeches, soiled and torn in several places, clung damply to a body heavy with sweat.

"Teran." She forced the words out of a throat tight with growing apprehension. "What is the matter? What's happened to you?"

A guttural growl was her only reply as Teran slowly advanced on her, his head lowering like some animal ready to attack. Instinctively, Alia took a step backward. "Teran, please, I beg you. Tell me what's—"

Before the words had left her mouth, he sprang at her. Strong hands, made even more powerful by the frenzy within, grabbed at Alia, pulling her to him. A hard, savage mouth came down upon hers, brutal and punishing. Stunned by the senselessness of his assault, Alia stood there, paralyzed.

Sharp awareness returned as Teran's hands tore at her robe, his fingers madly shredding the cloth from her body. Alia reacted then and flailed wildly at him. "Teran, Teran, let go of me! Listen to me! It's Alia, Teran. Alia!"

If he heard, he gave no sign of recognition. Instead, Teran continued his senseless onslaught, tearing Alia's gown apart to expose her sheer undershift. As she futilely fought him, she felt the shift rip. A rough hand enveloped her breast.

A horrible realization flashed through her mind. He was going to ravish her, no matter what she said or did. Teran, the tender lover, the man of honor, was going to brutally take her like some animal mired in the throes of mating lust.

The High Priestess' words echoed through her mind—*not what you imagined, dangerous, gone mad*.

Endlessly the phrases reverberated, growing in volume until Alia thought her skull would shatter, And all the while, the grabbing, grasping, tearing hands attacked her body.

Teran's hands? No. The hands of some slavering animal. She must stop him, no matter what the cost, no matter how dear the memories of what they'd once shared. Now. Before it was too late for either of them.

Tightly clenching her eyes, Alia clasped Teran's face between her hands, the soft, familiar feel of his beard causing her to momentarily falter. How could she bring herself to harm him, she who had vowed never to use the govern keys on him again? One final look at his contorted, almost bestial countenance and the decision was made.

From a place deep within her a power surged forth, flowing from her innermost being outward into her arms, hands and through her fingertips. The male before her gave a hoarse cry, then froze. A surprised expression floated across his face, before his features twisted in agony. Teran's limbs relaxed, and he fell, plummeting straight to the floor.

Alia stared down at him, sprawled motionless before her. She felt nothing, her heart and mind drained, devoid of all emotion. The man she had known and loved was dead.

The being that now inhabited the shell of the body on the floor was not Teran. Teran was gone. After all this time, all her hopes and dreams, she was still alone—alone, save for the Knowing Crystal. A sob rising in her throat, Alia fled the room.

Outside, in the dim light of the wall torches, the Sisters were waiting for her. From the High Priestess at its head, two parallel rows dipped and rose in height and breadth until ending with the white-gowned novices. Alia silently took her place with them.

The High Priestess noted her arrival. She slowly strode down the path left between the ranks of Sisters and halted beside Alia. "Come, child," the older femina murmured, her voice flat and emotionless. "This nocte of the Weaver's moon, your place is at the head of the line. As the Crystal's deliverer you will lead your Sisters into the Sanctuary for the ceremony. You will then array yourself beside me. Comport yourself honorably, as behooves your new status."

Alia bowed. "Yes, Domina Magna."

The large stone doors, intricately sculpted with the history of the Knowing Crystal, swung open, revealing a long, narrow chamber dimly lit by recessed lighting high on the walls near the ceiling. Alia's gaze traveled down the center aisle, bordered on both sides by long stone benches. There, at the far end of the room, stood the obsidian pedestal, legendary receptacle of the Knowing Crystal. Even from this distance she could see the shimmering carved words, glowing golden in the heavily shadowed room.

From behind her, the Sisters began chanting the Litany of the Crystal Gifts, the hauntingly beautiful song of the nearly limitless powers of the Knowing Crystal. The High Priestess tugged on Alia's sleeve, signaling her to begin the procession.

Alia stepped out, the hypnotic refrain seemingly all that followed her. Lulled by the soothing words and cherished lines that had never failed to fill her with radiant hope, it seemed but an instant later that Alia found herself before the throne of the High Priestess. Beside it was a smaller chair which she stepped in front of. Turning, she faced the slow procession of Sisters filing up the aisle before her.

In neat groups, they pivoted at their designated rows and walked to their places in front of the benches. As one, the eyes of the entire order raised to the High Priestess. She stood there, coldly proud, the ruler of the Sisterhood of the Crystal—and all Aranea.

"This is a happy nocte, the time of the Crystal's return," she began, her sharp voice carrying to the far reaches of the hall. "One of our own has brought honor to the order by rescuing the Knowing Crystal. We, in turn, honor her by allowing her to advance to the final Test of Worthiness. If she succeeds, on the morrow she will at last be truly one of us. Let us pray she finds the courage and discipline of heart to prevail."

A soft murmur of approval fluttered through the room. The High Priestess raised a silencing hand. "The time has come for Crystal Reinstatement. Alia, last of the Royal House Certare, step forward."

Alia felt a fleeting surge of panic, realizing that this was the culmination of all her dreams and the dreams of her people. Then it passed. She would not shame herself or her training by showing apprehension at the very moment of her victory. They had all doubted her ability to persevere until final Profession. Now she stood before them, exonorated by one no less than the High Priestess.

She stepped forward, her head held high. "I am at your command, Domina Magna," she said, her clear, young voice ringing throughout the Sanctuary.

A black-shrouded arm pointed in the direction of the pedestal. "Return the Knowing Crystal to its receptacle, child. Set us free of the tyranny of ignorance that has imprisoned us these hundreds of cycles. Key the Crystal and speak the first words of its homecoming."

Alia walked toward the smooth, shiny black repository, drawing the Crystal from her pocket as she did. She held it up to the assemblage, then turned to the receptacle once more. With both hands about it, Alia slowly replaced the Crystal in the hollowed-out space in the pedestal's center.

She stood before it and waited. Finally the Crystal began to flicker, then glow, until its luminous intensity filled the hall. A gasp spread through the congregation, then died, as the Sisters' attention riveted on the white-gowned figure before them.

The radiant peace filled her as before, the Crystal communing with its same soothing voice, the gladness swelling within her. Caught up in a whirling happiness, Alia felt insensible to time or space. Things she had never seen before, knowledge the stone had heretofore withheld, were finally granted. Past lifetimes and distant futures flashed before her.

Alia waited for what seemed an eternity for the final key that would unlock the door of knowledge—and waited in vain. She felt at a loss, as if the Crystal persisted in withholding the most vital information of all. Even now, after all she had suffered, all she had endured, there remained an impediment to total union.

Was she yet unworthy? her heart cried. *Yes*, it answered, and the glowing light faded, leaving her in confused darkness.

"Speak, child." The distant voice of the High Priestess called Alia. "Share the wisdom of the Crystal."

Alia forced herself to face the gathering, though the effort cost her dearly. She looked down upon faces eager for the first words of the Knowing Crystal, words not heard in their lifetime nor by many ancestors before them.

"The . . . the Crystal spoke of many things," she hesitantly began, "of ruined dreams, forfeited morality, man's inhumanity to man. Because of our failures it is sad, disheartened to discover how we have lost our way. It wonders if we are, perhaps, unable to learn, unable to profit from its past teachings. Its light dimmed as it told me this, as if greatly distressed.

"Then the Crystal began to speak of happier things, of hope, and slowly its light brightened. It foretold a new beginning for the peoples of the Imperium, but only if love and courage prevail. For hearts brave and true there must be a dying and a rebirth. Only then can we leave the darkness forever, only then . . ."

Alia's voice broke as she fought desperately to control the trembling that racked her body. What did it all mean? What was the Crystal really asking of her?

"Continue, child," the cold voice of the High Priestess prodded. "Was there more?"

Alia turned glazed, weary eyes toward the femina. "More?" Recovering herself, she shook her head. "No, Domina Magna, there was no more."

"Then come and follow your Sisters in the final procession. We go forward to announce the glorious news to all the people."

Alia watched the Sisters slowly file out of the Sanctuary, once more chanting the litany. When her turn came to follow, Alia forced her wooden limbs to join them, though she barely felt her feet touch the floor. The force of earlier habits moved her, the long cycles of unquestioning obedience to the smallest whim of the High Priestess.

Afterwards, when the cheering crowds were left behind, the emotionless eyes of the High Priestess greeted Alia outside the same stone doors. "We will go to the Room of Professions. It is past time you

334

were gowned in the robes of our order."

She led the way, Alia following in a numbed silence. The smaller Room of Professions was dimly lit by the eerie, flickering light of perpetual torches. Alia had always wondered, when she had dared peek into it as a child, why a room associated with such a joyous experience as Profession should look so dark and foreboding.

Without a backward glance, the High Priestess strode out of the room through a small side door. Alia remained where she was, wondering if she should follow. Her mind swam with questions and doubts if what she was about to do was correct. Could she now, even at this last moment, turn her back on the life she had dreamed of with Teran?

With a small sigh, she lowered herself onto the stool next to the High Priestess' throne. The thought of Teran filled her with a piercing sadness. There was no hope of a life with him now. He had destroyed it all in his senseless attack on her. Freedom might yet be his, but no longer with her. Her true destiny had been brought most forcibly home this nocte as she stood before the Knowing Crystal.

The older femina reentered, carrying a black gown folded over her arm. She stopped beside her chair and gazed down at Alia. "Rise, child," she commanded. "It is time for your robing in the colors of our order."

Shaky legs brought Alia to her feet. Was it actually happening? Was she to finally win the long-desired garb of the Professed? Her heart pounded in excitement. At long last!

"Shed your gown of youth, so I may clothe you in the black robes of maturity," the High Priestess said. The ritual words of robing dropped from her lips like so many precious jewels to Alia's longing ears. "Take it upon you as a symbol of eternal celibacy and obedience, and prepare for the revelation of your final test. It will give you the strength and courage to persevere, and earn for you, at long last, the hallowed title of Sister in the Order of the Crystal."

Celibacy. The meaning slashed through Alia, dampening the heady elation of achievement with the sobering memory of Teran. If she accepted the gown and its implications, their hopes of a life together were shattered, once and for all. Even now, with the harsh memory of his brutal assault upon her only horas before, the final reality was still more than she could bear. To give him up, the feel of his arms around her, the touch of his lips on her flesh . . .

"It was never meant to be, child," the High Priestess said, as if reading Alia's mind. "Your destiny lies with your people. To serve them as they truly deserve, you must deny yourself. The male is not for one such as you."

She held out the black and red gown, symbol of the choice between duty and fleeting pleasure. Alia stared at it, mesmerized, the programed phrases of honor and devotion to one's people flooding back to overwhelm her. Imperceptibly, the memory of Teran faded, the temporal joys of the body dimming in the bright light of consecrated service.

Finally she sighed. "Can you at least promise me Teran will be well-treated? He could not bear to be penned up like our males."

"His time of suffering is almost over, that I can promise you."

Alia unfastened her white gown. In the next instant, she stood there, clothed only in her sheer undershift. Beneath the piercing stare of the High Priestess, Alia suddenly felt vulnerable, as if she were the helpless prey of this femina before her. She

336

quickly took the black gown and slipped into its heavy, comforting weight.

"It is yours for life," the femina murmured, "for, indeed, your life depends on passing this final Test of Worthiness. There is no way to fail, except death. No one survives who has not the heart to complete the task I now set before you. Are you willing to suffer the possible consequences in order to gain final Profession in our hallowed order?"

"Yes, I am willing. May I have the courage to prevail."

The High Priestess moved closer, as if to tighten the web she now spun around the bewildered young femina. "Then hear my words and temper them with the knowledge and discipline of your cycles of training. Though harsh they may seem, trust in the ultimate wisdom of the act, an act long buried in perpetuity but still timely, still essential to the existence of our people.

"The task is simple, yet one only the true of heart can bear. As the representatives of the Aranean people, we of the Sisterhood have been chosen to perform a horrible but necessary service. I ask you once more, Alia of the House Certare, are you willing to hear this final test? Answer carefully, for once it leaves my lips there is no calling it back. Your life will be forever changed."

"My people require it of me," came the ritual reply. The time for thought had passed. Total, unquestioning acceptance was now all that mattered. "I am willing."

"Then hear your final test, and do not quail before it. To prove yourself worthy of Profession, you must sacrifice your lover. He must die on the morrow—by your hand and your hand alone."

CHAPTER 18

FOR A MOMENT SUSPENDED IN TIME ALIA GAZED AT THE High Priestess, her eyes wide with horror. Kill Teran? It was impossible. Yet hadn't she already acquiesced to the deed when she accepted the final test?

"You ask a thing I am incapable of fulfilling, Domina Magna," Alia finally whispered, choking out the words. A fierce trembling racked her body. Though she felt damp with terror, underneath it she was chilled, her palms icy. "Ask me anything else, and I will willingly comply, but not that I kill Teran. Is it not enough I've already agreed to part from him? I owe him too much for a reckoning such as you ask."

"And do you owe him more than your debt to your people?" was the frigid rejoinder. "Is one life of greater value than the lives of millions? He is nothing, a common criminal, an exile. You would forget him soon enough, whether he lived or died."

Alia shook her head, stunned disbelief etched into

her features. "You don't understand. Though I willingly choose to separate my life from his, I could never forget him. The child I bear would remind me of Teran everytime I gazed at it and held it in my arms."

Huge, grief-stricken eyes stared at the High Priestess. "Why is it necessary to kill Teran? Why would you require such a thing for my final test?"

Cold eyes glared back at her, remorseless and determined. "Think you this is but your test alone? All of us, all Sisters of the Crystal, are required to perform this act. It is the eventual fate of all Aranean males after mating and a successful number of impregnations has occurred. This task has been left to us, to protect our planet from the chaos of male domination. It is a sacred trust, a heavy responsibility, but one we must bear if Aranea is to survive. So ask me not why you have been unfairly chosen. I had thought you were trained better than to now snivel and bemoan your terrible fate."

"I . . . I do not wish to shirk my responsibility to my people, Domina Magna," Alia murmured. "I would willingly give my life if it would help Aranea, but how can Teran be a threat to our planet? He will eventually adapt; there is no need to kill him. In spite of what has happened he *is* a kind, compassionate man."

"And when, in your tender cycles, did you become capable of judging such matters?" the older femina retorted with dry sarcasm. "If I say the male is a danger, that should be enough for you. Would you rather trust someone you have known less than a monate over your Sisters? If you are to eventually rule, perhaps it is time to decide, once and for all, where your true loyalties lie."

Alia gave a strangled, desperate laugh. "Then you

will not tell me the reason for this cruel practice nor free me from its frightful course?"

"It is all part of the trial—the blind faith and obedience, the supreme sacrifice, the true test of your love for Aranea. Alia of the House Certare, are you worthy?"

The room began to whirl crazily, the humming in her ears rising to a deafening roar. Please, don't let me faint now, Alia frantically prayed. Don't let me shame myself anymore than I already have in this frightening, horrible moment of weakness. The words of the High Priestess echoed in her brain, hammering at her mind and beating at the very portals of her soul. If you are eventually to rule Aranea . . .

To rule Aranea—the responsibility, the self-sacrifice! It seemed this nocte would require not only the offering of Teran's life but her own as well—to her people and her planet. Did she not owe Aranea that ultimate loyalty?

A sudden, unbidden thought slipped into her mind. Was this what the Knowing Crystal had meant when it informed her she was still unworthy? Did it have yet its own Test of Worthiness—this final choice between love and duty? And how would she ever know if she didn't face it?

"Yes!" Alia cried, not knowing who she was really answering. "Yes, I *am* worthy. I am willing to do anything, sacrifice all, if it will help Aranea. I do not understand, but I accept the test."

"Then it is decided. On the morrow at the eighth hora you will await us in the Sacrifice Room. Your sisters will be there to support you. They, of all people, understand the supreme difficulty of the first immolation."

The High Priestess paused to carefully rearrange a

fold of her gown before glancing back at Alia. "Now go. The nocte is well advanced and you need to rest. The morrow will require all the strength you have. Your line has never been known for its overabundance of courage."

Alia tried to defend her family but gave it up. What was there to say, knowing as little as she did about them? She slowly walked from the room. If the High Priestess doubted her fortitude, the only way to settle the question was to prove herself at Sacrifice.

Sacrifice! The meaning of the word echoed in her mind—to give up one thing for the sake of another, to give up Teran for the sake of Aranea! With a muffled cry, Alia ran down the corridors in agony, fleeing the harsh deed that was hers, until she reached the haven of her own chamber.

The procession halted before a huge, stone door embellished only by a smooth, gleaming handle. Surprisingly, for its apparent weight, the portal swung open without difficulty at the merest touch of the High Priestess. With a grim twist to her mouth she stepped aside, elegantly motioning for Teran to enter. "Alia awaits you," she murmured silkily.

Teran hesitated, sensing a horrible danger emanating from the dimly lit room. He opened his mouth to refuse, when a soft voice issued from deep within the chamber.

"Teran, please come in," Alia called. "If you seek me, you have found what you sought."

He strode past the High Priestess, glowering at her as he swept by. Surveying the room, his eyes gradually adjusted to the semidarkness. His glance passed over the vague form of a table before finally coming to rest upon the figure of Alia, standing near the room's only window. She faced him, her form thrown into shadow.

"Alia," Teran rasped. Deep emotion surged through him. No matter what he may have done, if she'd even come to him last nocte, all that remained was the fact they were together at last.

His long legs carried him to her side. "I'm so glad to see you again." Though he tried mightily to hide it, there was a husky catch in his voice. "I was near mad with worry about you."

She stood there, looking at him without speaking, until Teran wondered if she had even heard him. The secundae plodded by, the tension building as the effort to contain his need for her rapidly dwindled. "Alia," he finally exploded, his words echoing harshly in the nearly empty room, "why won't you answer me?"

"It's over, Teran. Try to understand. My duty . . ." came the whispered reply.

A slender hand, slowly, reluctantly moved toward him. "Forgive me, Teran, if you can."

She touched his chest, her fingers grazing him in a gentle caress. Teran took a step forward to gather her into his arms, when an excrutiating pain jolted through him. His limbs froze. His body fell backward into the grasp of several Sisters who had silently surrounded him. Still fully conscious, he was lifted and carried across the chamber.

The realization of the High Priestess' machinations filled Teran with a sickening intensity, but the true agony was Alia's complicity in the scheme. How could he have been such a fool! Was it not she who had stunned him, she who had led him to this place? And surely it was she who had possessed the full knowledge of his eventual fate. The horror of the unknown was nothing in the face of such betrayal.

They lay him on the cold stone slab. A bright light appeared overhead, illuminating only the area in which he lay. The premonition of danger swelled inside him with the recognition of the scene as the one from his dream. Summoning all his strength Teran fought to move, to stir the limbs that felt everything except the command to action.

A fine sweat broke out on his brow as he strained every muscle in his body. They watched him in his futile struggles, the black-robed feminas who silently gathered around the table on which he lay. His mighty brawn eventually relaxed in exhaustion. Teran's gray eyes continued to move, though, sweeping the somber ring of unfriendly faces hovering over him. A movement near his head caught his attention, and he swiftly shifted his gaze in that direction.

The red and black-garbed form of the High Priestess stood there, malicious triumph gleaming in her eyes. "As much a fool as any male, your lust has led you to your death. At last you will pay the price for the indignities you have forced upon one of our Sisters. You will die, criminal, at her own hand!"

With a vicious snarl the High Priestess grasped the front of Teran's tunic, ripping it apart to completely bare his chest. She stepped back into the darkness that surrounded the slab. "Alia," she commanded, "your moment of Sacrifice is upon you. Come forward!"

His love, his betrayer, appeared at his side dressed in the same black and red robes as the other feminas. The face, though, was different than the rest. It was a face familiar and dear.

Drawn and white, Alia appeared possessed by a force outside herself. Her breath came in quick, shallow gasps. A spasmodic trembling shook her slender body.

But it was her eyes, wide and staring, that caught and held Teran's attention. They gazed down at him imploringly, as if begging for understanding and forgiveness. Their eyes locked. For an instant, they were alone in the room.

Gray orbs burned into honey-brown ones, the emotions arcing to and fro until Alia thought she would drown in the depths of Teran's expressive eyes. The things she saw there—infinite love and anguish, power and courage—seared into her very soul. If only he could give her a little of his strength, if only—

"Take up the weapon of his destruction," the High Priestess ordered, sharply intruding into Alia's wistful thoughts. "It is past time for the deed to be done, your worthiness proven."

Reluctantly, Alia raised a tortured face to the High Priestess. In the clawed hand of the older femina was a dagger, curved and intricately jeweled. In a moment frozen in time, Alia saw the dagger on another level in the form of her dreams. Even then she had feared its meaning, the blood-stained tip glinting horribly in her memory, but never in her worst fantasies, awake or sleeping, had she envisioned it as the instrument of Teran's destruction.

"Take it! Take it and perform the Sacrifice," the High Priestess rasped.

She shoved the dagger into Alia's hand, forcing her fingers to curve around the handle. "Prove your worthiness. Prove your love for your people, for Aranea."

Alia gazed at the weapon in dumb confusion. All the cycles of her painstaking training rose to torment her, to hurl derisive insults at her hesitation. The other Sisters moved imperceptibly closer, sensing the nearness of death and eager to witness the blood spilled.

A chanting arose, haunting and compelling. Through the growing mists of her despair, Alia wildly glanced about. Mouths in expressionless faces moved as her Sisters surged ever forward, urging her on with melodious, mesmerizing phrases.

"I will not fear; I will be strong. My courage true, my weakness wrong."

On and on it went, the familiar words lulling her into an almost hypnotic trance. It was true. She was simply afraid—afraid of facing her responsibilities and her innate weaknesses. But the vindication, for her as well as her family, was there, if only she found the courage to plunge that dagger into Teran's heart. Alia clasped her other hand around the weapon and raised her arms above her head.

In that last moment between life and death, she glanced down one last time at Teran. He lay there, an impotent prisoner, his silver eyes steadily gazing back at her. Her glance swept down his superbly hardened body, the cruel scars that marked his hair-whorled chest, the rippling ridges of his abdomen, the strong legs.

He had given her so much, shown her the universe within the expanse of but his arms. Her throat tightened until she thought she would strangle. She, too, was about to die.

The Crystal had spoken of a dying and rebirth. That very death was now upon her. She had only to take the next step.

The chanting grew louder, as if to sustain her faltering strength. It encompassed her, a smothering, clinging, tangible force. Choose. She must choose. How could Teran have known that nocte in the cave that such a heartrending decision would one sol be hers?

She jerked her eyes back to his. He *did* know. He

understood what she was feeling and suffering at this very moment. Teran knew her pain, her tormenting indecision, and still accepted her.

Still loved her.

"No!" Alia screamed in agony, throwing aside the dagger. "No!"

It slid across the stone floor until it struck a wall and broke into a multitude of tiny shards. The chanting ceased.

She defiantly stared back at them, her eyes diamond-bright. "I won't kill him, and you can't make me do it. It is wrong. Nothing any of you can ever say will make it right. Nothing, do you hear me? Nothing."

She fell upon Teran's chest, weeping hysterically. Yet even as Alia lay there, the warmth of Teran's body and the reassuring beat of his heart slowly calming her, she felt hard fingers dig into her arms, pulling her away from him.

"Come, child," the High Priestess murmured in a strangely soothing voice. "You are overwrought. Perhaps it was too soon to ask so much of you. The quest to Carcer has drained you more than I first imagined."

She drew Alia from the table, encircling her shoulders. "Come with me. We will talk, away from all this. The things I have to tell you may help you find your way through the confusion."

Teran strained to watch the High Priestess lead Alia from the room. With all his might he fought to rise, to go after them. He feared for Alia, alone in the malevolent clutches of that femina. She was yet so fragile in her newfound conscience; her sense of morality was still so fresh and untried. Yet the body that had always served him well failed in his greatest hora of need. He could do nothing but gaze after them in helpless silence, though his heart cried out.

The High Priestess led her into the Sanctuary. They silently walked the aisle where only the sol before Alia had triumphantly strode with the Knowing Crystal.

They paused before its obsidian pedestal to gaze down at the dull-faceted stone that lay therein. As Alia stared at it, all the love and pain in her heart flowed out of her, almost as if drawn by the Crystal. It began to glow, though its light was dim.

"See, child," the High Priestess said. "The Knowing Crystal is displeased with you and your family. Until you have righted the indignity to its honor, it will not commune with you."

Alia turned hurting, puzzled eyes to the femina next to her. "I . . . I don't understand. What have I and my family done to dishonor it?"

The High Priestess sighed deeply. Releasing her, she walked a few steps away. "I had hoped to spare you the humiliation of your mother's death. I had hoped to avert that same shame from you by the painstaking cycles of your training, and now it seems I have failed. Your blood runs too strong for any hope of salvation.

Alia reached out to tightly grip the black, stone receptacle, though all her attention was riveted on the High Priestess. "What happened to my mother that she failed Aranea and the Crystal?" she demanded hoarsely. "You have alluded to it these many cycles. Now you must finally tell me."

The tall, spare form wheeled around. "Must I now?" she snarled.

Her perpetual mask of control fell from her face. For the first time, Alia saw the unguarded look of envy and hatred in the High Priestess' eyes. Then, as quickly as it took for Alia to recognize it, the animosity was gone.

The High Priestess laughed, the sound shrill and harsh. "Yes, it is time, for if it does not shame you into your duty, it will not matter anyway. Your mother," she paused dramatically, "took her own life."

At Alia's swift intake of breath, a gloating smile spread across the High Priestess' face. "Yes, it is quite true. Your mother, who was to be crowned ruler of Aranea, chose instead to kill herself and leave you orphan."

"But why? Why would my mother leave me, when I know she loved me?"

Thin lips smirked at Alia. "Because she cared more for her mate, your father, than she did for her child and duty to her people. Sound familiar?"

Alia's eyes clouded in confusion. "I remember no father. If he still lived, why would my mother kill herself?"

"He was no longer alive. He had died before you were even born, sacrificed by your mother as her final Test of Worthiness. The problem arose when your mother found she lacked the courage to live with the consequences of her act. It seems she made the fatal mistake of falling in love with a male meant only for impregnation, and then she let her unruly emotions drive her into insanity—and death."

The High Priestess paused to rearrange a fold of her gown. "No matter," she continued. "It had become quite evident she was not fit to rule. If she had not taken her life, it would have been necessary to do it for her. It all worked out for the best. I became Regent for the child too young to rule, with the expectation of many cycles of molding her to my mind. I would have succeeded, too, if not for your unfortunate relationship with that male."

Horrified revulsion grew within Alia. "You never planned on letting me rule, did you? I was only a puppet, a royal facade behind which you pulled the strings. And when I arrived with Teran, you saw our love. You saw it and knew we must be separated as soon as possible. How convenient for you the final test required just the thing you needed—Teran's death! But what will you do now, now that I know of your cruel plan and refuse to cooperate?"

"What will I do, child?" the High Priestess silkily inquired. "Why exactly what I had planned all along —to rule Aranea. It matters not whether I do it with or without you. That choice is yours. If you wish to somesol wear the Crystal Crown, you will go back into the Sacrifice Room and kill that lover of yours. If not . . . well, you'll eventually die yourself."

"And who will allow you to harm me, the future queen?"

"The law is more powerful than any one ruler, child. You acquiesced to your death when you accepted the final Test of Worthiness. Don't you recall the terms of that agreement?"

Alia froze, harking back to that moment in the Room of Professions when the High Priestess had spoken of taking on the black robes of Profession.

"So you plan to see both of us, Teran and myself, dead, do you? And then who will you have to key the Crystal? The only two people you know of with the gift will then be gone."

"Did I say I would destroy all who have the gift?" the High Priestess archly inquired. "You forget your unborn child, whose gift will be even stronger, blessed as it is with the melding of the two royal lines. I never said I would kill you immediately. For the sake of your child, you would be allowed to live until its birth. After that, there would be no need for you. A wet nurse would do just as well."

"You wouldn't dare!" Alia cried.

"Wouldn't I? If you cannot see where your duty

lies, then it is up to me to take control. As I said before, it is your choice. I will leave you here for a time to ponder the consequences. We will expect you shortly."

She turned to go, then paused to glance back at Alia with a look almost akin to pity. "Tell me this. Is he worth it? Is he really worth your life, your child's life, the lives of your people?"

Breathless rage surged through Alia. How dare that horrible old femina stand there and exult as if she'd already won! And yet, hadn't she? What other alternatives were there for her, alone and pregnant, without any real power save what . . . what the Crystal could give her.

The Crystal. Perhaps there was a chance for them after all.

"We shall soon see, won't we, Domina Magna?" Alia replied, a fierce hope swelling within her. "You will have my decision soon enough."

The older femina's harsh laugh filled the room, reverberating against the walls long after she was gone. "Yes, soon enough, child. Soon enough."

> *Knowing Crystal, bright and fair*
> *Secret of the richest gain,*
> *Royal quest begins the cure*
> *For barren empire, deepest pain.*

For a long while Alia stared at the receptacle that held the Crystal, gazing down at the shimmering, prophetic words. All had been fulfilled, yet why did she still feel a sense of incompleteness? What *was* the richest gain of the Crystal? What was the deepest pain? And how had she really changed anything, bringing the Crystal back to be controlled by the same cruel ambitions that effected its loss in the first place?

She felt abandoned and confused. After all her hopes and all her efforts, what had she really accomplished? If only Vates were here now. He would know what to do, would clearly see the next path to be taken.

Alia stifled a sob. Ah, Vates, she thought, I need you now more than ever, and all I have left is the meager solace of your words. Yet what words they had been. Even now, harking back to them, they filled her with a warm comfort.

Seek the answers in your own heart . . . a heart brave and true . . . it is our only hope . . .

Was it possible? Had the solution to this dreadful dilemma always been there, just waiting to be found in her heart? Suddenly Alia's fears disappeared. She would find the answer and face the consequences, no matter the price.

Too long had the peoples of the Imperium refused to stand up for right and goodness and shirked their responsibilities, until at last there was nothing worth dying for—and nothing to live for, either. Her own mother had seen it and had taken the only path open to her. Could she do less? Did she dare turn from the choice that now lay before her?

A face full of strength, shining with a serene peace, turned once more to the Knowing Crystal. It would help her, this she now knew, if only she had the courage to listen and the strength to brave its truths.

The stone began to flicker, then glow, the soothing light bathing Alia's face. She gave herself over to it without reservation. Its luminous intensity filled the hall, but the brilliant light could not compare to the radiance that pervaded the soul of the femina before it. Time stood still as Alia and the Crystal joined, whirling across a vast universe of knowledge and history until, at long last, they parted. Time was once more the present, and reality lay beyond the walls—in a room of Sacrifice.

Teran felt numb, the cold from the thick stone slab seeping into his bones. As he lay there, awaiting Alia's return, he wondered how long the paralysis would last. He cursed himself for never having questioned her further on this particular aspect of her powers. If only she would stay away long enough for the effects of the stunning to wear off, perhaps then he would have a chance.

The High Priestess glided over to Teran's side. Bending low so no one could hear her words, she whispered to him in a hard and ruthless voice. "Think not for a moment you are saved, my handsome young animal. You will most certainly die, no matter what Alia's decision. The only riddle yet to be solved is whether she also chooses her own death. Either way, it matters not to me. I am still the ultimate victor."

The angry bits of silver that glared back at the black-gowned femina conveyed the fury of the man lying helplessly beneath her. With a malicious chuckle, the High Priestess pulled away from him, raking a long, pointed fingernail across Teran's chest. The thin line paled, then a trail of blood welled up in its place, a tiny river of red that intersected several white scars lacing the muscular terrain. She smiled down at him with a venomous pleasure, languorously licking her lips.

The ponderous stone door swung open. As one of the Sisters turned, an expectant hush settling over the room. Alia walked in.

A sharp, collective gasp effectively wrenched the High Priestess' attention away from her savage fascination with Teran. She turned, her hard features gleaming with anticipation, then gave a choked gurgle of surprise.

An aura of soft light illuminated Alia. In her hand she carried the Knowing Crystal, shining resplendently in the shadowy room. Inexorably, she advanced on the High Priestess, trailing a shimmering nimbus behind her. As she passed the Sisters stepped back, bowing low in reverence.

A spasmodic trembling shook the tall, thin frame of the femina beside Teran. She clenched her fists to try and staunch the revealing weakness, but the effort only intensified the shaking. At last they faced each other. For a long moment their eyes locked and battled fiercely—for life, for love, for Aranea.

Then, with a heavy sigh, the High Priestess stepped back. "What . . . what will become of me, child?" she asked in a quavering voice. "Think of all I have done for you—my painstaking efforts, the cycles of your training . . ."

A slender hand lifted to quench the terrified outpouring. "I do remember what you have done *to* me. That is why I'll allow the Crystal to determine your fate—a fate surely more kind than any I'd choose."

She held the stone before the trembling femina and watched as it began to whirl, its facets throwing brilliant, rainbow-hued beams across the room. Before the eyes of all, the form of the High Priestess began to pulsate, then rapidly shrink in size. Finally, only her gown remained. Out of the heap of fabric on the floor crawled a delicate, long-legged spider. As Alia watched, it quickly skittered away to hide in some dark, lonely corner.

Alia turned to Teran. She stroked his face, the tenderness in her gaze filling him with a soaring elation. In that brief moment he found all he had ever hoped to attain—the love and the eternal devotion of the femina he adored. With one last, lingering glance she turned from him to face the black-garbed feminas assembling before her.

"The loss of the Knowing Crystal has affected us all," Alia began, her voice rising clear and strong, "and none for the better."

She smiled in fond remembrance at words first spoken by Vates. "The time has come, however, to right the wrongs, to change for the better. Customs shrouded in hundreds of cycles at last must be understood and their origins uncovered, if we are to sort through the confusion and separate the good from the bad.

"The influence of the Knowing Crystal was too strong to ever find betrayal from outside. The treachery came from within, from one of our own High Priests who traded away the heart of the Imperium for some promise of even greater power. Hence came our tradition of male sacrifice. Originally a symbolic offering for return of the Crystal, as time went on it became a seething hatred, a token revenge against the ancestors of the first traitor—a male. Its original purpose lost in the mists of time, the killing of all Aranean males evolved into an issue of survival.

"It is our greatest shame, this murder of the fathers of our children, our own purchase price for our unthinking dependence on the Knowing Crystal. But no more," Alia cried, her voice fiercely exultant. "No longer will we wander in hopeless confusion. The Knowing Crystal will once again guide us. This much the Crystal has told me; this much I promise."

They watched her in fascinated wonder, like children waiting to be taken by the hand. Alia's heart filled with compassion. It was not their fault, this horrible adherence to the barbaric practice of legalized murder.

Alia motioned for her Sisters to go, a loving smile on her face. "We have much to discuss, but time enough another sol. Return to your duties. Ponder my words. On the morrow, we will begin anew."

The black forms silently filed out of the room. Alia returned to Teran's side. Laying the Crystal down beside him, she placed both hands on his forehead. With a mighty effort Alia drew out the paralysis. Teran struggled to a sitting position. When she made a move to pull back, he quickly grasped her hand. "Where do you think you're going?" he demanded, a rakish gleam in his eyes.

She smiled wanly. "Nowhere, if that is your wish. I only wonder what you think of me, after nearly dying at my hand."

Her honey-brown eyes glistened with barely suppressed tears. "If you want nothing further to do with me, I will understand. But before you say anything," Alia interrupted his attempt to speak by placing a silencing finger on his lips, "there is one more gift I have for you, one that asks no payment in return and requires no obligation from you."

Picking up the Crystal, Alia touched the stone to the govern collar. Sparks sprang from the site of union. With a loud click, the collar fell apart.

Teran reached up to his neck in wonder, touching the tiny, rapidly healing orifice now exposed over his spine. Then, with a rough motion, he tore the collar away.

He made a movement to fling it from him, when

Alia stopped him. "Let me have it as a memento, if you will, of the object that brought us together. Though you may hate it, I cherish it for the memories it has given me."

Teran's hand tightened around hers, his dark brows drawing together into a wary frown. "You speak as if that is all that is left you. Has the Crystal told you there's no place for me in your life? If it has, I won't rest until I've forced it to recant such cruel words."

One hot, hopeful tear trickled down Alia's face. "No," she whispered, choking back the sobs. "The Crystal would never ask such an unkind thing. I . . . I just thought you would no longer want me after all the terrible things I have done."

"Alia," he said, his voice husky as he stroked her arm, "I will always want you. I love you. But where can I possibly fit into your life, now that so much is demanded of you? With or without the collar, I'm still an outcast, exiled from my own planet, a convicted criminal by Imperium laws."

"No, not anymore," Alia fiercely said. "The Crystal has begun its new reign. New laws will be required. As a Crystal Master and joint ruler of Aranea, none would dare oppose you."

She lowered her head, suddenly abashed by the implications of her statement. "The choice is yours, but no matter what you choose, you are a free man from this moment on." She raised glowing eyes to him.

A smile teased the corner of Teran's mouth. "Are you proposing a life mating?"

Her cheeks flushed scarlet, but her glance did not waver. "Yes, Teran. I want you for my life mate, for I will have no other."

He looked at her, his eyes softly caressing. Then

Teran stroked her face, his touch almost hesitant in its tenderness.

"And I, too, will have no other. I will gladly rule at your side. Together, we will strive to return the Imperium to its former prosperity."

With a low moan, Alia came to him then, hungrily seeking the furry haven of his chest. "Ah, Teran, I don't know what I'd have done if you had turned from me. The task that lies ahead is so enormous. I fear I might have failed before I even began, if you weren't beside me, but now . . ."

She kissed him, her lips brushing his with the lightest of touches. "Now, all is possible. The Crystal lies in its pedestal of power, the Imperium will soon be at peace, and we are together. The prophecy spoke true. It has always been our destiny, even when it was so hard to trust in it."

"It has always been there for us," Teran agreed. "We've just been too blind, too afraid to accept it. Just like someone's inability to see that we have always been meant for each other," he slyly added.

Alia coyly tilted her head. "Are you perhaps implying I lack the good sense to appreciate you?"

"Well, you were one of my more difficult conquests." He grinned, a loving amusement glinting in his silver eyes.

"Conquest, am I?" she cried in mock outrage. "Just as I supposed from the beginning. You are no man of honor."

With a deep chuckle of satisfaction, Teran gathered her into his arms and rose to his feet. "Perhaps not, but then what I now have in mind for you is anything but honorable. Extremely pleasurable, perhaps, but anything but honorable."

Alia's only reply was a muffled giggle from a place

buried deep within Teran's chest. It mattered not what he had planned for her; she wanted it with all her heart. The morrow would bring fresh tasks, new quests for the pursuing, fruitfulness to be nurtured. But now, for this splendid moment in time, it was enough to be loved.

EPILOGUE

"ONLY FIVE SOLS, AND ALREADY IT SEEMS THE ENTIRE Imperium is clamoring for the Crystal's aid."

Alia turned away from the windy heights of the monastery parapets and the lushly crimson sunset to step into the warm haven of Teran's arms. She gave a small sigh. "Ah, my love, where do we begin?"

A deep, full-throated chuckle erupted from the broad chest she snuggled so closely to. "Are you already repenting your acceptance of the Crystal Crown? I've never known you to swerve from your duty, no matter what the obstacle."

"No, never would I desert Aranea, nor the Knowing Crystal, as long as they will have me. But all the petitions seem so imperative, so . . . so needing. How does one sort through and decide which to deal with first?" She gazed up at the rugged features of the man she loved. "Help me, Teran. Help me decide."

"Perhaps, for a short while, it would be prudent to divide our efforts," he said, as he thoughtfully stroked her upturned face. "The affairs of the mother planet must be set to order as quickly as possible. That, I think, should be your task. Mine must be to deal with the most pressing problems of the Imperium. From all I've heard, Agrica should be our first priority. My people have enslaved its inhabitants. It is fitting I visit the main Bellatorian garrison there."

"Yes, your plan is wise." Alia lowered her head to rest again on Teran's broad chest. "When will you leave?"

"On the morrow, I think."

She jerked back from him in dismay. "What? So soon? Can you not wait until after our life mating? The ceremony is only six sols away."

A strong, brown arm firmly clasped her waist. "I'll never enjoy parting from you, yet for a time I'm afraid it's necessary. But fear not. I've no intention of missing our life mating. If I leave on the morrow, I can at least begin to resolve some of Agrica's more serious problems in the next few sols. I'll be back in time. I promise."

"Indeed?" Alia gave him an arch smile. "Or is this perhaps a devious attempt to escape your commitments?"

Loving amusement flickered in Teran's silver eyes. "As if you and the Crystal would ever allow that."

His expression slowly sobered. "No, Alia, I will not shirk my responsibilities, nor the femina I love. The task that lies before us is enormous. We will need each other's support if we are to see it through."

Disengaging his arms from about her waist, Alia wound a hand through one of his. Together they turned and resumed a slow walk along the parapet.

"Yes, the task before us is large," she solemnly agreed. "For one, the Sisterhood must be diverted from its ancient role to one of more humane efforts. I think it only fair they now turn their labors to easing the transition of our males back into a more natural life. It will take time for the Aranean females to accept them. Some sol, though, the two sexes will again live as one. Children will know their fathers, and human love will flourish."

"An admirable goal. One I wholeheartedly approve of." He shot her a sly glance. "Perhaps our own example will help further that dream."

"Most certainly, Lord Ardane." Alia's mouth tilted up in a soft smile. "Most certainly, indeed. I envision, however, a far more glorious resolution to our man-made dilemma. Eventually, we must wean ourselves from our mindless dependence on the Knowing Crystal. Never again can we look to it for a soul each should develop within oneself. *That* must be our ultimate quest. It is the greatest knowledge the Crystal can ever impart."

He smiled. "We all have our secret dreams. Mine, it seems, will aid in yours. I hope to reintroduce the revered craft of teacher, to begin again the schools and the publication of books. A final tribute to Vates, however small it may be."

At the mention of the old man's name, Alia halted and turned to Teran. "Vates," she whispered, her heart swelling with emotion with all the old, poignant memories. "It is only fitting his hand should be in this, too. It was he who brought us together, he who sent us out on the true purpose of our quest. If only he were here to see it all come to fruition."

Teran pulled her to him then, holding her tightly. His love, like a warm, soothing balm, flowed over her, assuaging all the regrets and all the pain.

A voice husky with its own private recollections rumbled reassuringly in her ear. "He knows, Alia. Believe me. He knows."

Dear Reader:

I hope you have enjoyed reading *The Knowing Crystal*. My next Leisure Futuristic Romance, *Heart's Lair*, is scheduled for release in September, 1991. Also set in the Imperium of *The Knowing Crystal*, it is the tale of Karic, the young lord of the Cat People, and Liane, a Bellatorian psychic healer. When a power-crazed invader threatened Karic's people with mass extermination, Liane agreed to help him save his world. Her heart, however, was never part of the bargain.

Following *Heart's Lair*, in 1992, will be *Crystal Fire*, a tale of Teran's younger brother Brace Ardane and Marissa. Both are reluctantly drawn into a dangerous quest when the Knowing Crystal goes awry.

I would love to hear from my readers. For a reply, please send a SASE to me care of: Leisure Books; 276 Fifth Avenue; New York, NY 10001.

With Warmest Regards,

Kathleen Morgan

Kathleen Morgan